RANGER ACADEMY

Power Rangers

MARIA INGRANDE MORA
JO MI-GYEONG
FABIANA MASCOLO

VOLUME ONE

Published by

BOOM! BOX™

DESIGNER
MADISON GOYETTE

ASSISTANT EDITOR
KENZIE RZONCA

EDITOR
DAFNA PLEBAN

Ross Richie Chairman & Founder
Jen Harned CFO
Matt Gagnon Editor-in-Chief
Filip Sablik President, Publishing & Marketing
Stephen Christy President, Development
Adam Yoelin Senior Vice President, Film
Lance Kreiter Vice President, Licensing & Merchandising
Bryce Carlson Vice President, Editorial & Creative Strategy
Josh Hayes Vice President, Sales
Mette Norkjaer Vice President, Development
Eric Harburn Executive Editor
Ryan Matsunaga Director, Marketing
Stephanie Lazarski Director, Operations
Elyse Strandberg Manager, Finance
Michelle Ankley Manager, Production Design
Cheryl Parker Manager, Human Resources
Rosalind Morehead Manager, Retail Sales
Jason Lee Manager, Accounting

Licensed by:

HASBRO SPECIAL THANKS
TAYLA REO, MICHAEL KELLY, AND ED LANE

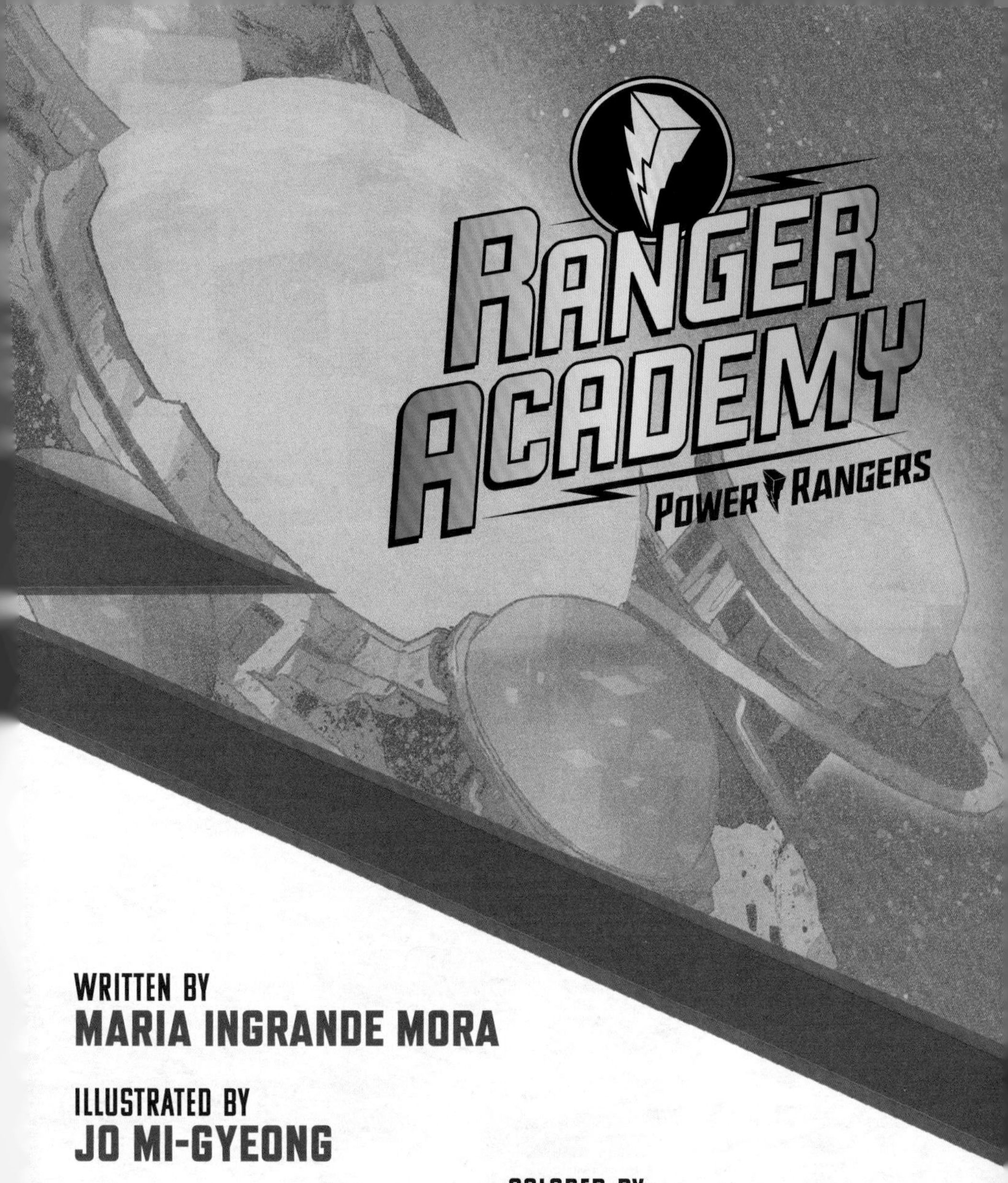

RANGER ACADEMY

POWER RANGERS

WRITTEN BY
MARIA INGRANDE MORA

ILLUSTRATED BY
JO MI-GYEONG

COLORED BY
FABIANA MASCOLO

LETTERED BY
ED DUKESHIRE & CARDINAL RAE
(CHAPTER ONE)

COVER BY
MIGUEL MERCADO

CHAPTER BREAK ART BY
JO MI-GYEONG

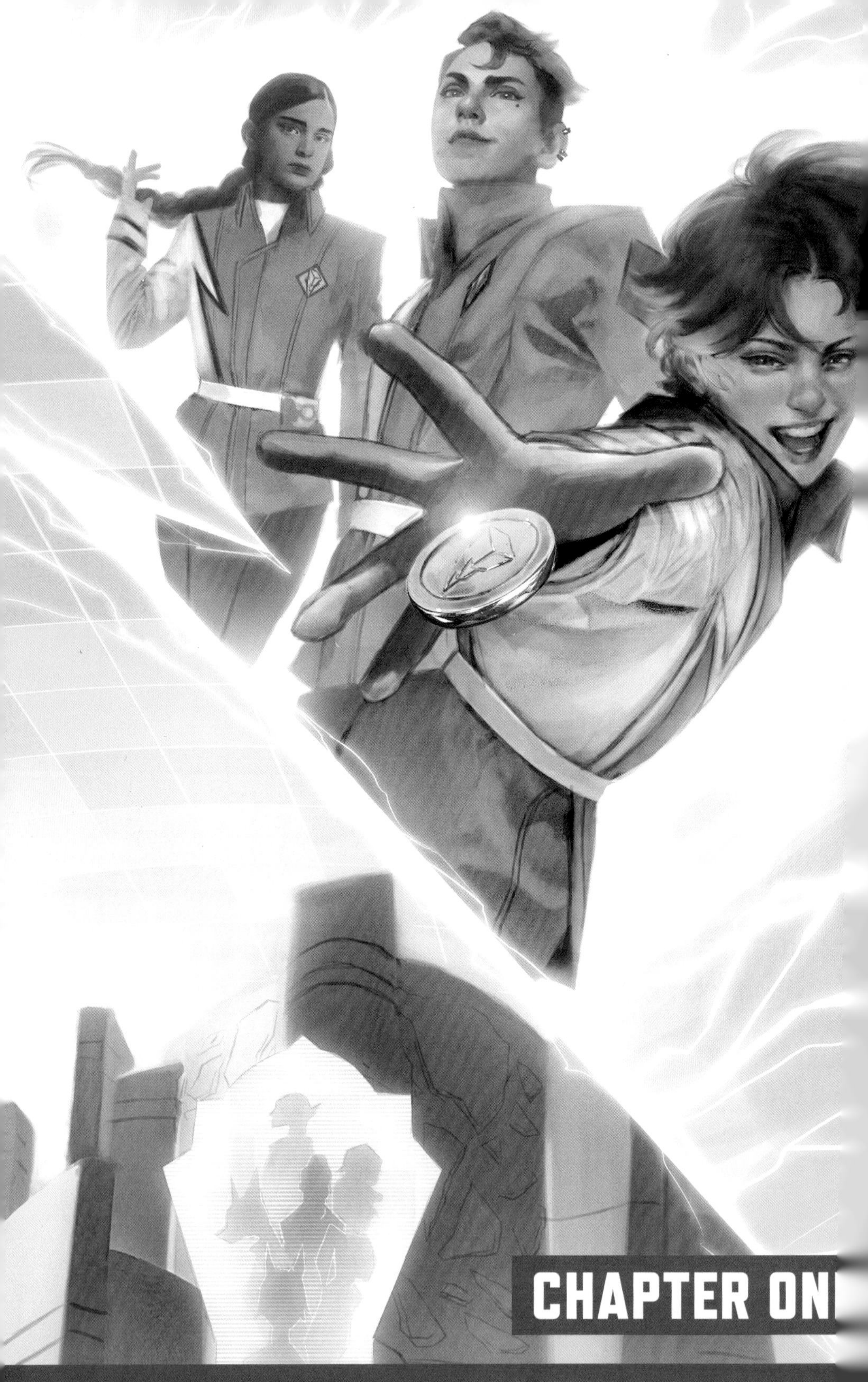

CHAPTER ON

ISSUE ONE COVER BY MIGUEL MERCADO

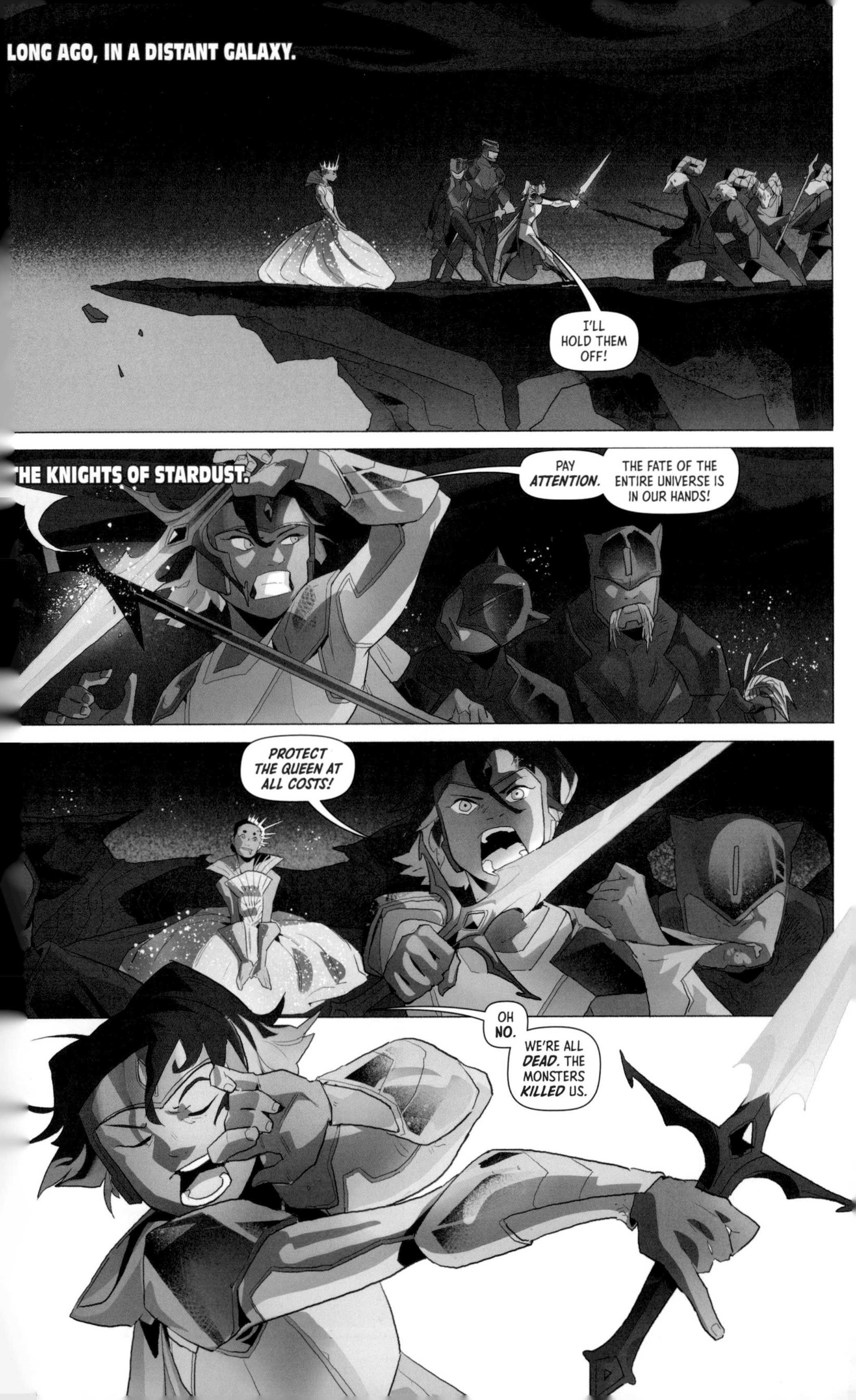

LONG AGO, IN A DISTANT GALAXY.
I'LL HOLD THEM OFF!
THE KNIGHTS OF STARDUST.
PAY ATTENTION.
THE FATE OF THE ENTIRE UNIVERSE IS IN OUR HANDS!
PROTECT THE QUEEN AT ALL COSTS!
OH NO.
WE'RE ALL DEAD. THE MONSTERS KILLED US.

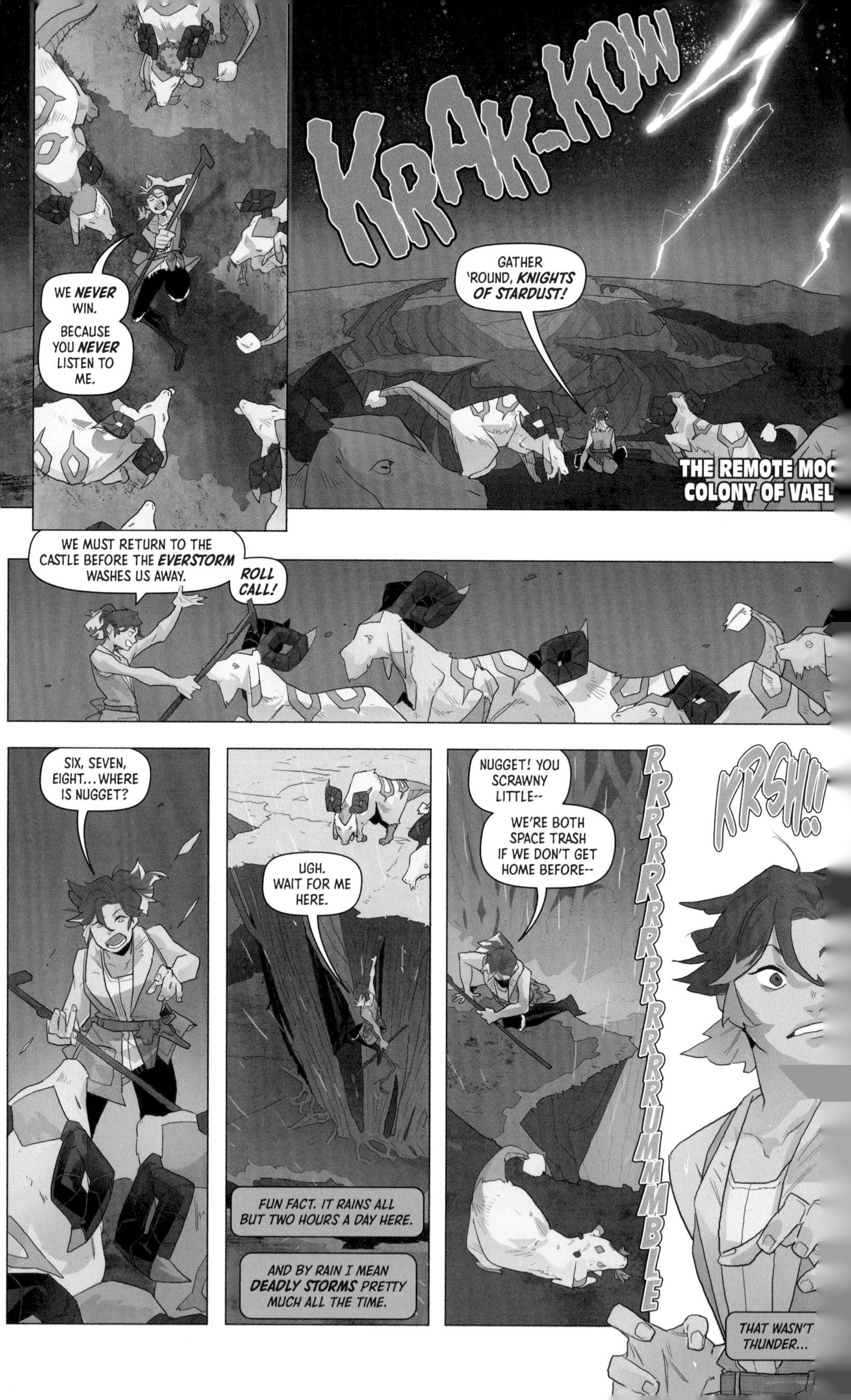
WE NEVER WIN.
BECAUSE YOU NEVER LISTEN TO ME.
KRAK-KOW
GATHER 'ROUND, KNIGHTS OF STARDUST!
THE REMOTE MOO COLONY OF VAEL
WE MUST RETURN TO THE CASTLE BEFORE THE EVERSTORM WASHES US AWAY.
ROLL CALL!
SIX, SEVEN, EIGHT... WHERE IS NUGGET?
UGH. WAIT FOR ME HERE.
FUN FACT. IT RAINS ALL BUT TWO HOURS A DAY HERE.
AND BY RAIN I MEAN DEADLY STORMS PRETTY MUCH ALL THE TIME.
NUGGET! YOU SCRAWNY LITTLE--
WE'RE BOTH SPACE TRASH IF WE DON'T GET HOME BEFORE--
RRRRRRRRRRRRRRUMMBLE
KRSH!!
THAT WASN'T THUNDER...

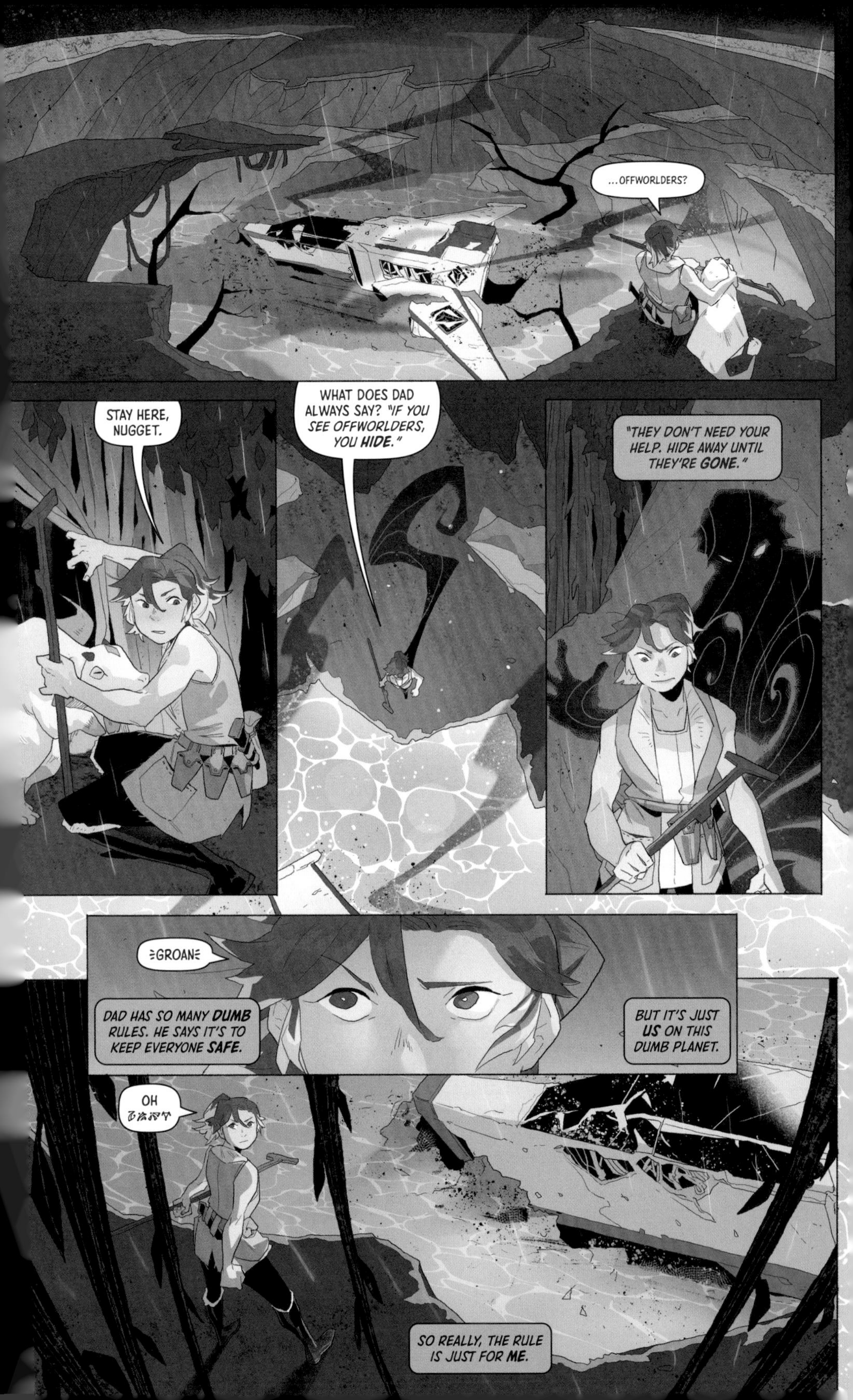

...OFFWORLDERS?
STAY HERE, NUGGET.
WHAT DOES DAD ALWAYS SAY? "IF YOU SEE OFFWORLDERS, YOU HIDE."
"THEY DON'T NEED YOUR HELP. HIDE AWAY UNTIL THEY'RE GONE."
GROAN
DAD HAS SO MANY DUMB RULES. HE SAYS IT'S TO KEEP EVERYONE SAFE.
BUT IT'S JUST US ON THIS DUMB PLANET.
OH
SO REALLY, THE RULE IS JUST FOR ME.

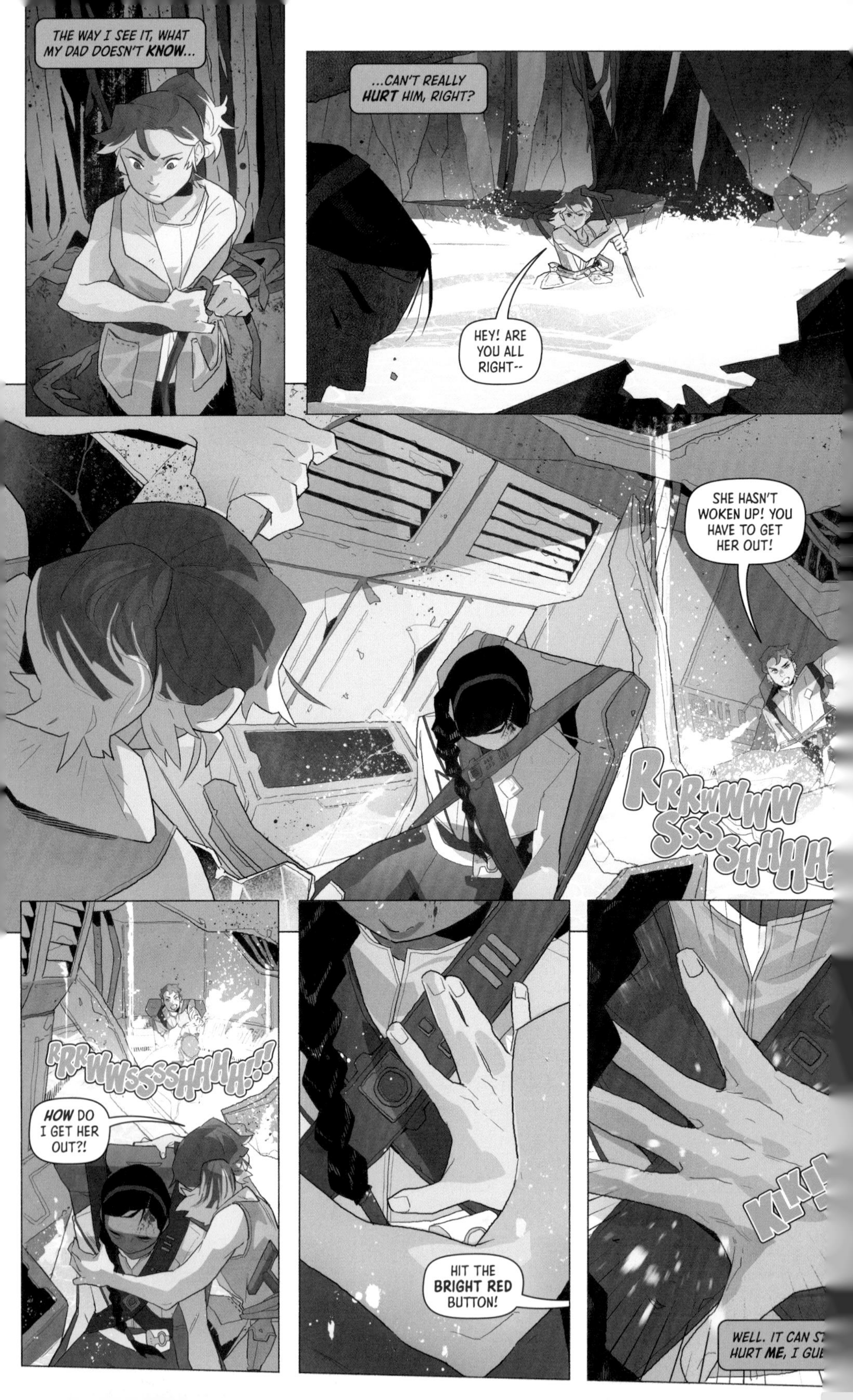
THE WAY I SEE IT, WHAT MY DAD DOESN'T **KNOW**...
...CAN'T REALLY **HURT** HIM, RIGHT?
HEY! ARE YOU ALL RIGHT--
SHE HASN'T WOKEN UP! YOU HAVE TO GET HER OUT!
RRRWWWWW SSSSHHHH!
RRRWWSSSSSHHHH!?!
HOW DO I GET HER OUT?!
HIT THE **BRIGHT RED** BUTTON!
KLK!
WELL. IT CAN ST
HURT **ME**, I GUE

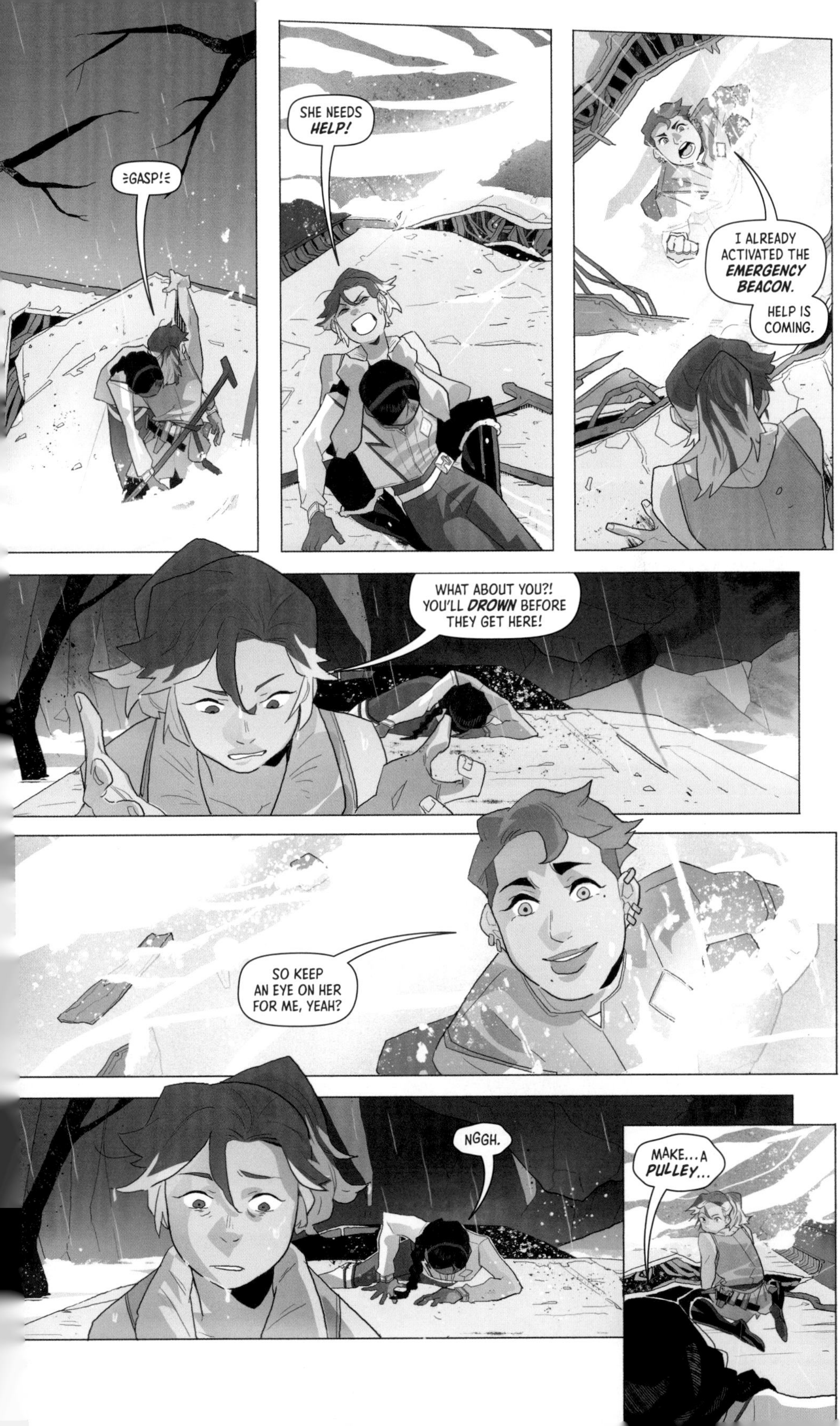
GASP!
SHE NEEDS HELP!
I ALREADY ACTIVATED THE EMERGENCY BEACON.
HELP IS COMING.
WHAT ABOUT YOU?! YOU'LL DROWN BEFORE THEY GET HERE!
SO KEEP AN EYE ON HER FOR ME, YEAH?
NGGH.
MAKE...A PULLEY...

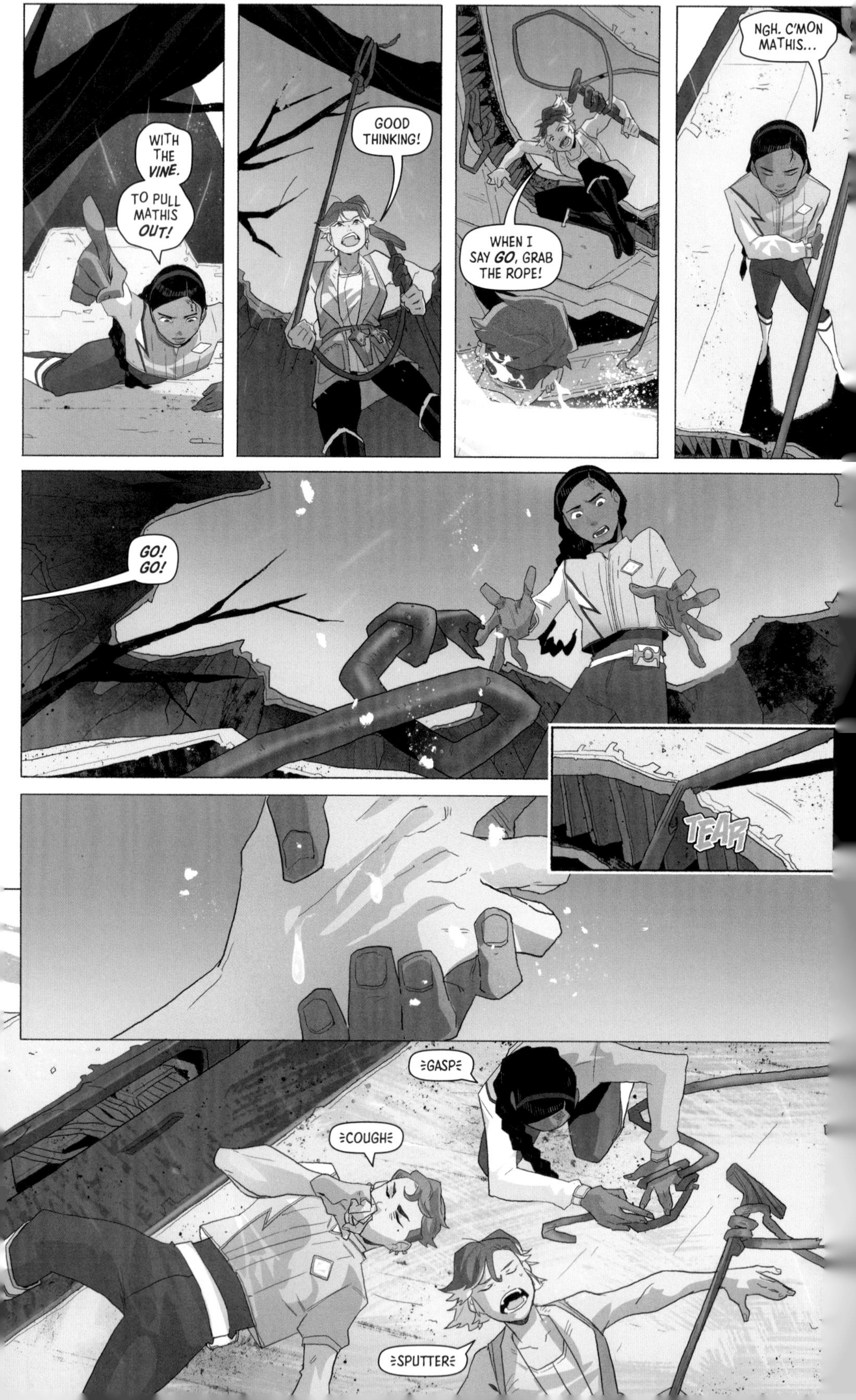
WITH THE VINE.
TO PULL MATHIS OUT!
GOOD THINKING!
WHEN I SAY GO, GRAB THE ROPE!
NGH. C'MON MATHIS...
GO! GO!
TEAR
GASP
COUGH
SPUTTER

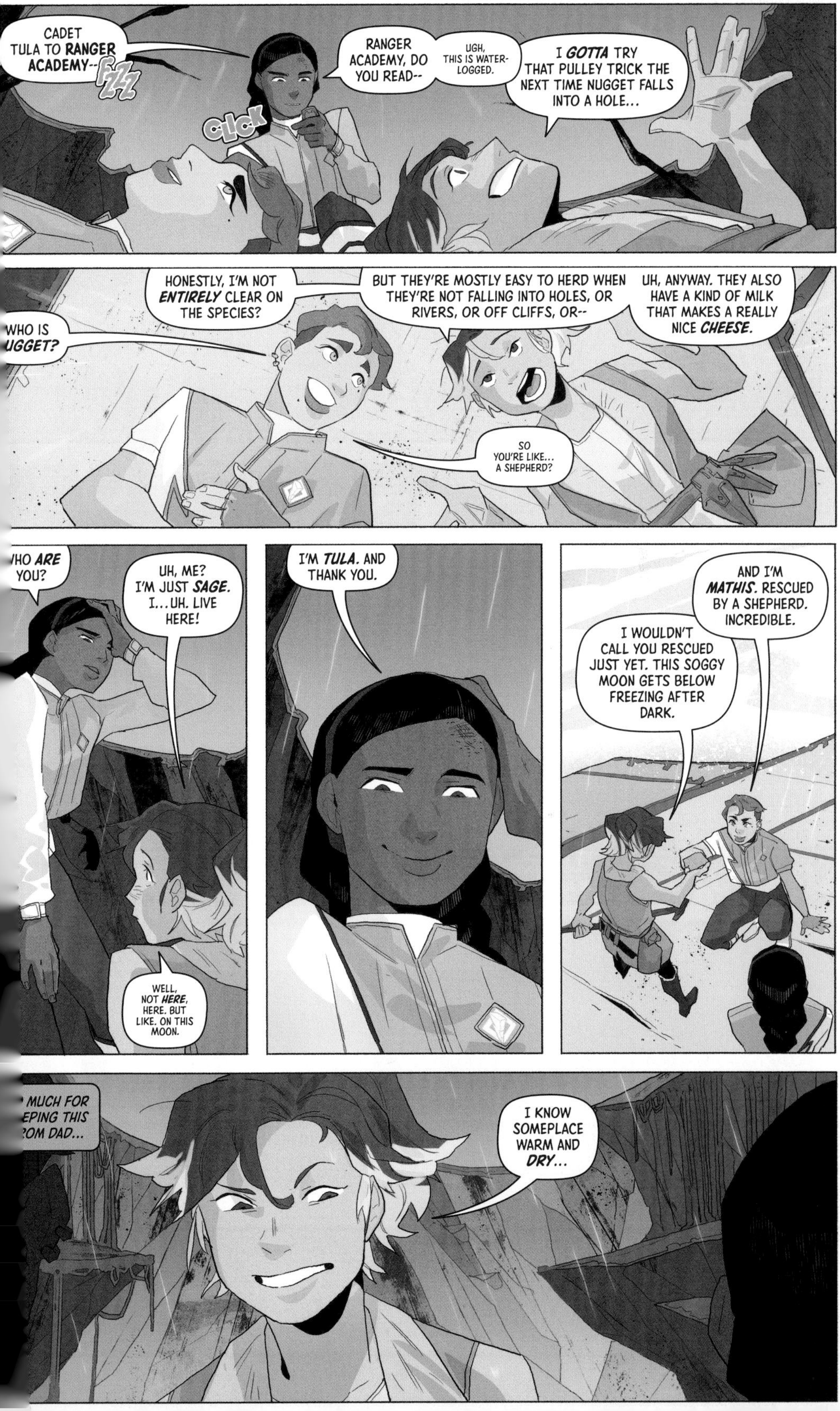

CADET TULA TO RANGER ACADEMY--
FZZZ
CLICK
RANGER ACADEMY, DO YOU READ--
UGH, THIS IS WATER-LOGGED.
I GOTTA TRY THAT PULLEY TRICK THE NEXT TIME NUGGET FALLS INTO A HOLE...
WHO IS NUGGET?
HONESTLY, I'M NOT ENTIRELY CLEAR ON THE SPECIES?
BUT THEY'RE MOSTLY EASY TO HERD WHEN THEY'RE NOT FALLING INTO HOLES, OR RIVERS, OR OFF CLIFFS, OR--
UH, ANYWAY. THEY ALSO HAVE A KIND OF MILK THAT MAKES A REALLY NICE CHEESE.
SO YOU'RE LIKE... A SHEPHERD?
WHO ARE YOU?
UH, ME? I'M JUST SAGE. I...UH. LIVE HERE!
WELL, NOT HERE, HERE. BUT LIKE. ON THIS MOON.
I'M TULA. AND THANK YOU.
AND I'M MATHIS. RESCUED BY A SHEPHERD. INCREDIBLE.
I WOULDN'T CALL YOU RESCUED JUST YET. THIS SOGGY MOON GETS BELOW FREEZING AFTER DARK.
MUCH FOR EPING THIS ROM DAD...
I KNOW SOMEPLACE WARM AND DRY...

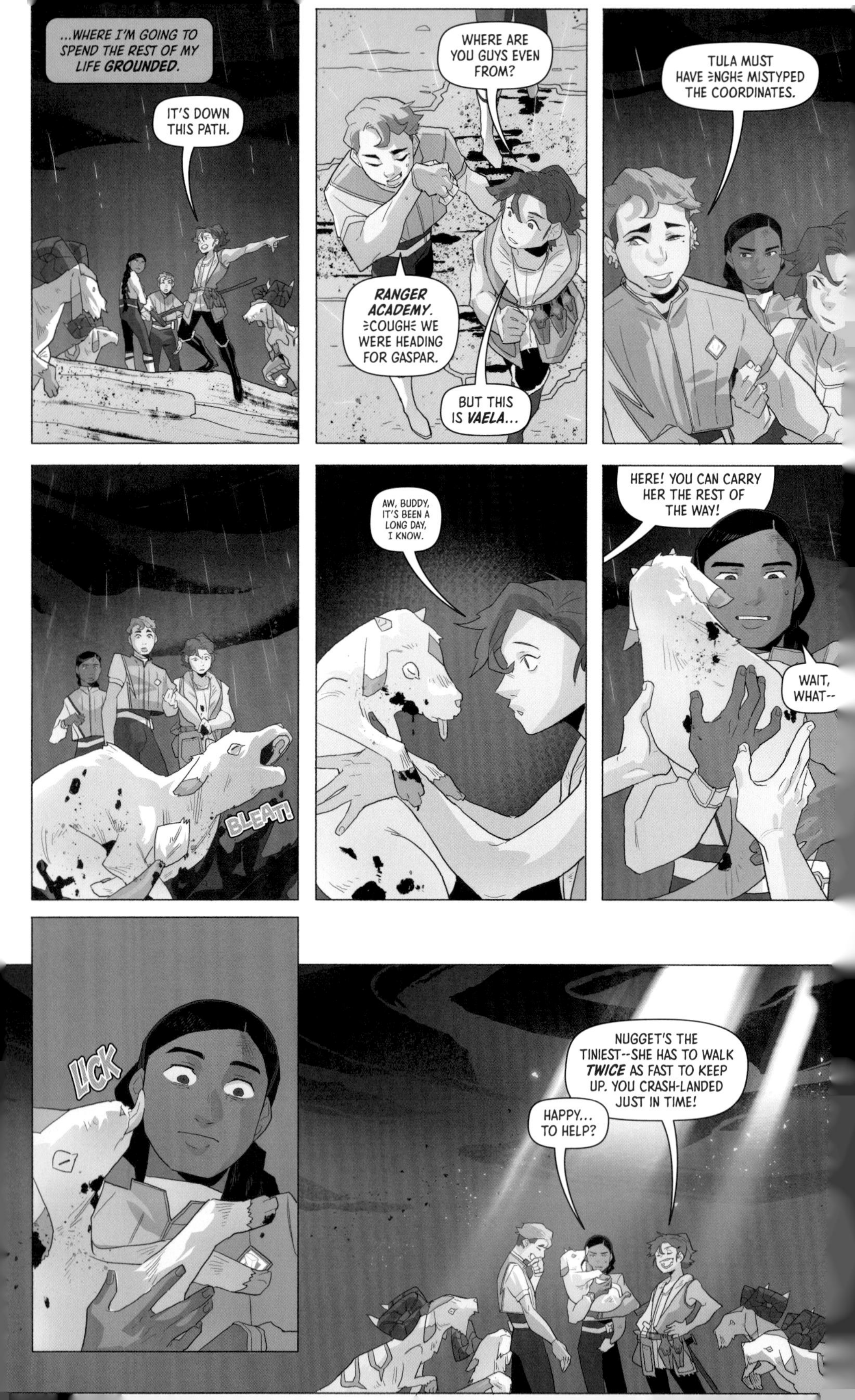
...WHERE I'M GOING TO SPEND THE REST OF MY LIFE **GROUNDED.**
IT'S DOWN THIS PATH.
WHERE ARE YOU GUYS EVEN FROM?
RANGER ACADEMY. ⋛COUGH⋛ WE WERE HEADING FOR GASPAR.
BUT THIS IS ***VAELA...***
TULA MUST HAVE ⋛NGH⋛ MISTYPED THE COORDINATES.
BLEAT!
AW, BUDDY, IT'S BEEN A LONG DAY, I KNOW.
HERE! YOU CAN CARRY HER THE REST OF THE WAY!
WAIT, WHAT--
LICK
NUGGET'S THE TINIEST--SHE HAS TO WALK ***TWICE*** AS FAST TO KEEP UP. YOU CRASH-LANDED JUST IN TIME!
HAPPY... TO HELP?

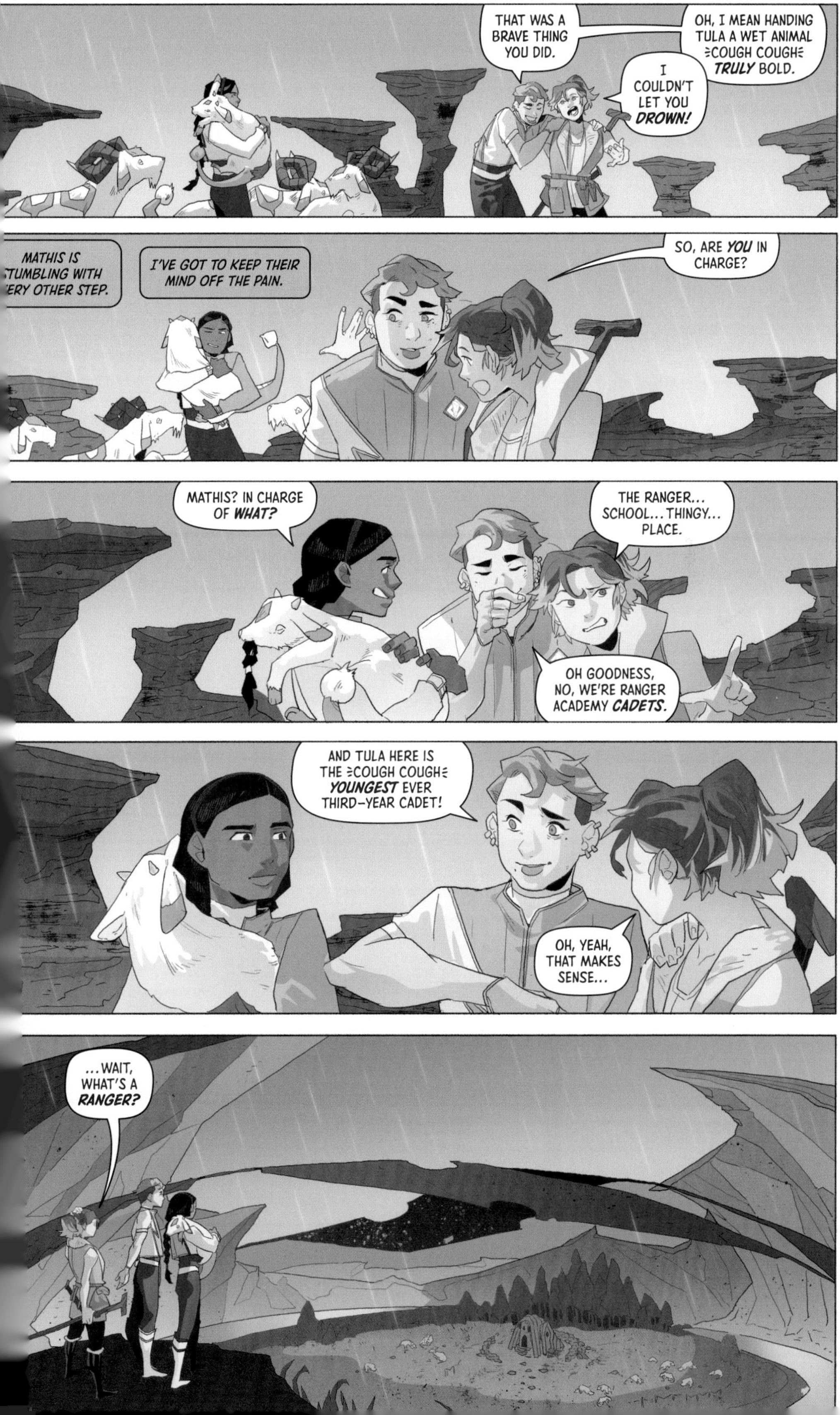
THAT WAS A BRAVE THING YOU DID.
I COULDN'T LET YOU *DROWN!*
OH, I MEAN HANDING TULA A WET ANIMAL ≋COUGH COUGH≋ *TRULY* BOLD.
MATHIS IS TUMBLING WITH ERY OTHER STEP.
I'VE GOT TO KEEP THEIR MIND OFF THE PAIN.
SO, ARE *YOU* IN CHARGE?
MATHIS? IN CHARGE OF *WHAT?*
THE RANGER... SCHOOL... THINGY... PLACE.
OH GOODNESS, NO, WE'RE RANGER ACADEMY *CADETS.*
AND TULA HERE IS THE ≋COUGH COUGH≋ *YOUNGEST* EVER THIRD-YEAR CADET!
OH, YEAH, THAT MAKES SENSE...
...WAIT, WHAT'S A *RANGER?*

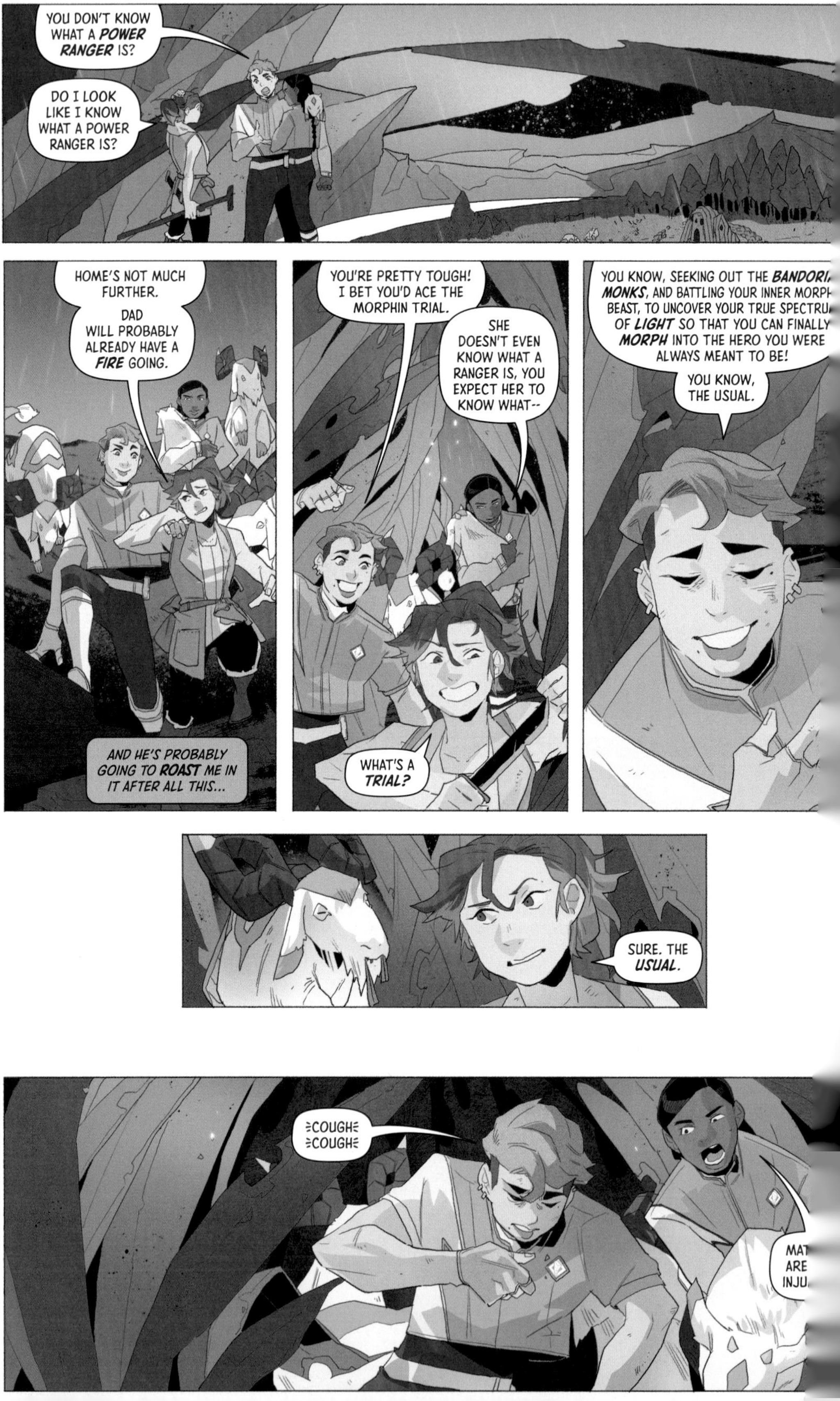
YOU DON'T KNOW WHAT A POWER RANGER IS?
DO I LOOK LIKE I KNOW WHAT A POWER RANGER IS?
HOME'S NOT MUCH FURTHER.
DAD WILL PROBABLY ALREADY HAVE A FIRE GOING.
AND HE'S PROBABLY GOING TO ROAST ME IN IT AFTER ALL THIS...
YOU'RE PRETTY TOUGH! I BET YOU'D ACE THE MORPHIN TRIAL.
SHE DOESN'T EVEN KNOW WHAT A RANGER IS, YOU EXPECT HER TO KNOW WHAT--
WHAT'S A TRIAL?
YOU KNOW, SEEKING OUT THE BANDORI MONKS, AND BATTLING YOUR INNER MORPH BEAST, TO UNCOVER YOUR TRUE SPECTRU OF LIGHT SO THAT YOU CAN FINALLY MORPH INTO THE HERO YOU WERE ALWAYS MEANT TO BE!
YOU KNOW, THE USUAL.
SURE. THE USUAL.
COUGH COUGH
MAT ARE INJU

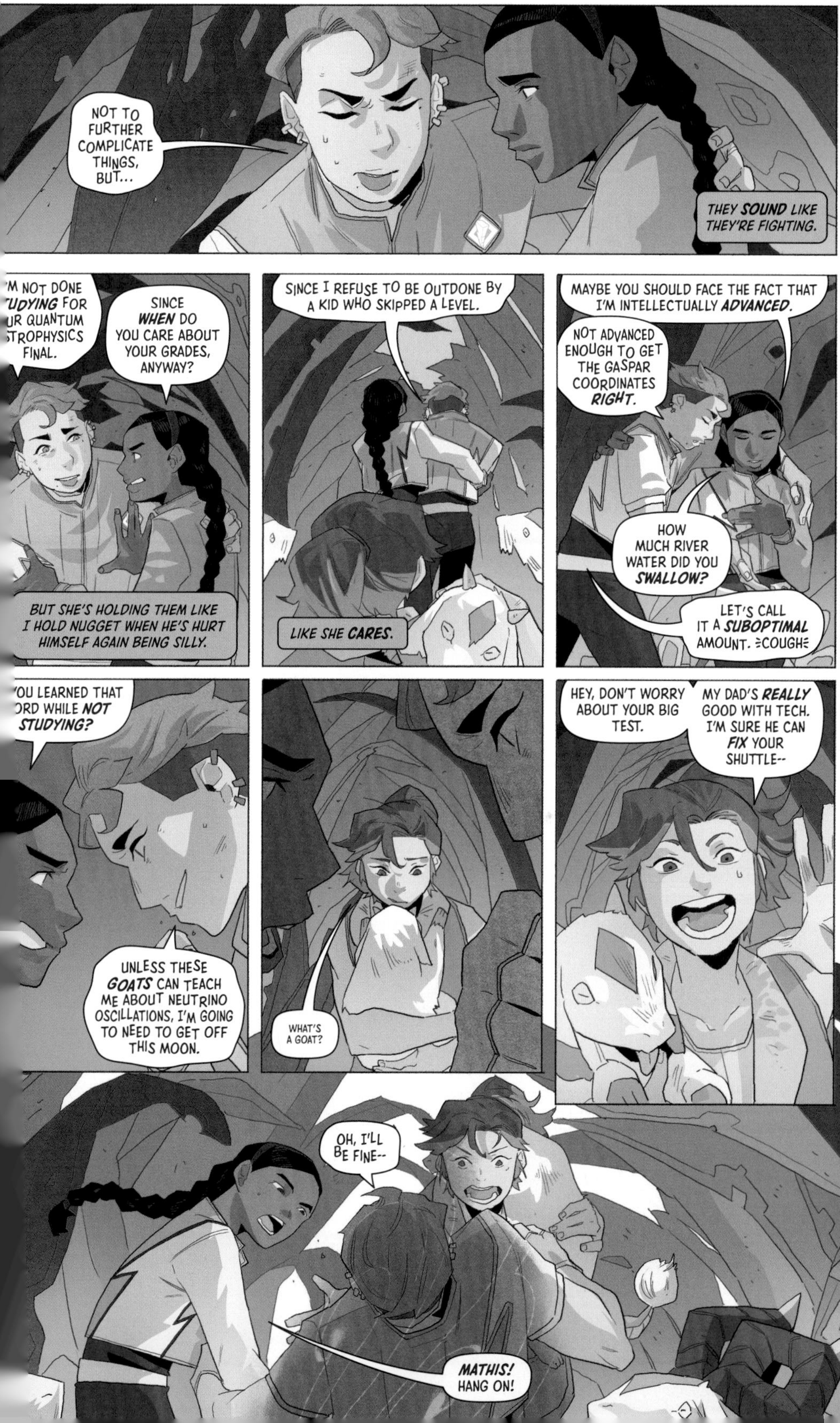
NOT TO FURTHER COMPLICATE THINGS, BUT...
THEY SOUND LIKE THEY'RE FIGHTING.
'M NOT DONE TUDYING FOR UR QUANTUM STROPHYSICS FINAL.
SINCE WHEN DO YOU CARE ABOUT YOUR GRADES, ANYWAY?
BUT SHE'S HOLDING THEM LIKE I HOLD NUGGET WHEN HE'S HURT HIMSELF AGAIN BEING SILLY.
SINCE I REFUSE TO BE OUTDONE BY A KID WHO SKIPPED A LEVEL.
LIKE SHE CARES.
MAYBE YOU SHOULD FACE THE FACT THAT I'M INTELLECTUALLY ADVANCED.
NOT ADVANCED ENOUGH TO GET THE GASPAR COORDINATES RIGHT.
HOW MUCH RIVER WATER DID YOU SWALLOW?
LET'S CALL IT A SUBOPTIMAL AMOUNT. ⁼COUGH⁼
OU LEARNED THAT ORD WHILE NOT STUDYING?
UNLESS THESE GOATS CAN TEACH ME ABOUT NEUTRINO OSCILLATIONS, I'M GOING TO NEED TO GET OFF THIS MOON.
WHAT'S A GOAT?
HEY, DON'T WORRY ABOUT YOUR BIG TEST.
MY DAD'S REALLY GOOD WITH TECH. I'M SURE HE CAN FIX YOUR SHUTTLE--
OH, I'LL BE FINE--
MATHIS! HANG ON!

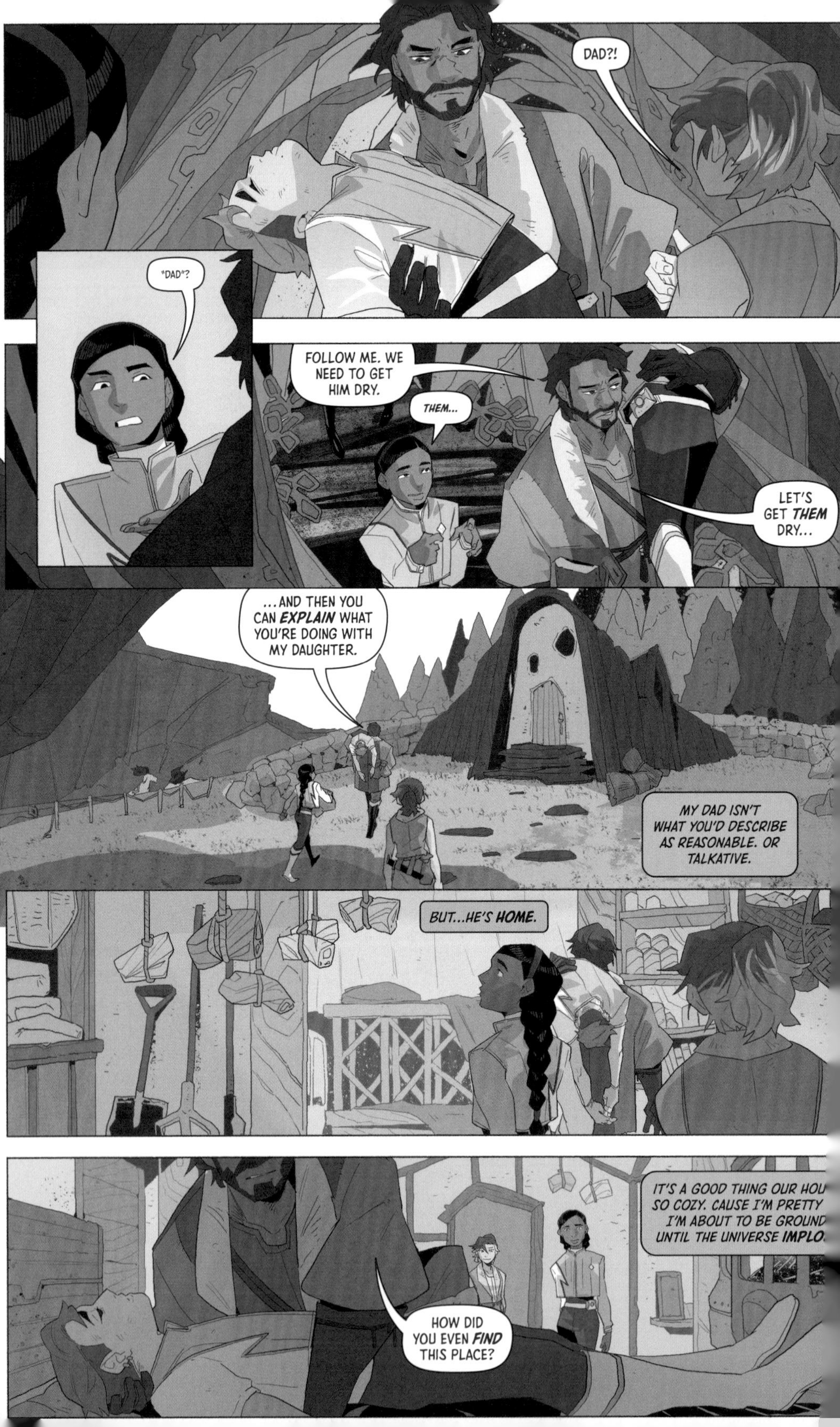
DAD?!
"DAD"?
FOLLOW ME. WE NEED TO GET HIM DRY.
THEM...
LET'S GET THEM DRY...
...AND THEN YOU CAN EXPLAIN WHAT YOU'RE DOING WITH MY DAUGHTER.
MY DAD ISN'T WHAT YOU'D DESCRIBE AS REASONABLE. OR TALKATIVE.
BUT...HE'S HOME.
IT'S A GOOD THING OUR HOU SO COZY. CAUSE I'M PRETTY I'M ABOUT TO BE GROUND UNTIL THE UNIVERSE IMPLO
HOW DID YOU EVEN FIND THIS PLACE?

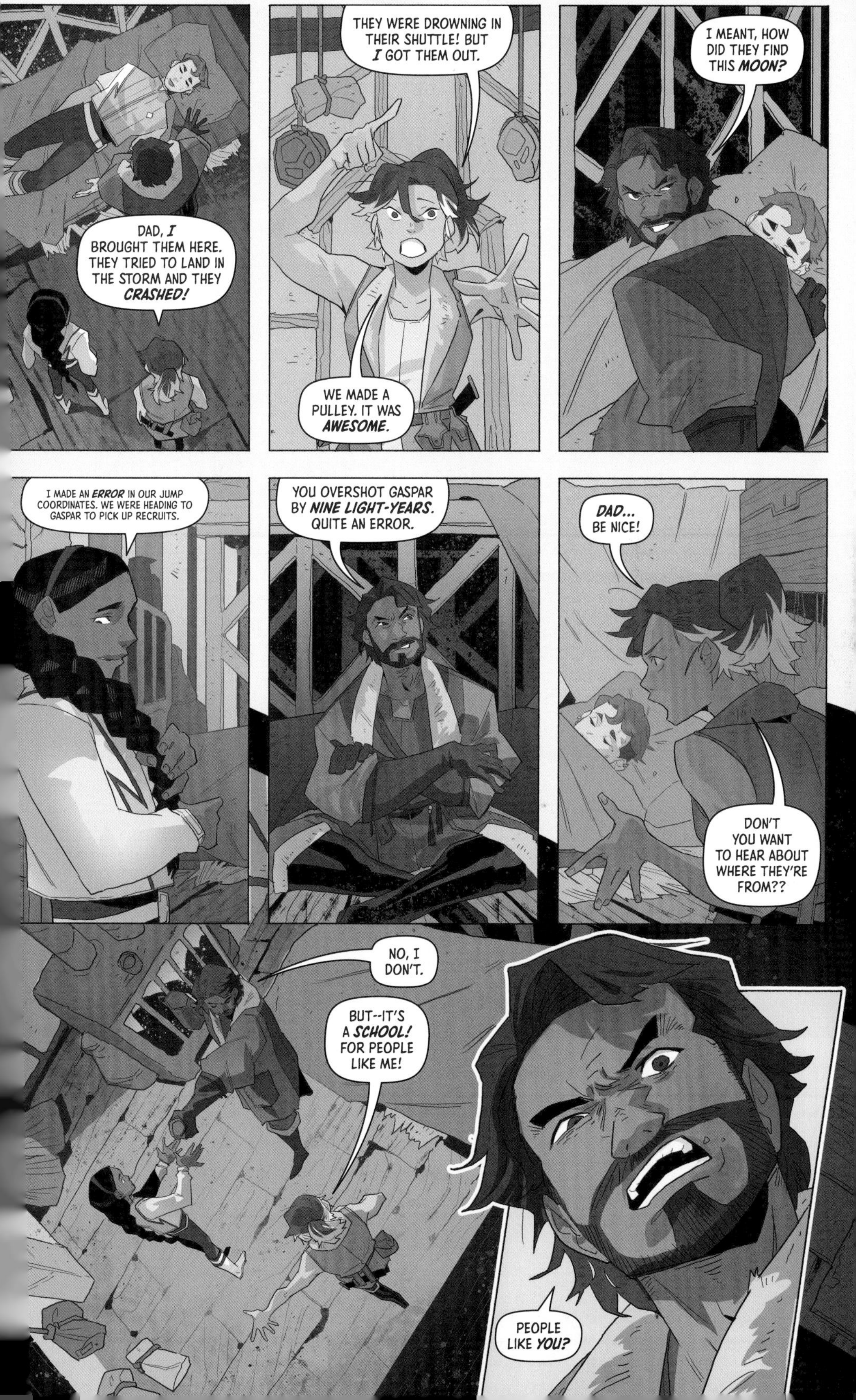
DAD, *I* BROUGHT THEM HERE. THEY TRIED TO LAND IN THE STORM AND THEY ***CRASHED!***
THEY WERE DROWNING IN THEIR SHUTTLE! BUT *I* GOT THEM OUT.
WE MADE A PULLEY. IT WAS ***AWESOME.***
I MEANT, HOW DID THEY FIND THIS ***MOON?***
I MADE AN ***ERROR*** IN OUR JUMP COORDINATES. WE WERE HEADING TO GASPAR TO PICK UP RECRUITS.
YOU OVERSHOT GASPAR BY ***NINE LIGHT-YEARS.*** QUITE AN ERROR.
DAD... BE NICE!
DON'T YOU WANT TO HEAR ABOUT WHERE THEY'RE FROM??
NO, I DON'T.
BUT--IT'S A ***SCHOOL!*** FOR PEOPLE LIKE ME!
PEOPLE LIKE ***YOU?***

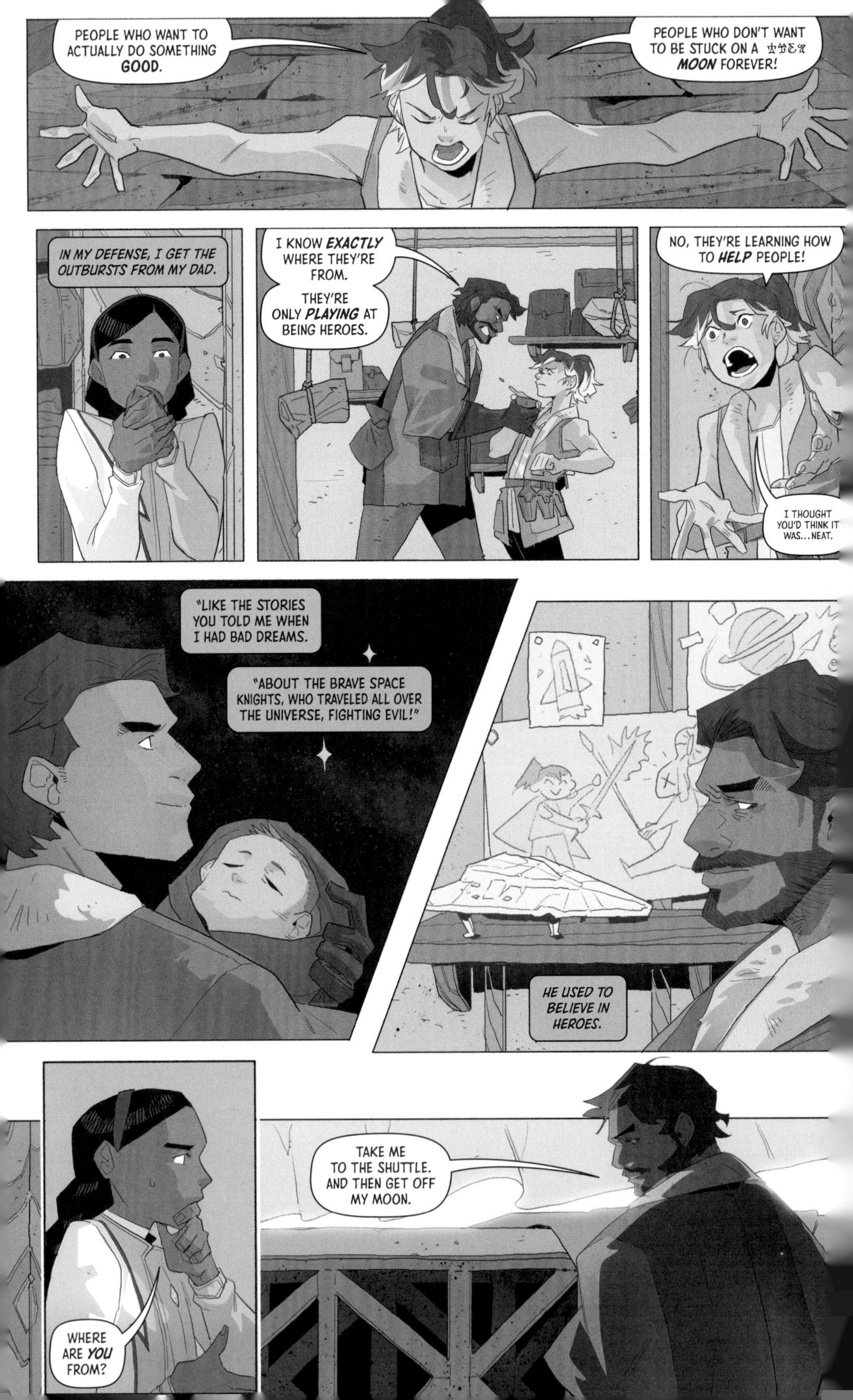
PEOPLE WHO WANT TO ACTUALLY DO SOMETHING GOOD.
PEOPLE WHO DON'T WANT TO BE STUCK ON A ⵜⵓⵔⵓ MOON FOREVER!
IN MY DEFENSE, I GET THE OUTBURSTS FROM MY DAD.
I KNOW EXACTLY WHERE THEY'RE FROM.
THEY'RE ONLY PLAYING AT BEING HEROES.
NO, THEY'RE LEARNING HOW TO HELP PEOPLE!
I THOUGHT YOU'D THINK IT WAS...NEAT.
"LIKE THE STORIES YOU TOLD ME WHEN I HAD BAD DREAMS.
"ABOUT THE BRAVE SPACE KNIGHTS, WHO TRAVELED ALL OVER THE UNIVERSE, FIGHTING EVIL!"
HE USED TO BELIEVE IN HEROES.
TAKE ME TO THE SHUTTLE. AND THEN GET OFF MY MOON.
WHERE ARE YOU FROM?

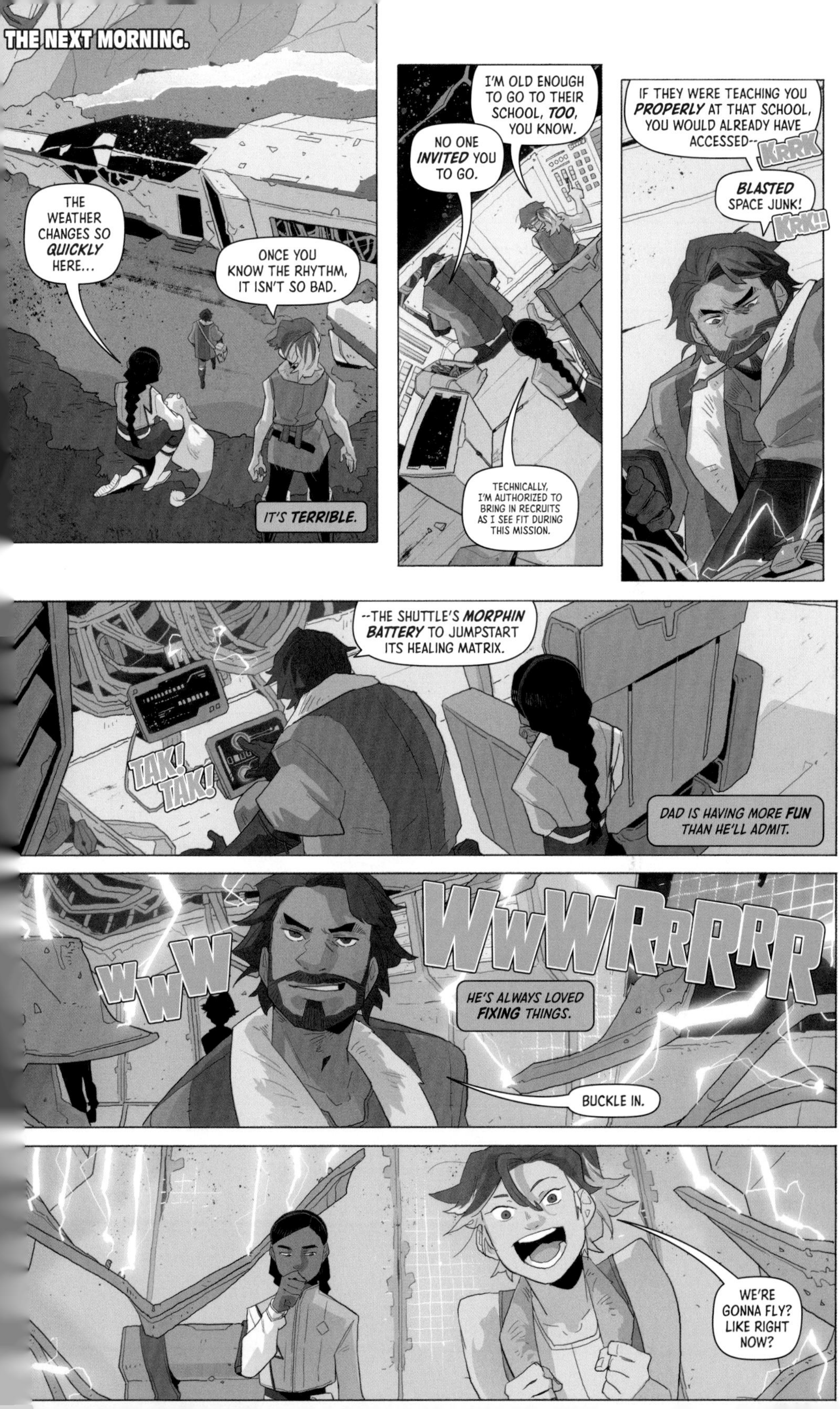
THE NEXT MORNING.
THE WEATHER CHANGES SO QUICKLY HERE...
ONCE YOU KNOW THE RHYTHM, IT ISN'T SO BAD.
IT'S TERRIBLE.
I'M OLD ENOUGH TO GO TO THEIR SCHOOL, TOO, YOU KNOW.
NO ONE INVITED YOU TO GO.
TECHNICALLY, I'M AUTHORIZED TO BRING IN RECRUITS AS I SEE FIT DURING THIS MISSION.
IF THEY WERE TEACHING YOU PROPERLY AT THAT SCHOOL, YOU WOULD ALREADY HAVE ACCESSED--
KRRK
BLASTED SPACE JUNK!
KRK!!
--THE SHUTTLE'S MORPHIN BATTERY TO JUMPSTART ITS HEALING MATRIX.
TAK! TAK!
DAD IS HAVING MORE FUN THAN HE'LL ADMIT.
WWW
WWWRRRRRR
HE'S ALWAYS LOVED FIXING THINGS.
BUCKLE IN.
WE'RE GONNA FLY? LIKE RIGHT NOW?

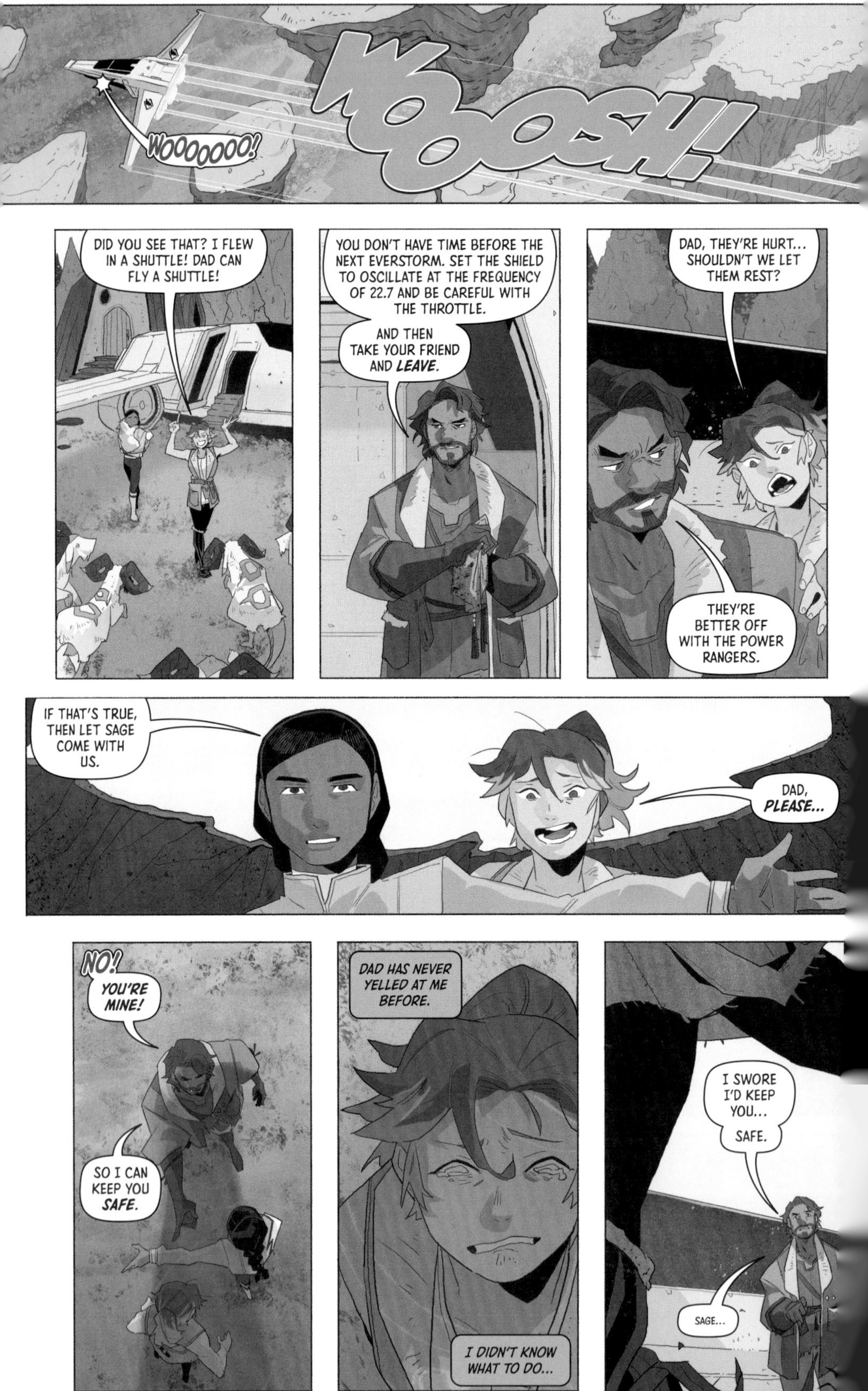
WOOOOOOO!
WOOOSH!!
DID YOU SEE THAT? I FLEW IN A SHUTTLE! DAD CAN FLY A SHUTTLE!
YOU DON'T HAVE TIME BEFORE THE NEXT EVERSTORM. SET THE SHIELD TO OSCILLATE AT THE FREQUENCY OF 22.7 AND BE CAREFUL WITH THE THROTTLE.
AND THEN TAKE YOUR FRIEND AND LEAVE.
DAD, THEY'RE HURT... SHOULDN'T WE LET THEM REST?
THEY'RE BETTER OFF WITH THE POWER RANGERS.
IF THAT'S TRUE, THEN LET SAGE COME WITH US.
DAD, PLEASE...
NO!
YOU'RE MINE!
SO I CAN KEEP YOU SAFE.
DAD HAS NEVER YELLED AT ME BEFORE.
I DIDN'T KNOW WHAT TO DO...
I SWORE I'D KEEP YOU...
SAFE.
SAGE...

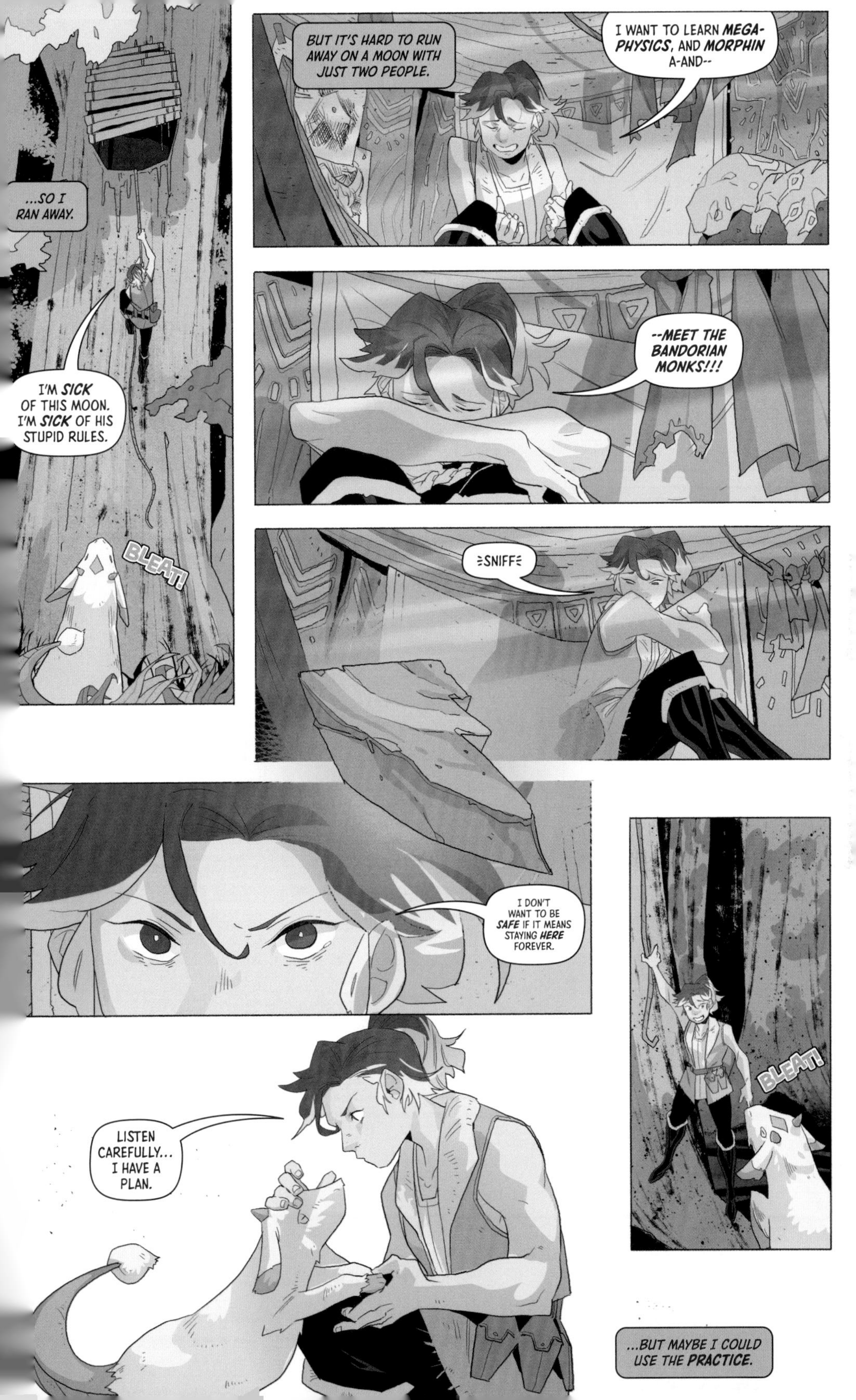
...SO I RAN AWAY.
I'M SICK OF THIS MOON. I'M SICK OF HIS STUPID RULES.
BLEAT!
BUT IT'S HARD TO RUN AWAY ON A MOON WITH JUST TWO PEOPLE.
I WANT TO LEARN MEGA-PHYSICS, AND MORPHIN A-AND--
--MEET THE BANDORIAN MONKS!!!
SNIFF
I DON'T WANT TO BE SAFE IF IT MEANS STAYING HERE FOREVER.
LISTEN CAREFULLY... I HAVE A PLAN.
BLEAT!
...BUT MAYBE I COULD USE THE PRACTICE.

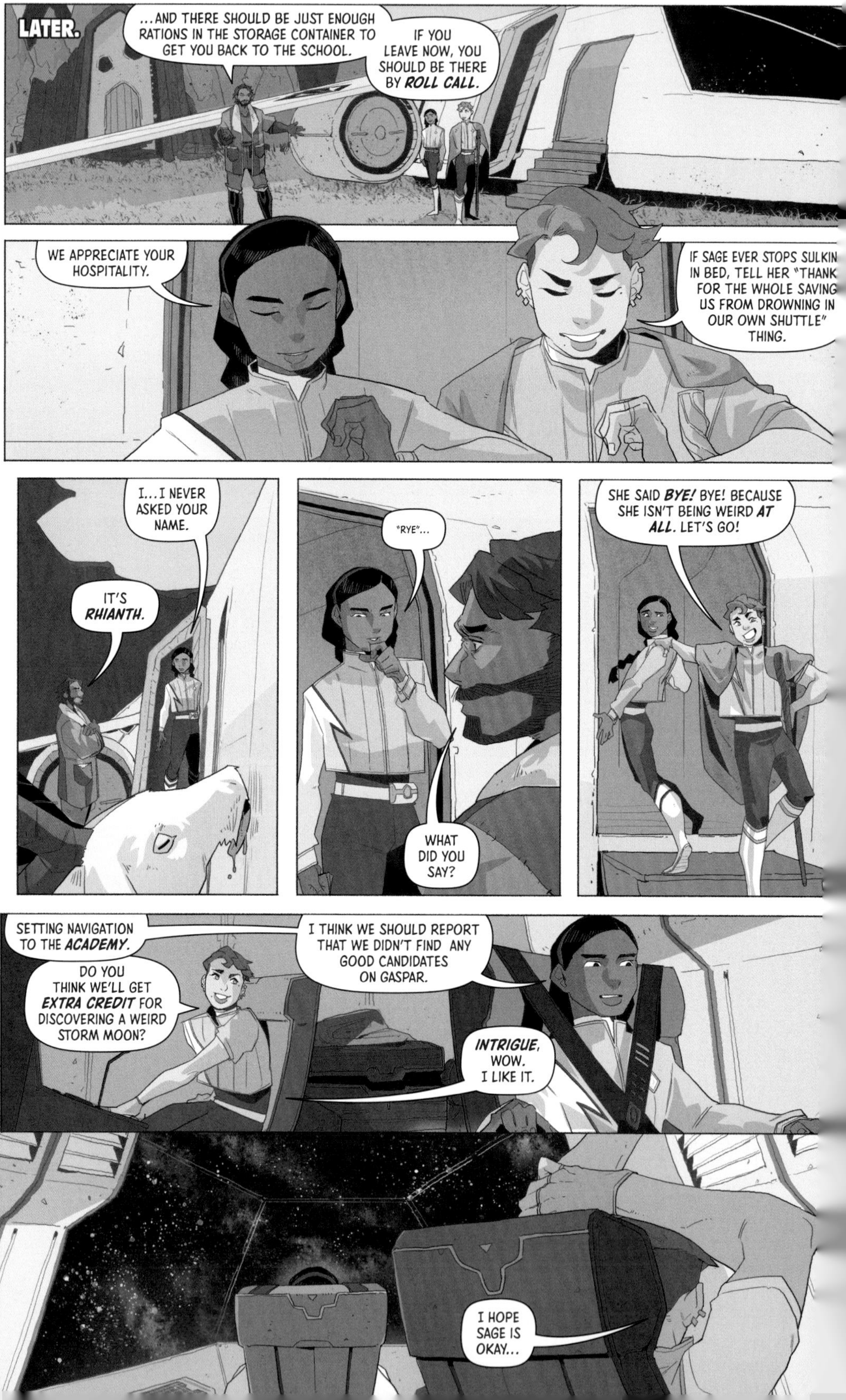
LATER.
...AND THERE SHOULD BE JUST ENOUGH RATIONS IN THE STORAGE CONTAINER TO GET YOU BACK TO THE SCHOOL.
IF YOU LEAVE NOW, YOU SHOULD BE THERE BY ROLL CALL.
WE APPRECIATE YOUR HOSPITALITY.
IF SAGE EVER STOPS SULKIN IN BED, TELL HER "THANK FOR THE WHOLE SAVING US FROM DROWNING IN OUR OWN SHUTTLE" THING.
I...I NEVER ASKED YOUR NAME.
IT'S RHIANTH.
"RYE"...
WHAT DID YOU SAY?
SHE SAID BYE! BYE! BECAUSE SHE ISN'T BEING WEIRD AT ALL. LET'S GO!
SETTING NAVIGATION TO THE ACADEMY.
DO YOU THINK WE'LL GET EXTRA CREDIT FOR DISCOVERING A WEIRD STORM MOON?
I THINK WE SHOULD REPORT THAT WE DIDN'T FIND ANY GOOD CANDIDATES ON GASPAR.
INTRIGUE, WOW. I LIKE IT.
I HOPE SAGE IS OKAY...

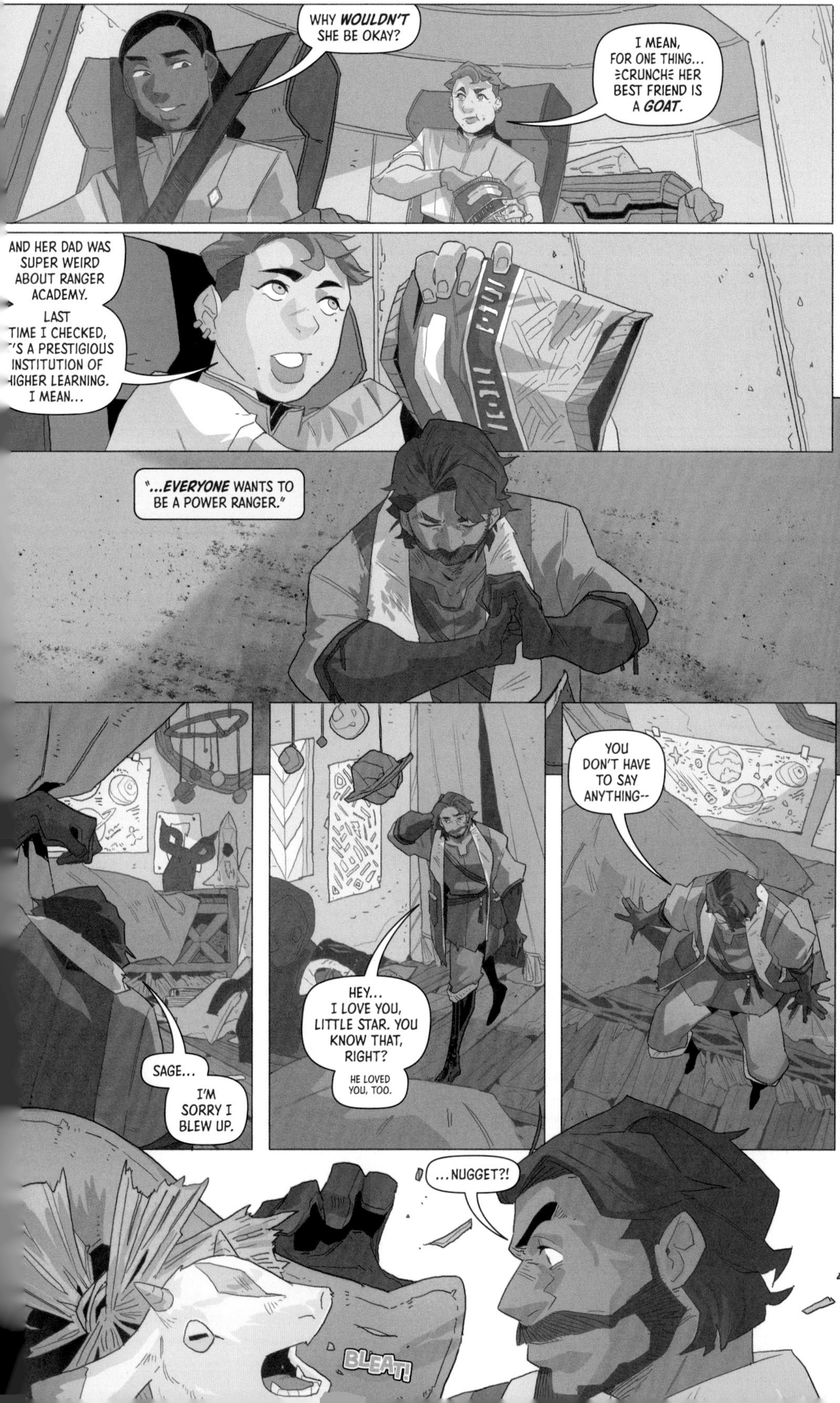
WHY WOULDN'T SHE BE OKAY?
I MEAN, FOR ONE THING... ≡CRUNCH≡ HER BEST FRIEND IS A GOAT.
AND HER DAD WAS SUPER WEIRD ABOUT RANGER ACADEMY.
LAST TIME I CHECKED, IT'S A PRESTIGIOUS INSTITUTION OF HIGHER LEARNING. I MEAN...
"...EVERYONE WANTS TO BE A POWER RANGER."
SAGE...
I'M SORRY I BLEW UP.
HEY... I LOVE YOU, LITTLE STAR. YOU KNOW THAT, RIGHT?
HE LOVED YOU, TOO.
YOU DON'T HAVE TO SAY ANYTHING--
...NUGGET?!
BLEAT!

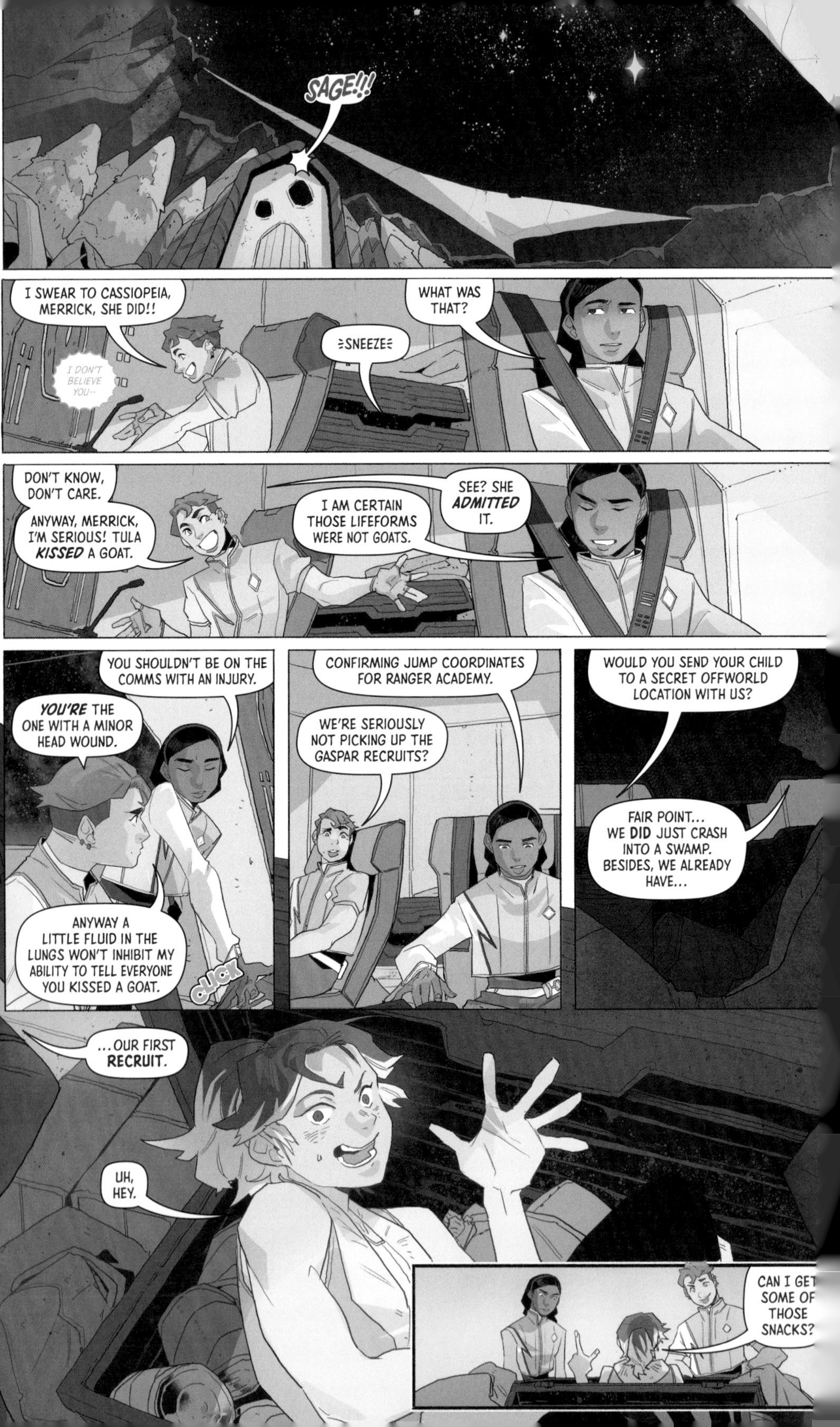
SAGE!!!
I SWEAR TO CASSIOPEIA, MERRICK, SHE DID!!
I DON'T BELIEVE YOU--
≡SNEEZE≡
WHAT WAS THAT?
DON'T KNOW, DON'T CARE.
ANYWAY, MERRICK, I'M SERIOUS! TULA *KISSED* A GOAT.
I AM CERTAIN THOSE LIFEFORMS WERE NOT GOATS.
SEE? SHE *ADMITTED* IT.
YOU SHOULDN'T BE ON THE COMMS WITH AN INJURY.
YOU'RE THE ONE WITH A MINOR HEAD WOUND.
ANYWAY A LITTLE FLUID IN THE LUNGS WON'T INHIBIT MY ABILITY TO TELL EVERYONE YOU KISSED A GOAT.
CLICK
CONFIRMING JUMP COORDINATES FOR RANGER ACADEMY.
WE'RE SERIOUSLY NOT PICKING UP THE GASPAR RECRUITS?
WOULD YOU SEND YOUR CHILD TO A SECRET OFFWORLD LOCATION WITH US?
FAIR POINT... WE **DID** JUST CRASH INTO A SWAMP. BESIDES, WE ALREADY HAVE...
...OUR FIRST **RECRUIT.**
UH, HEY.
CAN I GET SOME OF THOSE SNACKS?

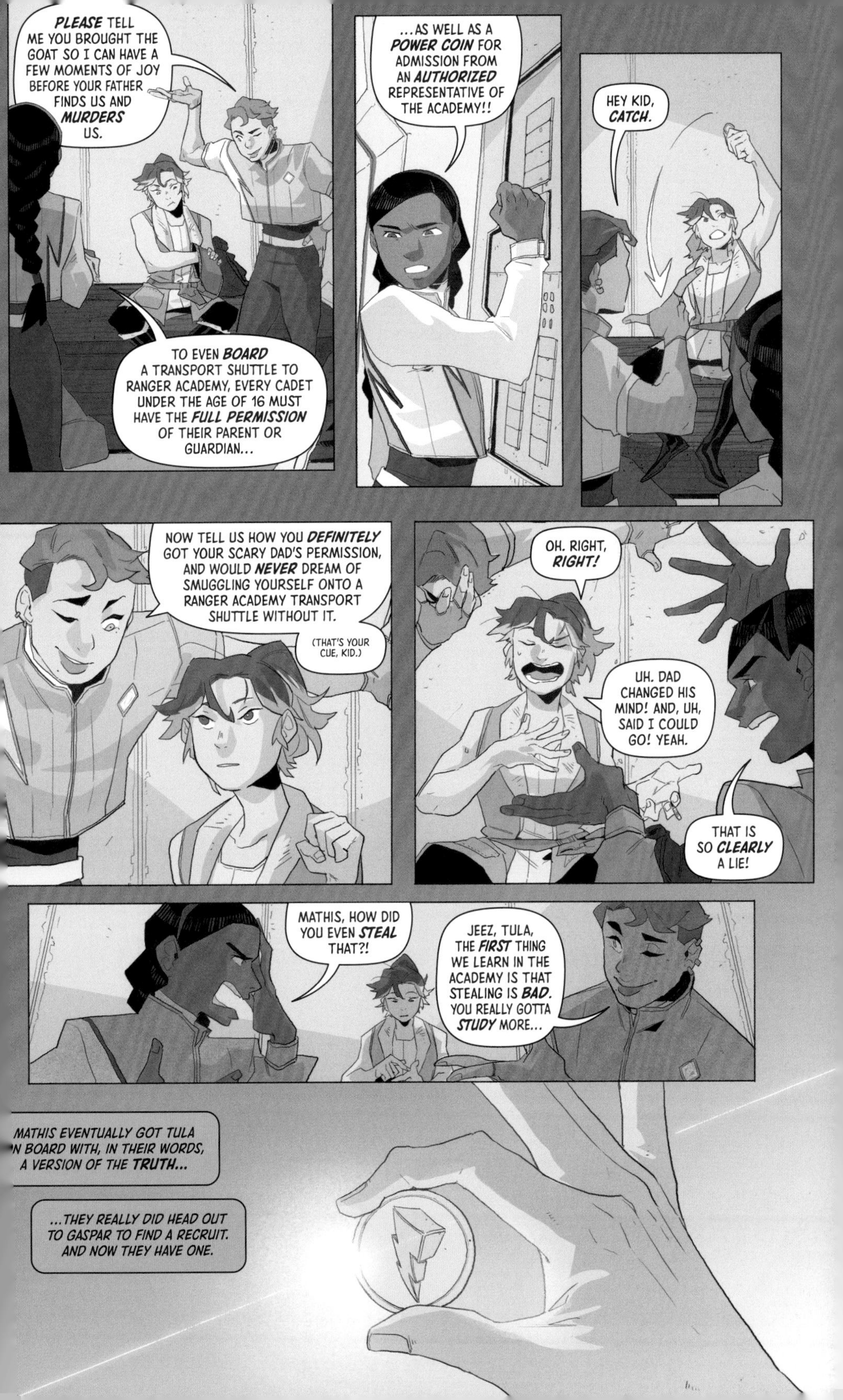
PLEASE TELL ME YOU BROUGHT THE GOAT SO I CAN HAVE A FEW MOMENTS OF JOY BEFORE YOUR FATHER FINDS US AND MURDERS US.
TO EVEN BOARD A TRANSPORT SHUTTLE TO RANGER ACADEMY, EVERY CADET UNDER THE AGE OF 16 MUST HAVE THE FULL PERMISSION OF THEIR PARENT OR GUARDIAN...
...AS WELL AS A POWER COIN FOR ADMISSION FROM AN AUTHORIZED REPRESENTATIVE OF THE ACADEMY!!
HEY KID, CATCH.
NOW TELL US HOW YOU DEFINITELY GOT YOUR SCARY DAD'S PERMISSION, AND WOULD NEVER DREAM OF SMUGGLING YOURSELF ONTO A RANGER ACADEMY TRANSPORT SHUTTLE WITHOUT IT.
(THAT'S YOUR CUE, KID.)
OH. RIGHT, RIGHT!
UH. DAD CHANGED HIS MIND! AND, UH, SAID I COULD GO! YEAH.
THAT IS SO CLEARLY A LIE!
MATHIS, HOW DID YOU EVEN STEAL THAT?!
JEEZ, TULA, THE FIRST THING WE LEARN IN THE ACADEMY IS THAT STEALING IS BAD. YOU REALLY GOTTA STUDY MORE...
MATHIS EVENTUALLY GOT TULA ON BOARD WITH, IN THEIR WORDS, A VERSION OF THE TRUTH...
...THEY REALLY DID HEAD OUT TO GASPAR TO FIND A RECRUIT. AND NOW THEY HAVE ONE.

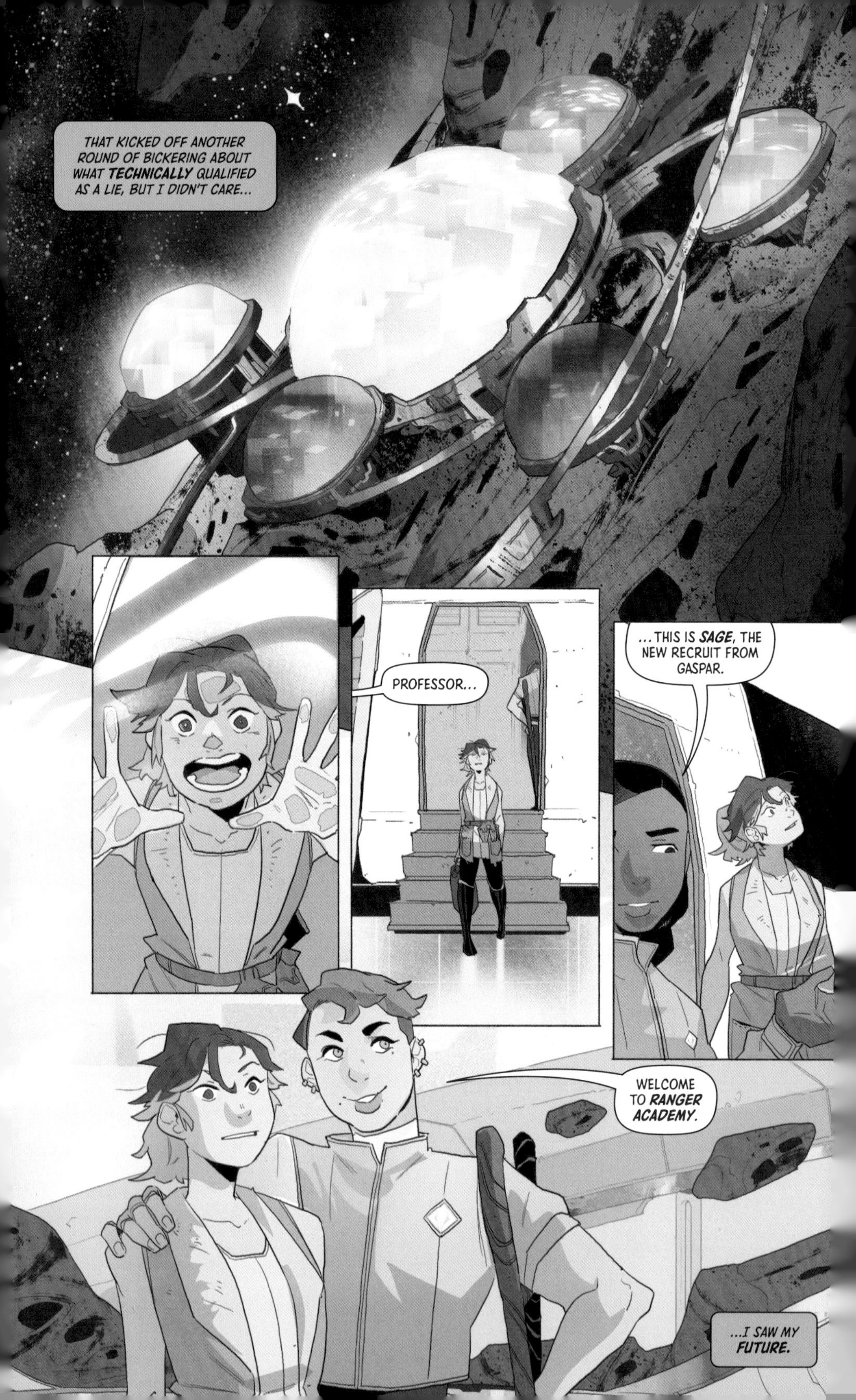
THAT KICKED OFF ANOTHER ROUND OF BICKERING ABOUT WHAT TECHNICALLY QUALIFIED AS A LIE, BUT I DIDN'T CARE...
PROFESSOR...
...THIS IS SAGE, THE NEW RECRUIT FROM GASPAR.
WELCOME TO RANGER ACADEMY.
...I SAW MY FUTURE.

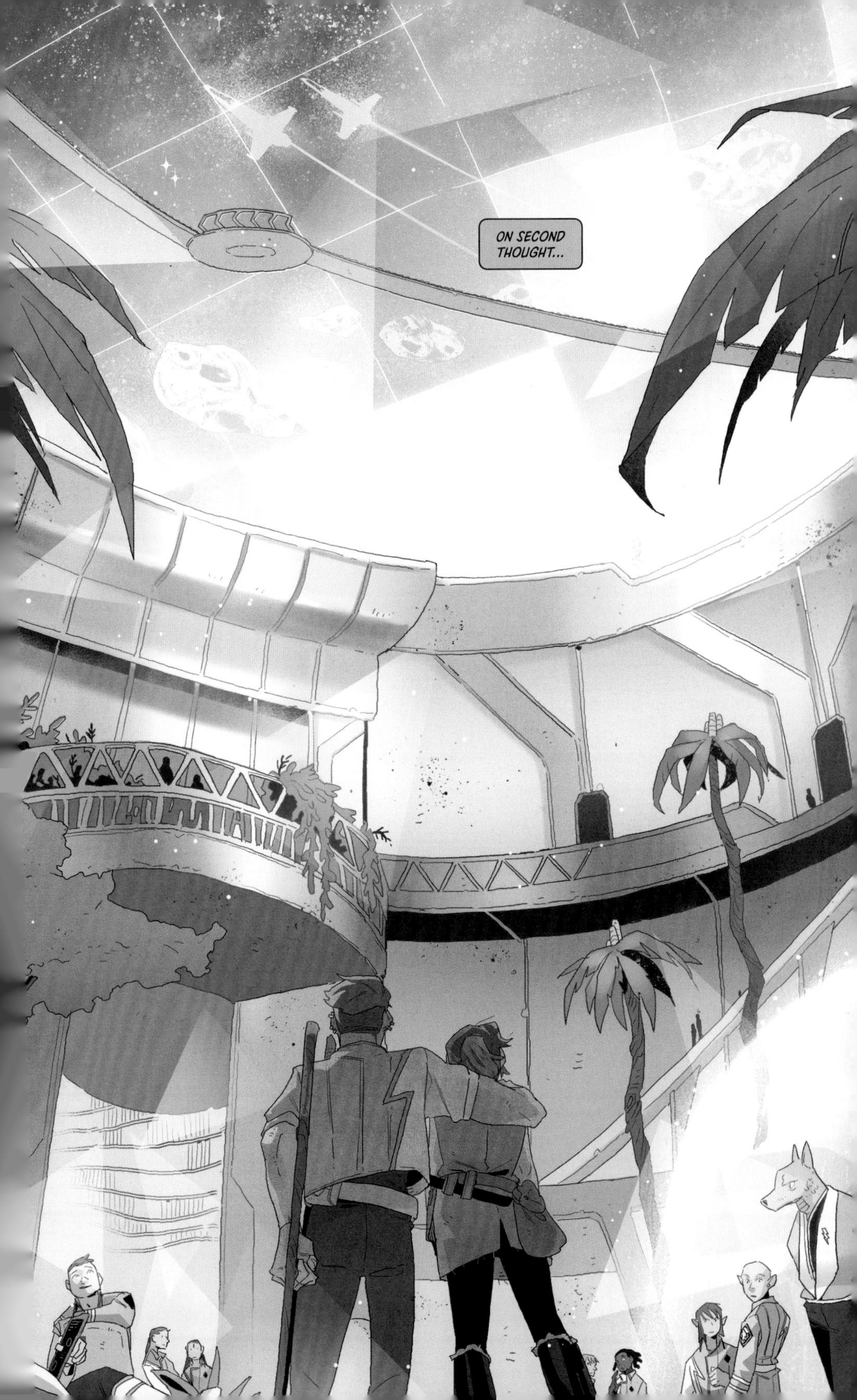
ON SECOND THOUGHT...

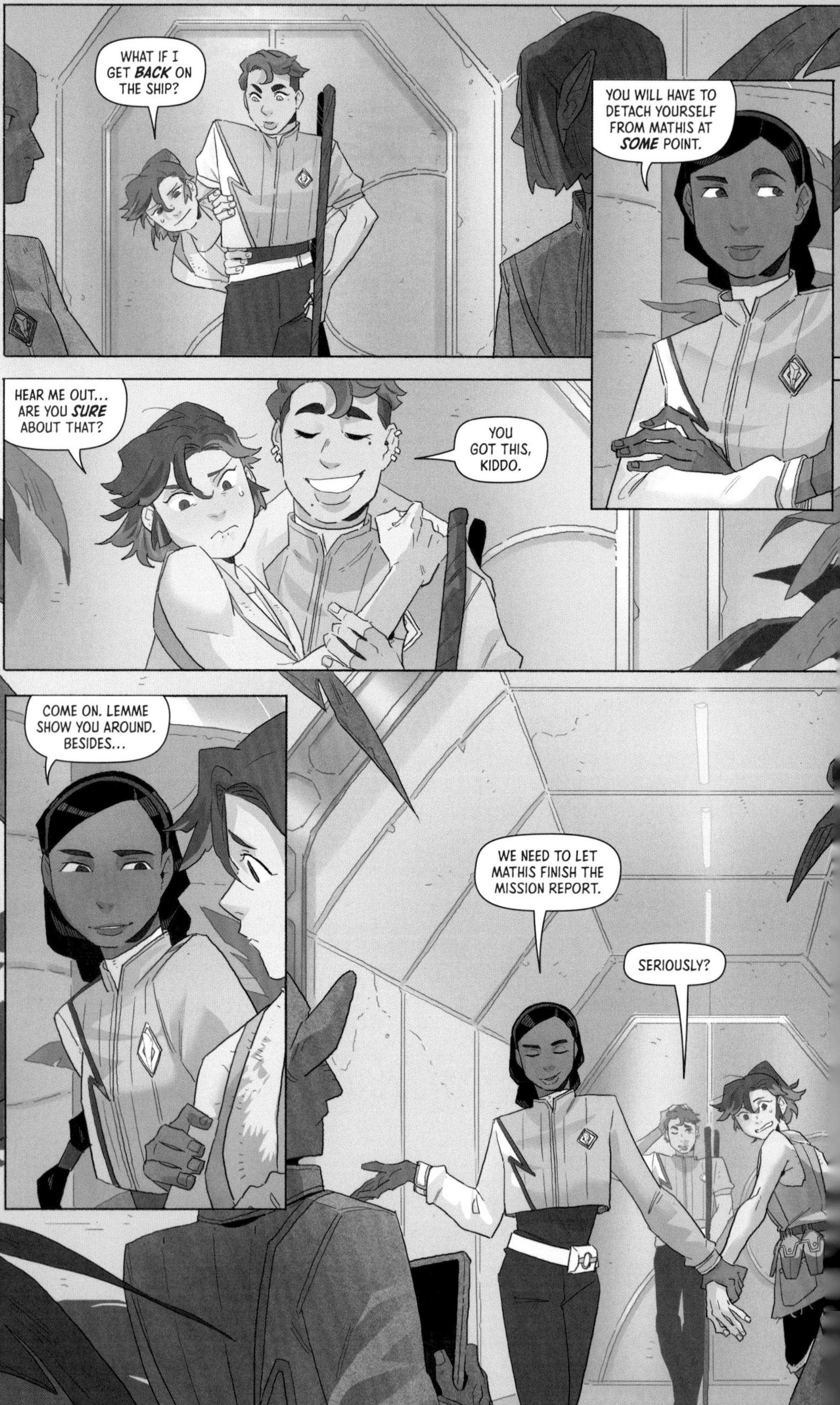
WHAT IF I GET ***BACK*** ON THE SHIP?
YOU WILL HAVE TO DETACH YOURSELF FROM MATHIS AT ***SOME*** POINT.
HEAR ME OUT... ARE YOU ***SURE*** ABOUT THAT?
YOU GOT THIS, KIDDO.
COME ON. LEMME SHOW YOU AROUND. BESIDES...
WE NEED TO LET MATHIS FINISH THE MISSION REPORT.
SERIOUSLY?

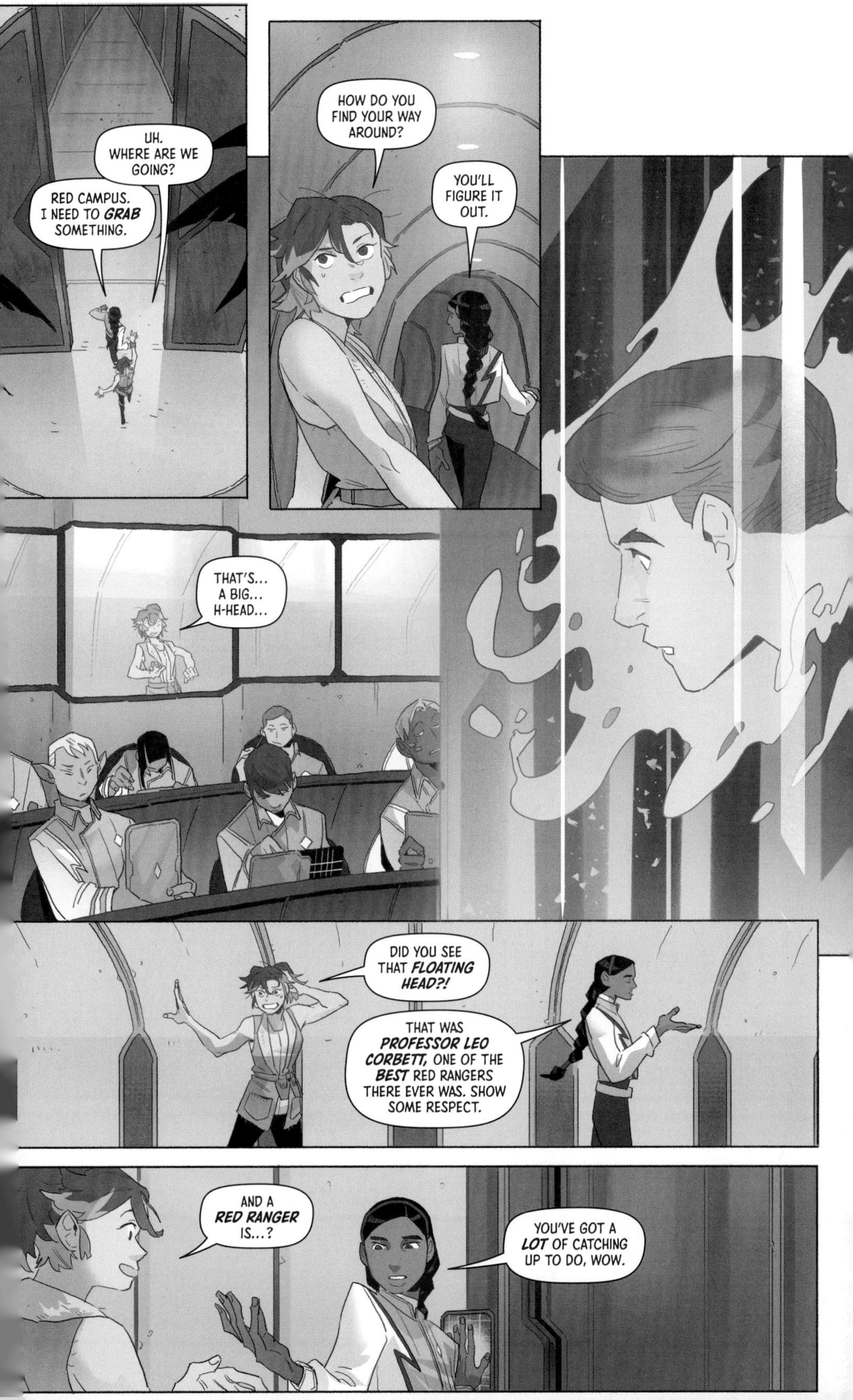
UH. WHERE ARE WE GOING?
RED CAMPUS. I NEED TO GRAB SOMETHING.
HOW DO YOU FIND YOUR WAY AROUND?
YOU'LL FIGURE IT OUT.
THAT'S... A BIG... H-HEAD...
DID YOU SEE THAT FLOATING HEAD?!
THAT WAS PROFESSOR LEO CORBETT, ONE OF THE BEST RED RANGERS THERE EVER WAS. SHOW SOME RESPECT.
AND A RED RANGER IS...?
YOU'VE GOT A LOT OF CATCHING UP TO DO, WOW.

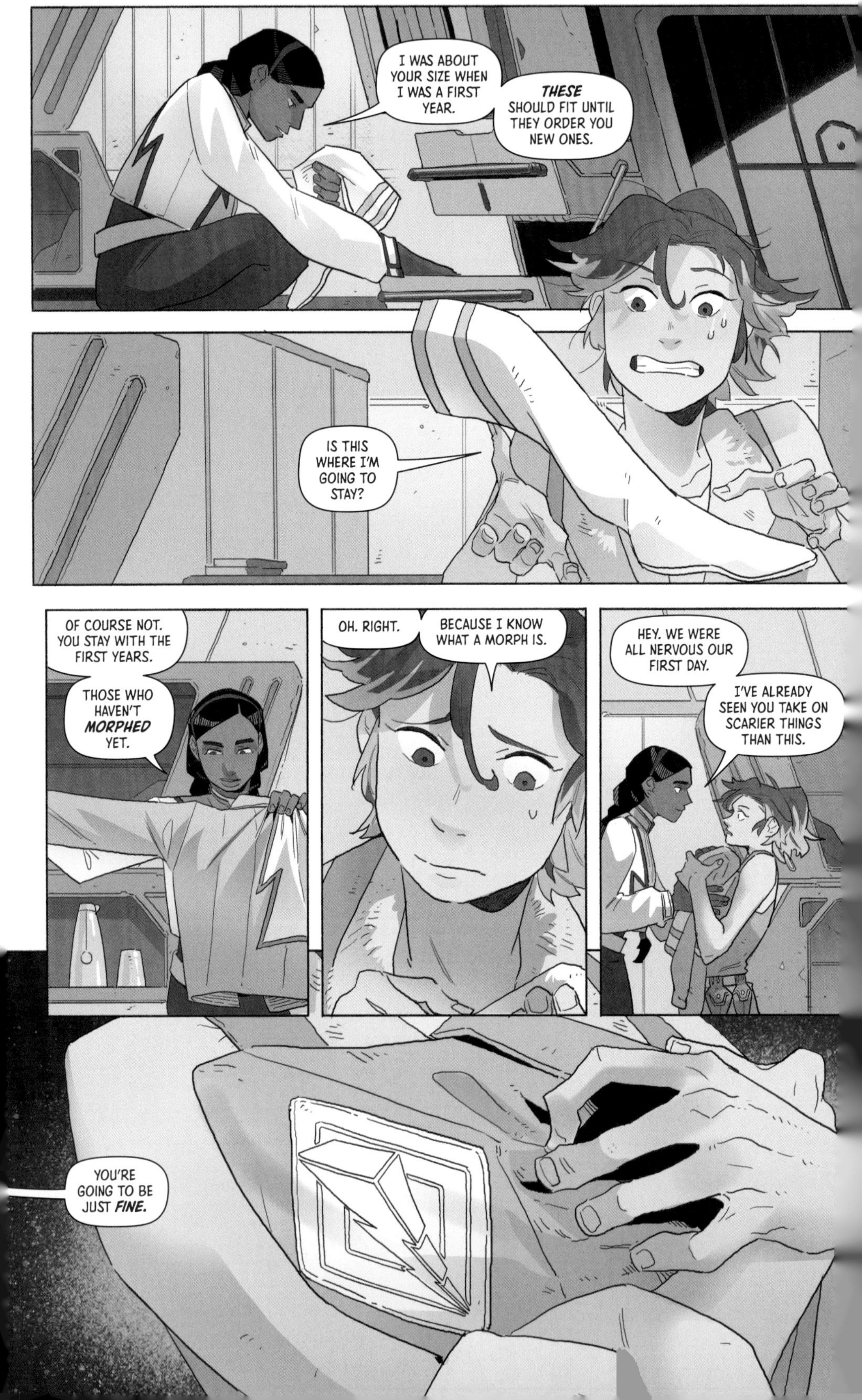
I WAS ABOUT YOUR SIZE WHEN I WAS A FIRST YEAR.
THESE SHOULD FIT UNTIL THEY ORDER YOU NEW ONES.
IS THIS WHERE I'M GOING TO STAY?
OF COURSE NOT. YOU STAY WITH THE FIRST YEARS.
THOSE WHO HAVEN'T *MORPHED* YET.
OH. RIGHT.
BECAUSE I KNOW WHAT A MORPH IS.
HEY. WE WERE ALL NERVOUS OUR FIRST DAY.
I'VE ALREADY SEEN YOU TAKE ON SCARIER THINGS THAN THIS.
YOU'RE GOING TO BE JUST *FINE.*

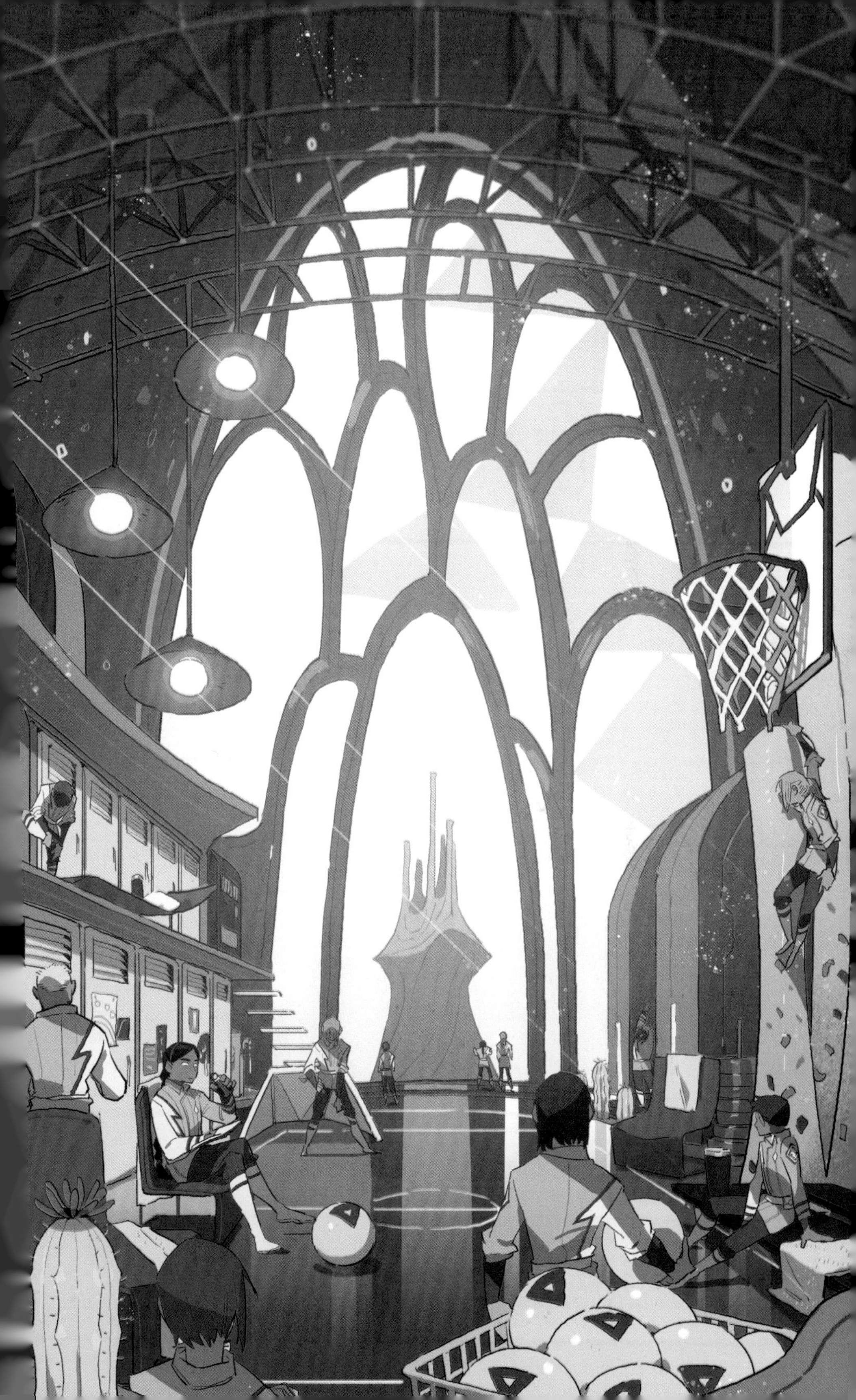

CHAPTER TWO

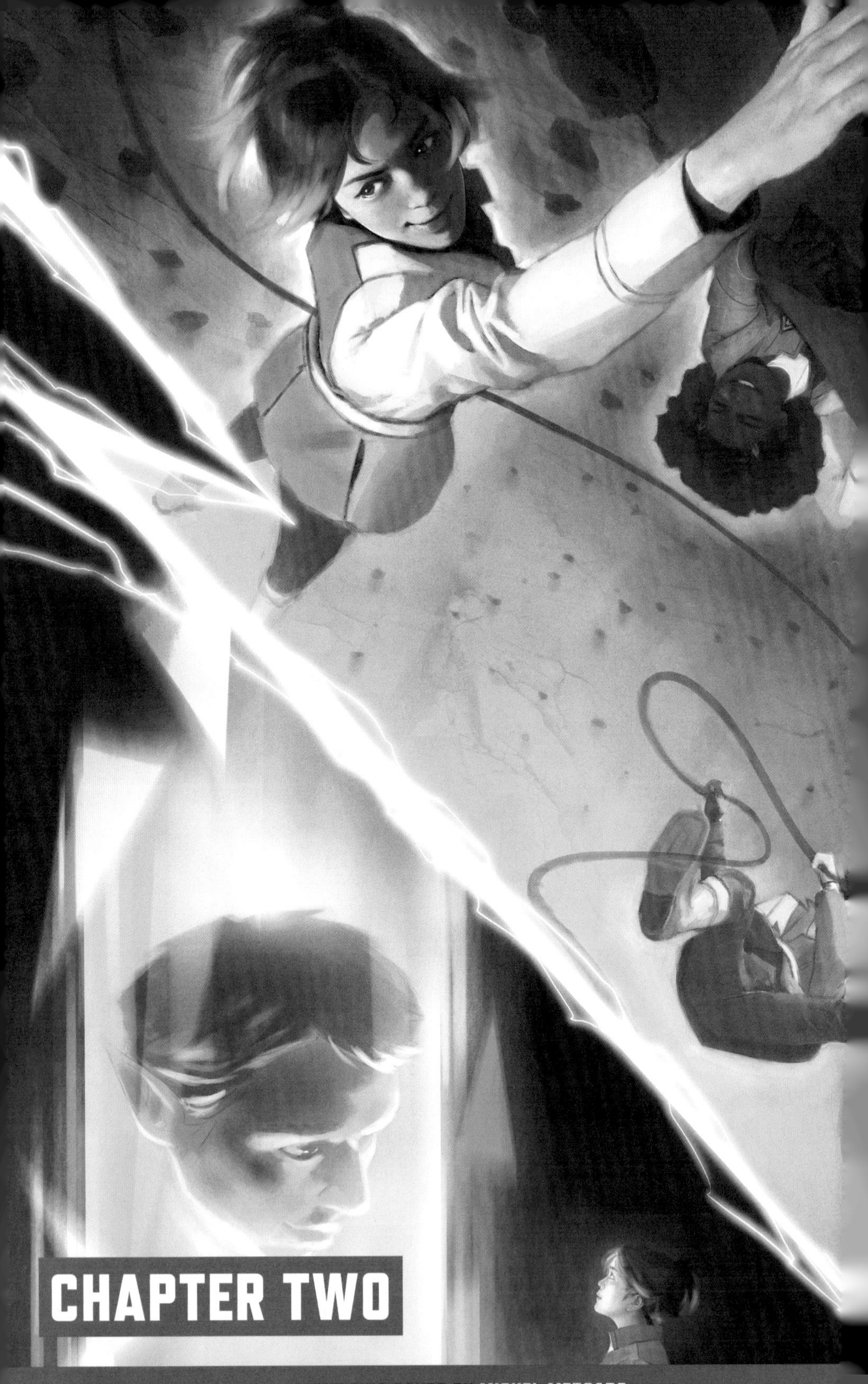

ISSUE TWO COVER BY MIGUEL MERCADO

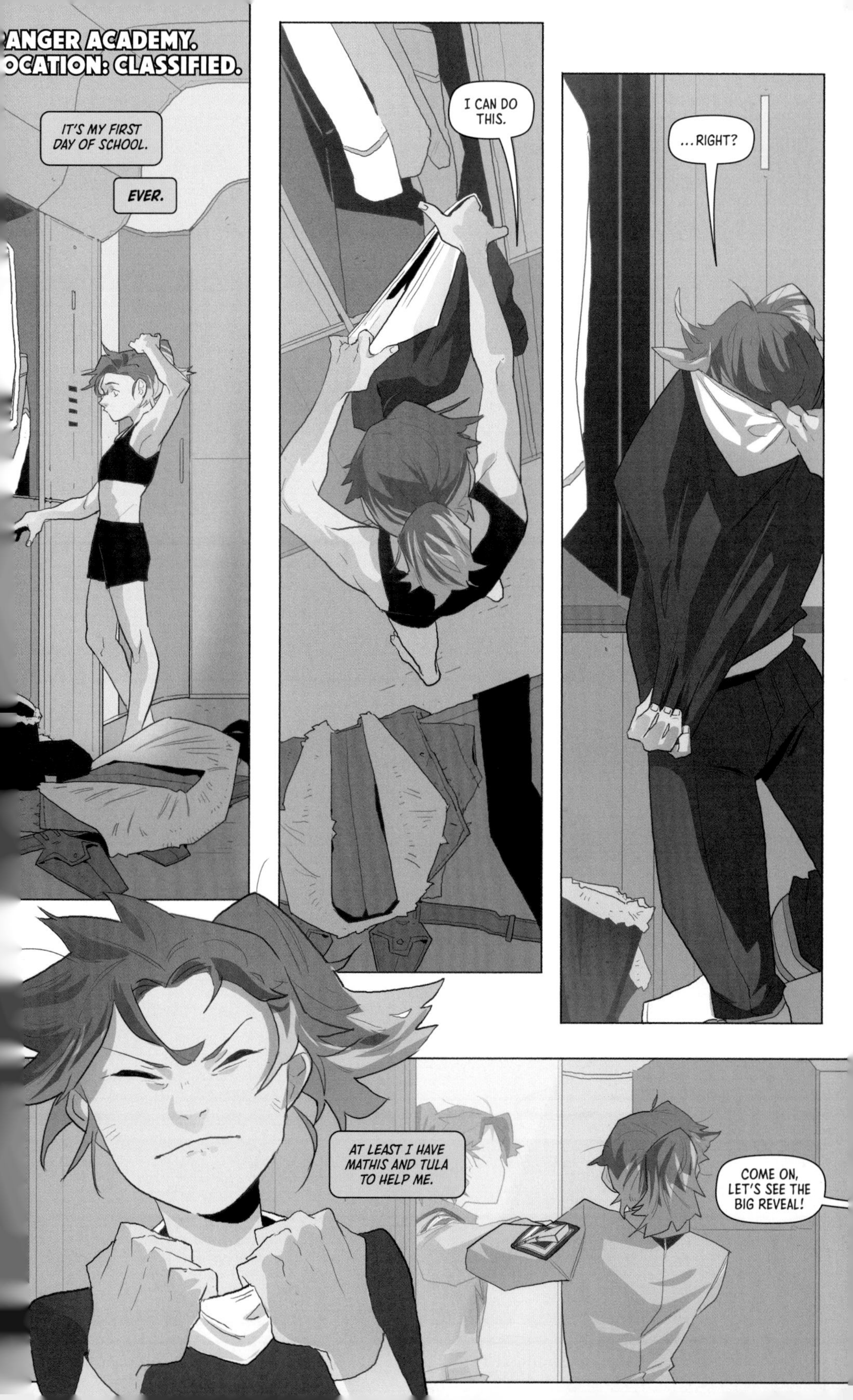
ANGER ACADEMY.
OCATION: CLASSIFIED.
IT'S MY FIRST DAY OF SCHOOL.
EVER.
I CAN DO THIS.
...RIGHT?
AT LEAST I HAVE MATHIS AND TULA TO HELP ME.
COME ON, LET'S SEE THE BIG REVEAL!

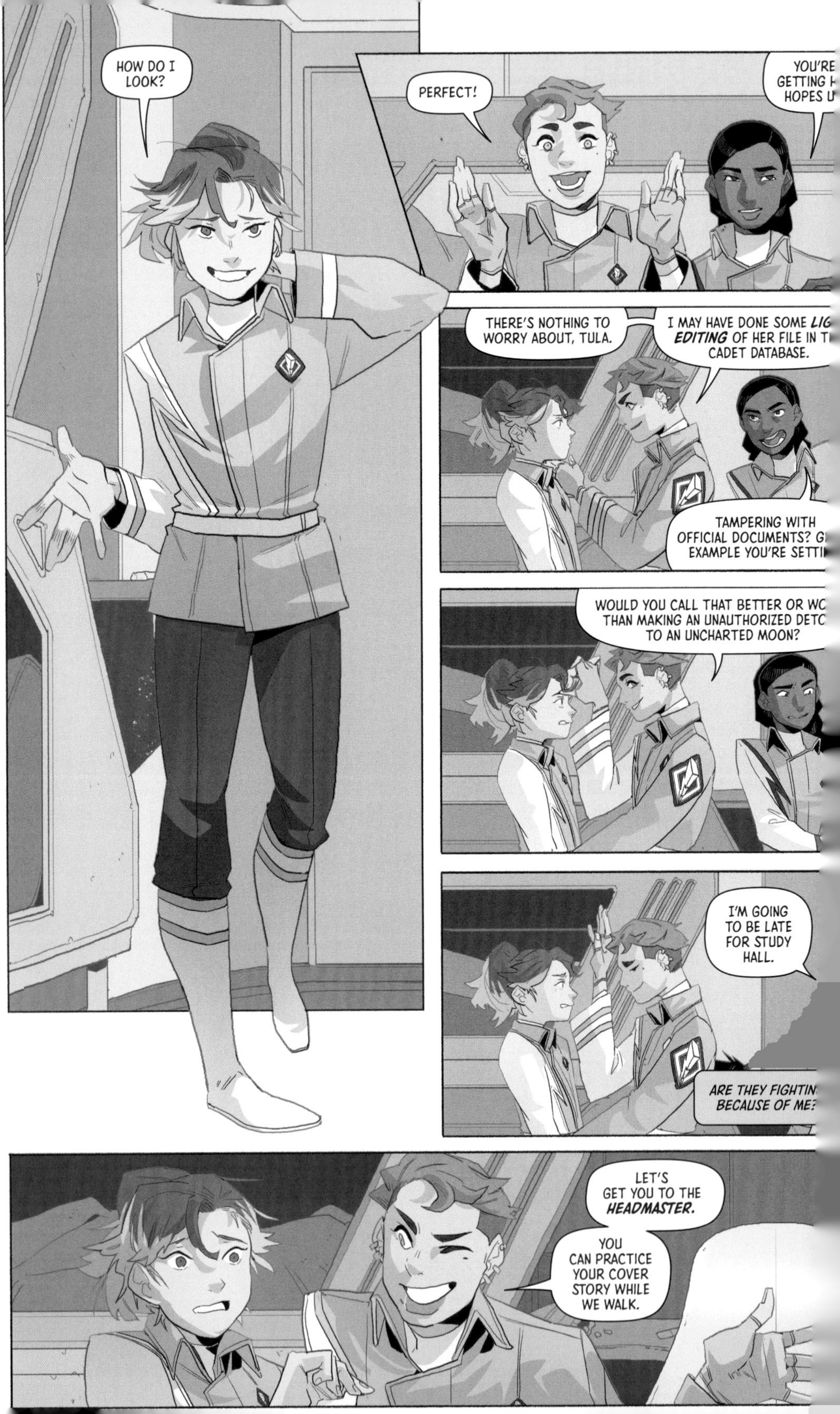
HOW DO I LOOK?
PERFECT!
YOU'RE GETTING H HOPES U
THERE'S NOTHING TO WORRY ABOUT, TULA.
I MAY HAVE DONE SOME ***LIG EDITING*** OF HER FILE IN T CADET DATABASE.
TAMPERING WITH OFFICIAL DOCUMENTS? G EXAMPLE YOU'RE SETTI
WOULD YOU CALL THAT BETTER OR WO THAN MAKING AN UNAUTHORIZED DETO TO AN UNCHARTED MOON?
I'M GOING TO BE LATE FOR STUDY HALL.
ARE THEY FIGHTIN BECAUSE OF ME?
LET'S GET YOU TO THE ***HEADMASTER.***
YOU CAN PRACTICE YOUR COVER STORY WHILE WE WALK.

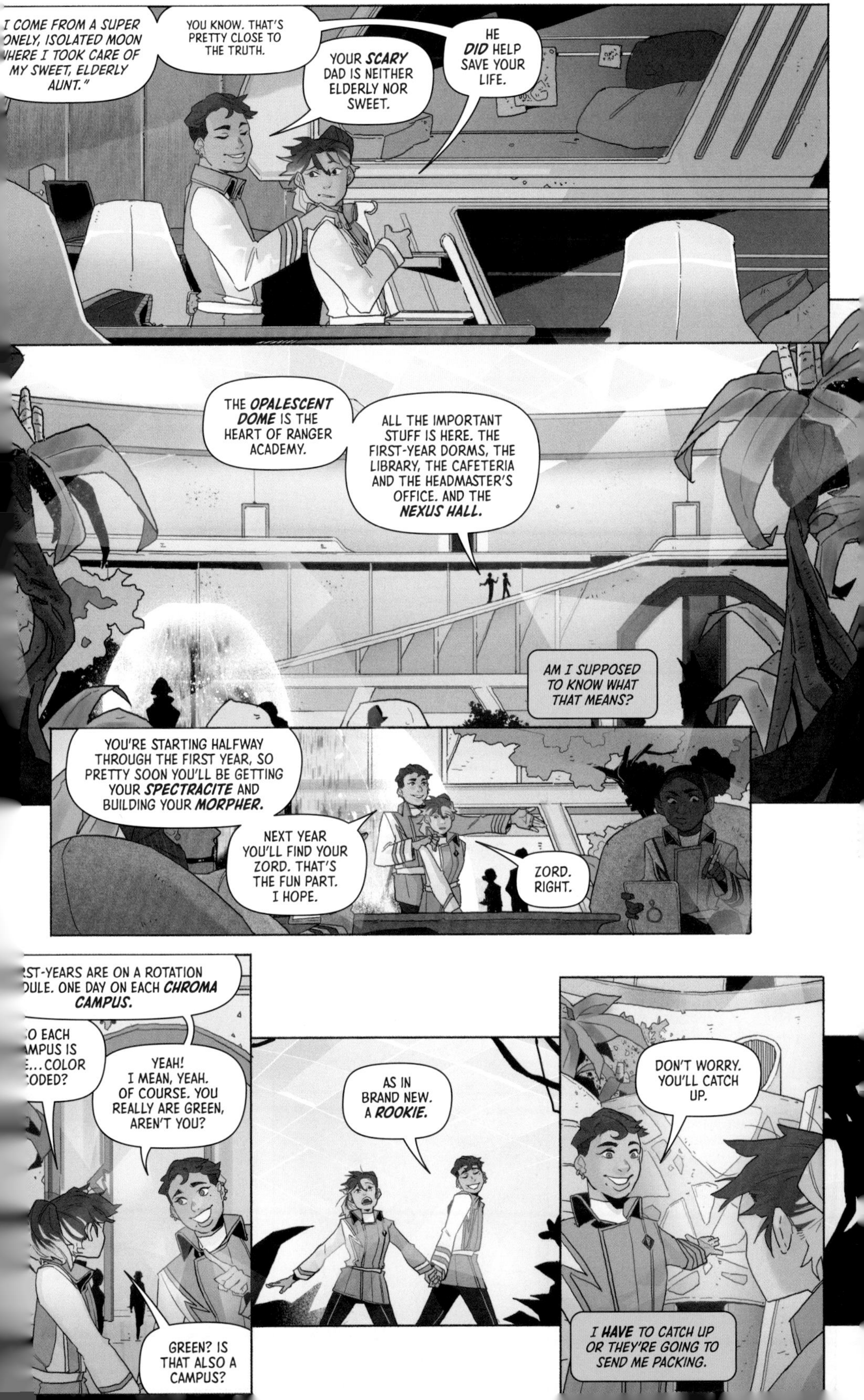
I COME FROM A SUPER
ONELY, ISOLATED MOON
WHERE I TOOK CARE OF
MY SWEET, ELDERLY
AUNT."
YOU KNOW. THAT'S PRETTY CLOSE TO THE TRUTH.
YOUR SCARY DAD IS NEITHER ELDERLY NOR SWEET.
HE DID HELP SAVE YOUR LIFE.
THE OPALESCENT DOME IS THE HEART OF RANGER ACADEMY.
ALL THE IMPORTANT STUFF IS HERE. THE FIRST-YEAR DORMS, THE LIBRARY, THE CAFETERIA AND THE HEADMASTER'S OFFICE. AND THE NEXUS HALL.
AM I SUPPOSED TO KNOW WHAT THAT MEANS?
YOU'RE STARTING HALFWAY THROUGH THE FIRST YEAR, SO PRETTY SOON YOU'LL BE GETTING YOUR SPECTRACITE AND BUILDING YOUR MORPHER.
NEXT YEAR YOU'LL FIND YOUR ZORD. THAT'S THE FUN PART. I HOPE.
ZORD. RIGHT.
RST-YEARS ARE ON A ROTATION
DULE. ONE DAY ON EACH CHROMA CAMPUS.
O EACH
MPUS IS
...COLOR
ODED?
YEAH! I MEAN, YEAH. OF COURSE. YOU REALLY ARE GREEN, AREN'T YOU?
GREEN? IS THAT ALSO A CAMPUS?
AS IN BRAND NEW. A ROOKIE.
DON'T WORRY. YOU'LL CATCH UP.
I HAVE TO CATCH UP OR THEY'RE GOING TO SEND ME PACKING.

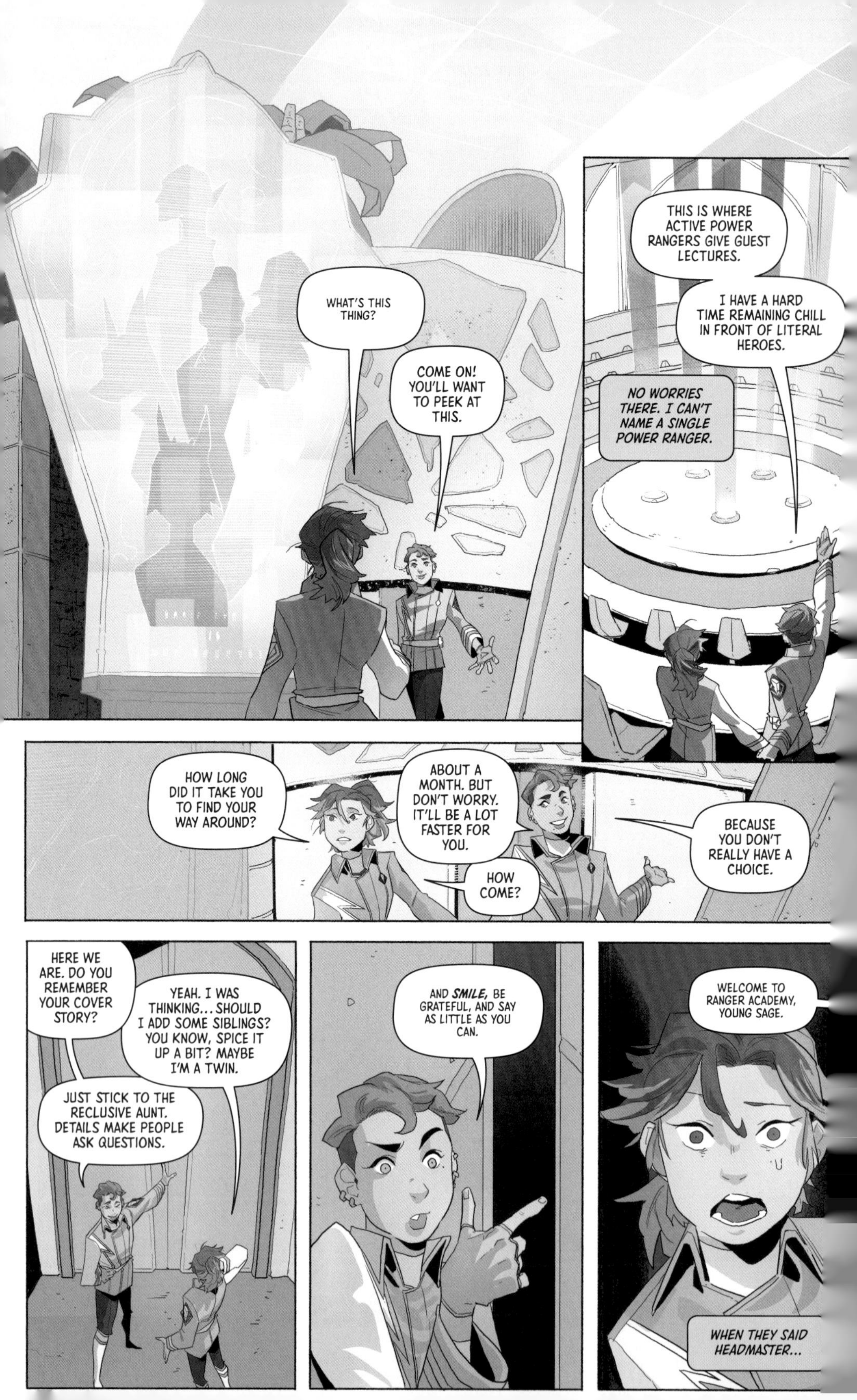
WHAT'S THIS THING?
COME ON! YOU'LL WANT TO PEEK AT THIS.
THIS IS WHERE ACTIVE POWER RANGERS GIVE GUEST LECTURES.
I HAVE A HARD TIME REMAINING CHILL IN FRONT OF LITERAL HEROES.
NO WORRIES THERE. I CAN'T NAME A SINGLE POWER RANGER.
HOW LONG DID IT TAKE YOU TO FIND YOUR WAY AROUND?
ABOUT A MONTH. BUT DON'T WORRY. IT'LL BE A LOT FASTER FOR YOU.
HOW COME?
BECAUSE YOU DON'T REALLY HAVE A CHOICE.
HERE WE ARE. DO YOU REMEMBER YOUR COVER STORY?
YEAH. I WAS THINKING... SHOULD I ADD SOME SIBLINGS? YOU KNOW, SPICE IT UP A BIT? MAYBE I'M A TWIN.
JUST STICK TO THE RECLUSIVE AUNT. DETAILS MAKE PEOPLE ASK QUESTIONS.
AND SMILE, BE GRATEFUL, AND SAY AS LITTLE AS YOU CAN.
WELCOME TO RANGER ACADEMY, YOUNG SAGE.
WHEN THEY SAID HEADMASTER...

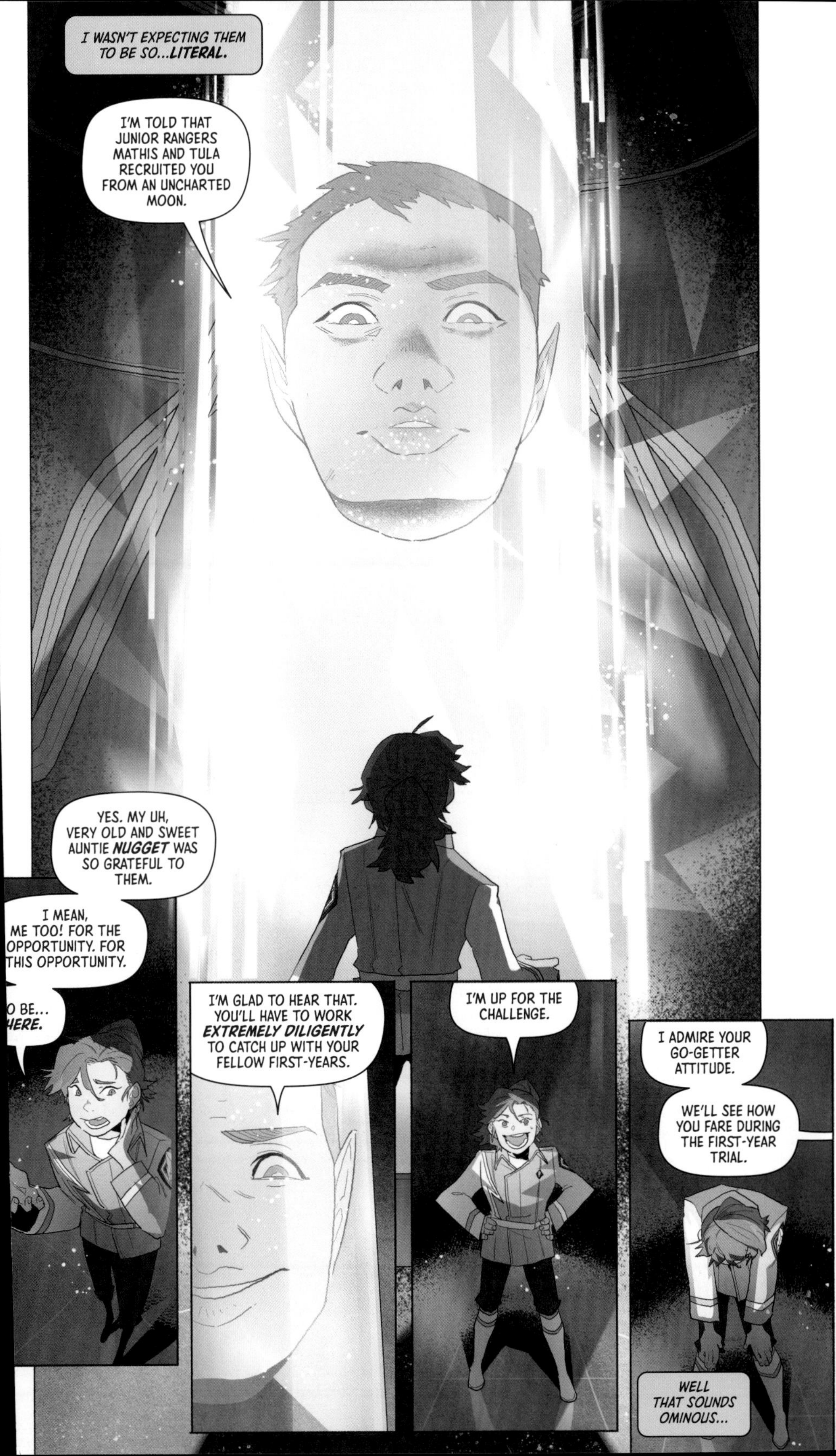
I WASN'T EXPECTING THEM TO BE SO...LITERAL.
I'M TOLD THAT JUNIOR RANGERS MATHIS AND TULA RECRUITED YOU FROM AN UNCHARTED MOON.
YES. MY UH, VERY OLD AND SWEET AUNTIE NUGGET WAS SO GRATEFUL TO THEM.
I MEAN, ME TOO! FOR THE OPPORTUNITY. FOR THIS OPPORTUNITY.
I'M GLAD TO HEAR THAT. YOU'LL HAVE TO WORK EXTREMELY DILIGENTLY TO CATCH UP WITH YOUR FELLOW FIRST-YEARS.
I'M UP FOR THE CHALLENGE.
I ADMIRE YOUR GO-GETTER ATTITUDE.
WE'LL SEE HOW YOU FARE DURING THE FIRST-YEAR TRIAL.
WELL THAT SOUNDS OMINOUS...

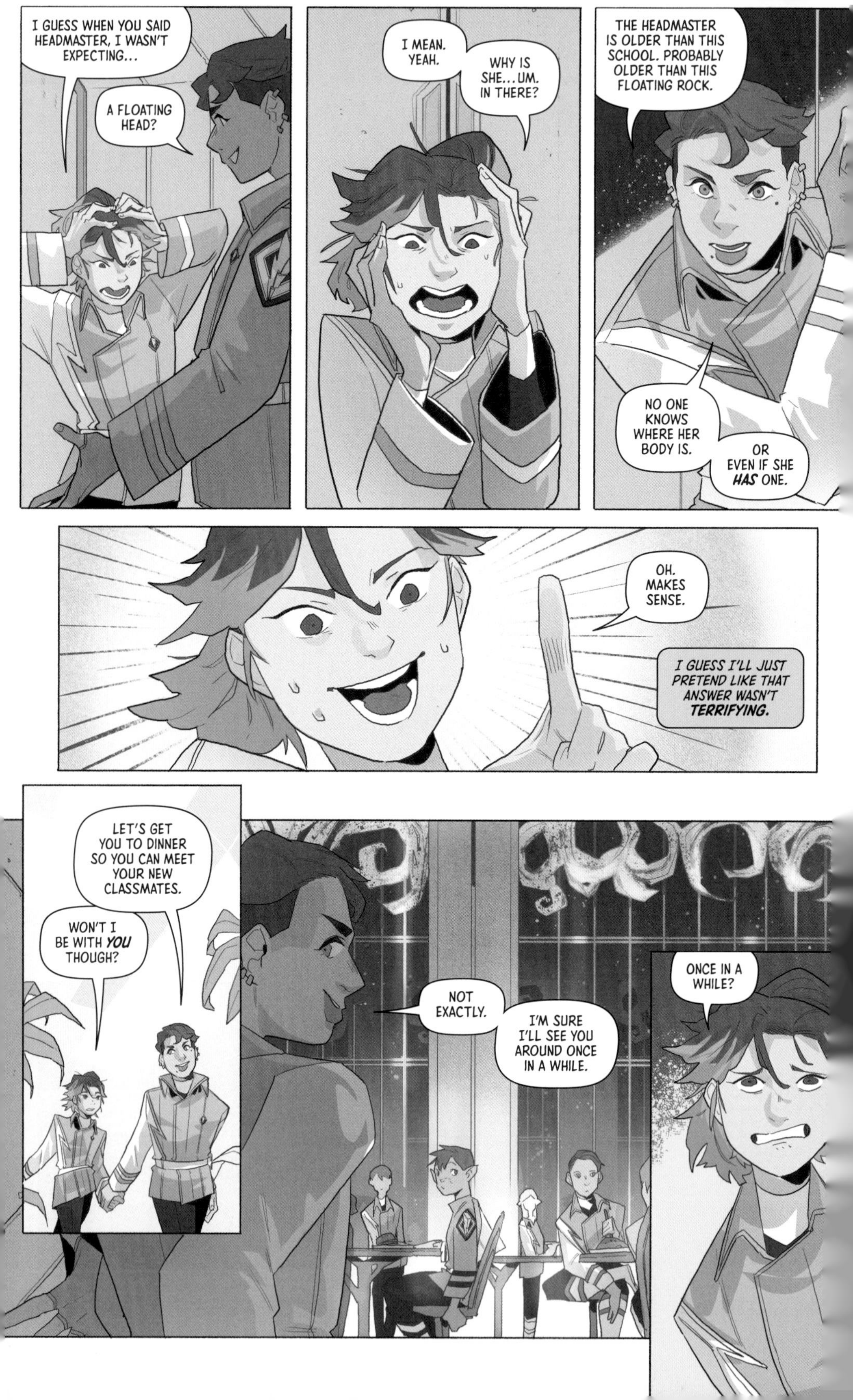
I GUESS WHEN YOU SAID HEADMASTER, I WASN'T EXPECTING...
A FLOATING HEAD?
I MEAN. YEAH.
WHY IS SHE... UM. IN THERE?
THE HEADMASTER IS OLDER THAN THIS SCHOOL. PROBABLY OLDER THAN THIS FLOATING ROCK.
NO ONE KNOWS WHERE HER BODY IS.
OR EVEN IF SHE ***HAS*** ONE.
OH. MAKES SENSE.
I GUESS I'LL JUST PRETEND LIKE THAT ANSWER WASN'T ***TERRIFYING.***
LET'S GET YOU TO DINNER SO YOU CAN MEET YOUR NEW CLASSMATES.
WON'T I BE WITH ***YOU*** THOUGH?
NOT EXACTLY.
I'M SURE I'LL SEE YOU AROUND ONCE IN A WHILE.
ONCE IN A WHILE?

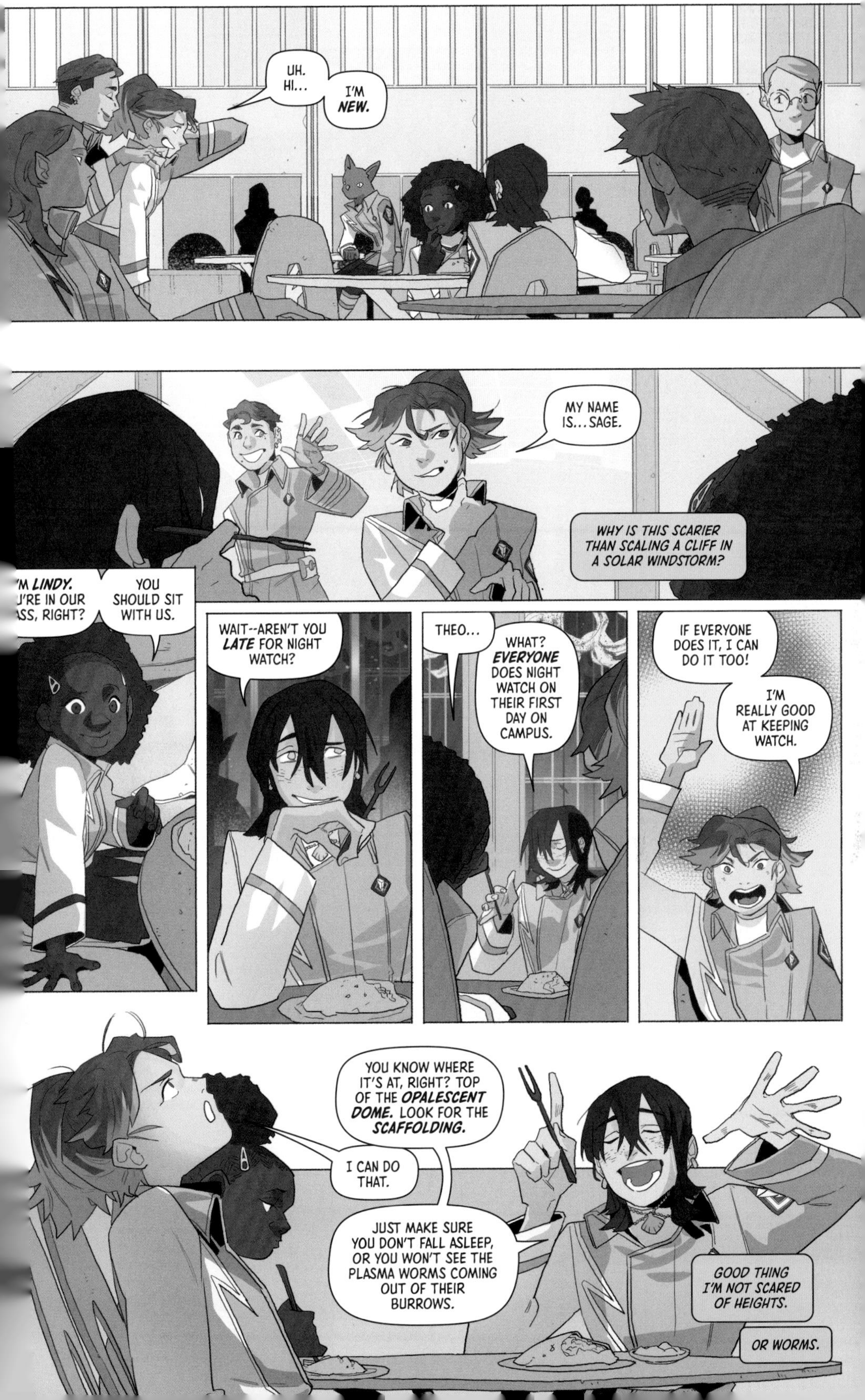
UH. HI...
I'M NEW.
MY NAME IS... SAGE.
WHY IS THIS SCARIER THAN SCALING A CLIFF IN A SOLAR WINDSTORM?
'M LINDY. U'RE IN OUR ASS, RIGHT?
YOU SHOULD SIT WITH US.
WAIT--AREN'T YOU LATE FOR NIGHT WATCH?
THEO...
WHAT? EVERYONE DOES NIGHT WATCH ON THEIR FIRST DAY ON CAMPUS.
IF EVERYONE DOES IT, I CAN DO IT TOO!
I'M REALLY GOOD AT KEEPING WATCH.
YOU KNOW WHERE IT'S AT, RIGHT? TOP OF THE OPALESCENT DOME. LOOK FOR THE SCAFFOLDING.
I CAN DO THAT.
JUST MAKE SURE YOU DON'T FALL ASLEEP, OR YOU WON'T SEE THE PLASMA WORMS COMING OUT OF THEIR BURROWS.
GOOD THING I'M NOT SCARED OF HEIGHTS.
OR WORMS.

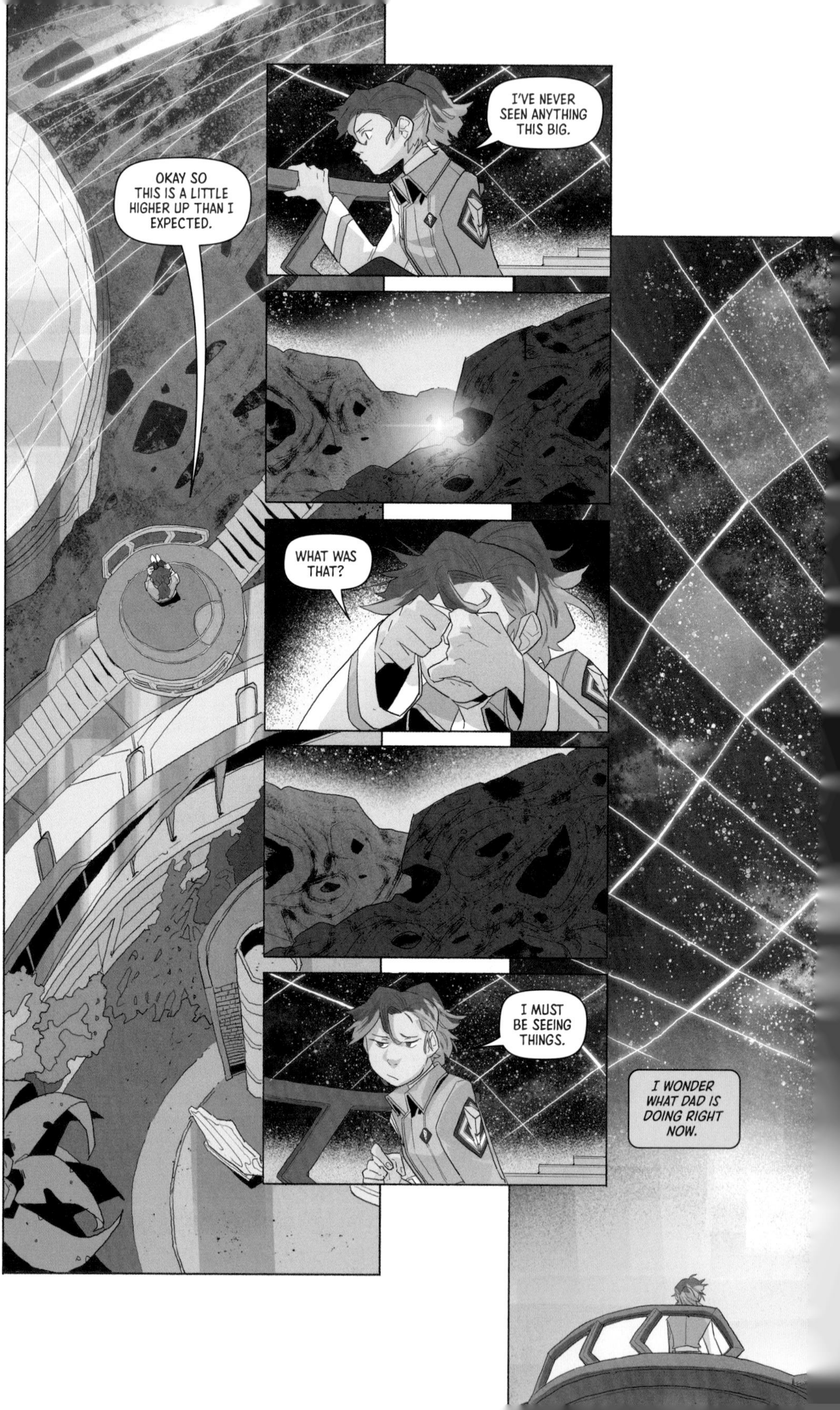
OKAY SO THIS IS A LITTLE HIGHER UP THAN I EXPECTED.
I'VE NEVER SEEN ANYTHING THIS BIG.
WHAT WAS THAT?
I MUST BE SEEING THINGS.
I WONDER WHAT DAD IS DOING RIGHT NOW.

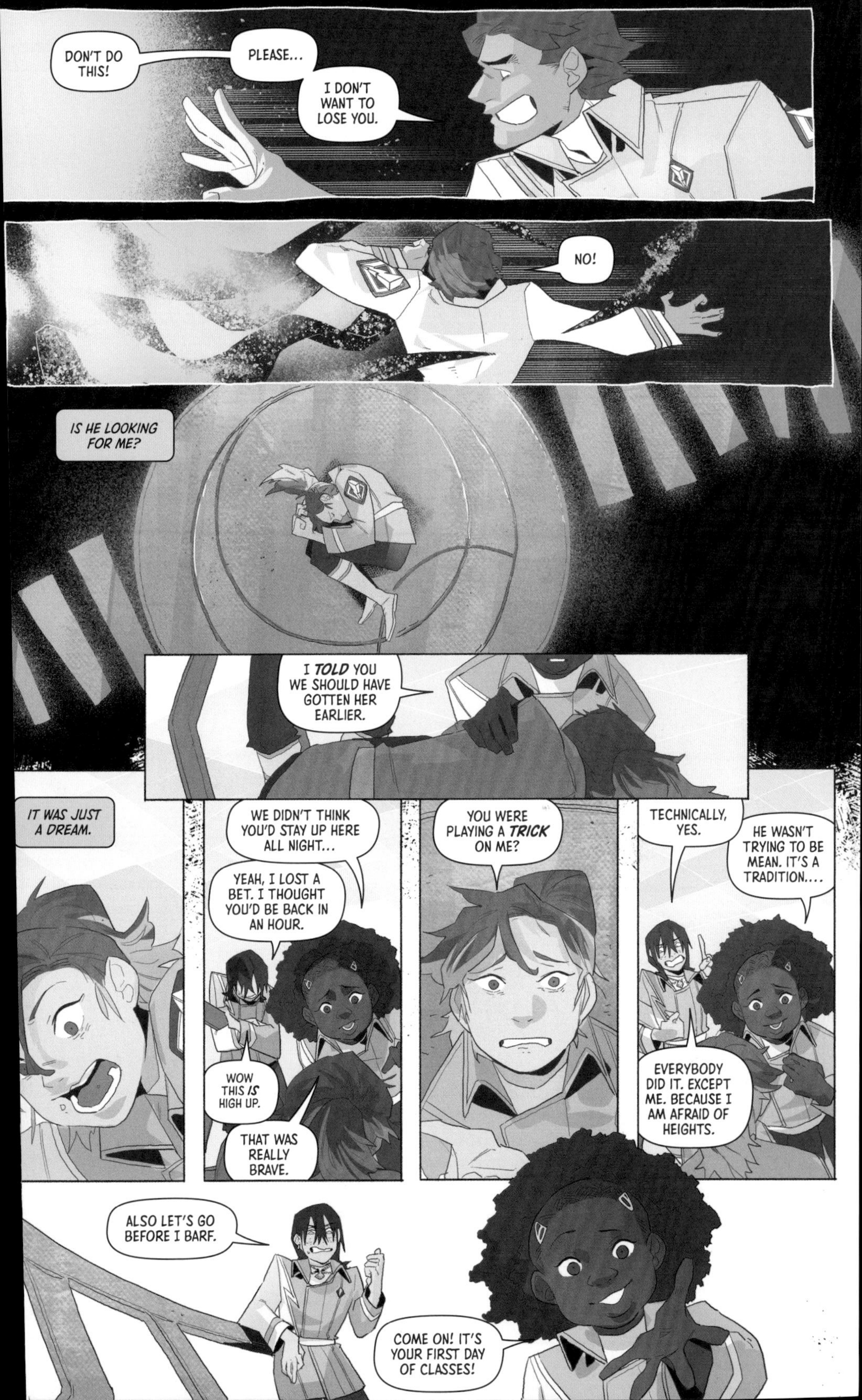
DON'T DO THIS!
PLEASE...
I DON'T WANT TO LOSE YOU.
NO!
IS HE LOOKING FOR ME?
I TOLD YOU WE SHOULD HAVE GOTTEN HER EARLIER.
IT WAS JUST A DREAM.
WE DIDN'T THINK YOU'D STAY UP HERE ALL NIGHT...
YEAH, I LOST A BET. I THOUGHT YOU'D BE BACK IN AN HOUR.
WOW THIS IS HIGH UP.
THAT WAS REALLY BRAVE.
YOU WERE PLAYING A TRICK ON ME?
TECHNICALLY, YES.
HE WASN'T TRYING TO BE MEAN. IT'S A TRADITION....
EVERYBODY DID IT. EXCEPT ME. BECAUSE I AM AFRAID OF HEIGHTS.
ALSO LET'S GO BEFORE I BARF.
COME ON! IT'S YOUR FIRST DAY OF CLASSES!

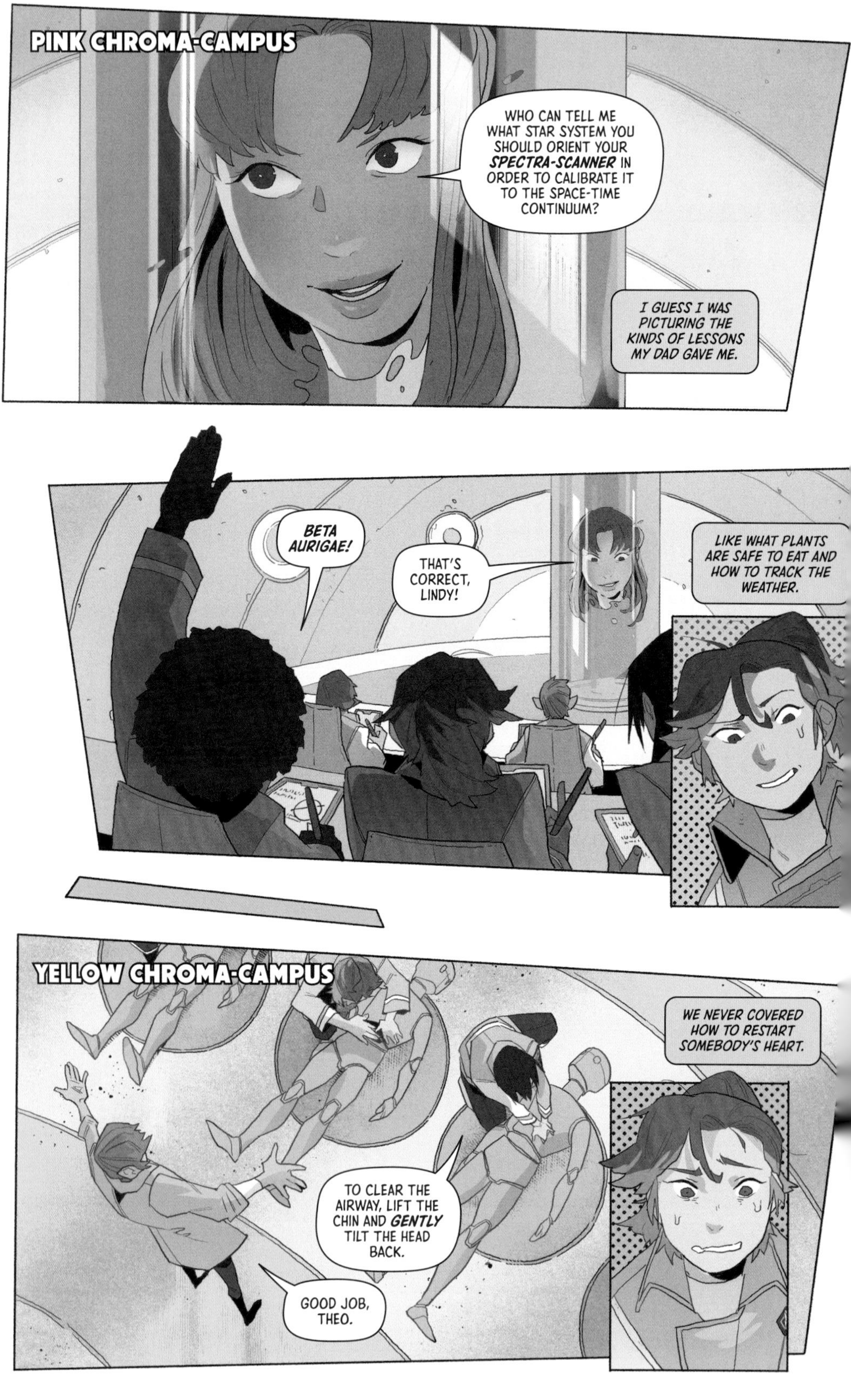
PINK CHROMA-CAMPUS
WHO CAN TELL ME WHAT STAR SYSTEM YOU SHOULD ORIENT YOUR SPECTRA-SCANNER IN ORDER TO CALIBRATE IT TO THE SPACE-TIME CONTINUUM?
I GUESS I WAS PICTURING THE KINDS OF LESSONS MY DAD GAVE ME.
BETA AURIGAE!
THAT'S CORRECT, LINDY!
LIKE WHAT PLANTS ARE SAFE TO EAT AND HOW TO TRACK THE WEATHER.
YELLOW CHROMA-CAMPUS
WE NEVER COVERED HOW TO RESTART SOMEBODY'S HEART.
TO CLEAR THE AIRWAY, LIFT THE CHIN AND GENTLY TILT THE HEAD BACK.
GOOD JOB, THEO.

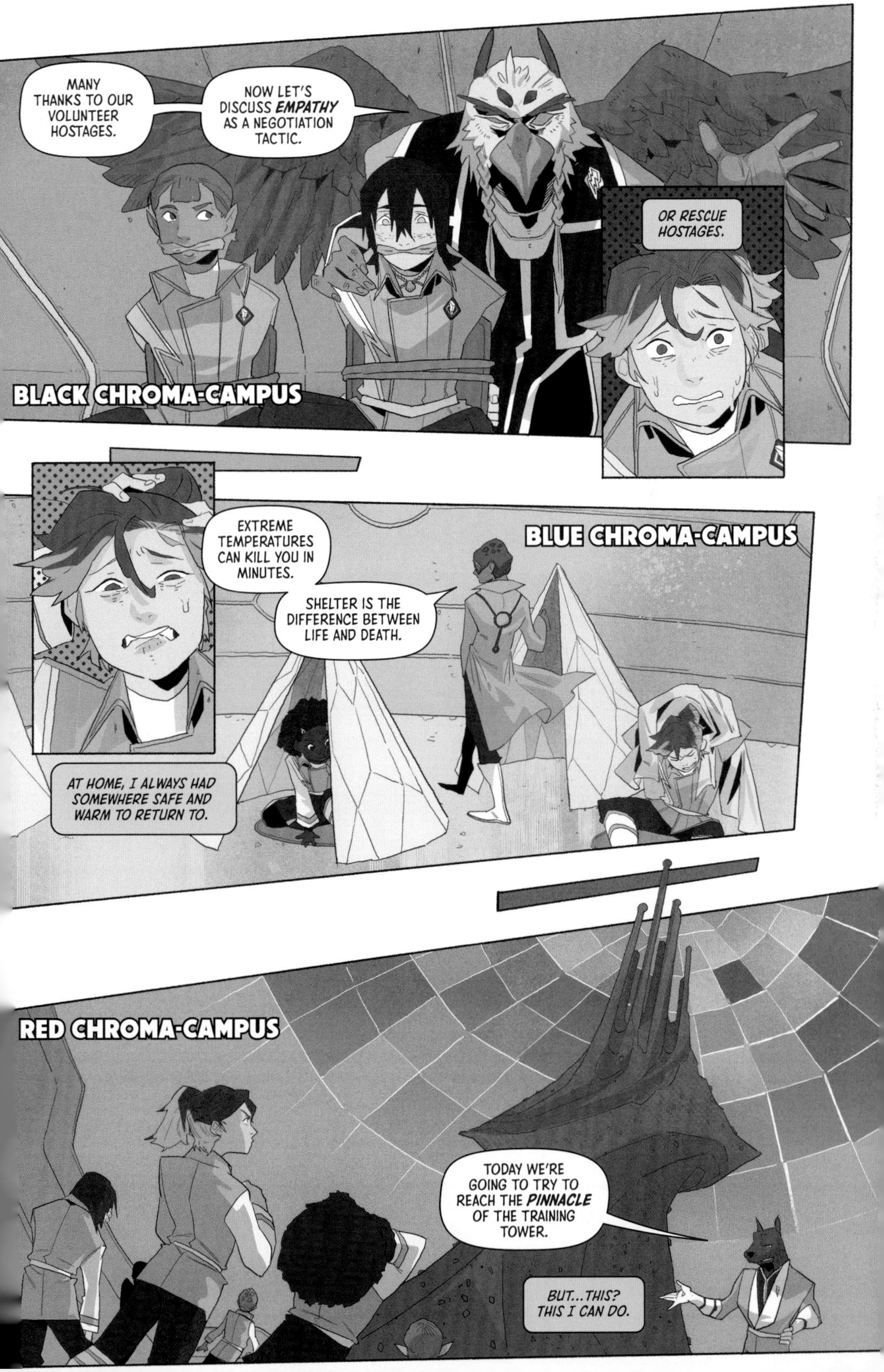

MANY THANKS TO OUR VOLUNTEER HOSTAGES.
NOW LET'S DISCUSS *EMPATHY* AS A NEGOTIATION TACTIC.
BLACK CHROMA-CAMPUS
OR RESCUE HOSTAGES.
BLUE CHROMA-CAMPUS
EXTREME TEMPERATURES CAN KILL YOU IN MINUTES.
SHELTER IS THE DIFFERENCE BETWEEN LIFE AND DEATH.
AT HOME, I ALWAYS HAD SOMEWHERE SAFE AND WARM TO RETURN TO.
RED CHROMA-CAMPUS
TODAY WE'RE GOING TO TRY TO REACH THE *PINNACLE* OF THE TRAINING TOWER.
BUT...THIS? THIS I CAN DO.

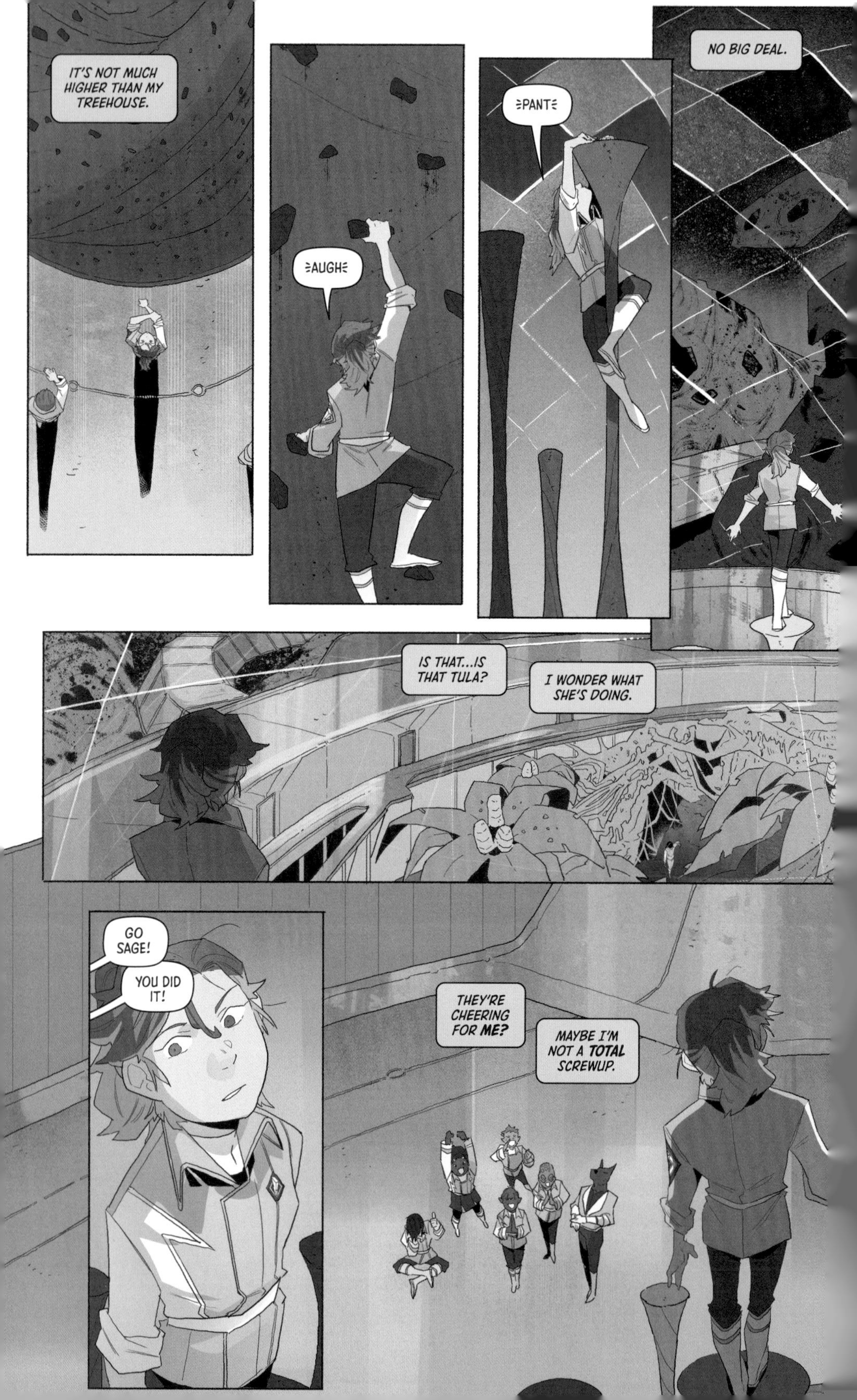
IT'S NOT MUCH HIGHER THAN MY TREEHOUSE.
AUGH
PANT
NO BIG DEAL.
IS THAT...IS THAT TULA?
I WONDER WHAT SHE'S DOING.
GO SAGE!
YOU DID IT!
THEY'RE CHEERING FOR ME?
MAYBE I'M NOT A TOTAL SCREWUP.

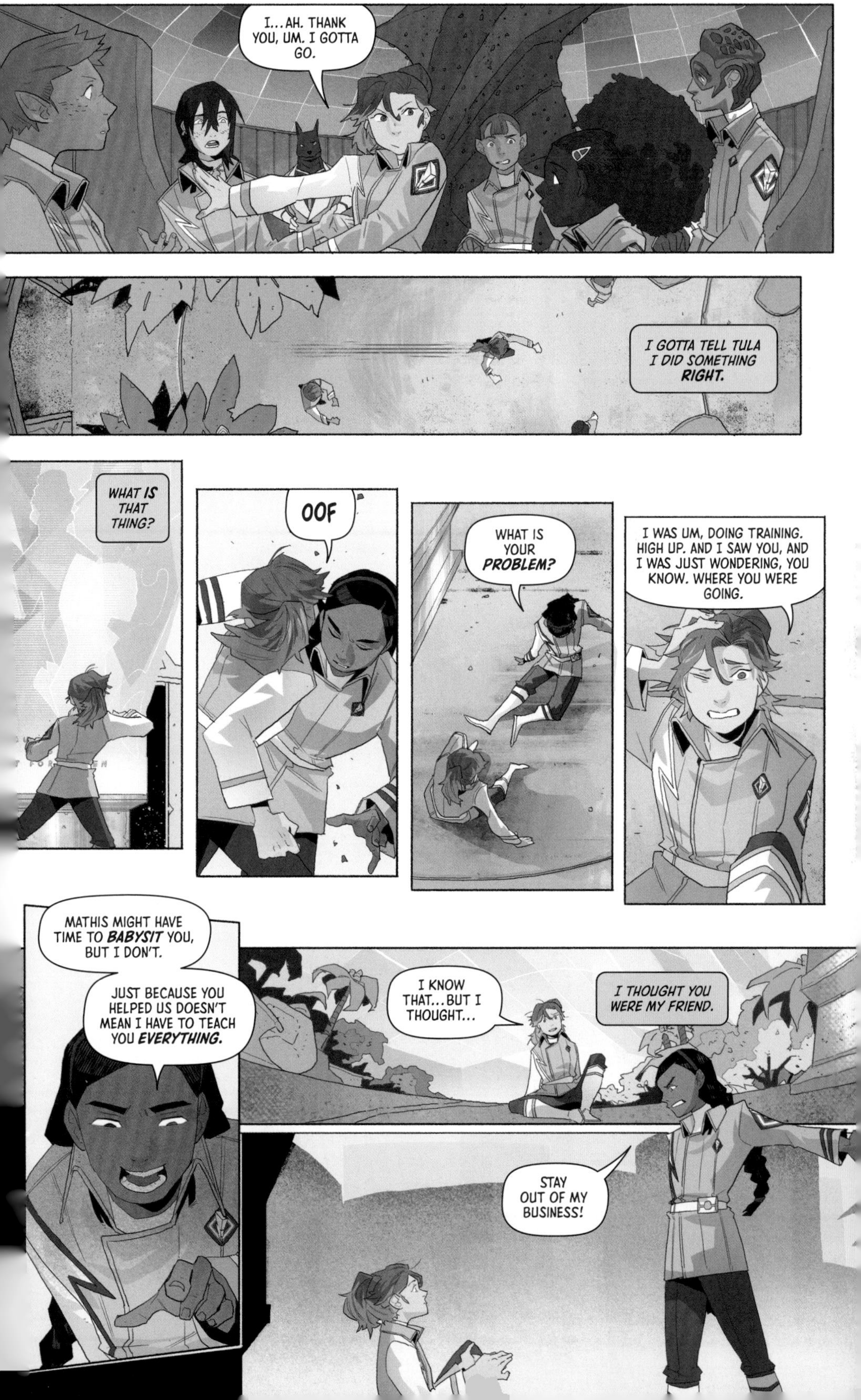
I...AH. THANK YOU, UM. I GOTTA GO.
I GOTTA TELL TULA I DID SOMETHING RIGHT.
WHAT IS THAT THING?
OOF
WHAT IS YOUR PROBLEM?
I WAS UM, DOING TRAINING. HIGH UP. AND I SAW YOU, AND I WAS JUST WONDERING, YOU KNOW. WHERE YOU WERE GOING.
MATHIS MIGHT HAVE TIME TO BABYSIT YOU, BUT I DON'T.
JUST BECAUSE YOU HELPED US DOESN'T MEAN I HAVE TO TEACH YOU EVERYTHING.
I KNOW THAT...BUT I THOUGHT...
I THOUGHT YOU WERE MY FRIEND.
STAY OUT OF MY BUSINESS!

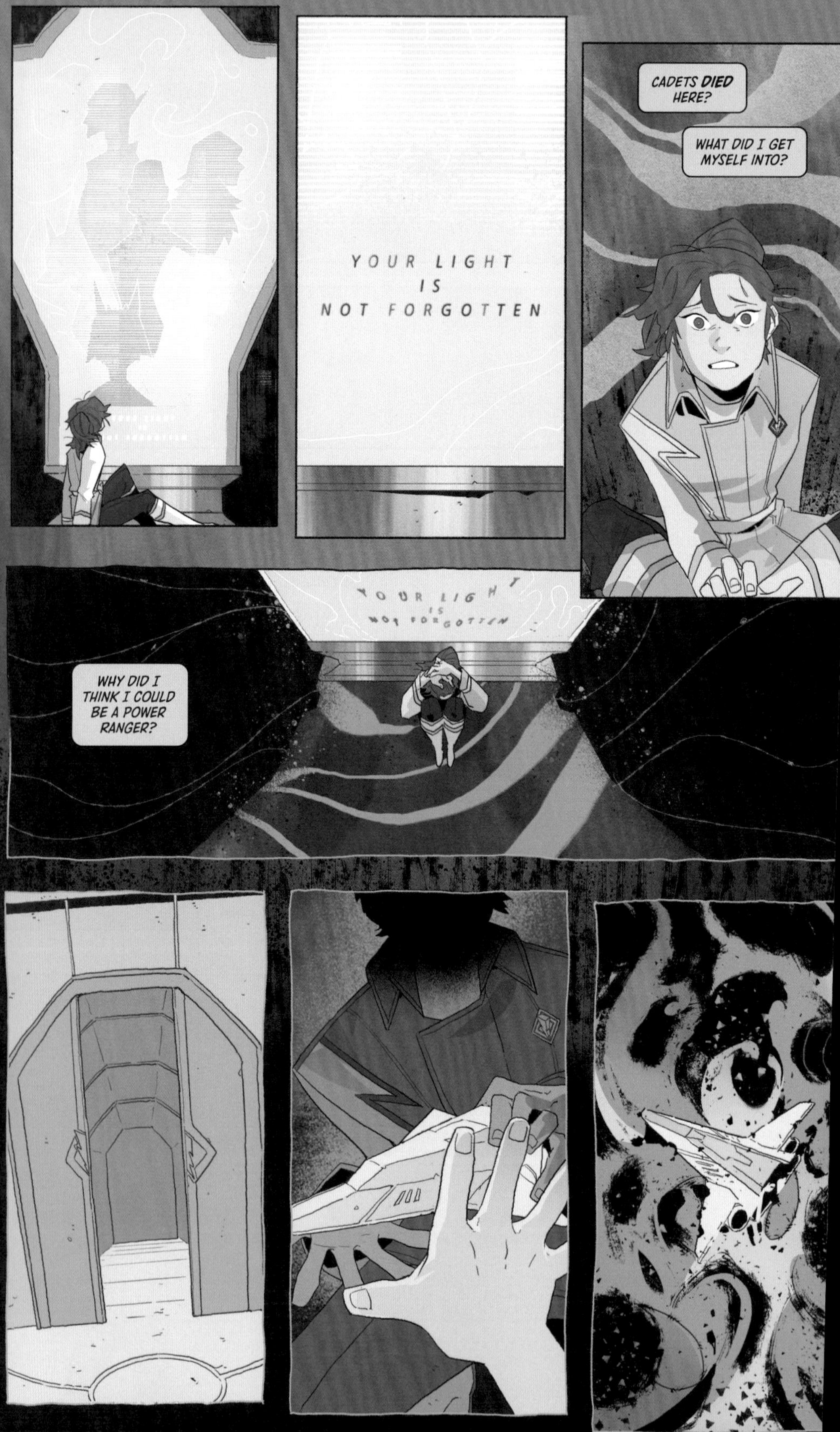
YOUR LIGHT
IS
NOT FORGOTTEN
CADETS DIED HERE?
WHAT DID I GET MYSELF INTO?
YOUR LIGHT IS NOT FORGOTTEN
WHY DID I THINK I COULD BE A POWER RANGER?

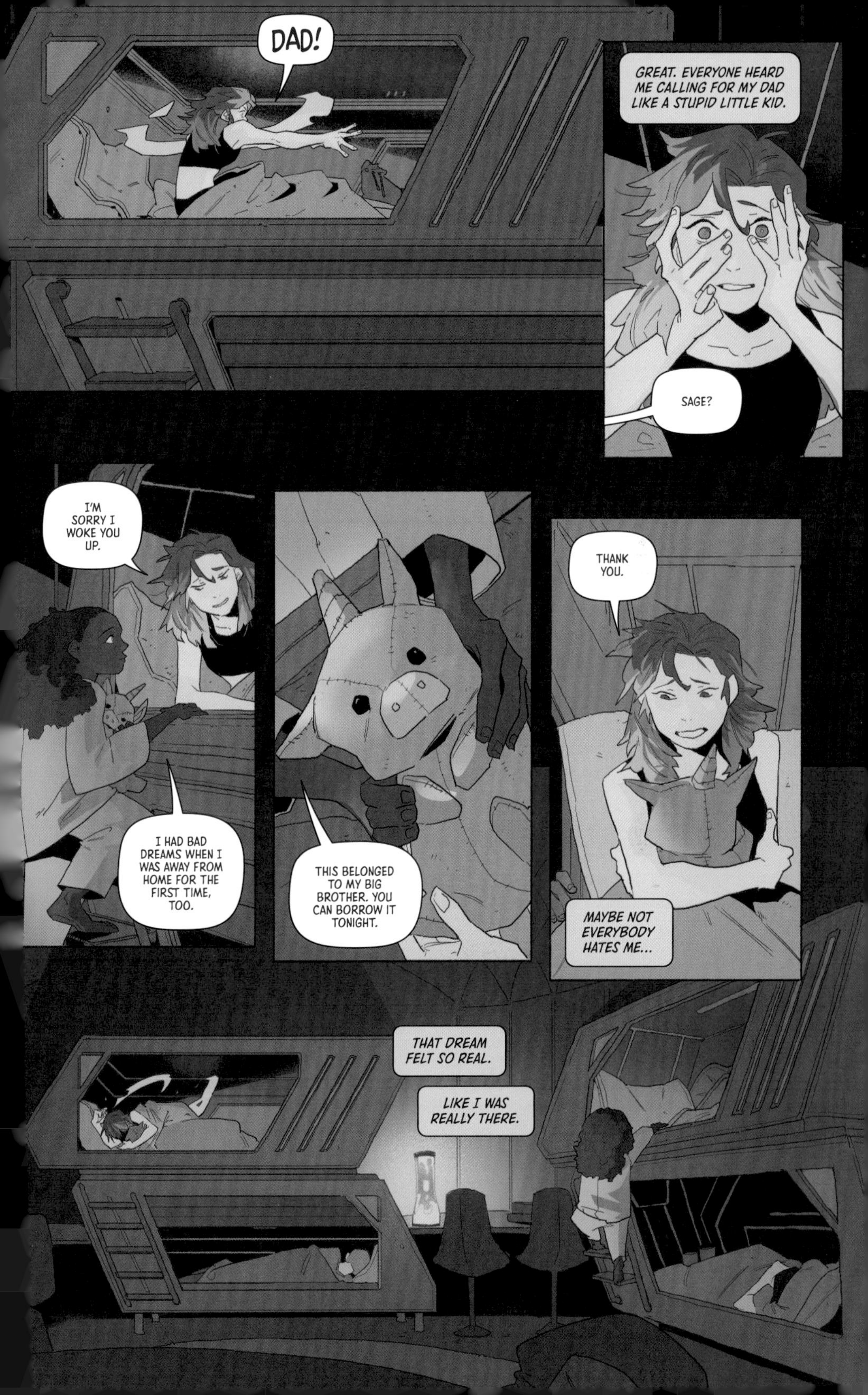
DAD!
GREAT. EVERYONE HEARD ME CALLING FOR MY DAD LIKE A STUPID LITTLE KID.
SAGE?
I'M SORRY I WOKE YOU UP.
I HAD BAD DREAMS WHEN I WAS AWAY FROM HOME FOR THE FIRST TIME, TOO.
THIS BELONGED TO MY BIG BROTHER. YOU CAN BORROW IT TONIGHT.
THANK YOU.
MAYBE NOT EVERYBODY HATES ME...
THAT DREAM FELT SO REAL.
LIKE I WAS REALLY THERE.

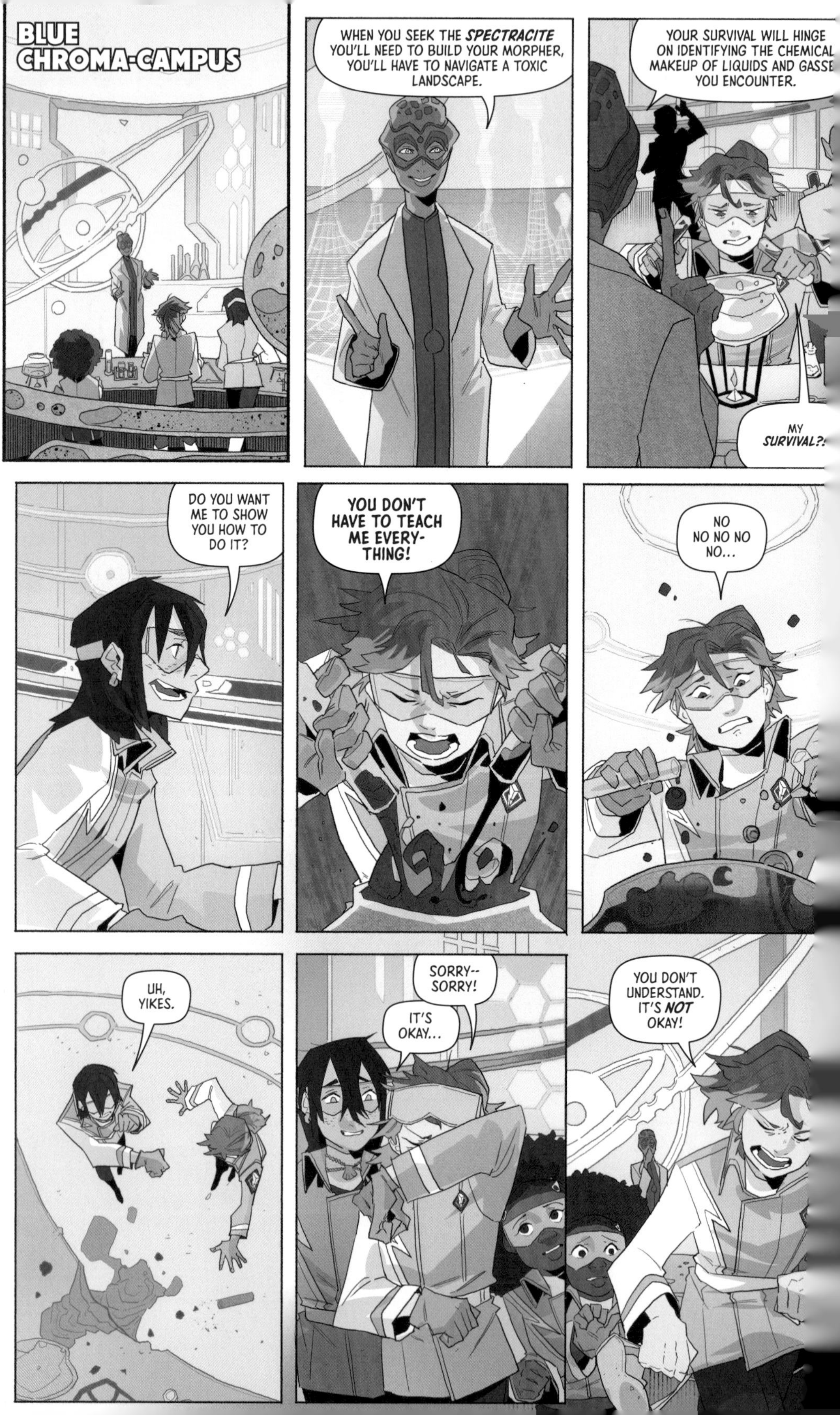
BLUE CHROMA-CAMPUS
WHEN YOU SEEK THE SPECTRACITE YOU'LL NEED TO BUILD YOUR MORPHER, YOU'LL HAVE TO NAVIGATE A TOXIC LANDSCAPE.
YOUR SURVIVAL WILL HINGE ON IDENTIFYING THE CHEMICAL MAKEUP OF LIQUIDS AND GASSE YOU ENCOUNTER.
MY SURVIVAL?!
DO YOU WANT ME TO SHOW YOU HOW TO DO IT?
YOU DON'T HAVE TO TEACH ME EVERY-THING!
NO NO NO NO NO...
UH, YIKES.
SORRY-- SORRY!
IT'S OKAY...
YOU DON'T UNDERSTAND. IT'S NOT OKAY!

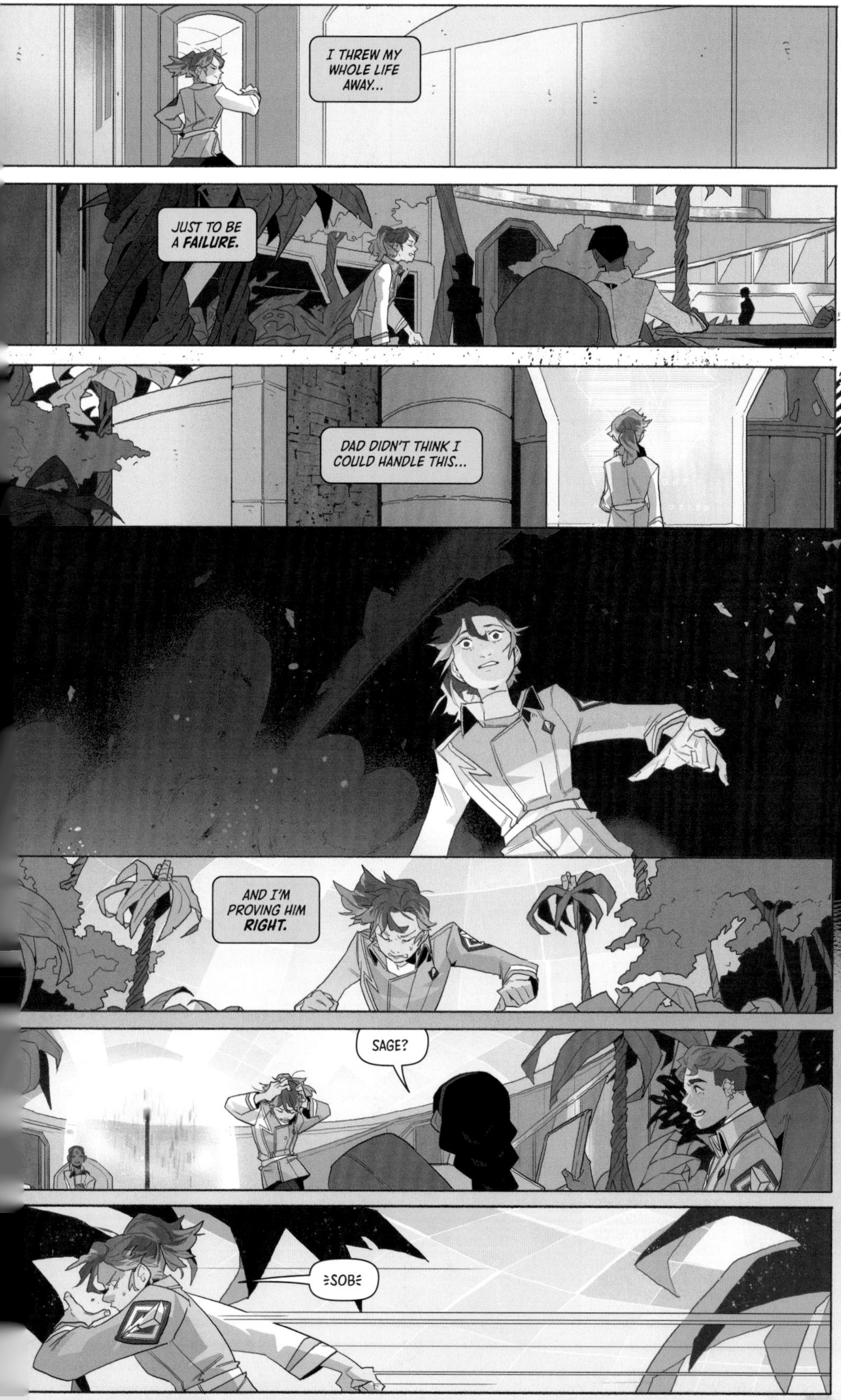
I THREW MY WHOLE LIFE AWAY...
JUST TO BE A **FAILURE.**
DAD DIDN'T THINK I COULD HANDLE THIS...
AND I'M PROVING HIM **RIGHT.**
SAGE?
SOB

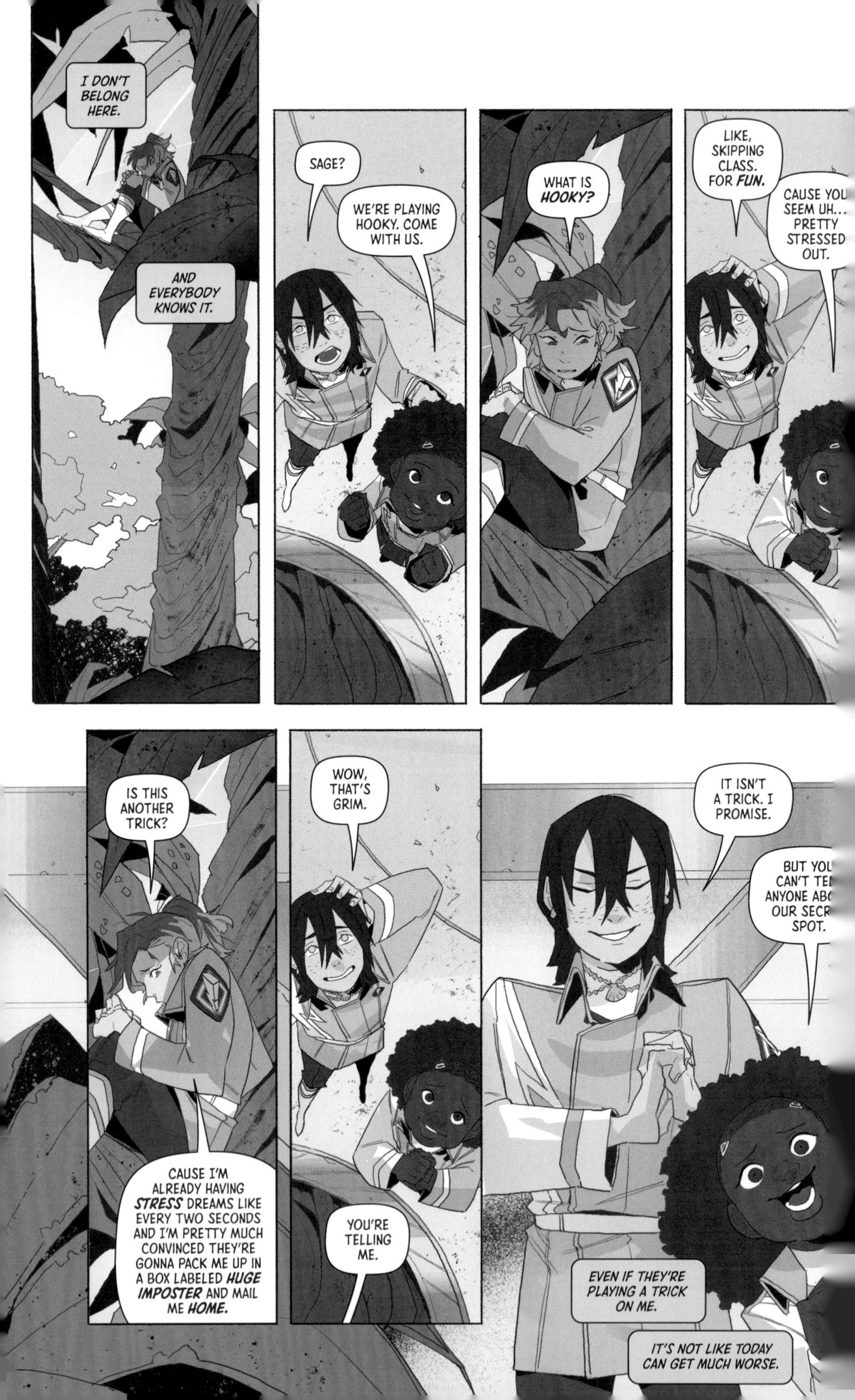
I DON'T BELONG HERE.
AND EVERYBODY KNOWS IT.
SAGE?
WE'RE PLAYING HOOKY. COME WITH US.
WHAT IS *HOOKY?*
LIKE, SKIPPING CLASS. FOR *FUN.*
CAUSE YOU SEEM UH... PRETTY STRESSED OUT.
IS THIS ANOTHER TRICK?
CAUSE I'M ALREADY HAVING *STRESS* DREAMS LIKE EVERY TWO SECONDS AND I'M PRETTY MUCH CONVINCED THEY'RE GONNA PACK ME UP IN A BOX LABELED *HUGE IMPOSTER* AND MAIL ME *HOME.*
WOW, THAT'S GRIM.
YOU'RE TELLING ME.
IT ISN'T A TRICK. I PROMISE.
BUT YOU CAN'T TE ANYONE ABO OUR SECR SPOT.
EVEN IF THEY'RE PLAYING A TRICK ON ME.
IT'S NOT LIKE TODAY CAN GET MUCH WORSE.

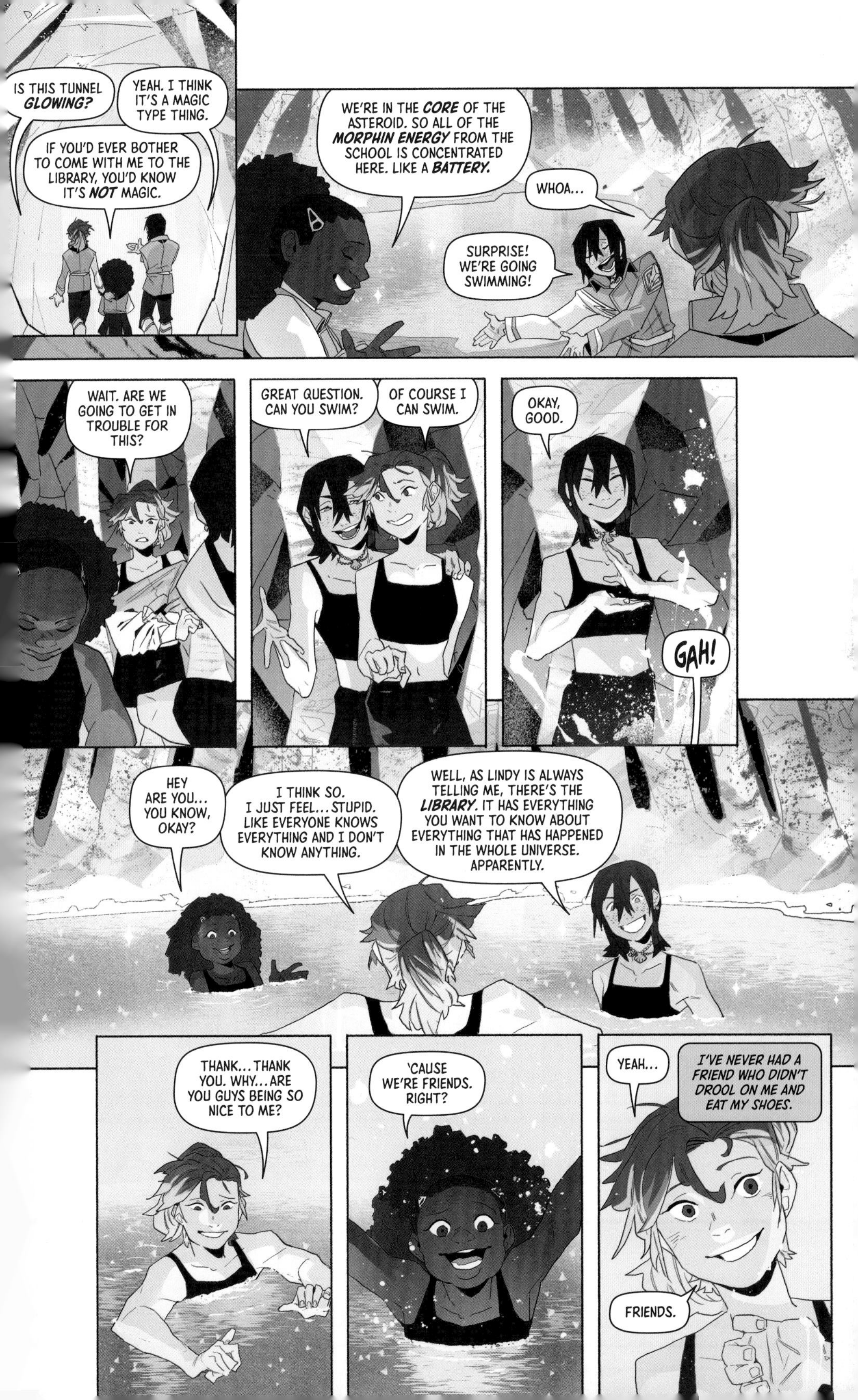
IS THIS TUNNEL GLOWING?
YEAH. I THINK IT'S A MAGIC TYPE THING.
IF YOU'D EVER BOTHER TO COME WITH ME TO THE LIBRARY, YOU'D KNOW IT'S NOT MAGIC.
WE'RE IN THE CORE OF THE ASTEROID. SO ALL OF THE MORPHIN ENERGY FROM THE SCHOOL IS CONCENTRATED HERE. LIKE A BATTERY.
WHOA...
SURPRISE! WE'RE GOING SWIMMING!
WAIT. ARE WE GOING TO GET IN TROUBLE FOR THIS?
GREAT QUESTION. CAN YOU SWIM?
OF COURSE I CAN SWIM.
OKAY, GOOD.
GAH!
HEY ARE YOU... YOU KNOW, OKAY?
I THINK SO. I JUST FEEL... STUPID. LIKE EVERYONE KNOWS EVERYTHING AND I DON'T KNOW ANYTHING.
WELL, AS LINDY IS ALWAYS TELLING ME, THERE'S THE LIBRARY. IT HAS EVERYTHING YOU WANT TO KNOW ABOUT EVERYTHING THAT HAS HAPPENED IN THE WHOLE UNIVERSE. APPARENTLY.
THANK... THANK YOU. WHY... ARE YOU GUYS BEING SO NICE TO ME?
'CAUSE WE'RE FRIENDS. RIGHT?
YEAH...
I'VE NEVER HAD A FRIEND WHO DIDN'T DROOL ON ME AND EAT MY SHOES.
FRIENDS.

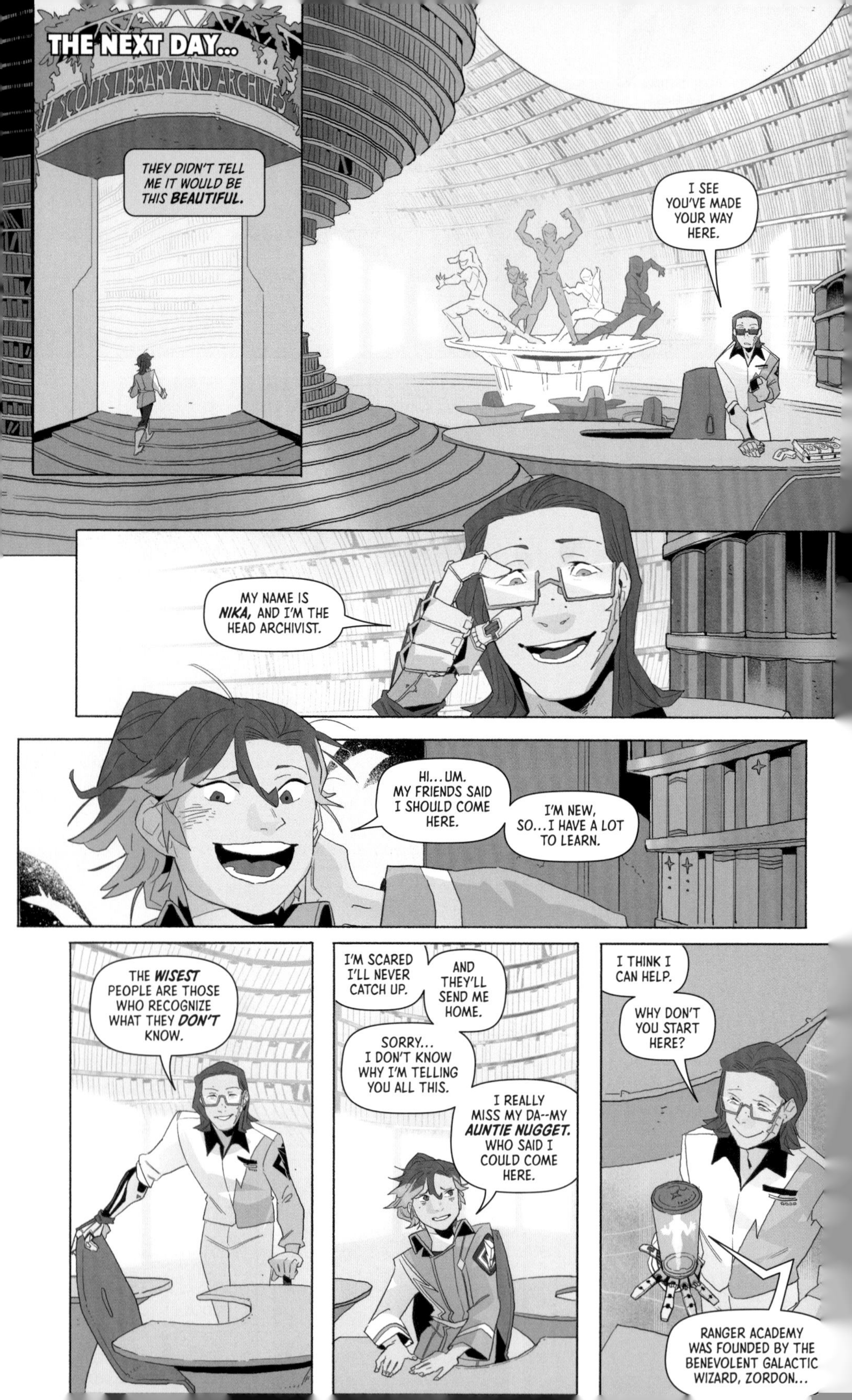
THE NEXT DAY...
SCOTTS LIBRARY AND ARCHIVES
THEY DIDN'T TELL ME IT WOULD BE THIS BEAUTIFUL.
I SEE YOU'VE MADE YOUR WAY HERE.
MY NAME IS NIKA, AND I'M THE HEAD ARCHIVIST.
HI... UM. MY FRIENDS SAID I SHOULD COME HERE.
I'M NEW, SO... I HAVE A LOT TO LEARN.
THE WISEST PEOPLE ARE THOSE WHO RECOGNIZE WHAT THEY DON'T KNOW.
I'M SCARED I'LL NEVER CATCH UP.
AND THEY'LL SEND ME HOME.
SORRY... I DON'T KNOW WHY I'M TELLING YOU ALL THIS.
I REALLY MISS MY DA--MY AUNTIE NUGGET. WHO SAID I COULD COME HERE.
I THINK I CAN HELP.
WHY DON'T YOU START HERE?
RANGER ACADEMY WAS FOUNDED BY THE BENEVOLENT GALACTIC WIZARD, ZORDON...

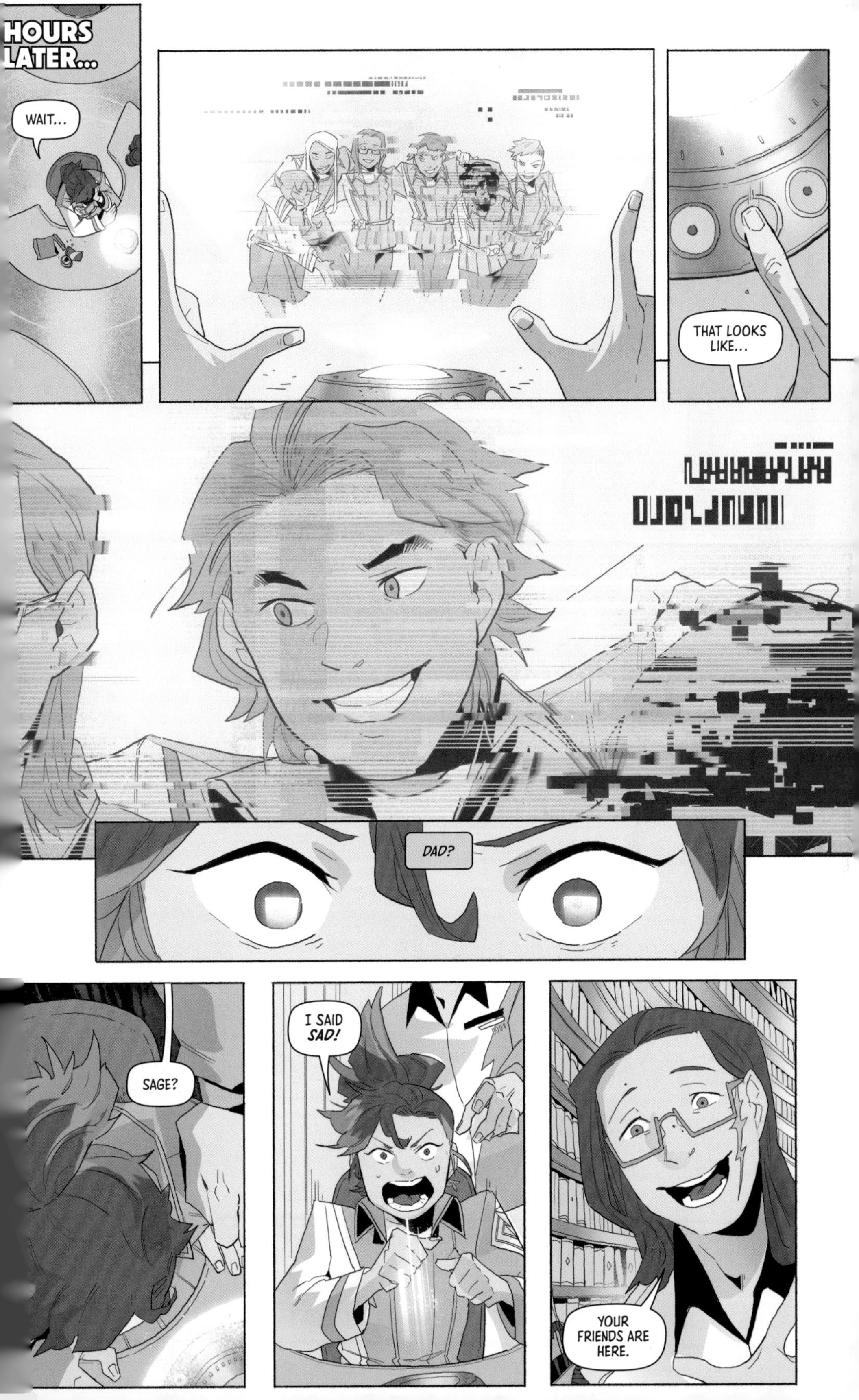
HOURS LATER...
WAIT...
THAT LOOKS LIKE...
DAD?
SAGE?
I SAID *SAD!*
YOUR FRIENDS ARE HERE.

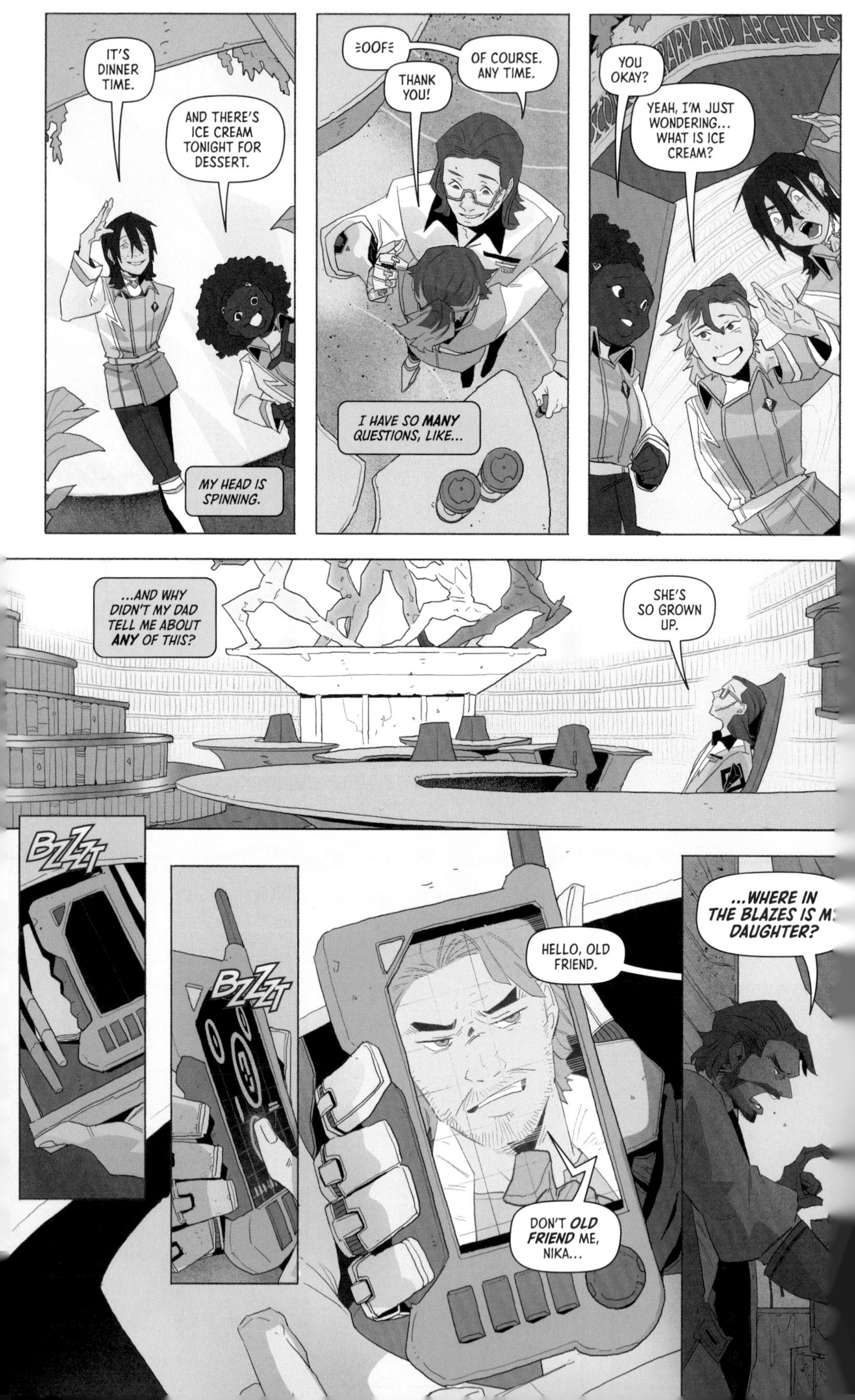
IT'S DINNER TIME.
AND THERE'S ICE CREAM TONIGHT FOR DESSERT.
MY HEAD IS SPINNING.
OOF
THANK YOU!
OF COURSE. ANY TIME.
I HAVE SO MANY QUESTIONS, LIKE...
YOU OKAY?
YEAH, I'M JUST WONDERING... WHAT IS ICE CREAM?
...AND WHY DIDN'T MY DAD TELL ME ABOUT ANY OF THIS?
SHE'S SO GROWN UP.
BZZZT
BZZZT
HELLO, OLD FRIEND.
DON'T OLD FRIEND ME, NIKA...
...WHERE IN THE BLAZES IS MY DAUGHTER?

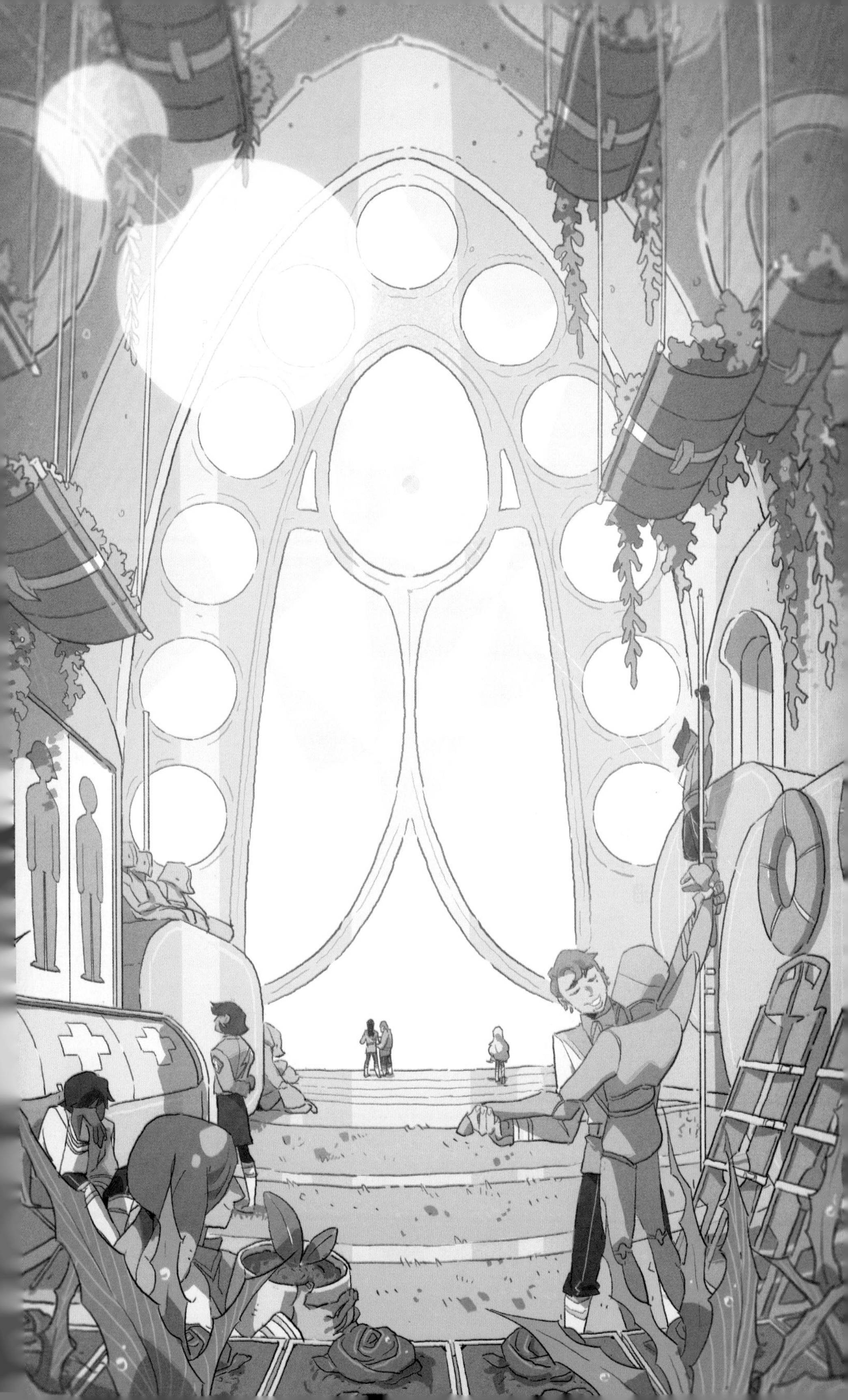

CHAPTER THRE

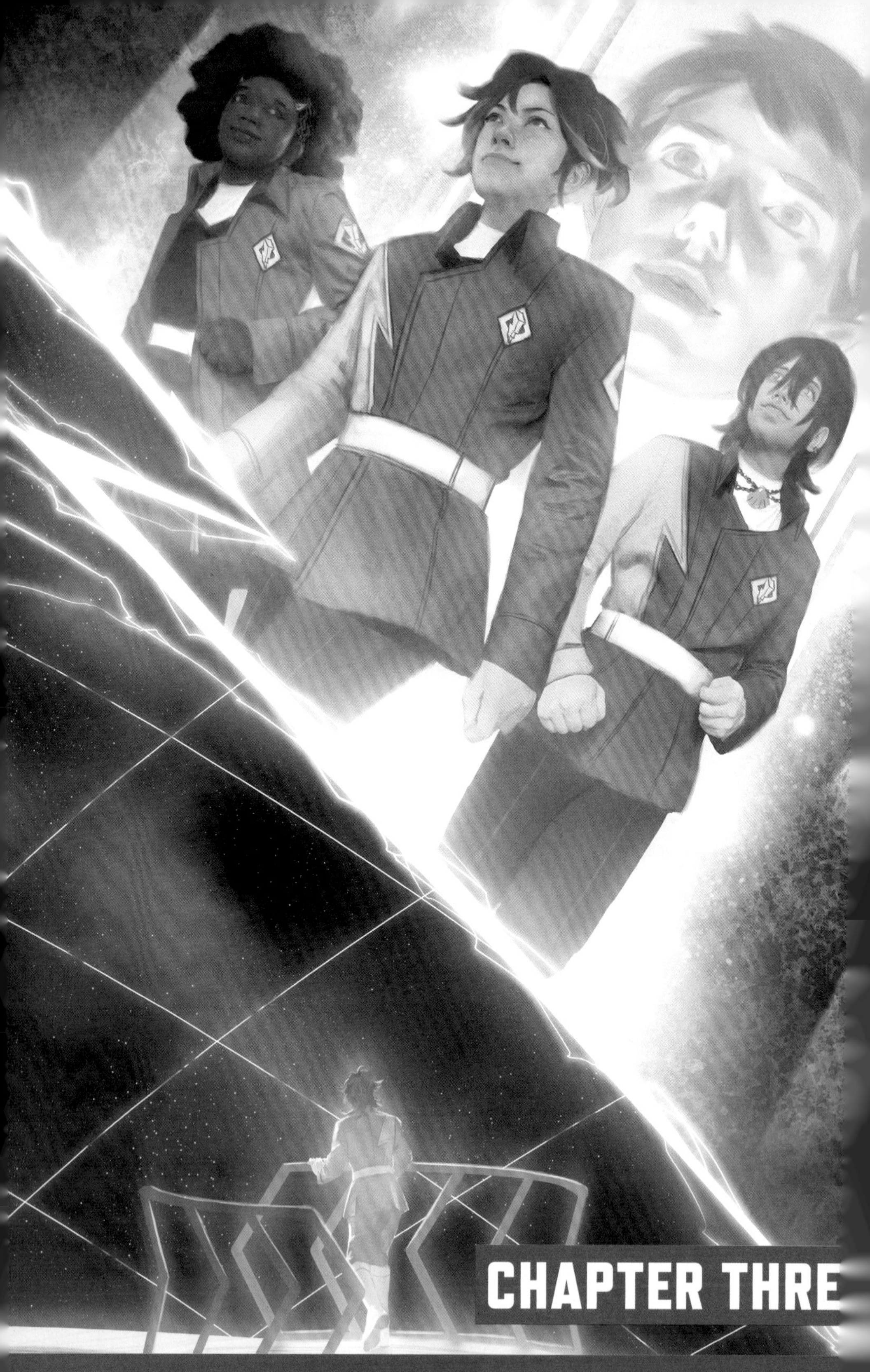

ISSUE THREE COVER BY MIGUEL MERCADO

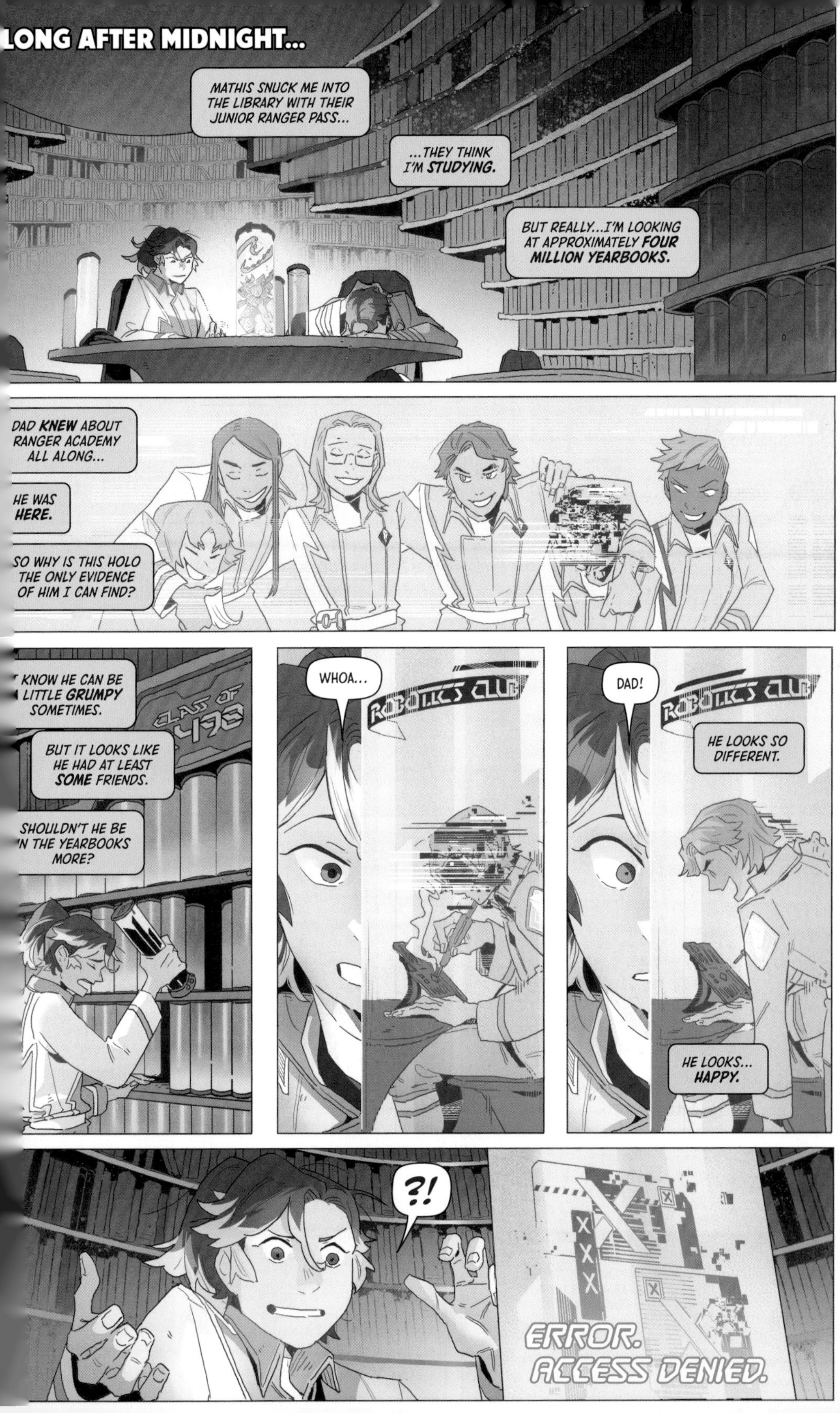
LONG AFTER MIDNIGHT...
MATHIS SNUCK ME INTO THE LIBRARY WITH THEIR JUNIOR RANGER PASS...
...THEY THINK I'M **STUDYING.**
BUT REALLY...I'M LOOKING AT APPROXIMATELY **FOUR MILLION YEARBOOKS.**
DAD **KNEW** ABOUT RANGER ACADEMY ALL ALONG...
HE WAS **HERE.**
SO WHY IS THIS HOLO THE ONLY EVIDENCE OF HIM I CAN FIND?
KNOW HE CAN BE LITTLE **GRUMPY** SOMETIMES.
BUT IT LOOKS LIKE HE HAD AT LEAST **SOME** FRIENDS.
SHOULDN'T HE BE N THE YEARBOOKS MORE?
WHOA...
ROBOTICS CLUB
DAD!
ROBOTICS CLUB
HE LOOKS SO DIFFERENT.
HE LOOKS... **HAPPY.**
?!
ERROR. ACCESS DENIED.

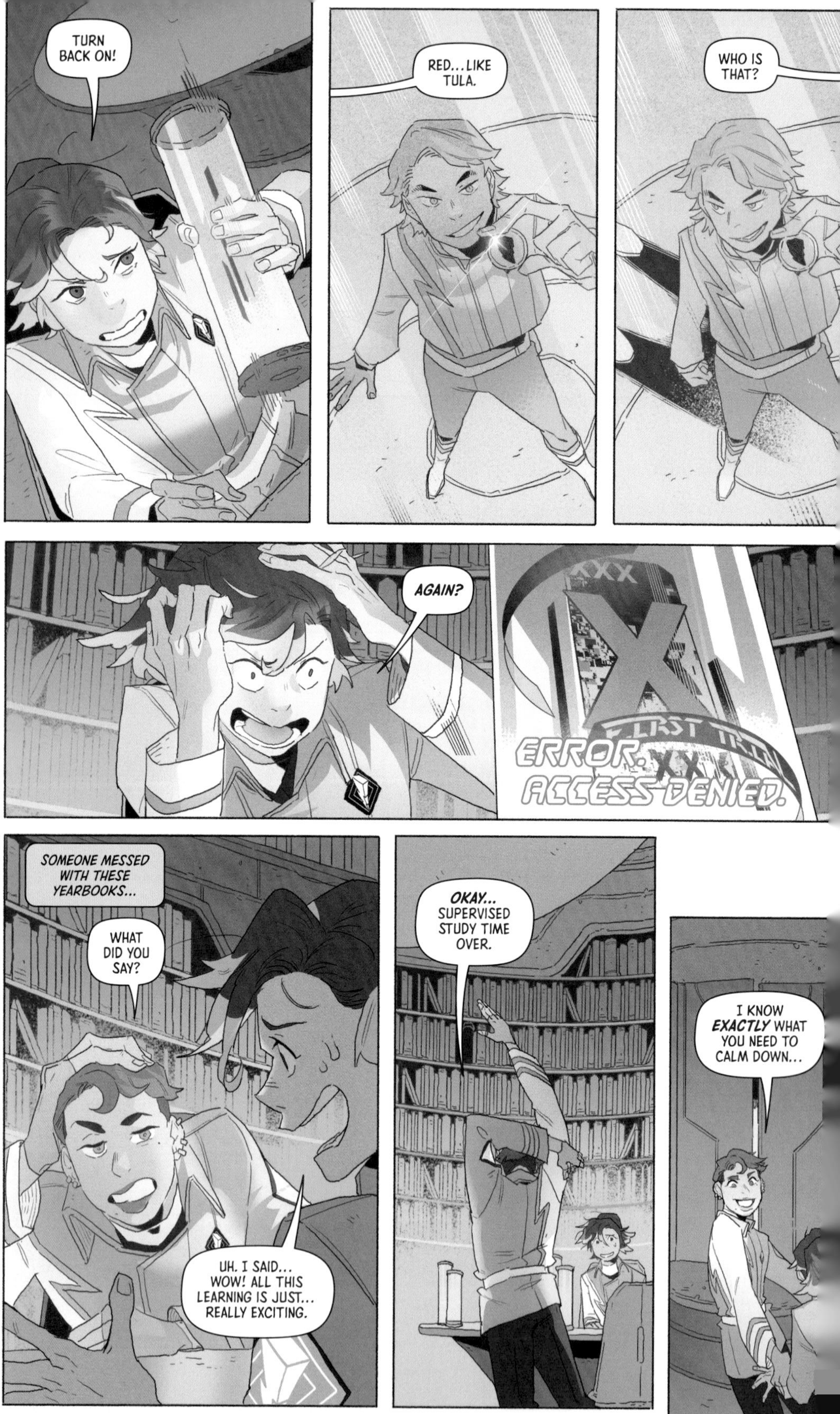
TURN BACK ON!
RED... LIKE TULA.
WHO IS THAT?
AGAIN?
ERROR. ACCESS DENIED.
SOMEONE MESSED WITH THESE YEARBOOKS...
WHAT DID YOU SAY?
UH. I SAID... WOW! ALL THIS LEARNING IS JUST... REALLY EXCITING.
OKAY... SUPERVISED STUDY TIME OVER.
I KNOW EXACTLY WHAT YOU NEED TO CALM DOWN...

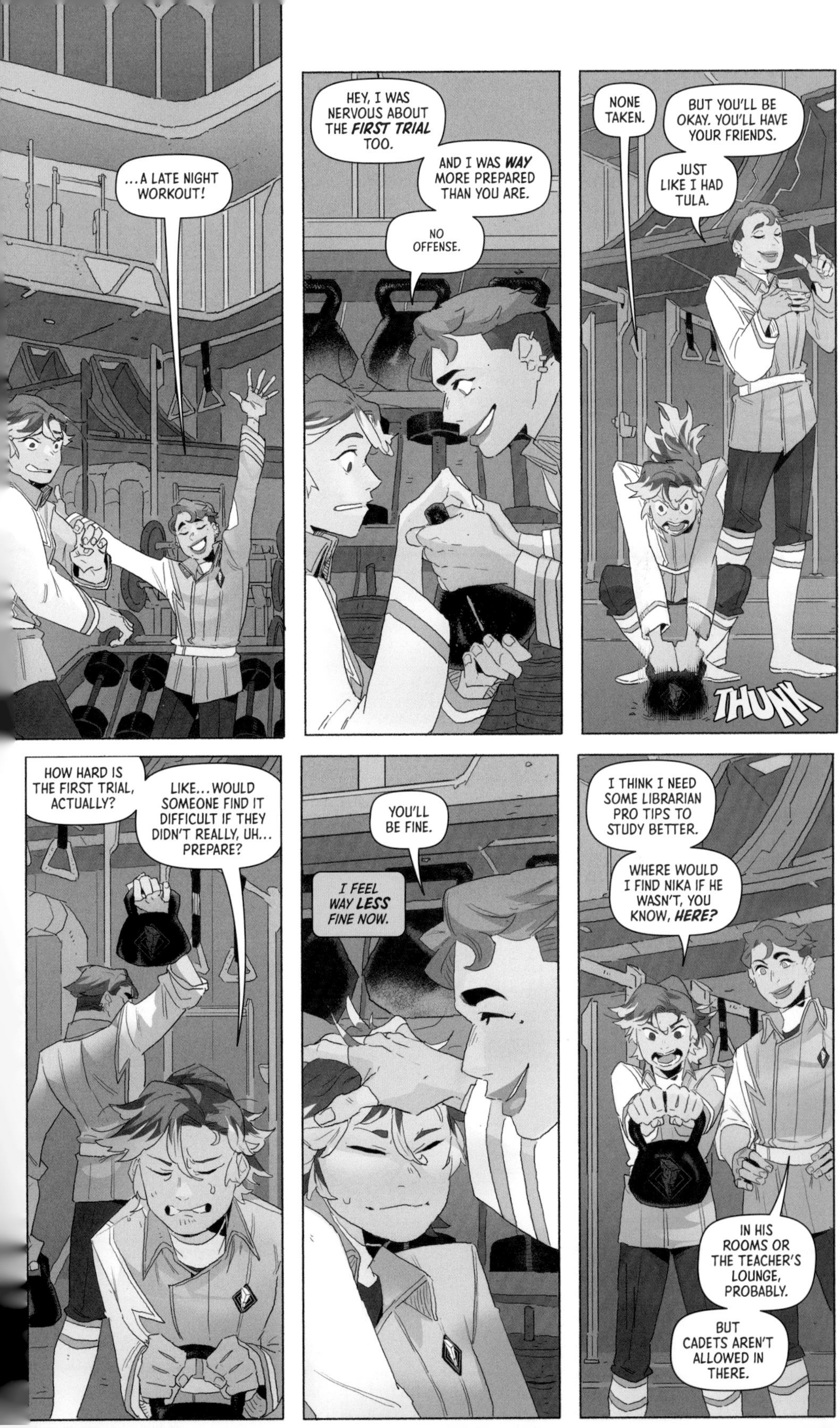
...A LATE NIGHT WORKOUT!
HEY, I WAS NERVOUS ABOUT THE **FIRST TRIAL** TOO.
AND I WAS **WAY** MORE PREPARED THAN YOU ARE.
NO OFFENSE.
NONE TAKEN.
BUT YOU'LL BE OKAY. YOU'LL HAVE YOUR FRIENDS.
JUST LIKE I HAD TULA.
THUNK
HOW HARD IS THE FIRST TRIAL, ACTUALLY?
LIKE...WOULD SOMEONE FIND IT DIFFICULT IF THEY DIDN'T REALLY, UH... PREPARE?
YOU'LL BE FINE.
*I FEEL WAY **LESS** FINE NOW.*
I THINK I NEED SOME LIBRARIAN PRO TIPS TO STUDY BETTER.
WHERE WOULD I FIND NIKA IF HE WASN'T, YOU KNOW, **HERE?**
IN HIS ROOMS OR THE TEACHER'S LOUNGE, PROBABLY.
BUT CADETS AREN'T ALLOWED IN THERE.

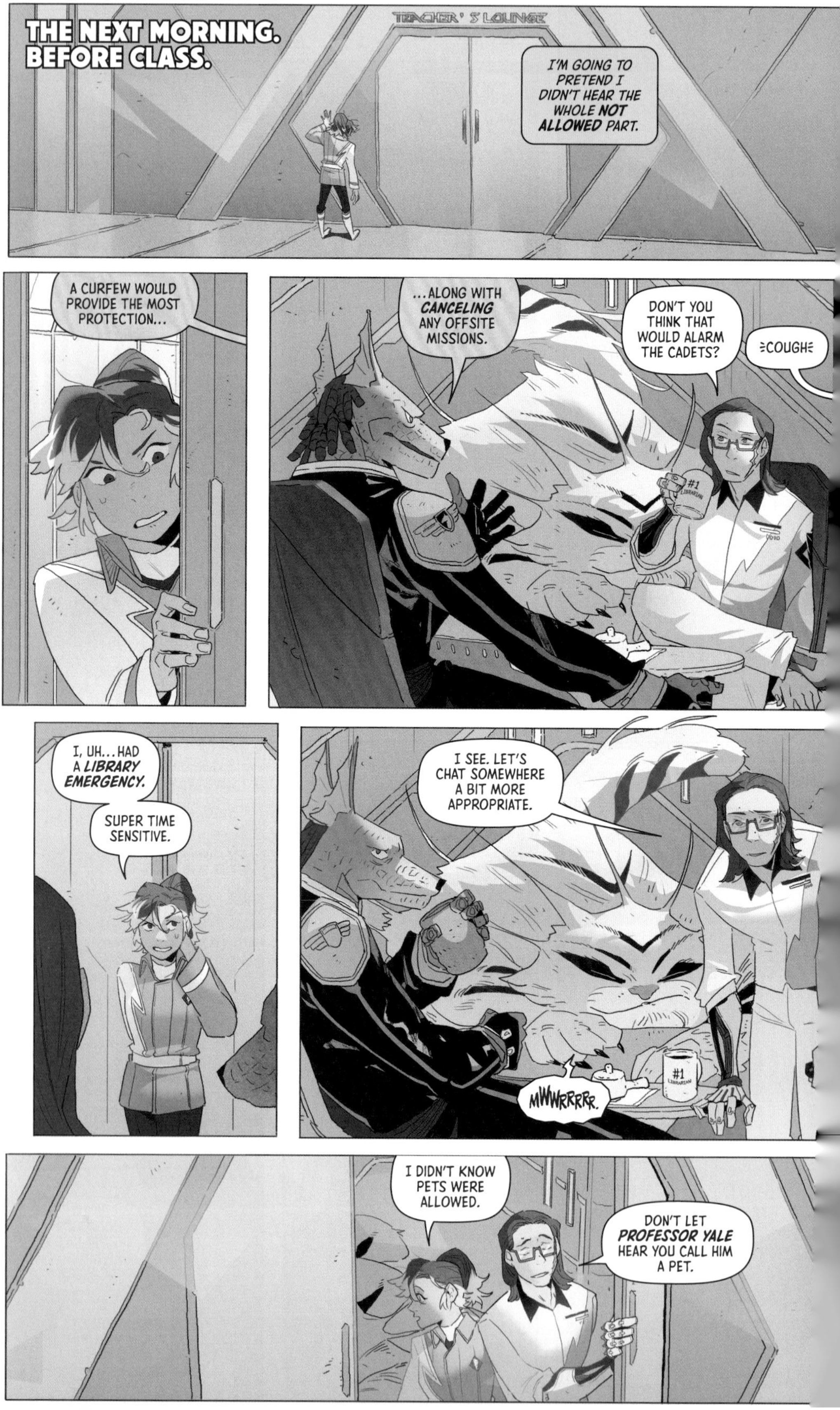
THE NEXT MORNING. BEFORE CLASS.
TEACHER'S LOUNGE
I'M GOING TO PRETEND I DIDN'T HEAR THE WHOLE NOT ALLOWED PART.
A CURFEW WOULD PROVIDE THE MOST PROTECTION...
...ALONG WITH CANCELING ANY OFFSITE MISSIONS.
DON'T YOU THINK THAT WOULD ALARM THE CADETS?
COUGH
#1 LIBRARIAN
I, UH...HAD A LIBRARY EMERGENCY.
SUPER TIME SENSITIVE.
I SEE. LET'S CHAT SOMEWHERE A BIT MORE APPROPRIATE.
MWWRRRRR.
#1 LIBRARIAN
I DIDN'T KNOW PETS WERE ALLOWED.
DON'T LET PROFESSOR YALE HEAR YOU CALL HIM A PET.

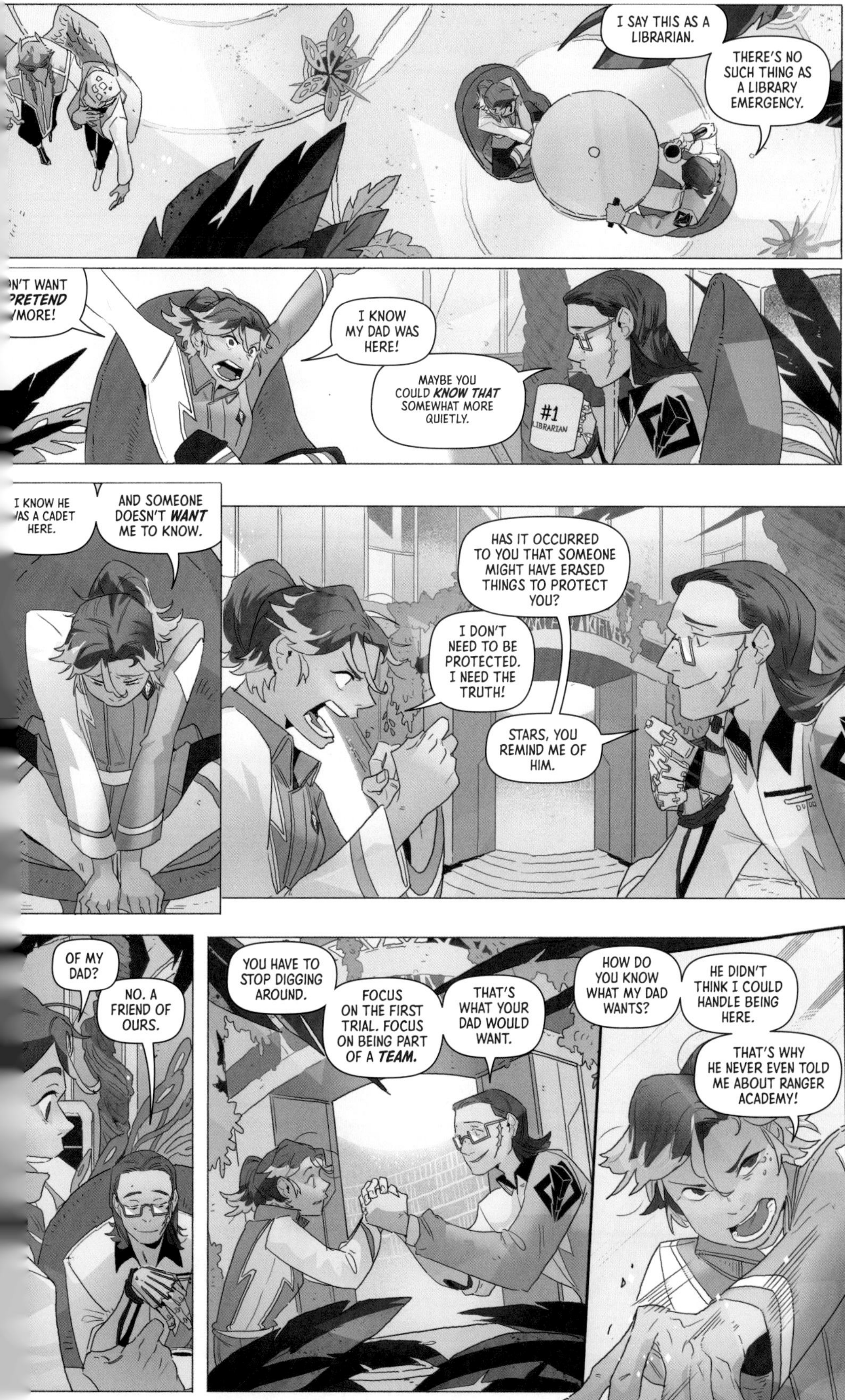
I SAY THIS AS A LIBRARIAN.
THERE'S NO SUCH THING AS A LIBRARY EMERGENCY.
N'T WANT PRETEND MORE!
I KNOW MY DAD WAS HERE!
MAYBE YOU COULD KNOW THAT SOMEWHAT MORE QUIETLY.
#1 LIBRARIAN
I KNOW HE WAS A CADET HERE.
AND SOMEONE DOESN'T WANT ME TO KNOW.
HAS IT OCCURRED TO YOU THAT SOMEONE MIGHT HAVE ERASED THINGS TO PROTECT YOU?
I DON'T NEED TO BE PROTECTED. I NEED THE TRUTH!
STARS, YOU REMIND ME OF HIM.
OF MY DAD?
NO. A FRIEND OF OURS.
YOU HAVE TO STOP DIGGING AROUND.
FOCUS ON THE FIRST TRIAL. FOCUS ON BEING PART OF A TEAM.
THAT'S WHAT YOUR DAD WOULD WANT.
HOW DO YOU KNOW WHAT MY DAD WANTS?
HE DIDN'T THINK I COULD HANDLE BEING HERE.
THAT'S WHY HE NEVER EVEN TOLD ME ABOUT RANGER ACADEMY!

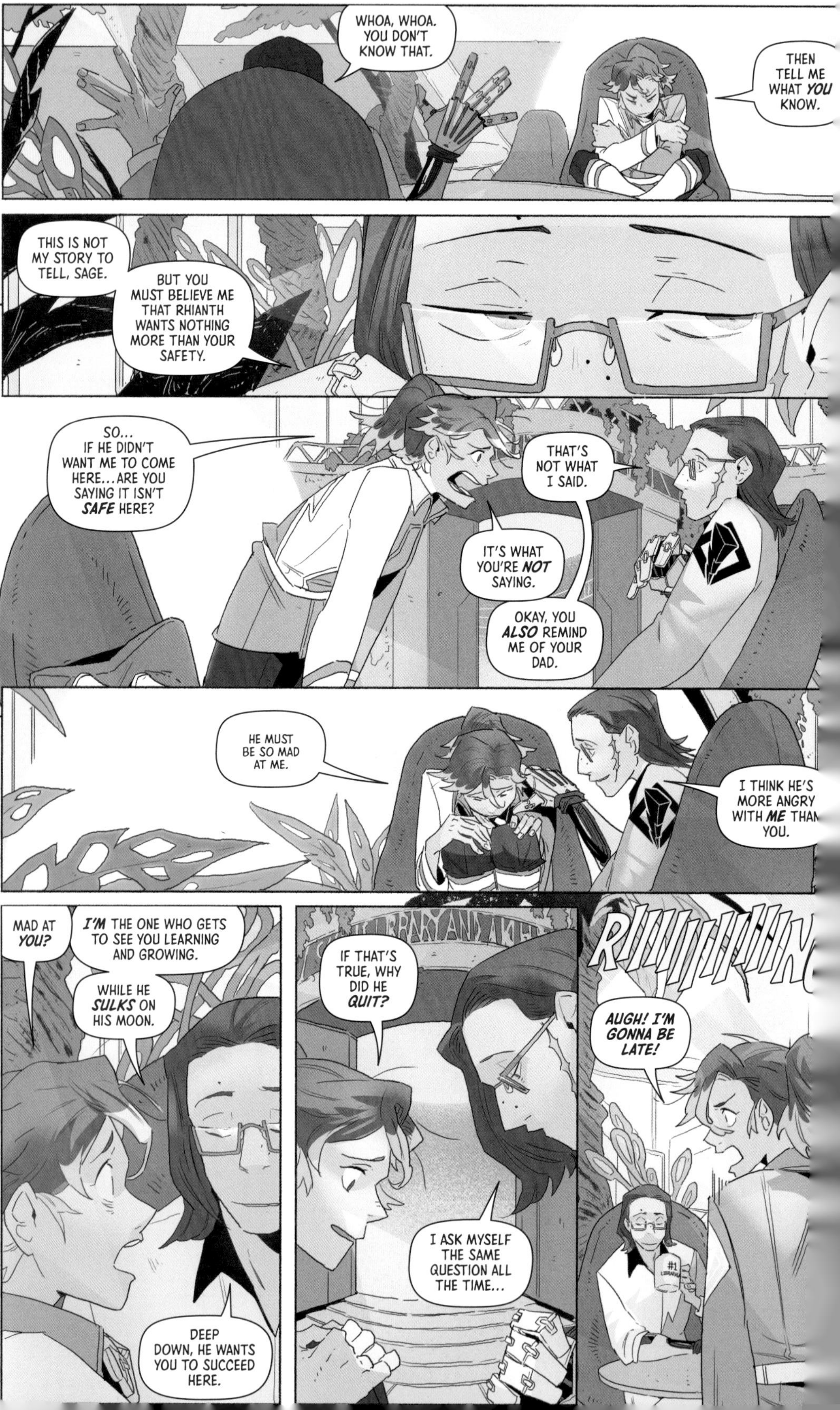
WHOA, WHOA. YOU DON'T KNOW THAT.
THEN TELL ME WHAT *YOU* KNOW.
THIS IS NOT MY STORY TO TELL, SAGE.
BUT YOU MUST BELIEVE ME THAT RHIANTH WANTS NOTHING MORE THAN YOUR SAFETY.
SO... IF HE DIDN'T WANT ME TO COME HERE...ARE YOU SAYING IT ISN'T *SAFE* HERE?
THAT'S NOT WHAT I SAID.
IT'S WHAT YOU'RE *NOT* SAYING.
OKAY, YOU *ALSO* REMIND ME OF YOUR DAD.
HE MUST BE SO MAD AT ME.
I THINK HE'S MORE ANGRY WITH *ME* THAN YOU.
MAD AT *YOU?*
I'M THE ONE WHO GETS TO SEE YOU LEARNING AND GROWING.
WHILE HE *SULKS* ON HIS MOON.
DEEP DOWN, HE WANTS YOU TO SUCCEED HERE.
IF THAT'S TRUE, WHY DID HE *QUIT?*
I ASK MYSELF THE SAME QUESTION ALL THE TIME...
RIIIIIIIIIIIIING
AUGH! I'M GONNA BE LATE!
#1 LIBRARIAN

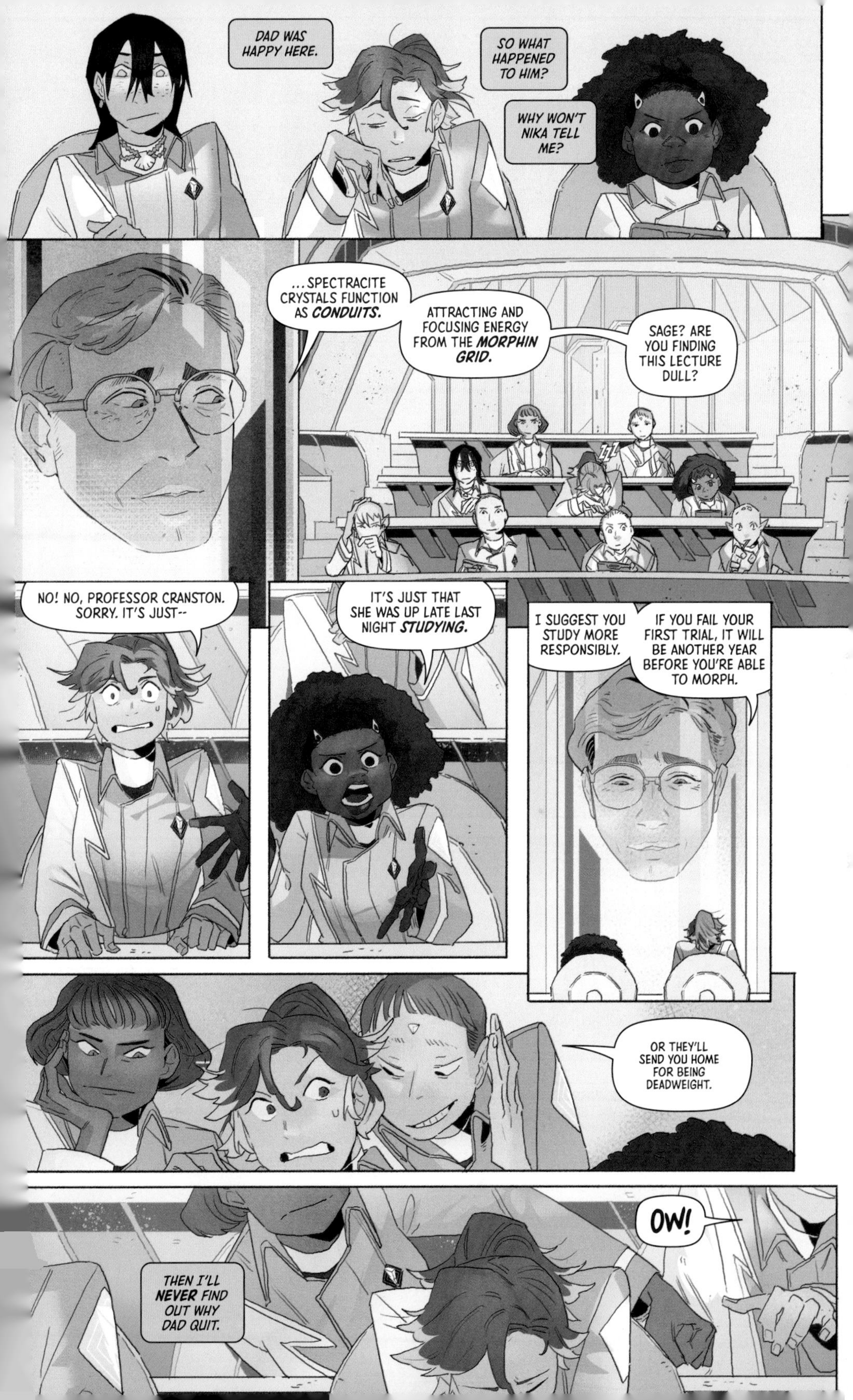
DAD WAS HAPPY HERE.
SO WHAT HAPPENED TO HIM?
WHY WON'T NIKA TELL ME?
...SPECTRACITE CRYSTALS FUNCTION AS CONDUITS.
ATTRACTING AND FOCUSING ENERGY FROM THE MORPHIN GRID.
SAGE? ARE YOU FINDING THIS LECTURE DULL?
ZZZ
NO! NO, PROFESSOR CRANSTON. SORRY. IT'S JUST--
IT'S JUST THAT SHE WAS UP LATE LAST NIGHT STUDYING.
I SUGGEST YOU STUDY MORE RESPONSIBLY.
IF YOU FAIL YOUR FIRST TRIAL, IT WILL BE ANOTHER YEAR BEFORE YOU'RE ABLE TO MORPH.
OR THEY'LL SEND YOU HOME FOR BEING DEADWEIGHT.
OW!
THEN I'LL NEVER FIND OUT WHY DAD QUIT.

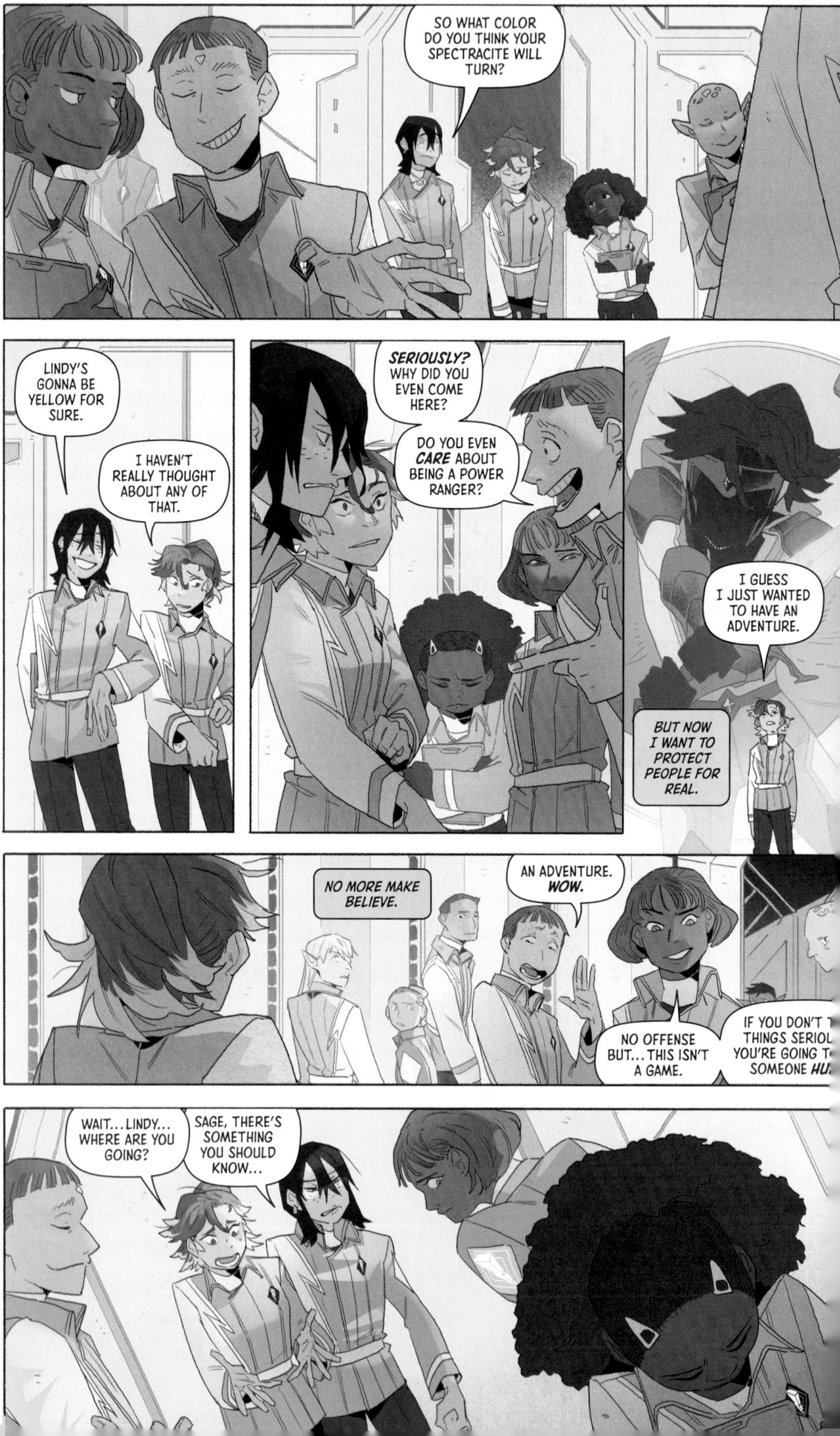
SO WHAT COLOR DO YOU THINK YOUR SPECTRACITE WILL TURN?
LINDY'S GONNA BE YELLOW FOR SURE.
I HAVEN'T REALLY THOUGHT ABOUT ANY OF THAT.
SERIOUSLY? WHY DID YOU EVEN COME HERE?
DO YOU EVEN CARE ABOUT BEING A POWER RANGER?
I GUESS I JUST WANTED TO HAVE AN ADVENTURE.
BUT NOW I WANT TO PROTECT PEOPLE FOR REAL.
NO MORE MAKE BELIEVE.
AN ADVENTURE. WOW.
NO OFFENSE BUT... THIS ISN'T A GAME.
IF YOU DON'T
THINGS SERIO
YOU'RE GOING T
SOMEONE HU
WAIT... LINDY... WHERE ARE YOU GOING?
SAGE, THERE'S SOMETHING YOU SHOULD KNOW...

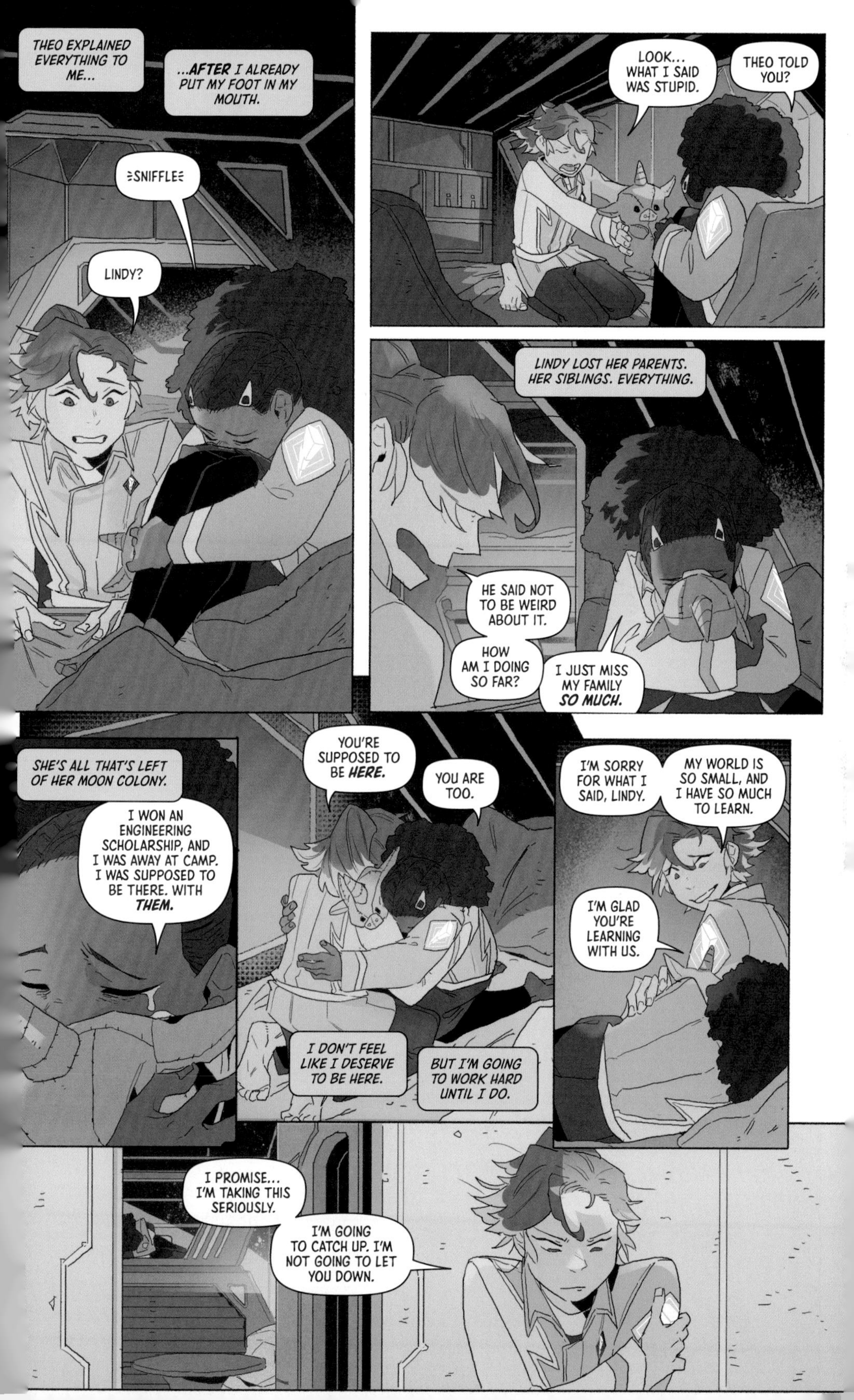
THEO EXPLAINED EVERYTHING TO ME...
...AFTER I ALREADY PUT MY FOOT IN MY MOUTH.
SNIFFLE
LINDY?
LOOK... WHAT I SAID WAS STUPID.
THEO TOLD YOU?
LINDY LOST HER PARENTS. HER SIBLINGS. EVERYTHING.
HE SAID NOT TO BE WEIRD ABOUT IT.
HOW AM I DOING SO FAR?
I JUST MISS MY FAMILY SO MUCH.
SHE'S ALL THAT'S LEFT OF HER MOON COLONY.
I WON AN ENGINEERING SCHOLARSHIP, AND I WAS AWAY AT CAMP. I WAS SUPPOSED TO BE THERE. WITH THEM.
YOU'RE SUPPOSED TO BE HERE.
YOU ARE TOO.
I DON'T FEEL LIKE I DESERVE TO BE HERE.
BUT I'M GOING TO WORK HARD UNTIL I DO.
I'M SORRY FOR WHAT I SAID, LINDY.
MY WORLD IS SO SMALL, AND I HAVE SO MUCH TO LEARN.
I'M GLAD YOU'RE LEARNING WITH US.
I PROMISE... I'M TAKING THIS SERIOUSLY.
I'M GOING TO CATCH UP. I'M NOT GOING TO LET YOU DOWN.

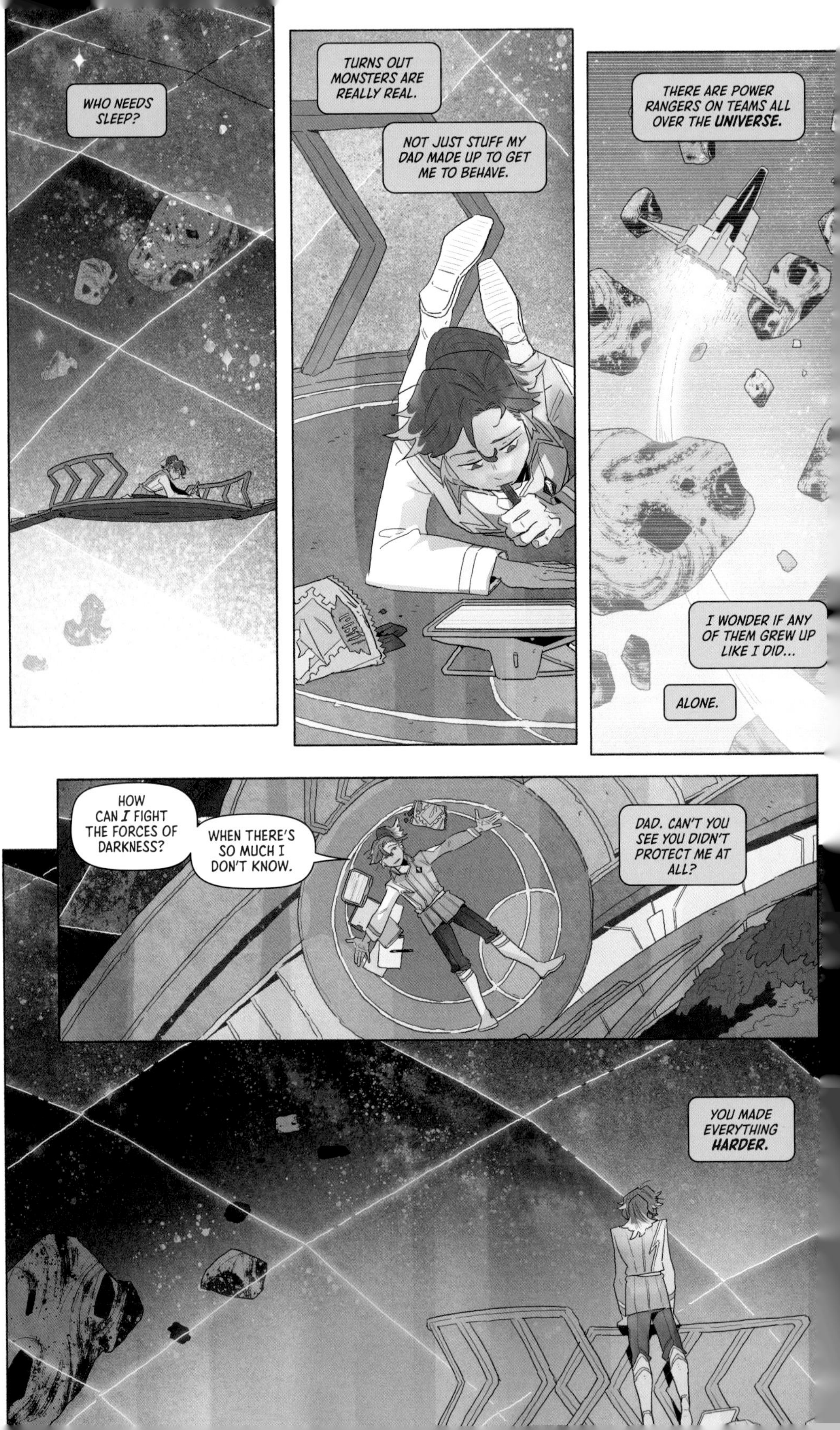
WHO NEEDS SLEEP?
TURNS OUT MONSTERS ARE REALLY REAL.
NOT JUST STUFF MY DAD MADE UP TO GET ME TO BEHAVE.
THERE ARE POWER RANGERS ON TEAMS ALL OVER THE UNIVERSE.
I WONDER IF ANY OF THEM GREW UP LIKE I DID...
ALONE.
HOW CAN I FIGHT THE FORCES OF DARKNESS?
WHEN THERE'S SO MUCH I DON'T KNOW.
DAD. CAN'T YOU SEE YOU DIDN'T PROTECT ME AT ALL?
YOU MADE EVERYTHING HARDER.

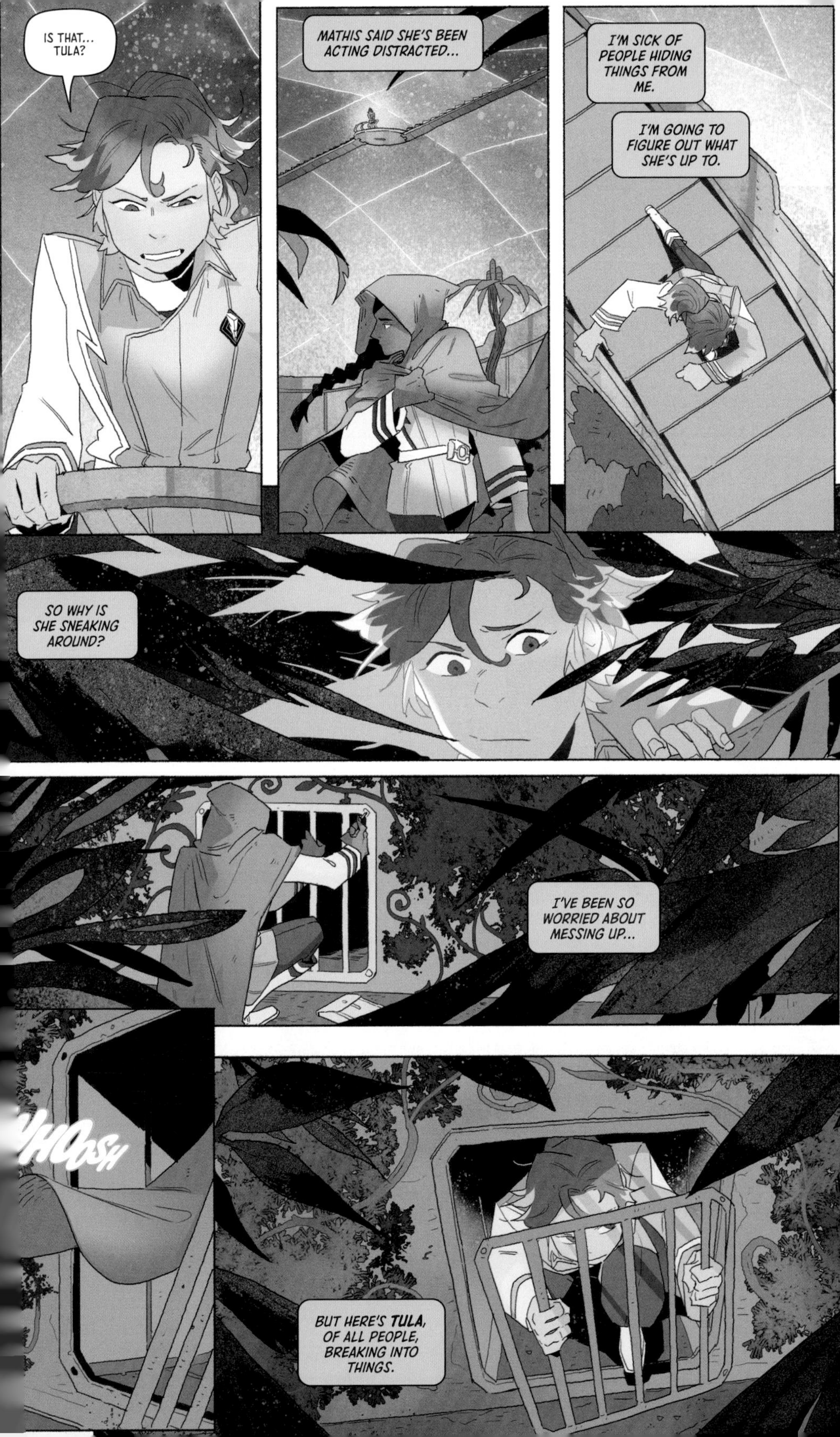
IS THAT... TULA?
MATHIS SAID SHE'S BEEN ACTING DISTRACTED...
I'M SICK OF PEOPLE HIDING THINGS FROM ME.
I'M GOING TO FIGURE OUT WHAT SHE'S UP TO.
SO WHY IS SHE SNEAKING AROUND?
I'VE BEEN SO WORRIED ABOUT MESSING UP...
WHOOSH
BUT HERE'S TULA, OF ALL PEOPLE, BREAKING INTO THINGS.

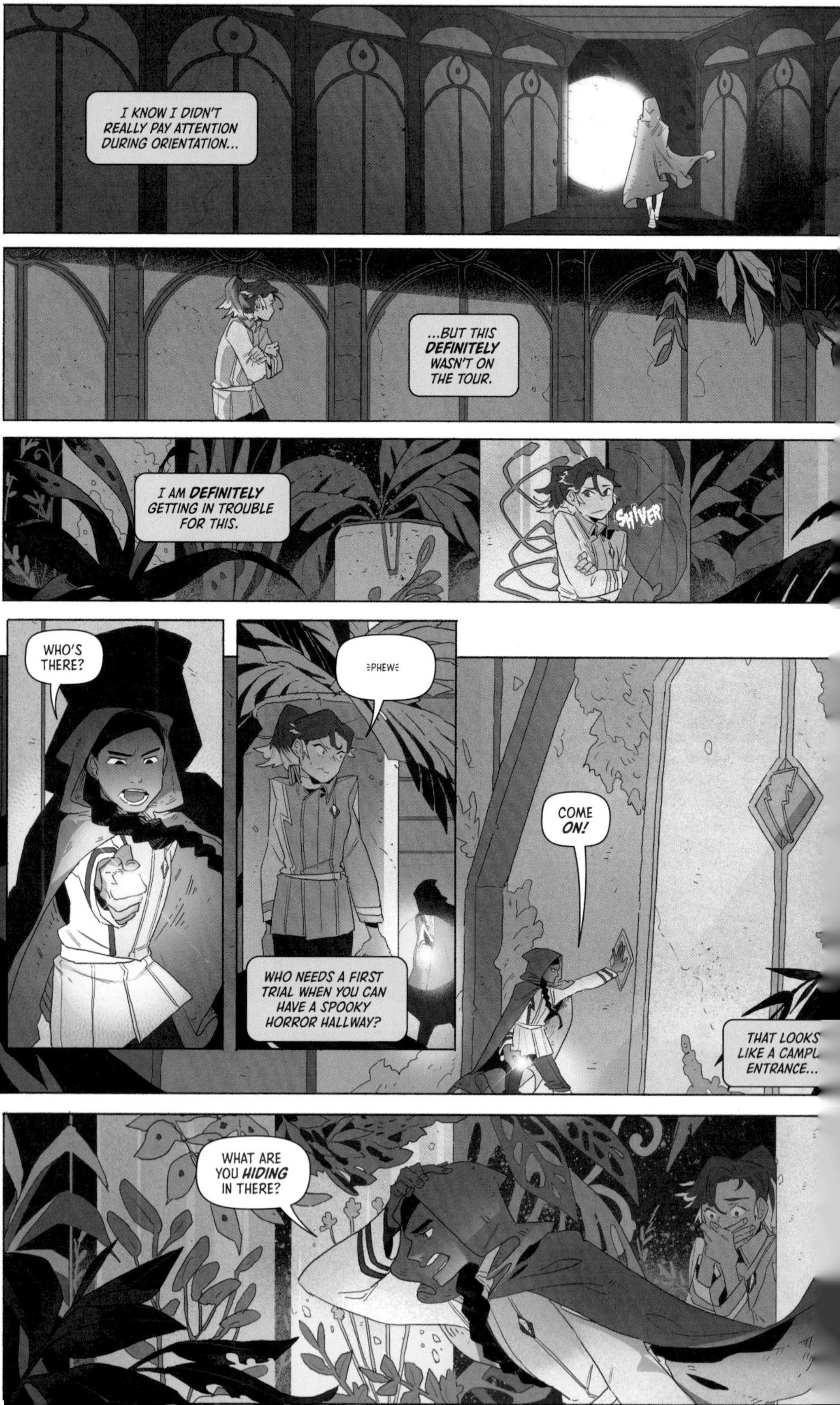

I KNOW I DIDN'T REALLY PAY ATTENTION DURING ORIENTATION...
...BUT THIS DEFINITELY WASN'T ON THE TOUR.
I AM DEFINITELY GETTING IN TROUBLE FOR THIS.
SHIVER
WHO'S THERE?
PHEW
WHO NEEDS A FIRST TRIAL WHEN YOU CAN HAVE A SPOOKY HORROR HALLWAY?
COME ON!
THAT LOOKS LIKE A CAMP
ENTRANCE...
WHAT ARE YOU HIDING IN THERE?

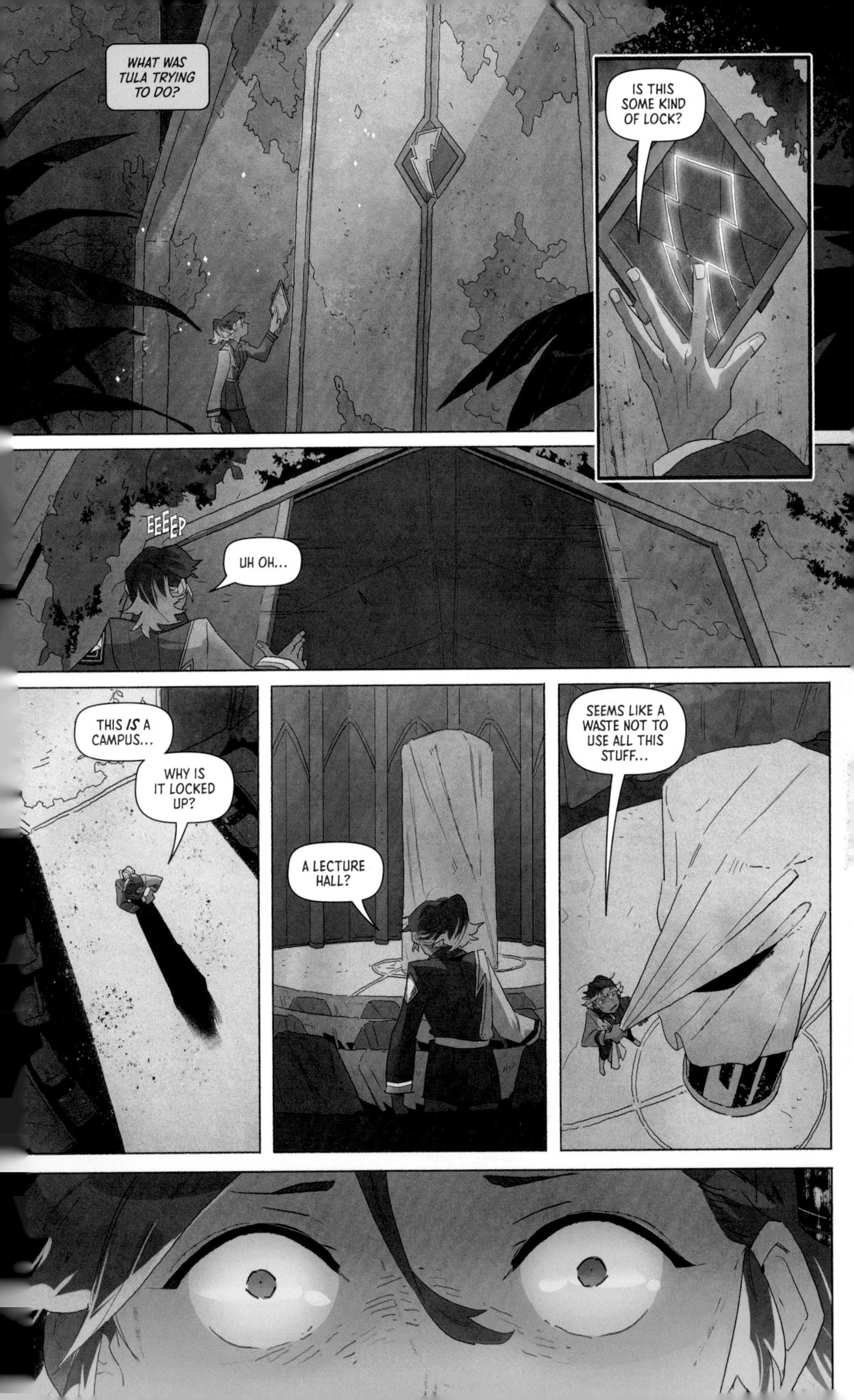

WHAT WAS TULA TRYING TO DO?
IS THIS SOME KIND OF LOCK?
EEEEP
UH OH...
THIS IS A CAMPUS...
WHY IS IT LOCKED UP?
A LECTURE HALL?
SEEMS LIKE A WASTE NOT TO USE ALL THIS STUFF...

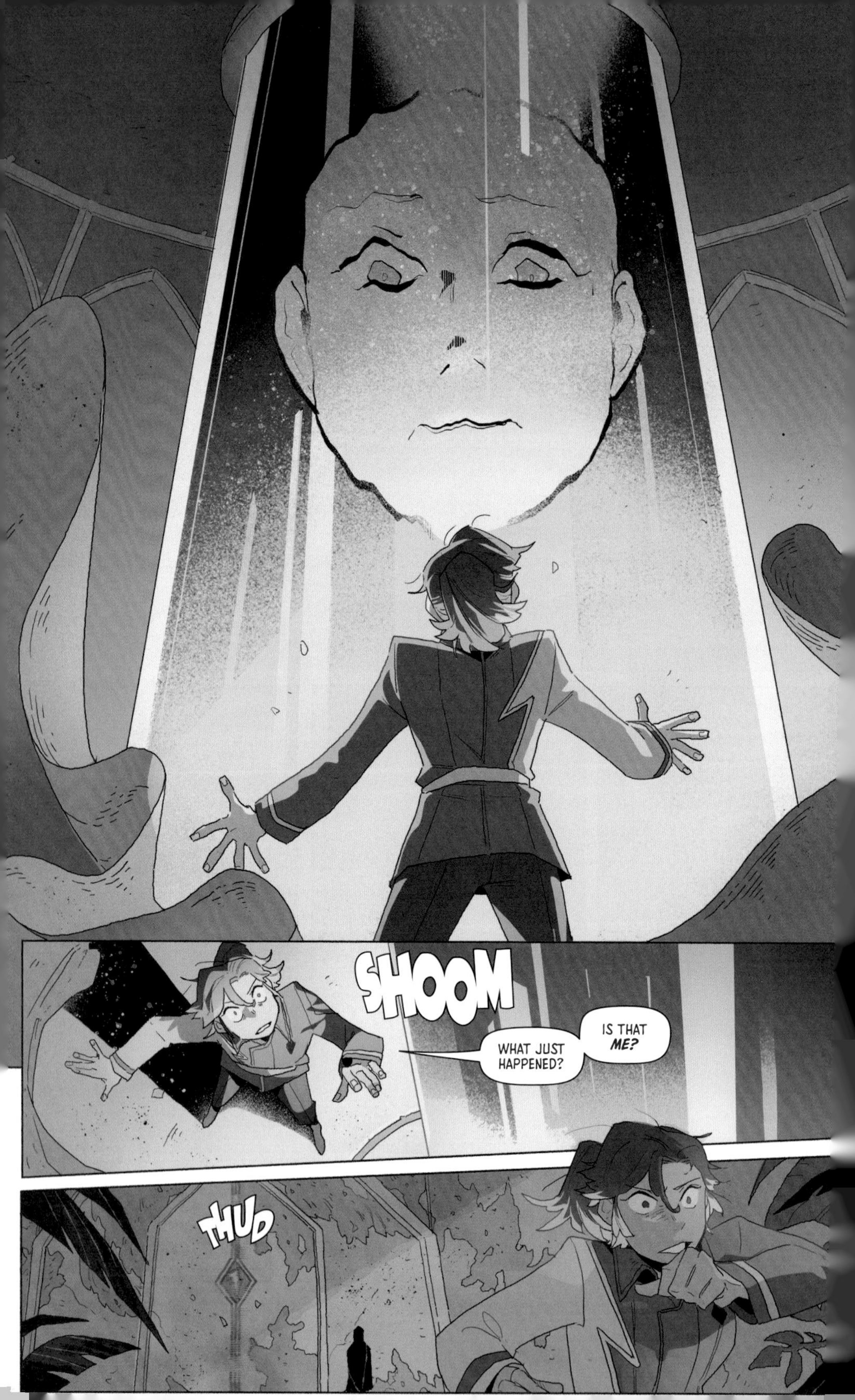
SHOOM
WHAT JUST HAPPENED?
IS THAT *ME?*
THUD

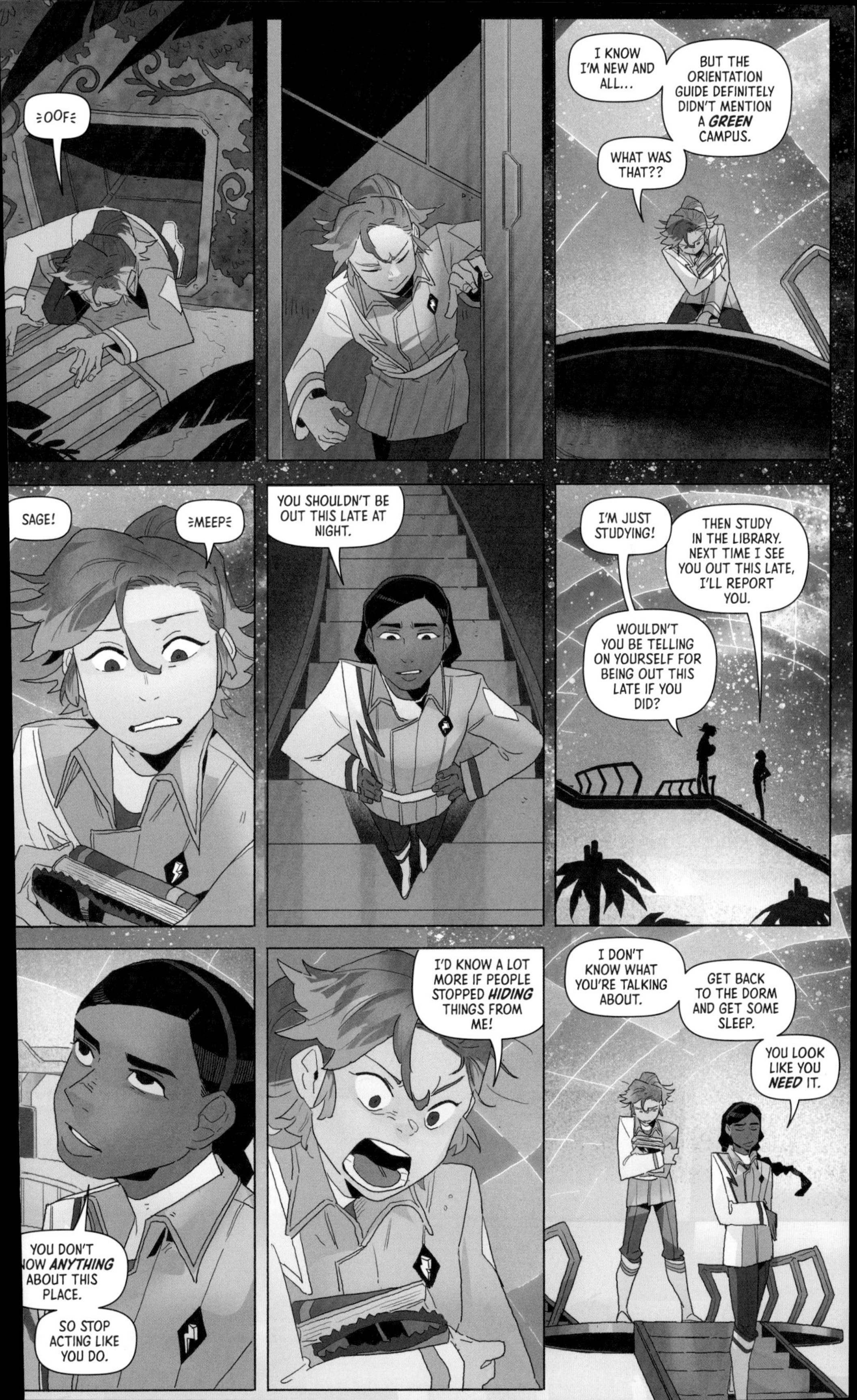
OOF
I KNOW I'M NEW AND ALL...
BUT THE ORIENTATION GUIDE DEFINITELY DIDN'T MENTION A *GREEN* CAMPUS.
WHAT WAS THAT??
SAGE!
MEEP
YOU SHOULDN'T BE OUT THIS LATE AT NIGHT.
I'M JUST STUDYING!
THEN STUDY IN THE LIBRARY. NEXT TIME I SEE YOU OUT THIS LATE, I'LL REPORT YOU.
WOULDN'T YOU BE TELLING ON YOURSELF FOR BEING OUT THIS LATE IF YOU DID?
YOU DON'T
OW *ANYTHING* ABOUT THIS PLACE.
SO STOP ACTING LIKE YOU DO.
I'D KNOW A LOT MORE IF PEOPLE STOPPED *HIDING* THINGS FROM ME!
I DON'T KNOW WHAT YOU'RE TALKING ABOUT.
GET BACK TO THE DORM AND GET SOME SLEEP.
YOU LOOK LIKE YOU *NEED* IT.

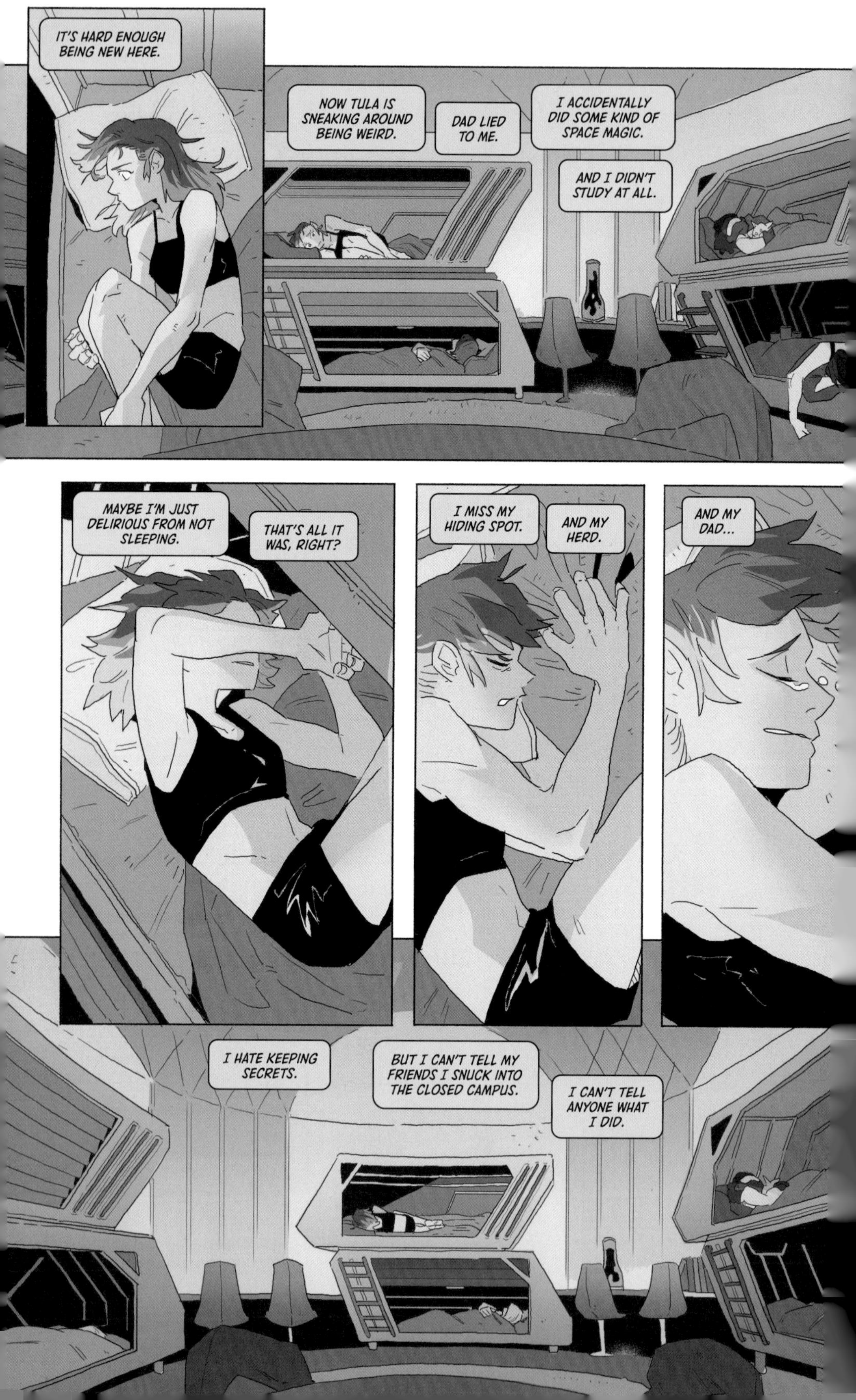
IT'S HARD ENOUGH BEING NEW HERE.
NOW TULA IS SNEAKING AROUND BEING WEIRD.
DAD LIED TO ME.
I ACCIDENTALLY DID SOME KIND OF SPACE MAGIC.
AND I DIDN'T STUDY AT ALL.
MAYBE I'M JUST DELIRIOUS FROM NOT SLEEPING.
THAT'S ALL IT WAS, RIGHT?
I MISS MY HIDING SPOT.
AND MY HERD.
AND MY DAD...
I HATE KEEPING SECRETS.
BUT I CAN'T TELL MY FRIENDS I SNUCK INTO THE CLOSED CAMPUS.
I CAN'T TELL ANYONE WHAT I DID.

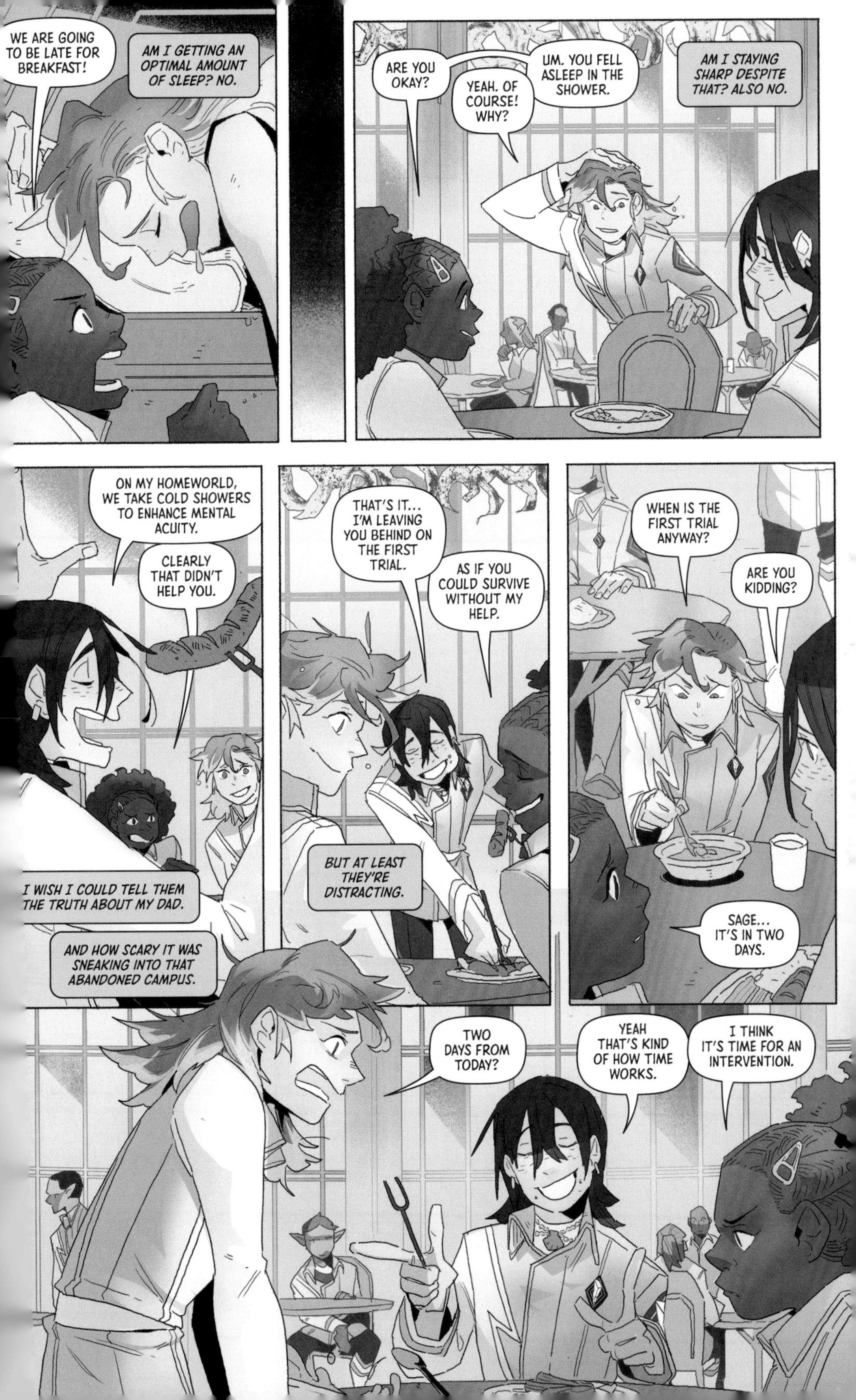
WE ARE GOING TO BE LATE FOR BREAKFAST!
AM I GETTING AN OPTIMAL AMOUNT OF SLEEP? NO.
ARE YOU OKAY?
YEAH. OF COURSE! WHY?
UM. YOU FELL ASLEEP IN THE SHOWER.
AM I STAYING SHARP DESPITE THAT? ALSO NO.
ON MY HOMEWORLD, WE TAKE COLD SHOWERS TO ENHANCE MENTAL ACUITY.
CLEARLY THAT DIDN'T HELP YOU.
I WISH I COULD TELL THEM THE TRUTH ABOUT MY DAD.
AND HOW SCARY IT WAS SNEAKING INTO THAT ABANDONED CAMPUS.
THAT'S IT... I'M LEAVING YOU BEHIND ON THE FIRST TRIAL.
AS IF YOU COULD SURVIVE WITHOUT MY HELP.
BUT AT LEAST THEY'RE DISTRACTING.
WHEN IS THE FIRST TRIAL ANYWAY?
ARE YOU KIDDING?
SAGE... IT'S IN TWO DAYS.
TWO DAYS FROM TODAY?
YEAH THAT'S KIND OF HOW TIME WORKS.
I THINK IT'S TIME FOR AN INTERVENTION.

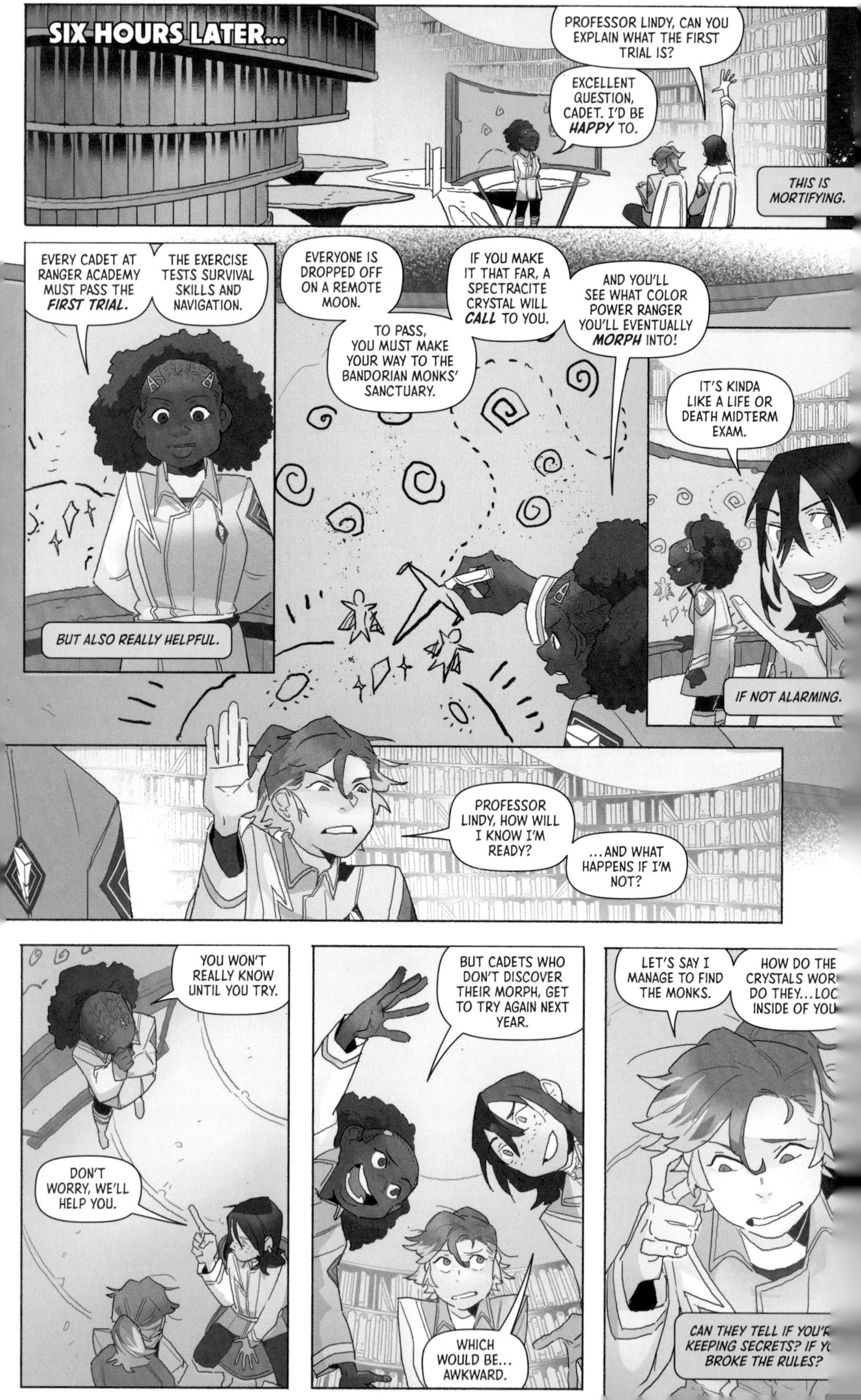
SIX HOURS LATER...
PROFESSOR LINDY, CAN YOU EXPLAIN WHAT THE FIRST TRIAL IS?
EXCELLENT QUESTION, CADET. I'D BE HAPPY TO.
THIS IS MORTIFYING.
EVERY CADET AT RANGER ACADEMY MUST PASS THE FIRST TRIAL.
THE EXERCISE TESTS SURVIVAL SKILLS AND NAVIGATION.
BUT ALSO REALLY HELPFUL.
EVERYONE IS DROPPED OFF ON A REMOTE MOON.
TO PASS, YOU MUST MAKE YOUR WAY TO THE BANDORIAN MONKS' SANCTUARY.
IF YOU MAKE IT THAT FAR, A SPECTRACITE CRYSTAL WILL CALL TO YOU.
AND YOU'LL SEE WHAT COLOR POWER RANGER YOU'LL EVENTUALLY MORPH INTO!
IT'S KINDA LIKE A LIFE OR DEATH MIDTERM EXAM.
IF NOT ALARMING.
PROFESSOR LINDY, HOW WILL I KNOW I'M READY?
...AND WHAT HAPPENS IF I'M NOT?
YOU WON'T REALLY KNOW UNTIL YOU TRY.
DON'T WORRY, WE'LL HELP YOU.
BUT CADETS WHO DON'T DISCOVER THEIR MORPH, GET TO TRY AGAIN NEXT YEAR.
WHICH WOULD BE... AWKWARD.
LET'S SAY I MANAGE TO FIND THE MONKS.
HOW DO THE CRYSTALS WOR DO THEY...LOC INSIDE OF YOU
CAN THEY TELL IF YOU' KEEPING SECRETS? IF Y BROKE THE RULES?

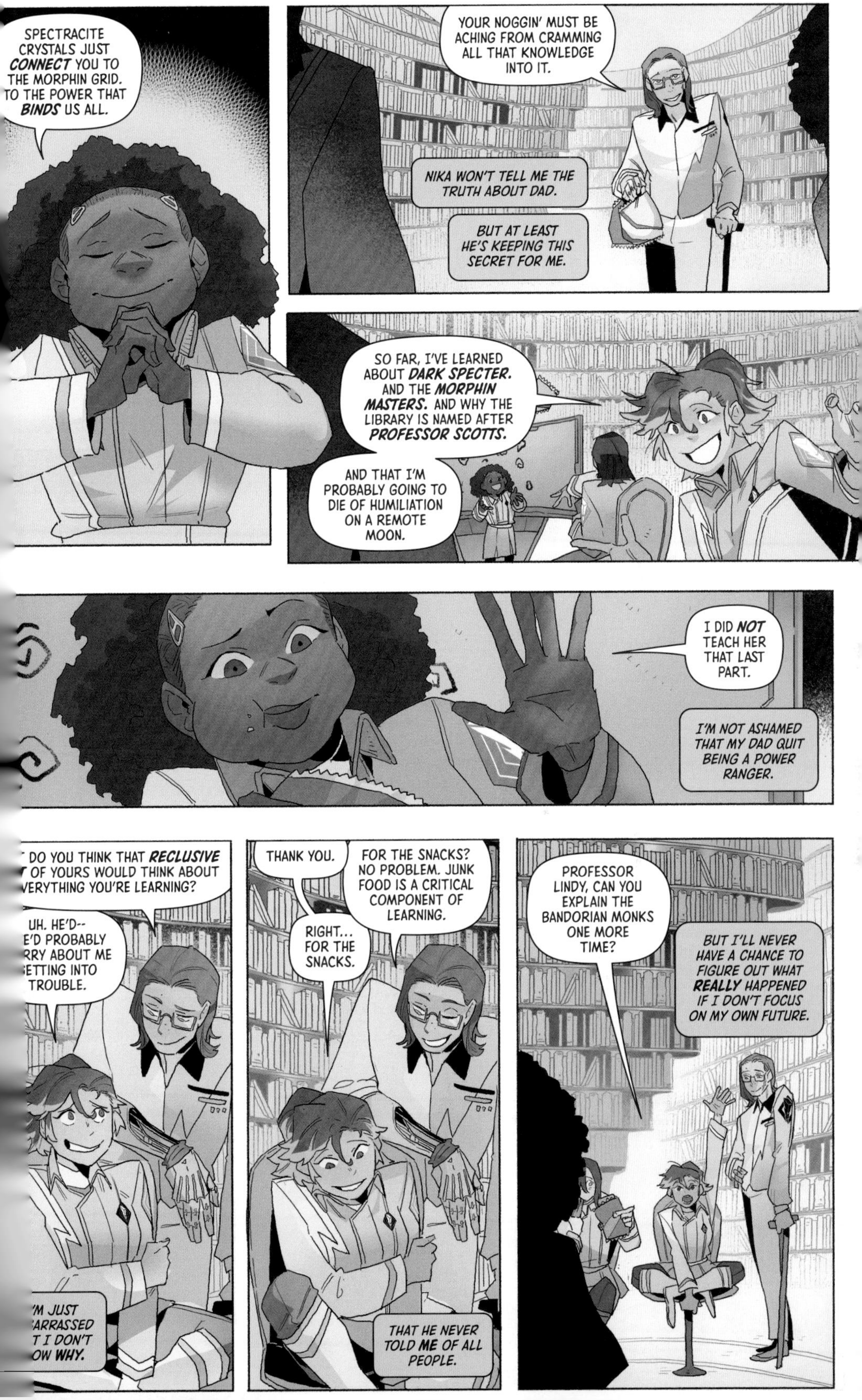

SPECTRACITE CRYSTALS JUST CONNECT YOU TO THE MORPHIN GRID. TO THE POWER THAT BINDS US ALL.
YOUR NOGGIN' MUST BE ACHING FROM CRAMMING ALL THAT KNOWLEDGE INTO IT.
NIKA WON'T TELL ME THE TRUTH ABOUT DAD.
BUT AT LEAST HE'S KEEPING THIS SECRET FOR ME.
SO FAR, I'VE LEARNED ABOUT DARK SPECTER. AND THE MORPHIN MASTERS. AND WHY THE LIBRARY IS NAMED AFTER PROFESSOR SCOTTS.
AND THAT I'M PROBABLY GOING TO DIE OF HUMILIATION ON A REMOTE MOON.
I DID NOT TEACH HER THAT LAST PART.
I'M NOT ASHAMED THAT MY DAD QUIT BEING A POWER RANGER.
DO YOU THINK THAT RECLUSIVE OF YOURS WOULD THINK ABOUT VERYTHING YOU'RE LEARNING?
UH. HE'D-- E'D PROBABLY RRY ABOUT ME ETTING INTO TROUBLE.
M JUST ARRASSED T I DON'T OW WHY.
THANK YOU.
FOR THE SNACKS? NO PROBLEM. JUNK FOOD IS A CRITICAL COMPONENT OF LEARNING.
RIGHT... FOR THE SNACKS.
THAT HE NEVER TOLD ME OF ALL PEOPLE.
PROFESSOR LINDY, CAN YOU EXPLAIN THE BANDORIAN MONKS ONE MORE TIME?
BUT I'LL NEVER HAVE A CHANCE TO FIGURE OUT WHAT REALLY HAPPENED IF I DON'T FOCUS ON MY OWN FUTURE.

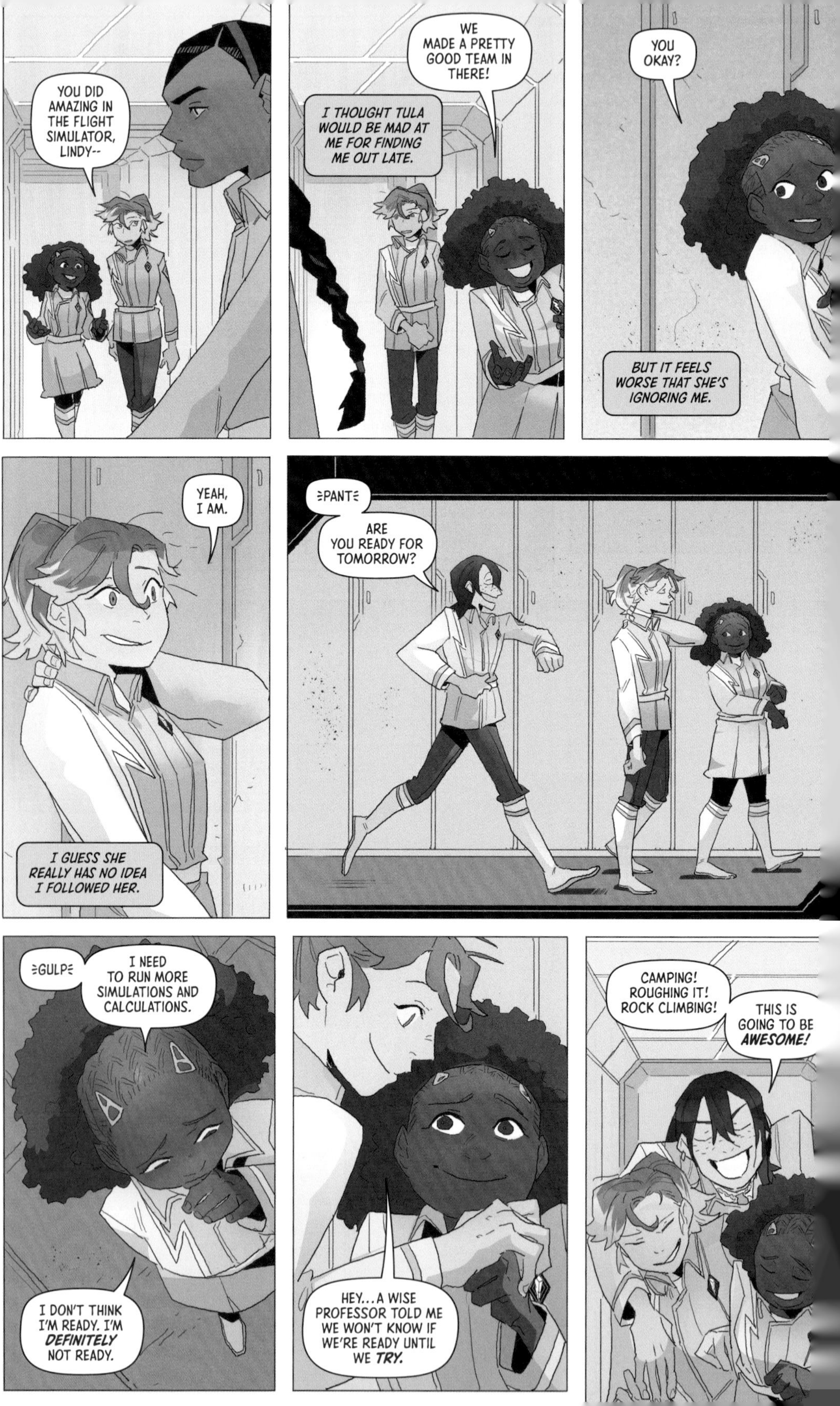
YOU DID AMAZING IN THE FLIGHT SIMULATOR, LINDY--
WE MADE A PRETTY GOOD TEAM IN THERE!
I THOUGHT TULA WOULD BE MAD AT ME FOR FINDING ME OUT LATE.
YOU OKAY?
BUT IT FEELS WORSE THAT SHE'S IGNORING ME.
YEAH, I AM.
I GUESS SHE REALLY HAS NO IDEA I FOLLOWED HER.
PANT
ARE YOU READY FOR TOMORROW?
GULP
I NEED TO RUN MORE SIMULATIONS AND CALCULATIONS.
I DON'T THINK I'M READY. I'M *DEFINITELY* NOT READY.
HEY... A WISE PROFESSOR TOLD ME WE WON'T KNOW IF WE'RE READY UNTIL WE *TRY.*
CAMPING! ROUGHING IT! ROCK CLIMBING!
THIS IS GOING TO BE ***AWESOME!***

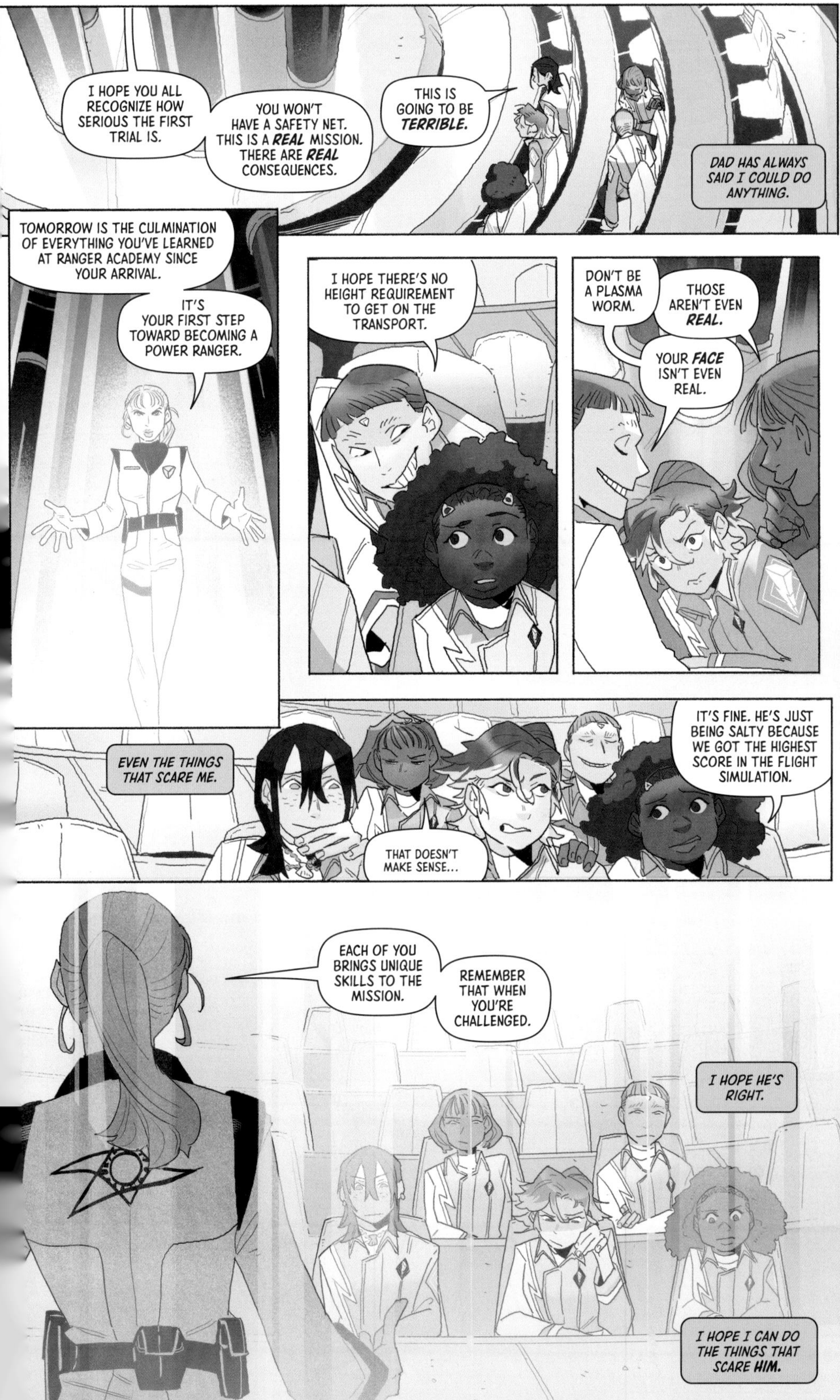

I HOPE YOU ALL RECOGNIZE HOW SERIOUS THE FIRST TRIAL IS.
YOU WON'T HAVE A SAFETY NET. THIS IS A **REAL** MISSION. THERE ARE **REAL** CONSEQUENCES.
THIS IS GOING TO BE ***TERRIBLE.***
DAD HAS ALWAYS SAID I COULD DO ANYTHING.
TOMORROW IS THE CULMINATION OF EVERYTHING YOU'VE LEARNED AT RANGER ACADEMY SINCE YOUR ARRIVAL.
IT'S YOUR FIRST STEP TOWARD BECOMING A POWER RANGER.
I HOPE THERE'S NO HEIGHT REQUIREMENT TO GET ON THE TRANSPORT.
DON'T BE A PLASMA WORM.
THOSE AREN'T EVEN **REAL.**
YOUR **FACE** ISN'T EVEN REAL.
EVEN THE THINGS THAT SCARE ME.
THAT DOESN'T MAKE SENSE...
IT'S FINE. HE'S JUST BEING SALTY BECAUSE WE GOT THE HIGHEST SCORE IN THE FLIGHT SIMULATION.
EACH OF YOU BRINGS UNIQUE SKILLS TO THE MISSION.
REMEMBER THAT WHEN YOU'RE CHALLENGED.
I HOPE HE'S RIGHT.
I HOPE I CAN DO THE THINGS THAT SCARE ***HIM.***

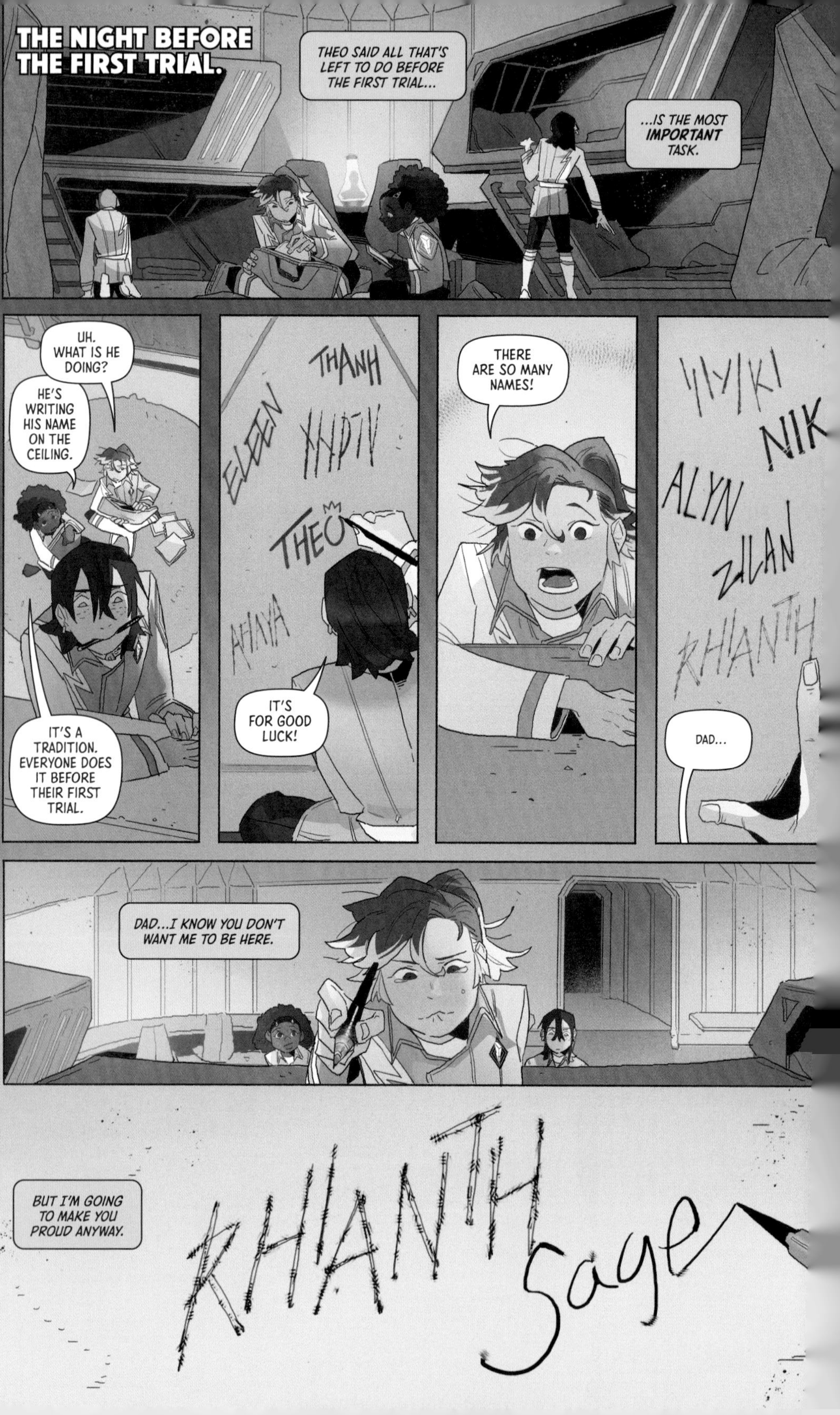
THE NIGHT BEFORE THE FIRST TRIAL.
THEO SAID ALL THAT'S LEFT TO DO BEFORE THE FIRST TRIAL...
...IS THE MOST IMPORTANT TASK.
UH. WHAT IS HE DOING?
HE'S WRITING HIS NAME ON THE CEILING.
IT'S A TRADITION. EVERYONE DOES IT BEFORE THEIR FIRST TRIAL.
THANH
ELDEN
THEO
IT'S FOR GOOD LUCK!
THERE ARE SO MANY NAMES!
NIK
ALYN
RHIANTH
DAD...
DAD...I KNOW YOU DON'T WANT ME TO BE HERE.
BUT I'M GOING TO MAKE YOU PROUD ANYWAY.
RHIANTH
Sage

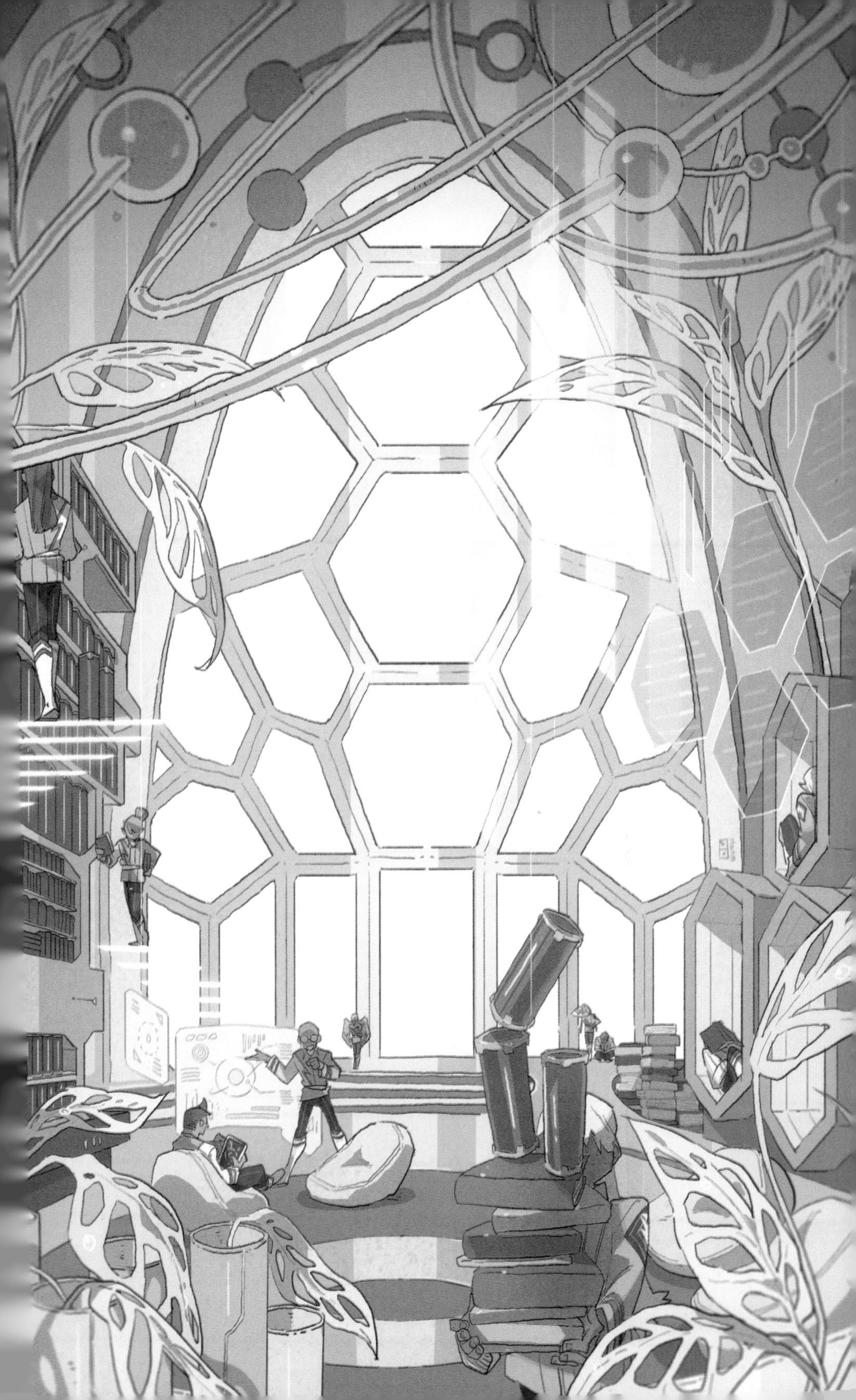

CHAPTER FOUR

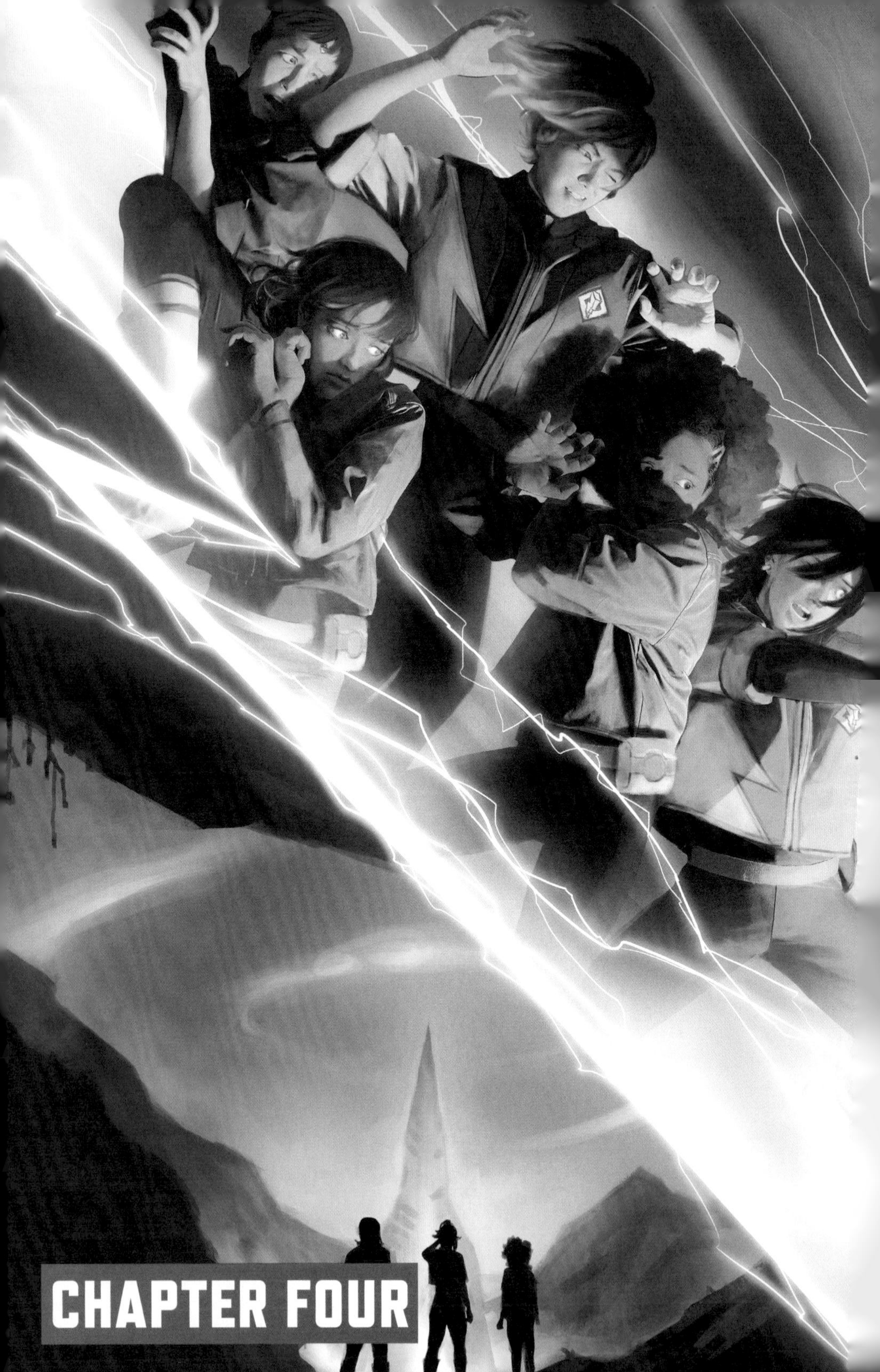

ISSUE FOUR COVER BY **MIGUEL MERCADO**

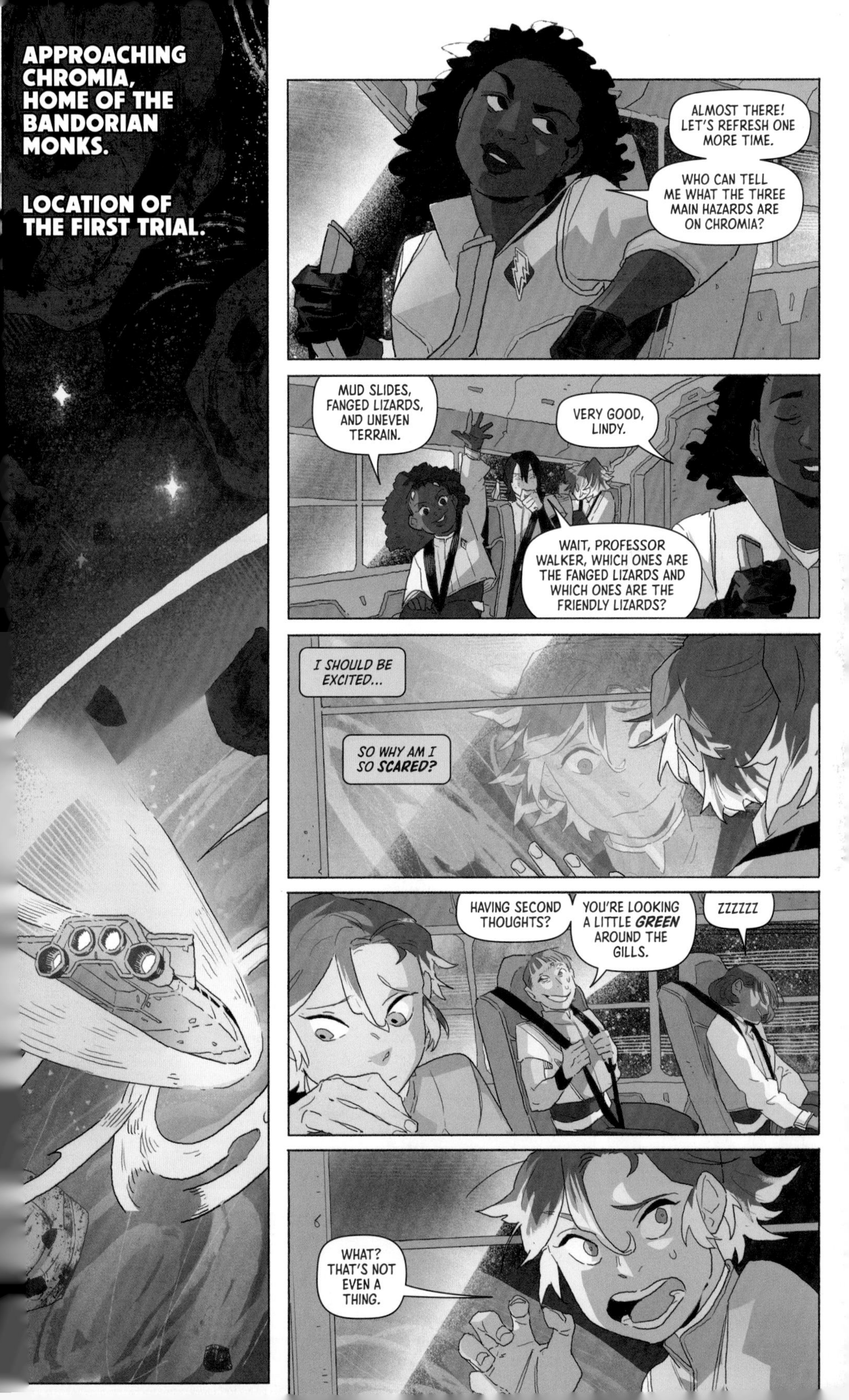
APPROACHING CHROMIA, HOME OF THE BANDORIAN MONKS.
LOCATION OF THE FIRST TRIAL.
ALMOST THERE! LET'S REFRESH ONE MORE TIME.
WHO CAN TELL ME WHAT THE THREE MAIN HAZARDS ARE ON CHROMIA?
MUD SLIDES, FANGED LIZARDS, AND UNEVEN TERRAIN.
VERY GOOD, LINDY.
WAIT, PROFESSOR WALKER, WHICH ONES ARE THE FANGED LIZARDS AND WHICH ONES ARE THE FRIENDLY LIZARDS?
I SHOULD BE EXCITED...
SO WHY AM I SO *SCARED?*
HAVING SECOND THOUGHTS?
YOU'RE LOOKING A LITTLE *GREEN* AROUND THE GILLS.
ZZZZZZ
WHAT? THAT'S NOT EVEN A THING.

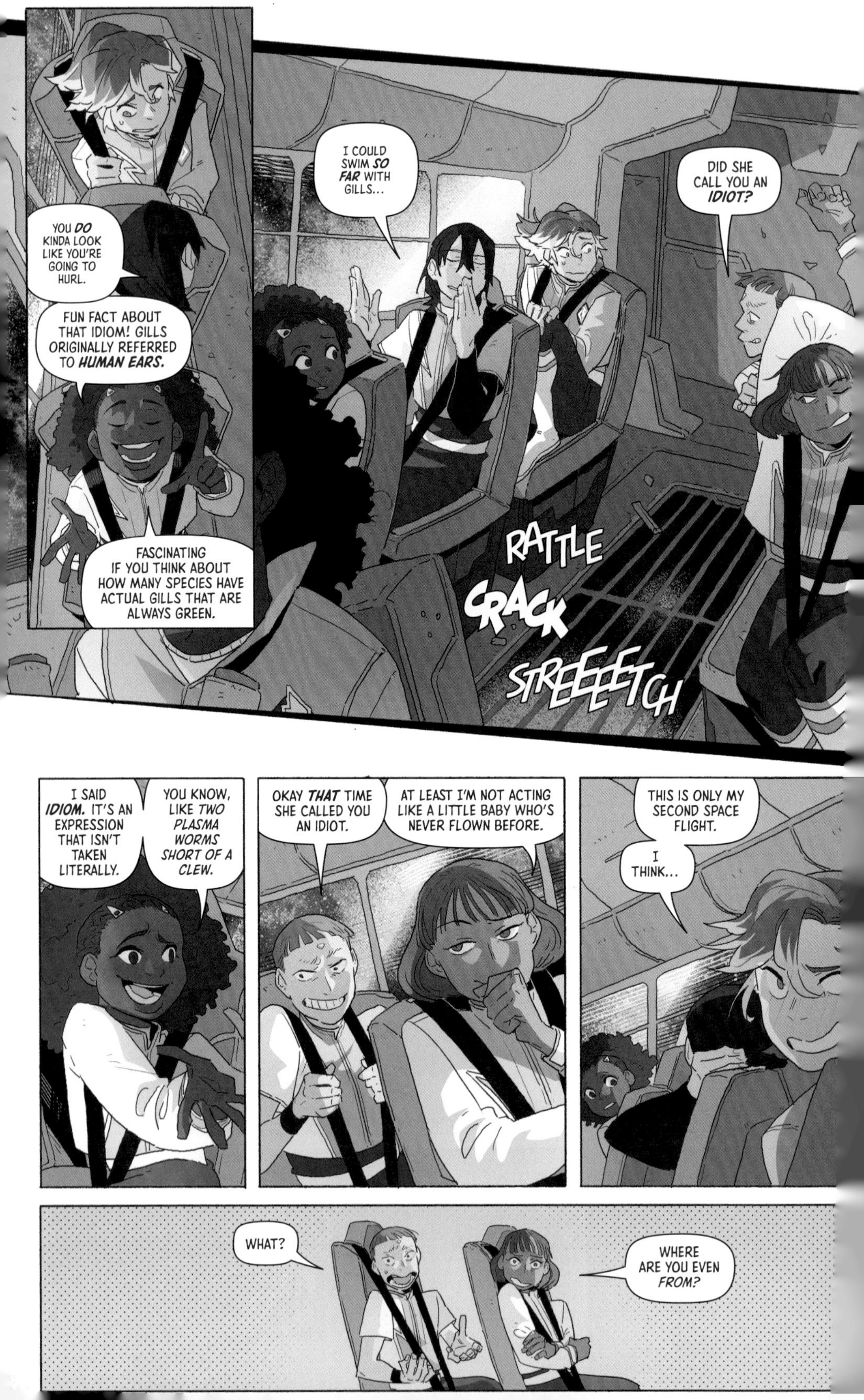
YOU *DO* KINDA LOOK LIKE YOU'RE GOING TO HURL.
FUN FACT ABOUT THAT IDIOM! GILLS ORIGINALLY REFERRED TO ***HUMAN EARS.***
FASCINATING IF YOU THINK ABOUT HOW MANY SPECIES HAVE ACTUAL GILLS THAT ARE ALWAYS GREEN.
I COULD SWIM ***SO FAR*** WITH GILLS...
DID SHE CALL YOU AN ***IDIOT?***
RATTLE
CRACK
STREEEETCH
I SAID ***IDIOM.*** IT'S AN EXPRESSION THAT ISN'T TAKEN LITERALLY.
YOU KNOW, LIKE *TWO PLASMA WORMS SHORT OF A CLEW.*
OKAY ***THAT*** TIME SHE CALLED YOU AN IDIOT.
AT LEAST I'M NOT ACTING LIKE A LITTLE BABY WHO'S NEVER FLOWN BEFORE.
THIS IS ONLY MY SECOND SPACE FLIGHT.
I THINK...
WHAT?
WHERE ARE YOU EVEN *FROM?*

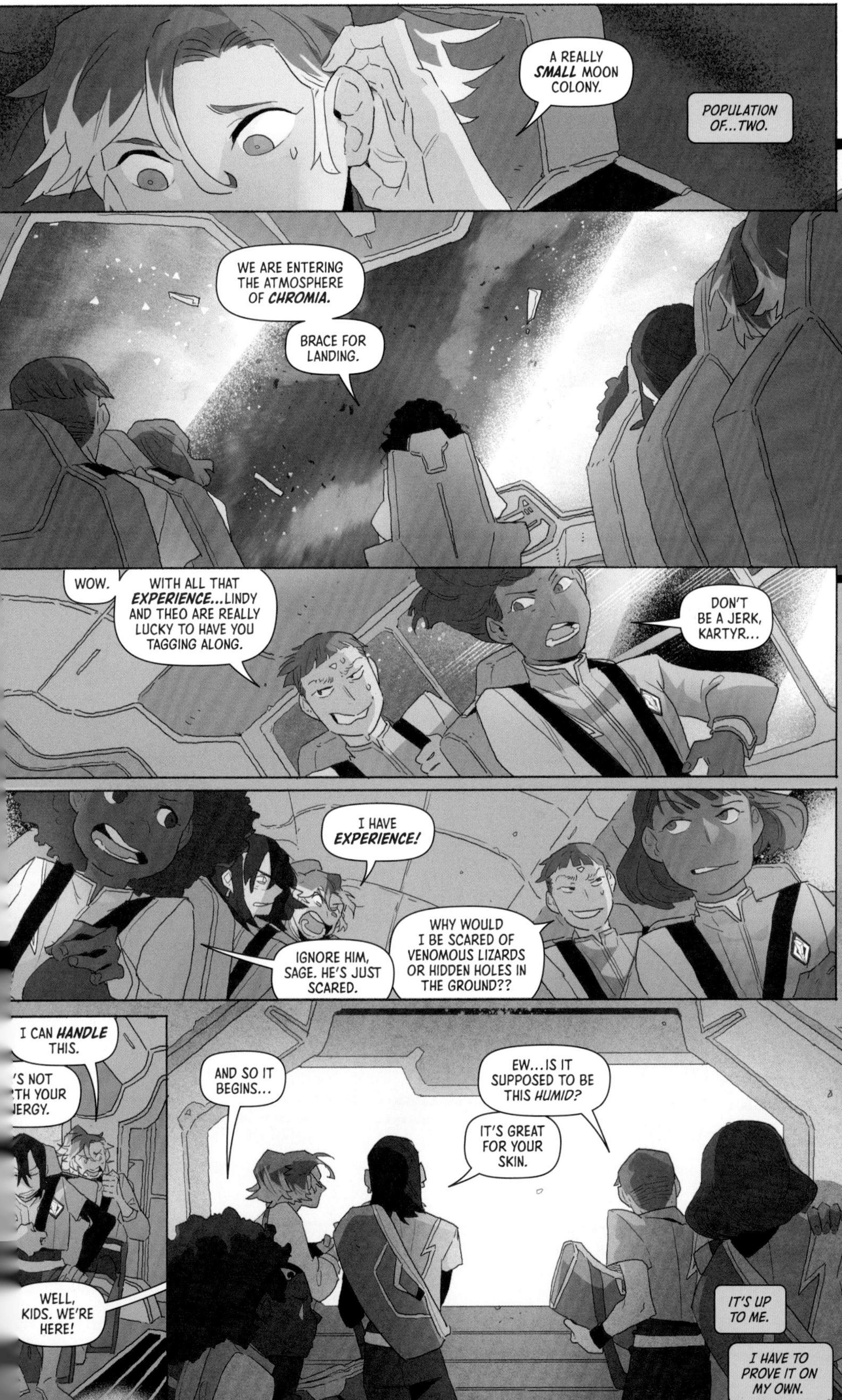
A REALLY SMALL MOON COLONY.
POPULATION OF...TWO.
WE ARE ENTERING THE ATMOSPHERE OF CHROMIA.
BRACE FOR LANDING.
WOW.
WITH ALL THAT EXPERIENCE...LINDY AND THEO ARE REALLY LUCKY TO HAVE YOU TAGGING ALONG.
DON'T BE A JERK, KARTYR...
I HAVE EXPERIENCE!
IGNORE HIM, SAGE. HE'S JUST SCARED.
WHY WOULD I BE SCARED OF VENOMOUS LIZARDS OR HIDDEN HOLES IN THE GROUND??
I CAN HANDLE THIS.
WELL, KIDS. WE'RE HERE!
AND SO IT BEGINS...
EW...IS IT SUPPOSED TO BE THIS HUMID?
IT'S GREAT FOR YOUR SKIN.
IT'S UP TO ME.
I HAVE TO PROVE IT ON MY OWN.

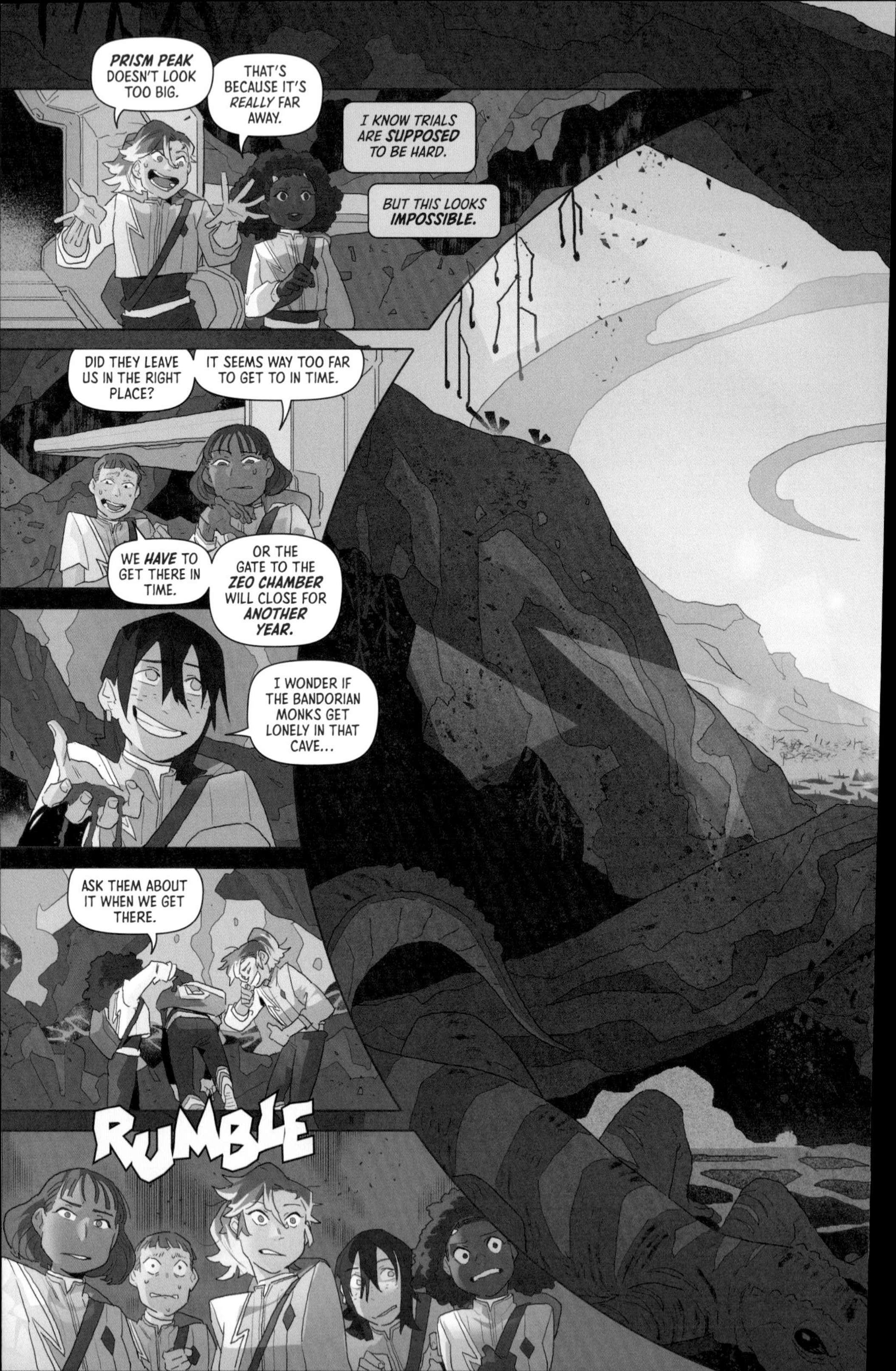
PRISM PEAK DOESN'T LOOK TOO BIG.
THAT'S BECAUSE IT'S REALLY FAR AWAY.
I KNOW TRIALS ARE SUPPOSED TO BE HARD.
BUT THIS LOOKS IMPOSSIBLE.
DID THEY LEAVE US IN THE RIGHT PLACE?
IT SEEMS WAY TOO FAR TO GET TO IN TIME.
WE HAVE TO GET THERE IN TIME.
OR THE GATE TO THE ZEO CHAMBER WILL CLOSE FOR ANOTHER YEAR.
I WONDER IF THE BANDORIAN MONKS GET LONELY IN THAT CAVE...
ASK THEM ABOUT IT WHEN WE GET THERE.
RUMBLE

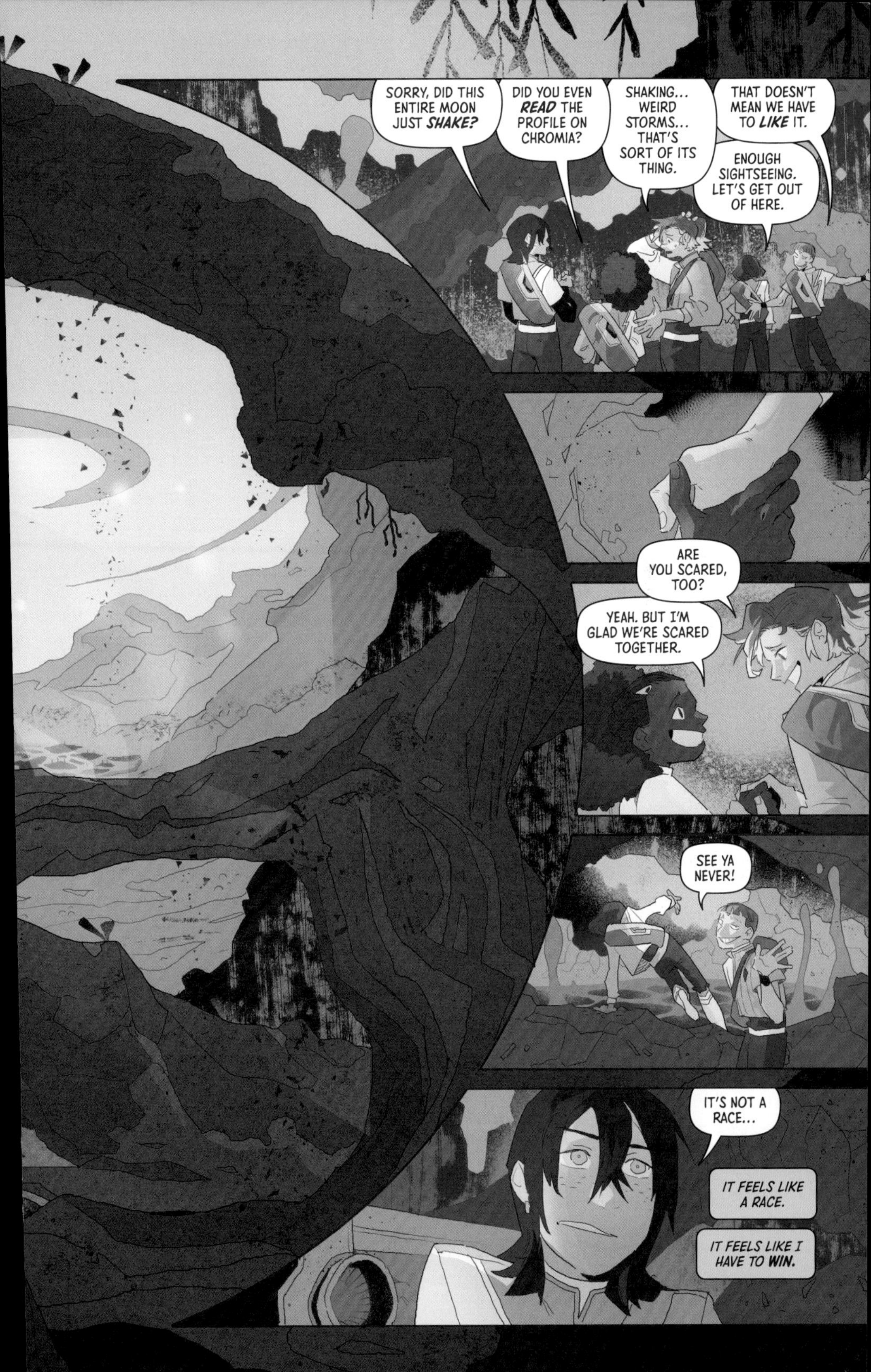
SORRY, DID THIS ENTIRE MOON JUST SHAKE?
DID YOU EVEN READ THE PROFILE ON CHROMIA?
SHAKING... WEIRD STORMS... THAT'S SORT OF ITS THING.
THAT DOESN'T MEAN WE HAVE TO LIKE IT.
ENOUGH SIGHTSEEING. LET'S GET OUT OF HERE.
ARE YOU SCARED, TOO?
YEAH. BUT I'M GLAD WE'RE SCARED TOGETHER.
SEE YA NEVER!
IT'S NOT A RACE...
IT FEELS LIKE A RACE.
IT FEELS LIKE I HAVE TO WIN.

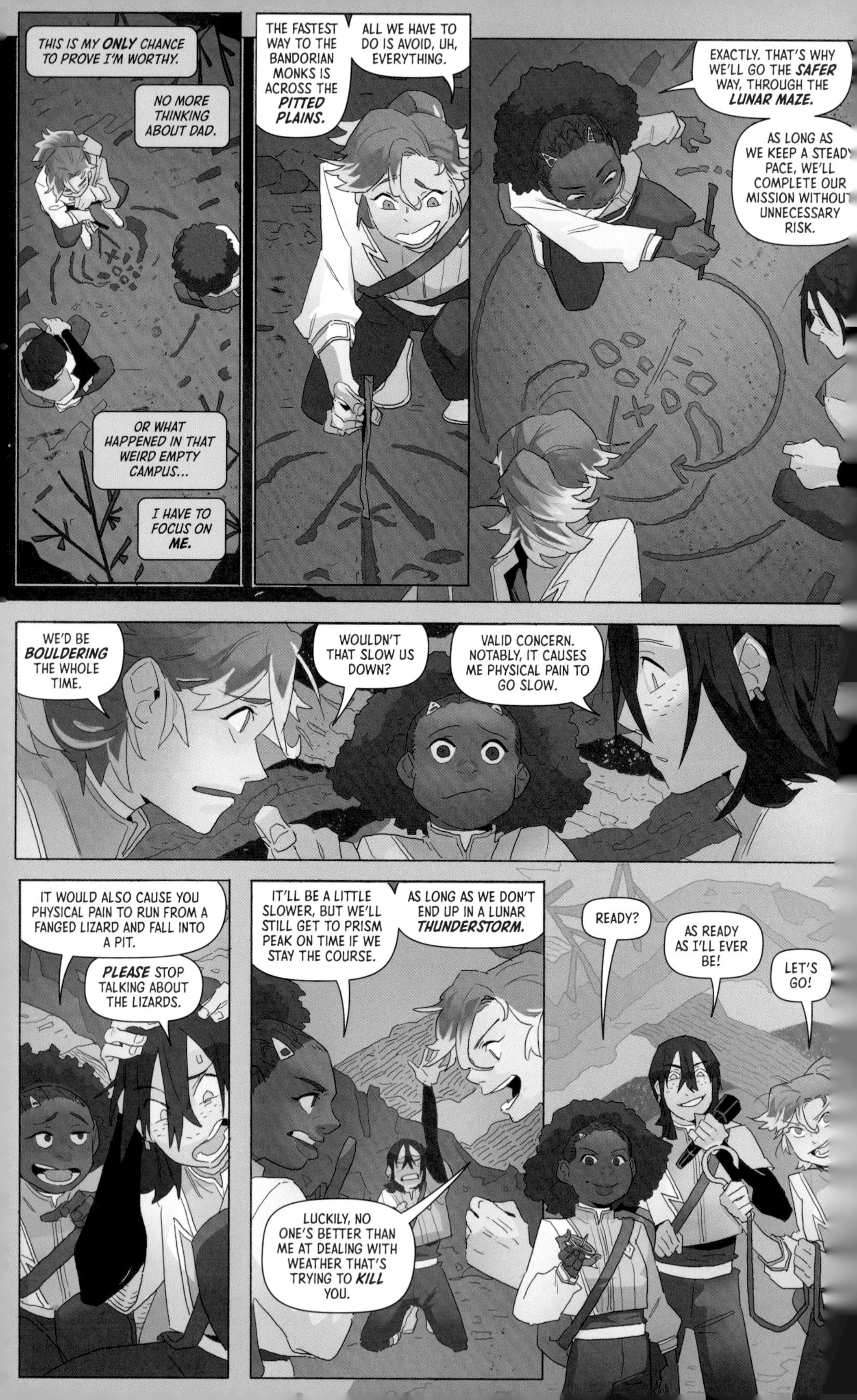
THIS IS MY ONLY CHANCE TO PROVE I'M WORTHY.
NO MORE THINKING ABOUT DAD.
OR WHAT HAPPENED IN THAT WEIRD EMPTY CAMPUS...
I HAVE TO FOCUS ON ME.
THE FASTEST WAY TO THE BANDORIAN MONKS IS ACROSS THE PITTED PLAINS.
ALL WE HAVE TO DO IS AVOID, UH, EVERYTHING.
EXACTLY. THAT'S WHY WE'LL GO THE SAFER WAY, THROUGH THE LUNAR MAZE.
AS LONG AS WE KEEP A STEADY PACE, WE'LL COMPLETE OUR MISSION WITHOUT UNNECESSARY RISK.
WE'D BE BOULDERING THE WHOLE TIME.
WOULDN'T THAT SLOW US DOWN?
VALID CONCERN. NOTABLY, IT CAUSES ME PHYSICAL PAIN TO GO SLOW.
IT WOULD ALSO CAUSE YOU PHYSICAL PAIN TO RUN FROM A FANGED LIZARD AND FALL INTO A PIT.
PLEASE STOP TALKING ABOUT THE LIZARDS.
IT'LL BE A LITTLE SLOWER, BUT WE'LL STILL GET TO PRISM PEAK ON TIME IF WE STAY THE COURSE.
AS LONG AS WE DON'T END UP IN A LUNAR THUNDERSTORM.
LUCKILY, NO ONE'S BETTER THAN ME AT DEALING WITH WEATHER THAT'S TRYING TO KILL YOU.
READY?
AS READY AS I'LL EVER BE!
LET'S GO!

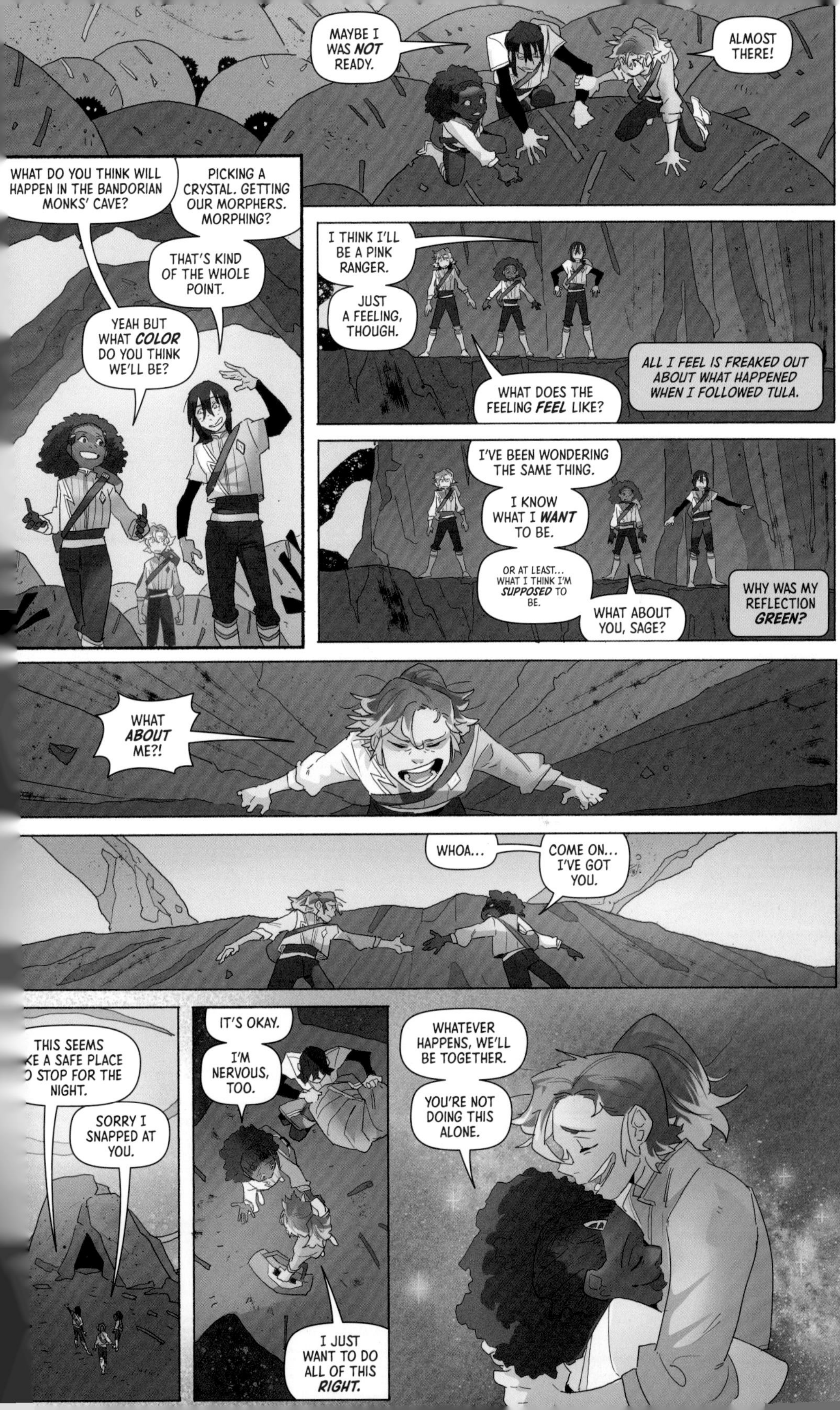
MAYBE I WAS NOT READY.
ALMOST THERE!
WHAT DO YOU THINK WILL HAPPEN IN THE BANDORIAN MONKS' CAVE?
PICKING A CRYSTAL. GETTING OUR MORPHERS. MORPHING?
THAT'S KIND OF THE WHOLE POINT.
YEAH BUT WHAT COLOR DO YOU THINK WE'LL BE?
I THINK I'LL BE A PINK RANGER.
JUST A FEELING, THOUGH.
WHAT DOES THE FEELING FEEL LIKE?
ALL I FEEL IS FREAKED OUT ABOUT WHAT HAPPENED WHEN I FOLLOWED TULA.
I'VE BEEN WONDERING THE SAME THING.
I KNOW WHAT I WANT TO BE.
OR AT LEAST... WHAT I THINK I'M SUPPOSED TO BE.
WHAT ABOUT YOU, SAGE?
WHY WAS MY REFLECTION GREEN?
WHAT ABOUT ME?!
WHOA...
COME ON... I'VE GOT YOU.
THIS SEEMS KE A SAFE PLACE O STOP FOR THE NIGHT.
SORRY I SNAPPED AT YOU.
IT'S OKAY.
I'M NERVOUS, TOO.
I JUST WANT TO DO ALL OF THIS RIGHT.
WHATEVER HAPPENS, WE'LL BE TOGETHER.
YOU'RE NOT DOING THIS ALONE.

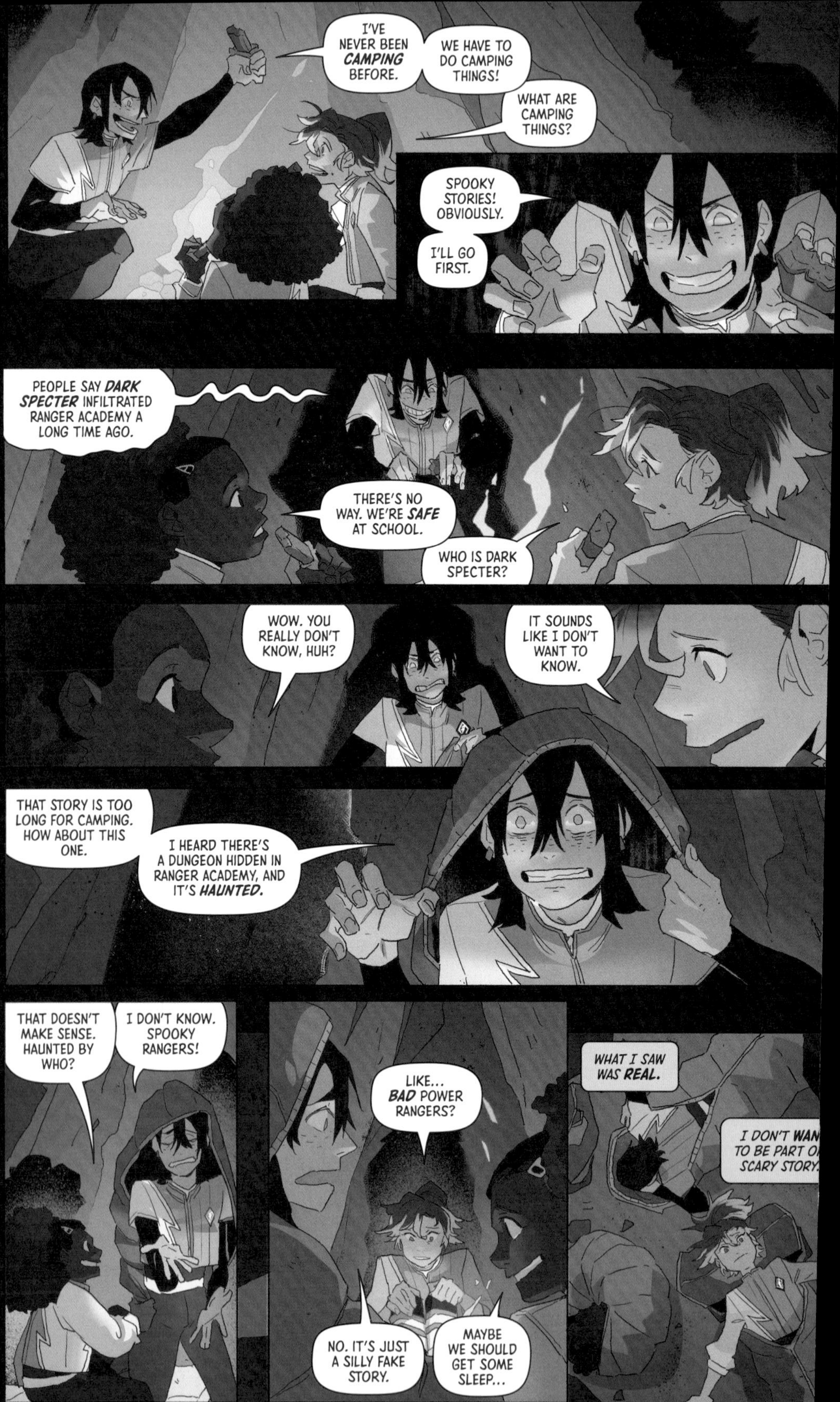

I'VE NEVER BEEN CAMPING BEFORE.
WE HAVE TO DO CAMPING THINGS!
WHAT ARE CAMPING THINGS?
SPOOKY STORIES! OBVIOUSLY.
I'LL GO FIRST.
PEOPLE SAY DARK SPECTER INFILTRATED RANGER ACADEMY A LONG TIME AGO.
THERE'S NO WAY. WE'RE SAFE AT SCHOOL.
WHO IS DARK SPECTER?
WOW. YOU REALLY DON'T KNOW, HUH?
IT SOUNDS LIKE I DON'T WANT TO KNOW.
THAT STORY IS TOO LONG FOR CAMPING. HOW ABOUT THIS ONE.
I HEARD THERE'S A DUNGEON HIDDEN IN RANGER ACADEMY, AND IT'S HAUNTED.
THAT DOESN'T MAKE SENSE. HAUNTED BY WHO?
I DON'T KNOW. SPOOKY RANGERS!
LIKE... BAD POWER RANGERS?
NO. IT'S JUST A SILLY FAKE STORY.
MAYBE WE SHOULD GET SOME SLEEP...
WHAT I SAW WAS REAL.

I FELL ASLEEP JUST AS THE SUN WAS RISING.

THOSE ARE *STORM CLOUDS*.

WE NEED TO MOVE QUICKLY.

SAGE... WE HAVE TO GET GOING.

I COULDN'T STOP *THINKING*.

HOW [COU]LD YOU [T]ELL?

THEY JUST LOOKED LIKE NORMAL CLOUDS TO ME.

RUMBLE

[W]HERE I [GRE]W UP, BAD [WE]ATHER [COU]LD *KILL* YOU.

[G]UESS I [LEA]RNED [TO] LISTEN.

I CAN BARELY GET MY FOOTING.

SO MUCH FOR KEEPING A STEADY PACE.

THE MUD SLIDE IS ONLY GOING TO GET *WORSE*.

LET ME TRY SOMETHING.

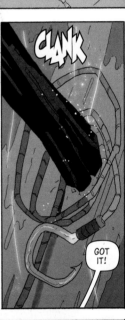

CLANK

GOT IT!

NICE AIM!

IT WAS A LUCKY THROW.

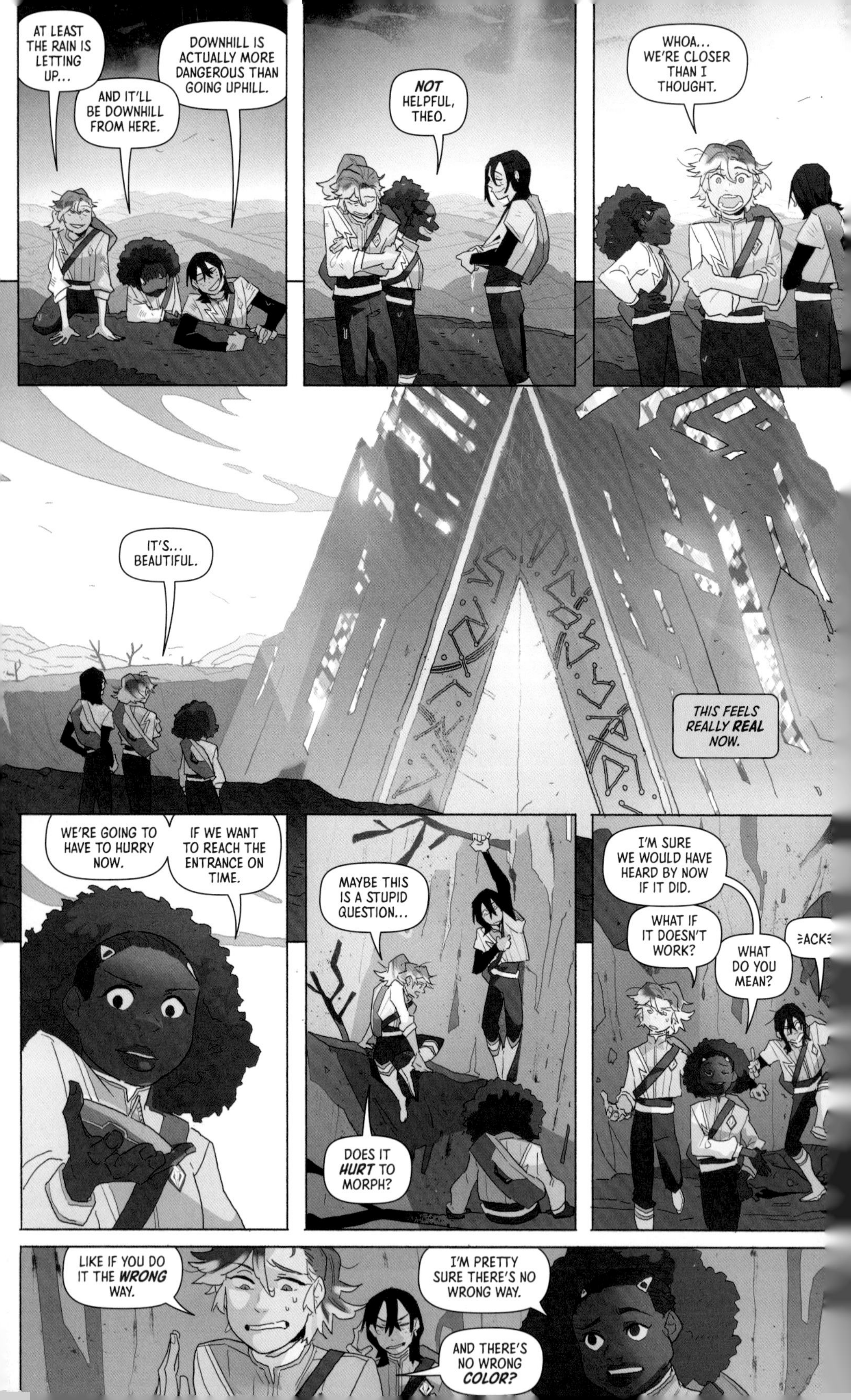

AT LEAST THE RAIN IS LETTING UP...
AND IT'LL BE DOWNHILL FROM HERE.
DOWNHILL IS ACTUALLY MORE DANGEROUS THAN GOING UPHILL.
NOT HELPFUL, THEO.
WHOA... WE'RE CLOSER THAN I THOUGHT.
IT'S... BEAUTIFUL.
THIS FEELS REALLY REAL NOW.
WE'RE GOING TO HAVE TO HURRY NOW.
IF WE WANT TO REACH THE ENTRANCE ON TIME.
MAYBE THIS IS A STUPID QUESTION...
DOES IT HURT TO MORPH?
I'M SURE WE WOULD HAVE HEARD BY NOW IF IT DID.
WHAT IF IT DOESN'T WORK?
WHAT DO YOU MEAN?
ACK
LIKE IF YOU DO IT THE WRONG WAY.
I'M PRETTY SURE THERE'S NO WRONG WAY.
AND THERE'S NO WRONG COLOR?

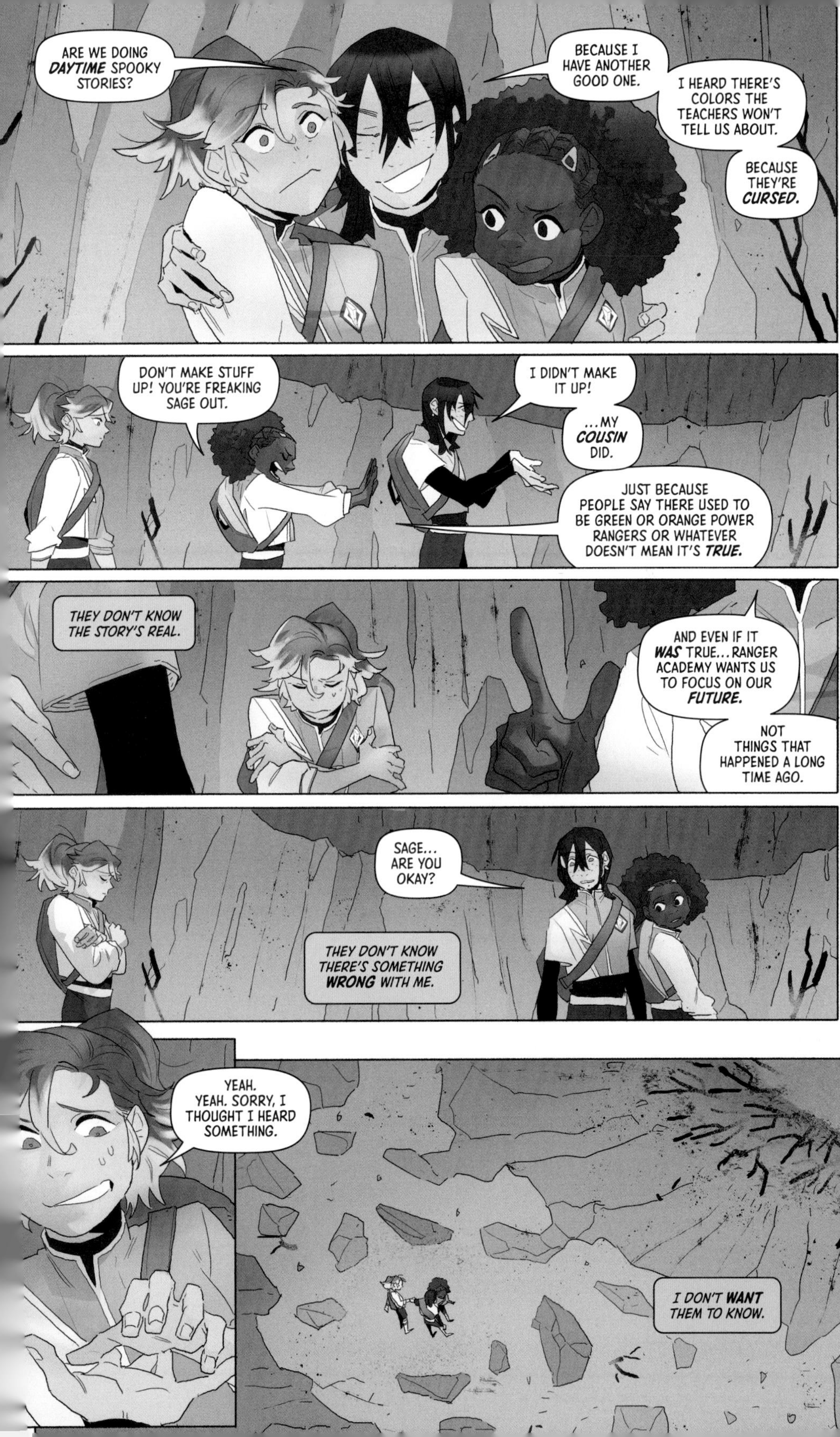
ARE WE DOING DAYTIME SPOOKY STORIES?
BECAUSE I HAVE ANOTHER GOOD ONE.
I HEARD THERE'S COLORS THE TEACHERS WON'T TELL US ABOUT.
BECAUSE THEY'RE CURSED.
DON'T MAKE STUFF UP! YOU'RE FREAKING SAGE OUT.
I DIDN'T MAKE IT UP!
...MY COUSIN DID.
JUST BECAUSE PEOPLE SAY THERE USED TO BE GREEN OR ORANGE POWER RANGERS OR WHATEVER DOESN'T MEAN IT'S TRUE.
THEY DON'T KNOW THE STORY'S REAL.
AND EVEN IF IT WAS TRUE...RANGER ACADEMY WANTS US TO FOCUS ON OUR FUTURE.
NOT THINGS THAT HAPPENED A LONG TIME AGO.
SAGE... ARE YOU OKAY?
THEY DON'T KNOW THERE'S SOMETHING WRONG WITH ME.
YEAH. YEAH. SORRY, I THOUGHT I HEARD SOMETHING.
I DON'T WANT THEM TO KNOW.

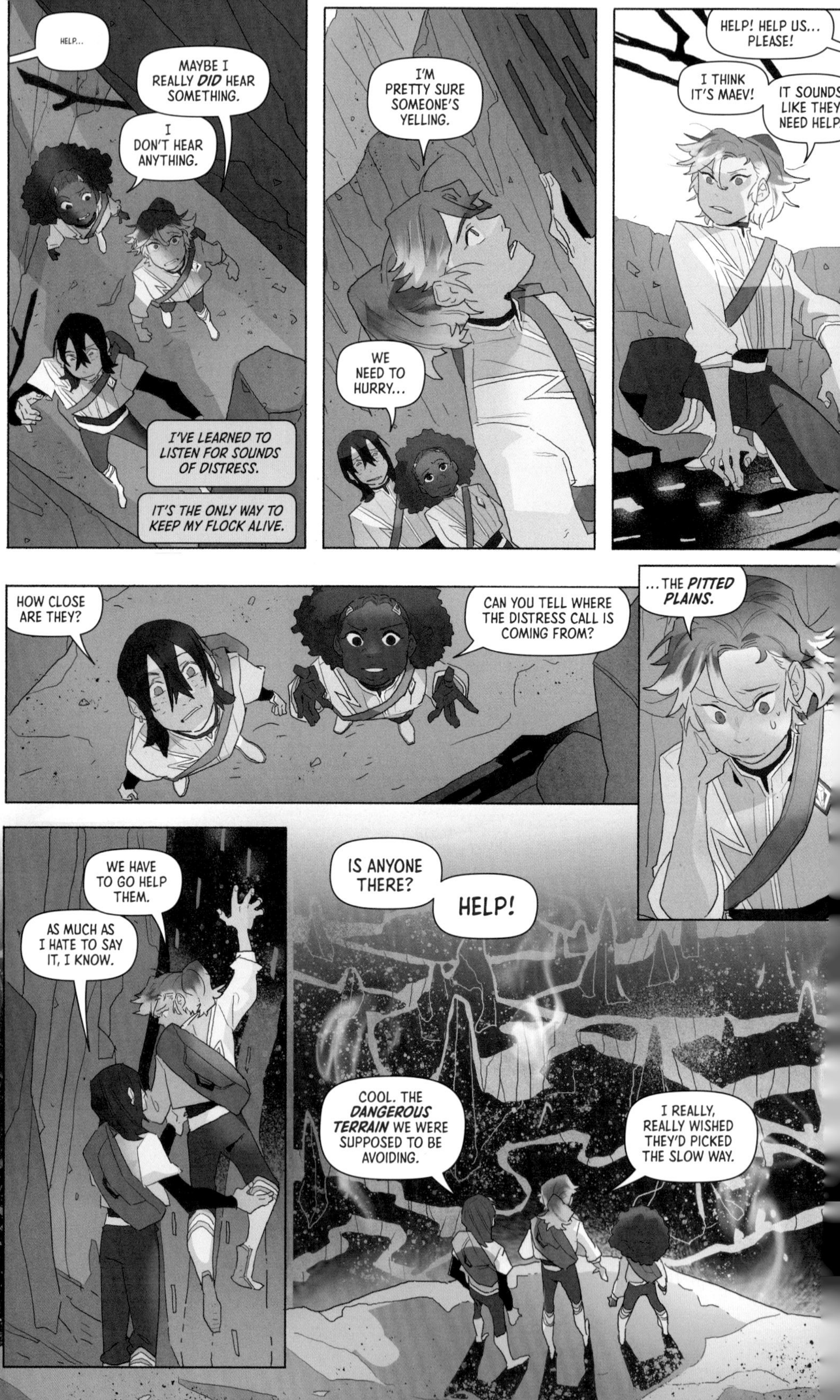
HELP...
MAYBE I REALLY DID HEAR SOMETHING.
I DON'T HEAR ANYTHING.
I'VE LEARNED TO LISTEN FOR SOUNDS OF DISTRESS.
IT'S THE ONLY WAY TO KEEP MY FLOCK ALIVE.
I'M PRETTY SURE SOMEONE'S YELLING.
WE NEED TO HURRY...
HELP! HELP US... PLEASE!
I THINK IT'S MAEV!
IT SOUNDS LIKE THEY NEED HELP.
HOW CLOSE ARE THEY?
CAN YOU TELL WHERE THE DISTRESS CALL IS COMING FROM?
...THE PITTED PLAINS.
WE HAVE TO GO HELP THEM.
AS MUCH AS I HATE TO SAY IT, I KNOW.
IS ANYONE THERE?
HELP!
COOL. THE DANGEROUS TERRAIN WE WERE SUPPOSED TO BE AVOIDING.
I REALLY, REALLY WISHED THEY'D PICKED THE SLOW WAY.

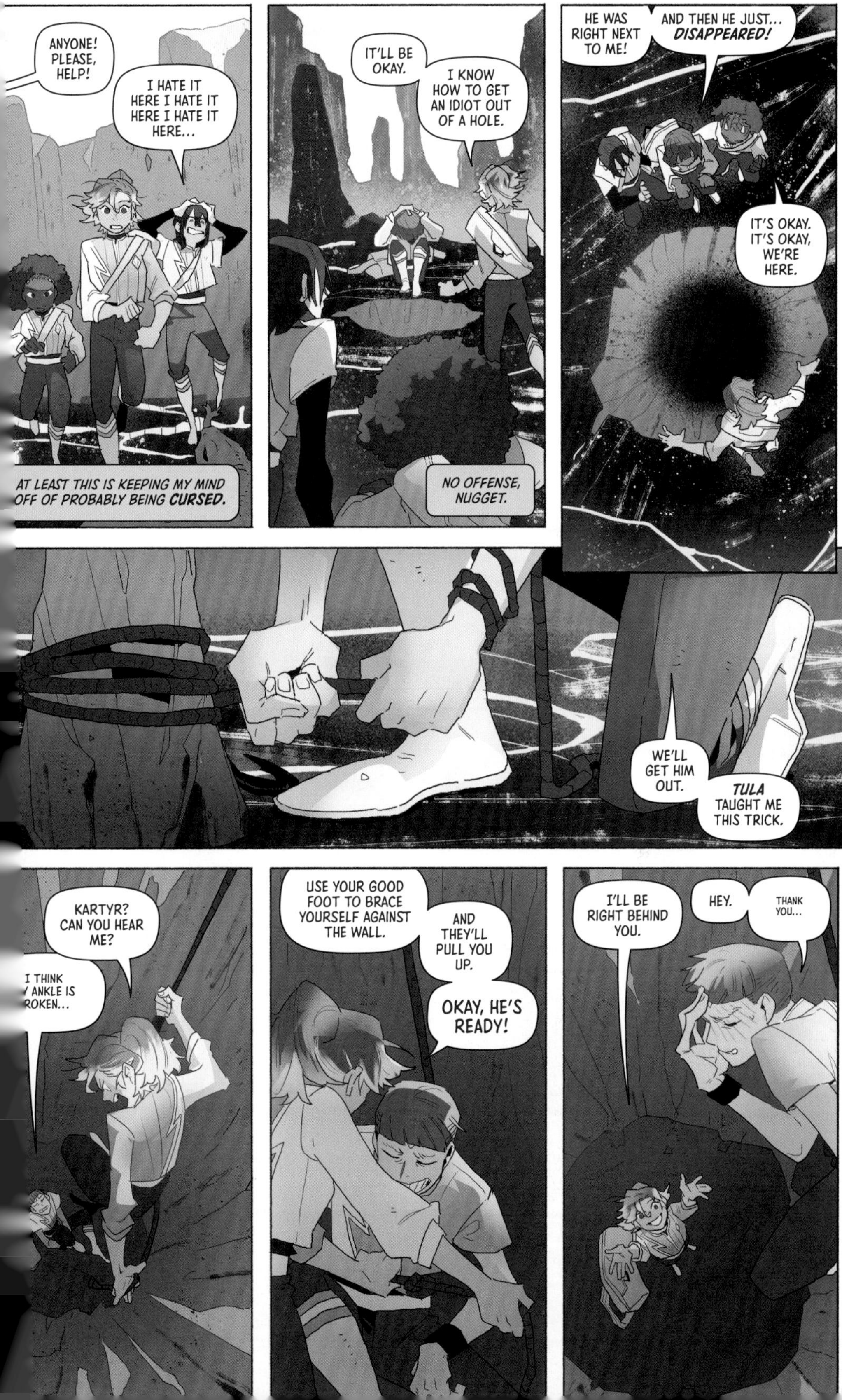
ANYONE! PLEASE, HELP!
I HATE IT HERE I HATE IT HERE I HATE IT HERE...
AT LEAST THIS IS KEEPING MY MIND OFF OF PROBABLY BEING CURSED.
IT'LL BE OKAY.
I KNOW HOW TO GET AN IDIOT OUT OF A HOLE.
NO OFFENSE, NUGGET.
HE WAS RIGHT NEXT TO ME!
AND THEN HE JUST... DISAPPEARED!
IT'S OKAY. IT'S OKAY, WE'RE HERE.
WE'LL GET HIM OUT.
TULA TAUGHT ME THIS TRICK.
KARTYR? CAN YOU HEAR ME?
I THINK Y ANKLE IS ROKEN...
USE YOUR GOOD FOOT TO BRACE YOURSELF AGAINST THE WALL.
AND THEY'LL PULL YOU UP.
OKAY, HE'S READY!
I'LL BE RIGHT BEHIND YOU.
HEY.
THANK YOU...

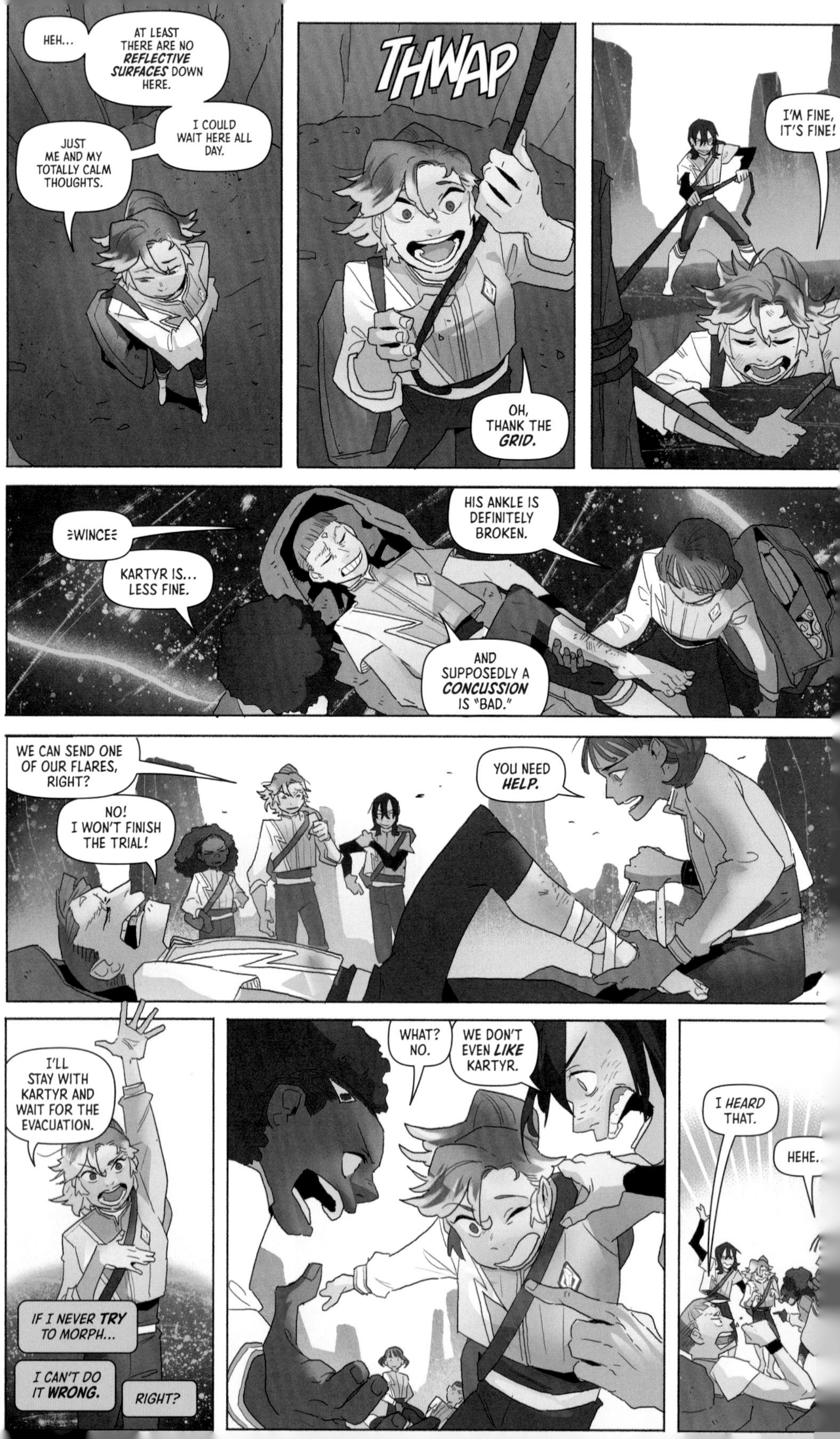
HEH...
AT LEAST THERE ARE NO REFLECTIVE SURFACES DOWN HERE.
I COULD WAIT HERE ALL DAY.
JUST ME AND MY TOTALLY CALM THOUGHTS.
THWAP
OH, THANK THE GRID.
I'M FINE, IT'S FINE!
HIS ANKLE IS DEFINITELY BROKEN.
≡WINCE≡
KARTYR IS... LESS FINE.
AND SUPPOSEDLY A CONCUSSION IS "BAD."
WE CAN SEND ONE OF OUR FLARES, RIGHT?
NO! I WON'T FINISH THE TRIAL!
YOU NEED HELP.
I'LL STAY WITH KARTYR AND WAIT FOR THE EVACUATION.
IF I NEVER TRY TO MORPH...
I CAN'T DO IT WRONG.
RIGHT?
WHAT? NO.
WE DON'T EVEN LIKE KARTYR.
I HEARD THAT.
HEHE...

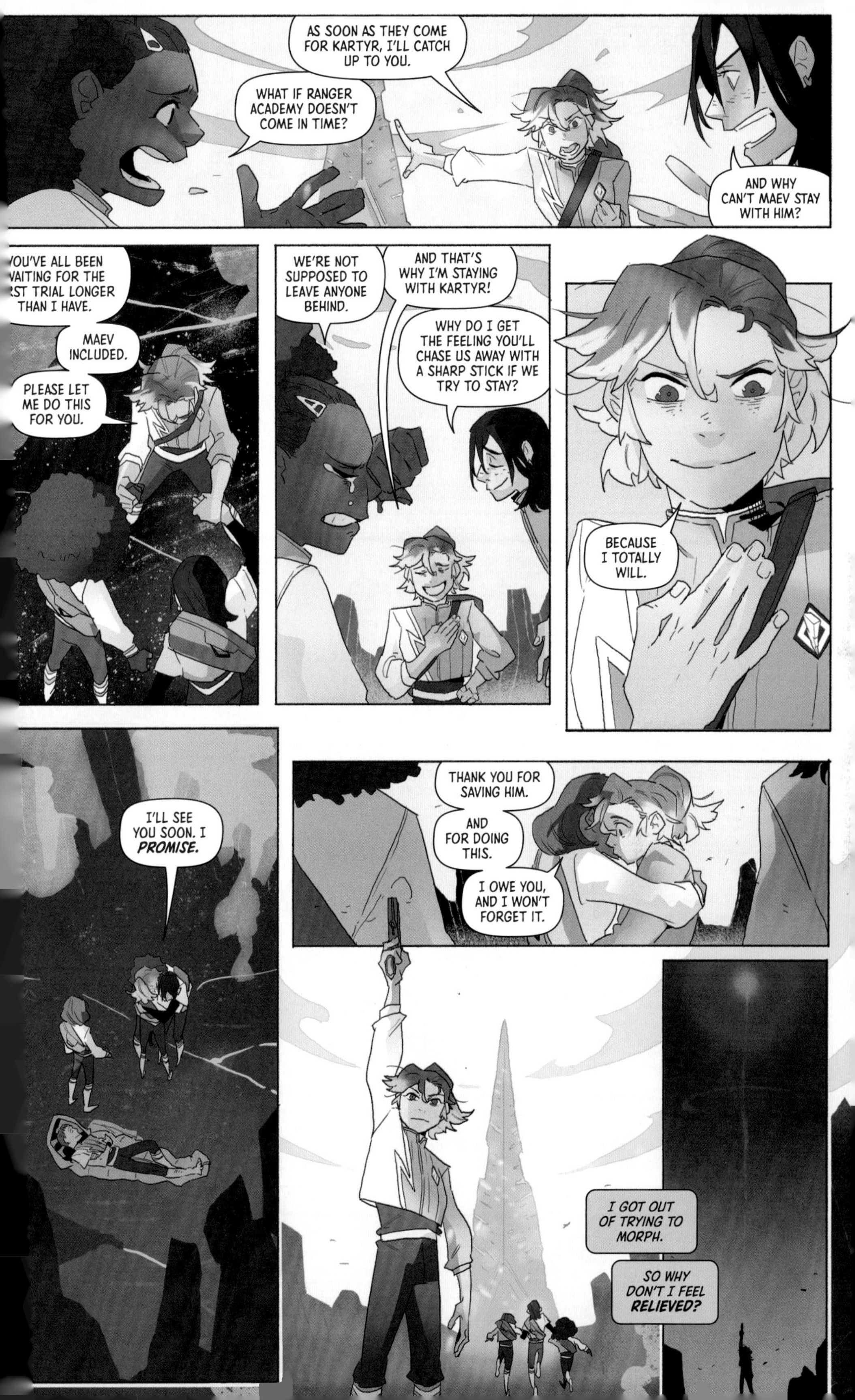
AS SOON AS THEY COME FOR KARTYR, I'LL CATCH UP TO YOU.
WHAT IF RANGER ACADEMY DOESN'T COME IN TIME?
AND WHY CAN'T MAEV STAY WITH HIM?
YOU'VE ALL BEEN WAITING FOR THE FIRST TRIAL LONGER THAN I HAVE.
MAEV INCLUDED.
PLEASE LET ME DO THIS FOR YOU.
WE'RE NOT SUPPOSED TO LEAVE ANYONE BEHIND.
AND THAT'S WHY I'M STAYING WITH KARTYR!
WHY DO I GET THE FEELING YOU'LL CHASE US AWAY WITH A SHARP STICK IF WE TRY TO STAY?
BECAUSE I TOTALLY WILL.
I'LL SEE YOU SOON. I ***PROMISE.***
THANK YOU FOR SAVING HIM.
AND FOR DOING THIS.
I OWE YOU, AND I WON'T FORGET IT.
I GOT OUT OF TRYING TO MORPH.
*SO WHY DON'T I FEEL **RELIEVED?***

SO YOU'RE SCARED OF THE BANDORIAN MONKS, HUH?

I'M NOT SCARED. *YOU'RE* SCARED.

ISN'T THAT WHY YOU THREW YOURSELF INTO A PIT?

HOW DID YOU KNOW THAT?

UH. I WAS *KIDDING.*

PLEASE TELL ME YOU DIDN'T DO THAT ON PURPOSE.

IF I WAS GOING TO FAIL ANYWAY, IT MIGHT AS WELL HAVE BEEN BECAUSE OF AN "ACCIDENT."

INSTEAD OF NOT BEING GOOD *ENOUGH.*

SKITTE

NONE OF US KNOW IF WE'RE GOOD ENOUGH YET.

ISN'T THAT THE WHOLE POINT OF THIS?

THE BANDORIAN MONKS ARE THE MOST POWERFUL SAGES IN THE UNIVERSE.

THEY'LL KNOW I'M SCARED.

WHOOSH

MAYBE... YOU'LL GET A DO-OVER?

YEAH. A *YEAR* FROM NOW. BY THEN EVERYONE ELSE WILL ALREADY BE JUNIOR RANGERS.

AND WE'LL BE PATHETIC LOSERS.

MY DAD DIDN'T THINK I WAS *GOOD ENOUGH* TO BE HERE.

HE'S PROBABLY RIGHT.

SHUT

YOU'RE NOT THE ONE WH JUMP--*FELL* A HOLE.

AND IF IT WASN'T FOR ME, YOU'D BE THE FIRST LATE STARTER TO EVER MAKE IT THROUGH THE FIRST TRIAL.

DON'T TAKE THAT AS A COMPLIMENT.

I STILL THINK YOU'RE...A LOSER, OR WHATEVER.

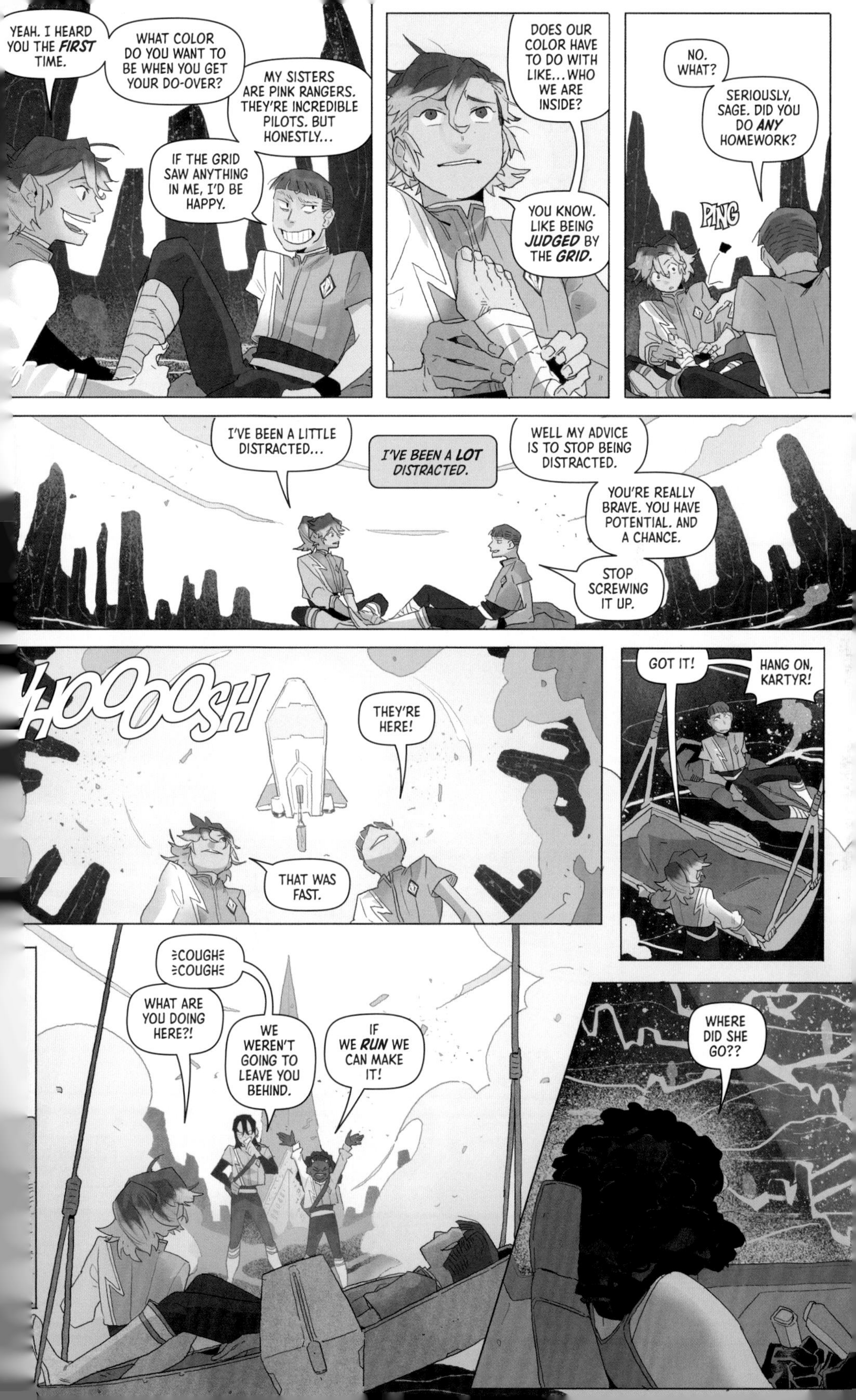
YEAH. I HEARD YOU THE FIRST TIME.
WHAT COLOR DO YOU WANT TO BE WHEN YOU GET YOUR DO-OVER?
MY SISTERS ARE PINK RANGERS. THEY'RE INCREDIBLE PILOTS. BUT HONESTLY...
IF THE GRID SAW ANYTHING IN ME, I'D BE HAPPY.
DOES OUR COLOR HAVE TO DO WITH LIKE...WHO WE ARE INSIDE?
YOU KNOW. LIKE BEING JUDGED BY THE GRID.
NO. WHAT?
SERIOUSLY, SAGE. DID YOU DO ANY HOMEWORK?
PING
I'VE BEEN A LITTLE DISTRACTED...
I'VE BEEN A LOT DISTRACTED.
WELL MY ADVICE IS TO STOP BEING DISTRACTED.
YOU'RE REALLY BRAVE. YOU HAVE POTENTIAL. AND A CHANCE.
STOP SCREWING IT UP.
WHOOOOSH
THEY'RE HERE!
THAT WAS FAST.
GOT IT!
HANG ON, KARTYR!
COUGH COUGH
WHAT ARE YOU DOING HERE?!
WE WEREN'T GOING TO LEAVE YOU BEHIND.
IF WE RUN WE CAN MAKE IT!
WHERE DID SHE GO??

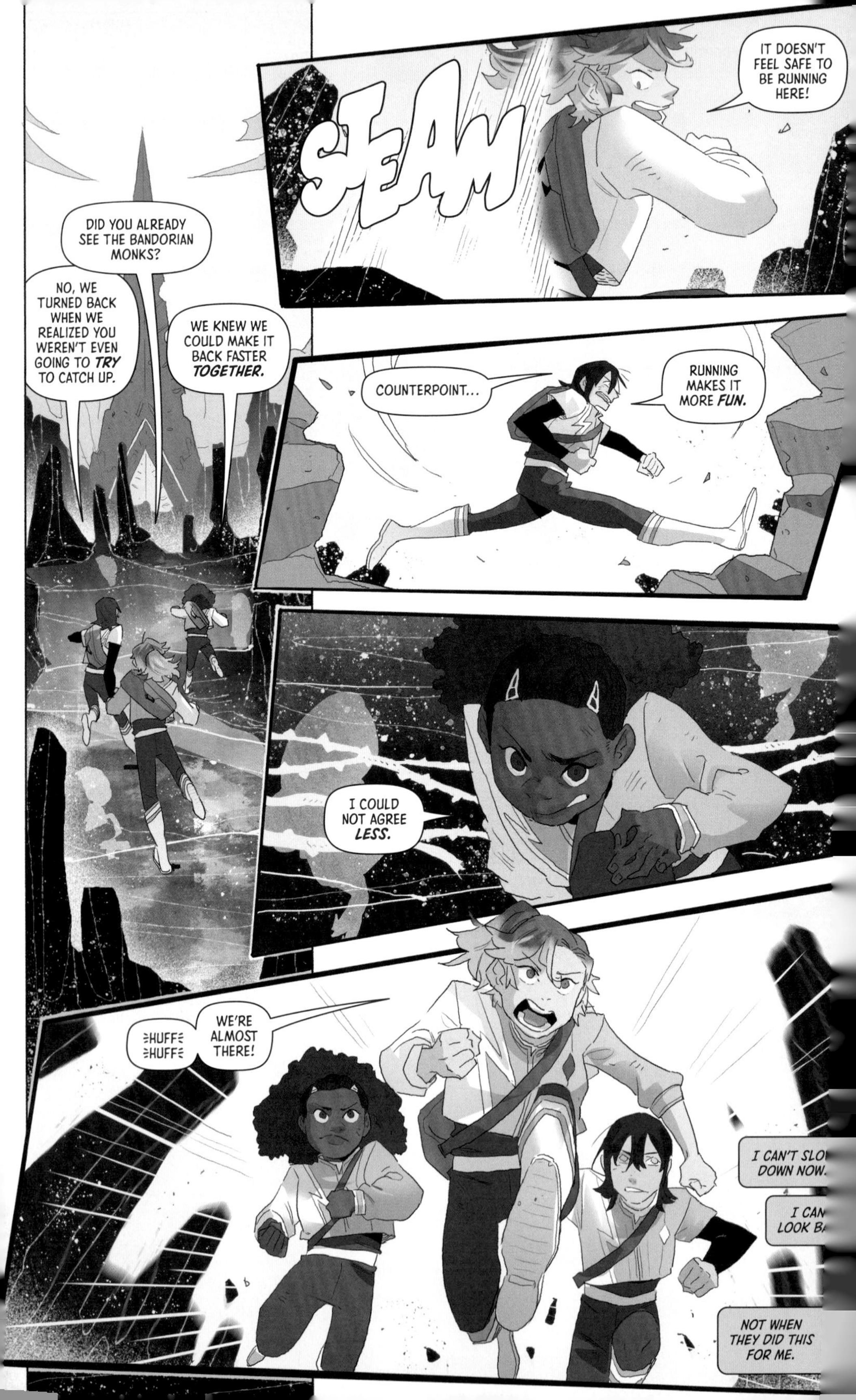
DID YOU ALREADY SEE THE BANDORIAN MONKS?
NO, WE TURNED BACK WHEN WE REALIZED YOU WEREN'T EVEN GOING TO *TRY* TO CATCH UP.
WE KNEW WE COULD MAKE IT BACK FASTER *TOGETHER.*
SLAM
IT DOESN'T FEEL SAFE TO BE RUNNING HERE!
COUNTERPOINT...
RUNNING MAKES IT MORE *FUN.*
I COULD NOT AGREE *LESS.*
HUFF HUFF
WE'RE ALMOST THERE!
I CAN'T SLO DOWN NOW.
I CAN LOOK BA
NOT WHEN THEY DID THIS FOR ME.

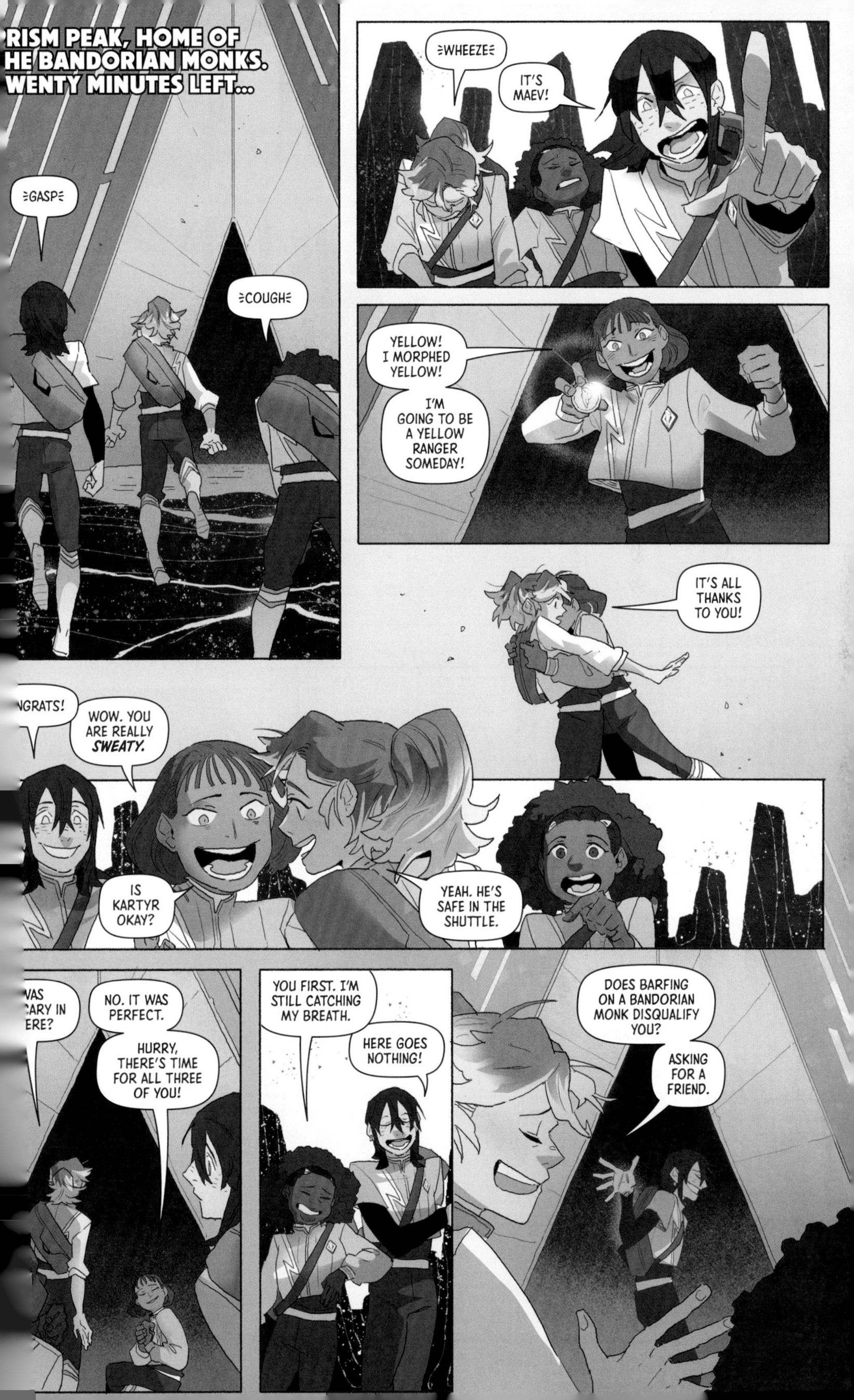
RISM PEAK, HOME OF
HE BANDORIAN MONKS.
WENTY MINUTES LEFT...
GASP
COUGH
WHEEZE
IT'S MAEV!
YELLOW! I MORPHED YELLOW!
I'M GOING TO BE A YELLOW RANGER SOMEDAY!
IT'S ALL THANKS TO YOU!
NGRATS!
WOW. YOU ARE REALLY SWEATY.
IS KARTYR OKAY?
YEAH. HE'S SAFE IN THE SHUTTLE.
WAS
CARY IN
ERE?
NO. IT WAS PERFECT.
HURRY, THERE'S TIME FOR ALL THREE OF YOU!
YOU FIRST. I'M STILL CATCHING MY BREATH.
HERE GOES NOTHING!
DOES BARFING ON A BANDORIAN MONK DISQUALIFY YOU?
ASKING FOR A FRIEND.

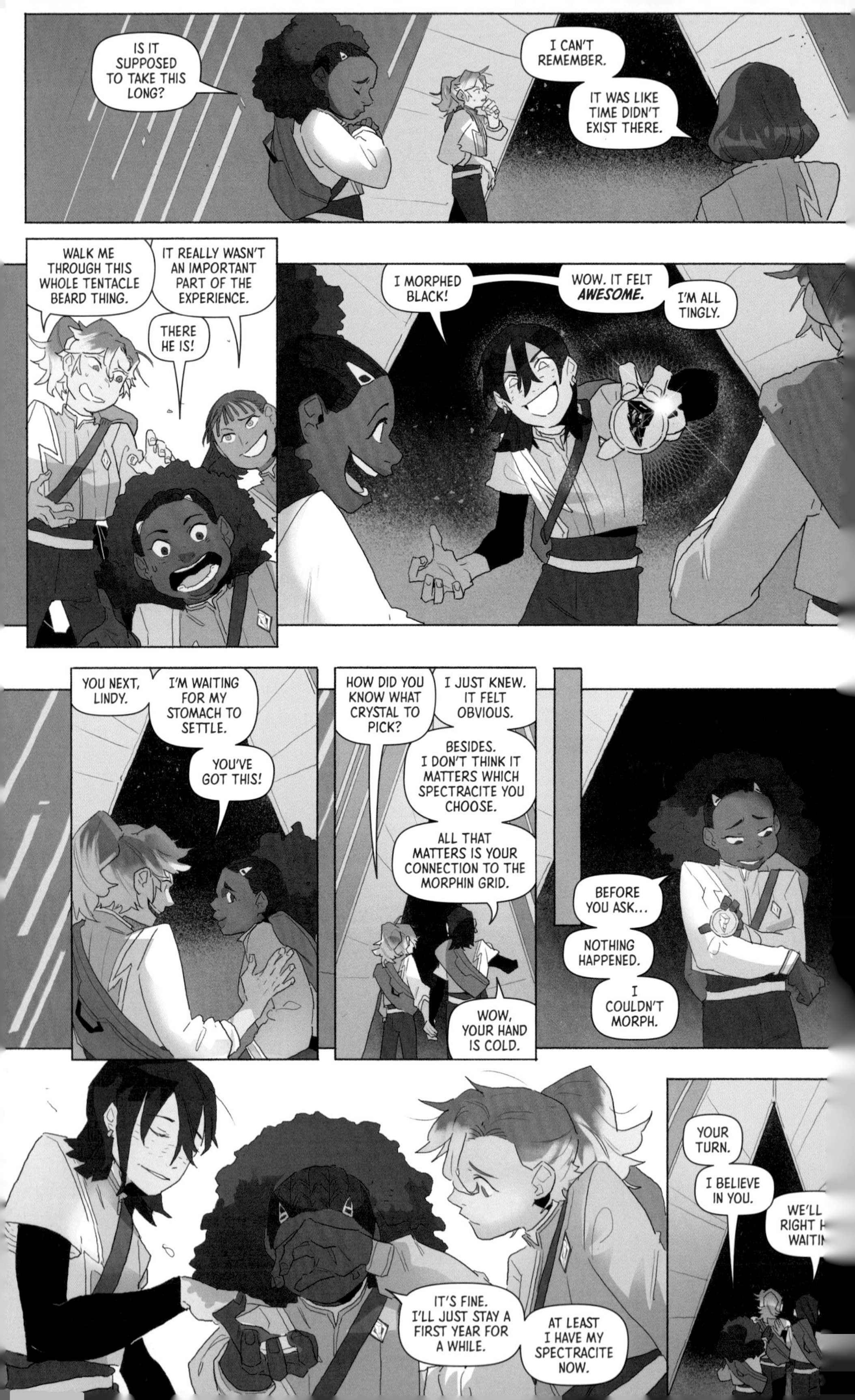
IS IT SUPPOSED TO TAKE THIS LONG?
I CAN'T REMEMBER.
IT WAS LIKE TIME DIDN'T EXIST THERE.
WALK ME THROUGH THIS WHOLE TENTACLE BEARD THING.
IT REALLY WASN'T AN IMPORTANT PART OF THE EXPERIENCE.
THERE HE IS!
I MORPHED BLACK!
WOW. IT FELT AWESOME.
I'M ALL TINGLY.
YOU NEXT, LINDY.
I'M WAITING FOR MY STOMACH TO SETTLE.
YOU'VE GOT THIS!
HOW DID YOU KNOW WHAT CRYSTAL TO PICK?
I JUST KNEW. IT FELT OBVIOUS.
BESIDES. I DON'T THINK IT MATTERS WHICH SPECTRACITE YOU CHOOSE.
ALL THAT MATTERS IS YOUR CONNECTION TO THE MORPHIN GRID.
WOW, YOUR HAND IS COLD.
BEFORE YOU ASK...
NOTHING HAPPENED.
I COULDN'T MORPH.
IT'S FINE. I'LL JUST STAY A FIRST YEAR FOR A WHILE.
AT LEAST I HAVE MY SPECTRACITE NOW.
YOUR TURN.
I BELIEVE IN YOU.

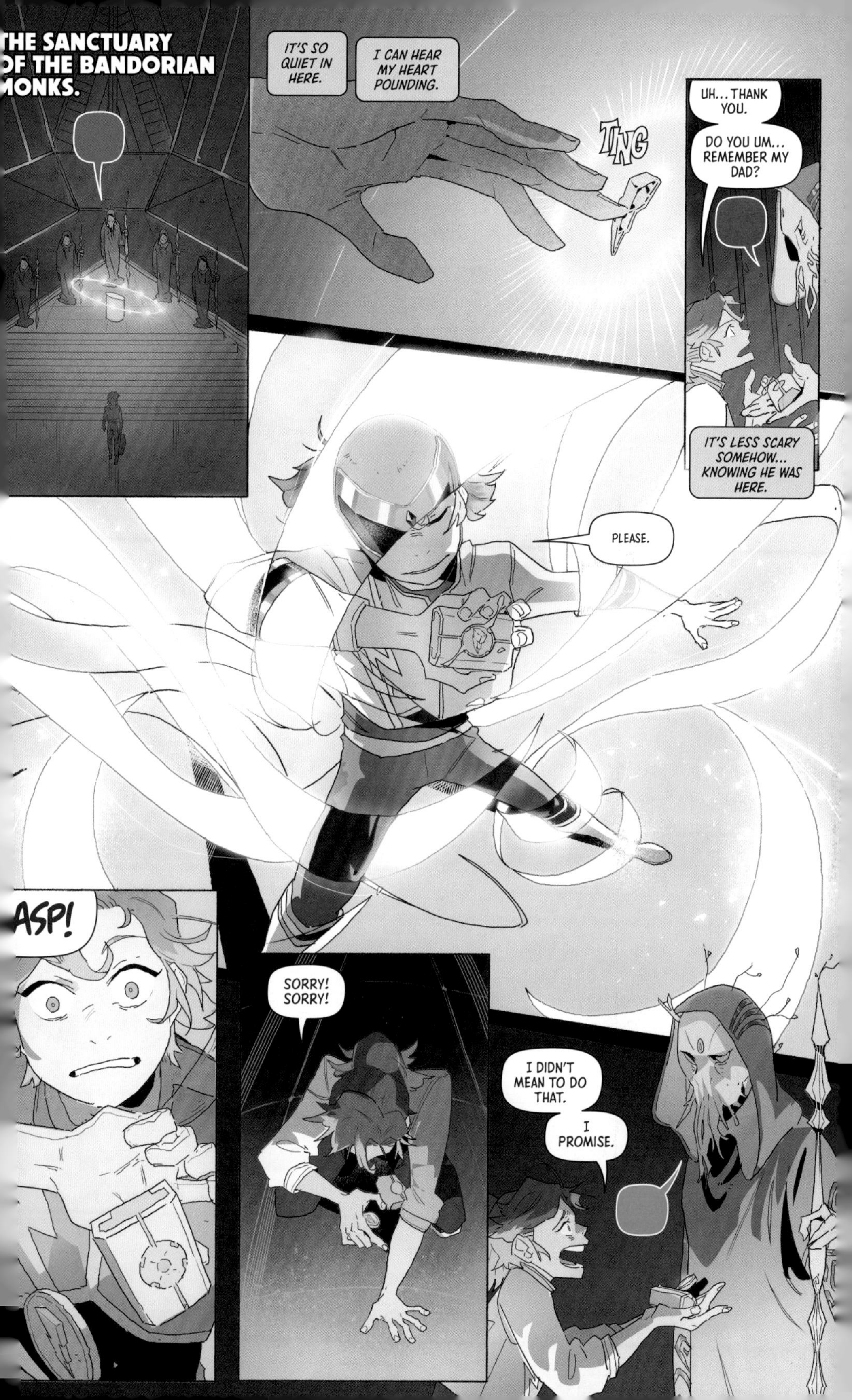
THE SANCTUARY OF THE BANDORIAN MONKS.
IT'S SO QUIET IN HERE.
I CAN HEAR MY HEART POUNDING.
TING
UH...THANK YOU.
DO YOU UM... REMEMBER MY DAD?
IT'S LESS SCARY SOMEHOW... KNOWING HE WAS HERE.
PLEASE.
ASP!
SORRY! SORRY!
I DIDN'T MEAN TO DO THAT.
I PROMISE.

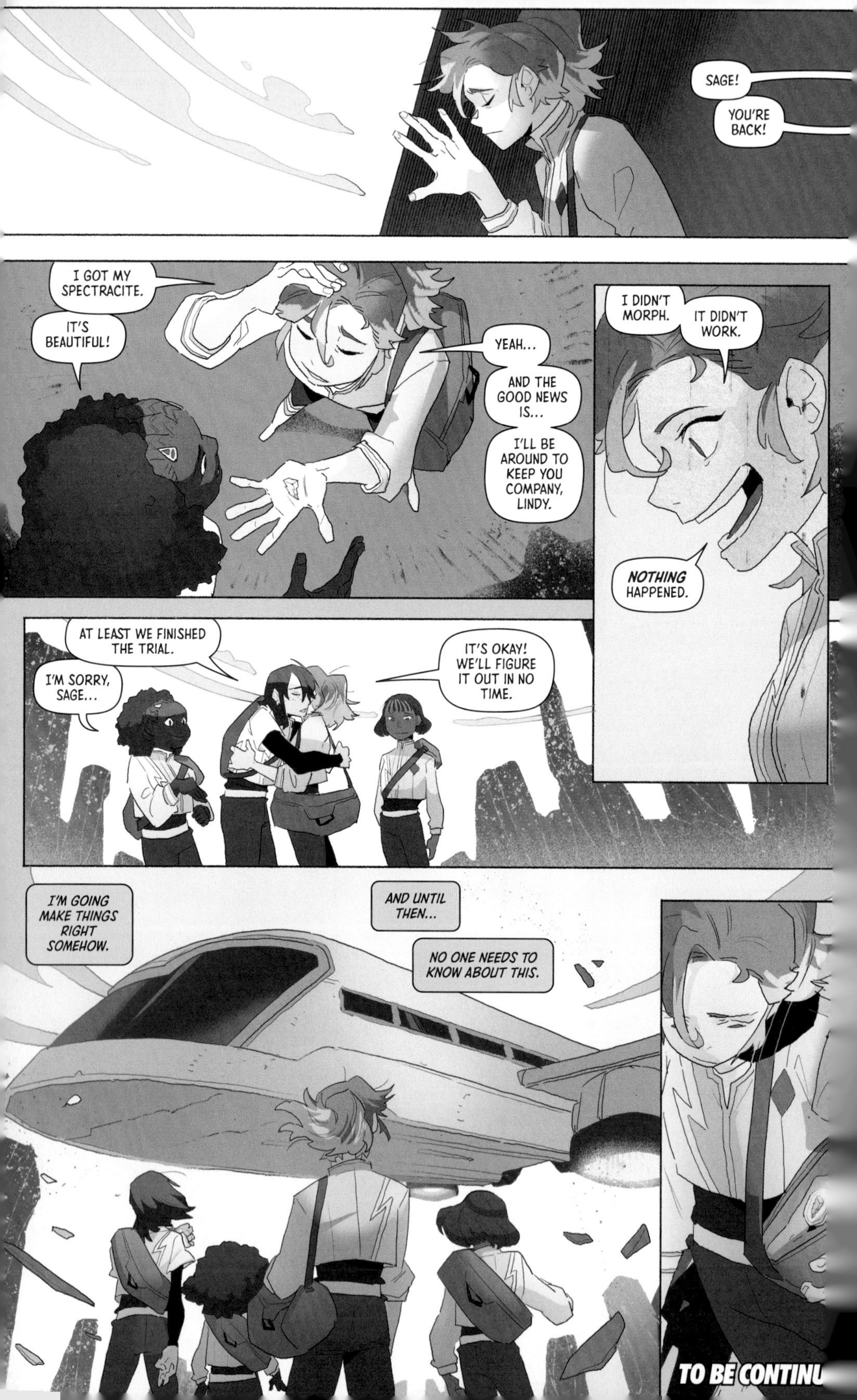
SAGE!
YOU'RE BACK!
I GOT MY SPECTRACITE.
IT'S BEAUTIFUL!
YEAH...
AND THE GOOD NEWS IS...
I'LL BE AROUND TO KEEP YOU COMPANY, LINDY.
I DIDN'T MORPH.
IT DIDN'T WORK.
NOTHING HAPPENED.
AT LEAST WE FINISHED THE TRIAL.
I'M SORRY, SAGE...
IT'S OKAY! WE'LL FIGURE IT OUT IN NO TIME.
I'M GOING MAKE THINGS RIGHT SOMEHOW.
AND UNTIL THEN...
NO ONE NEEDS TO KNOW ABOUT THIS.
TO BE CONTINU

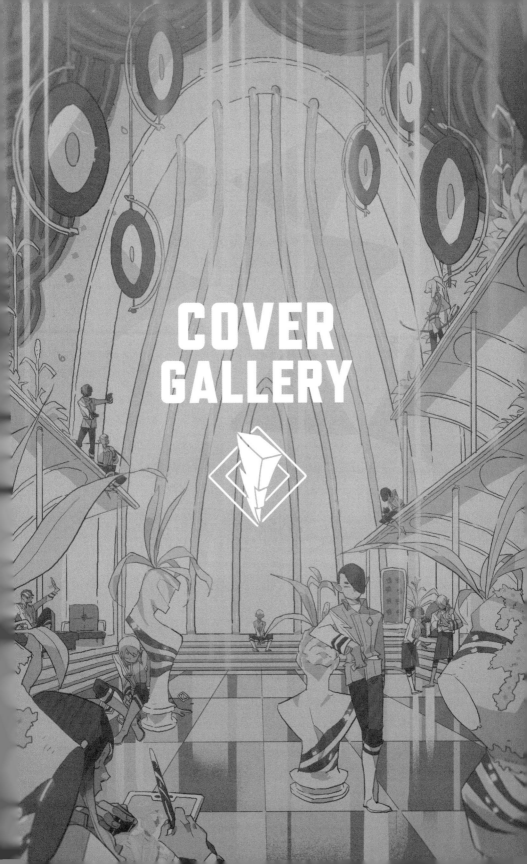

COVER GALLERY

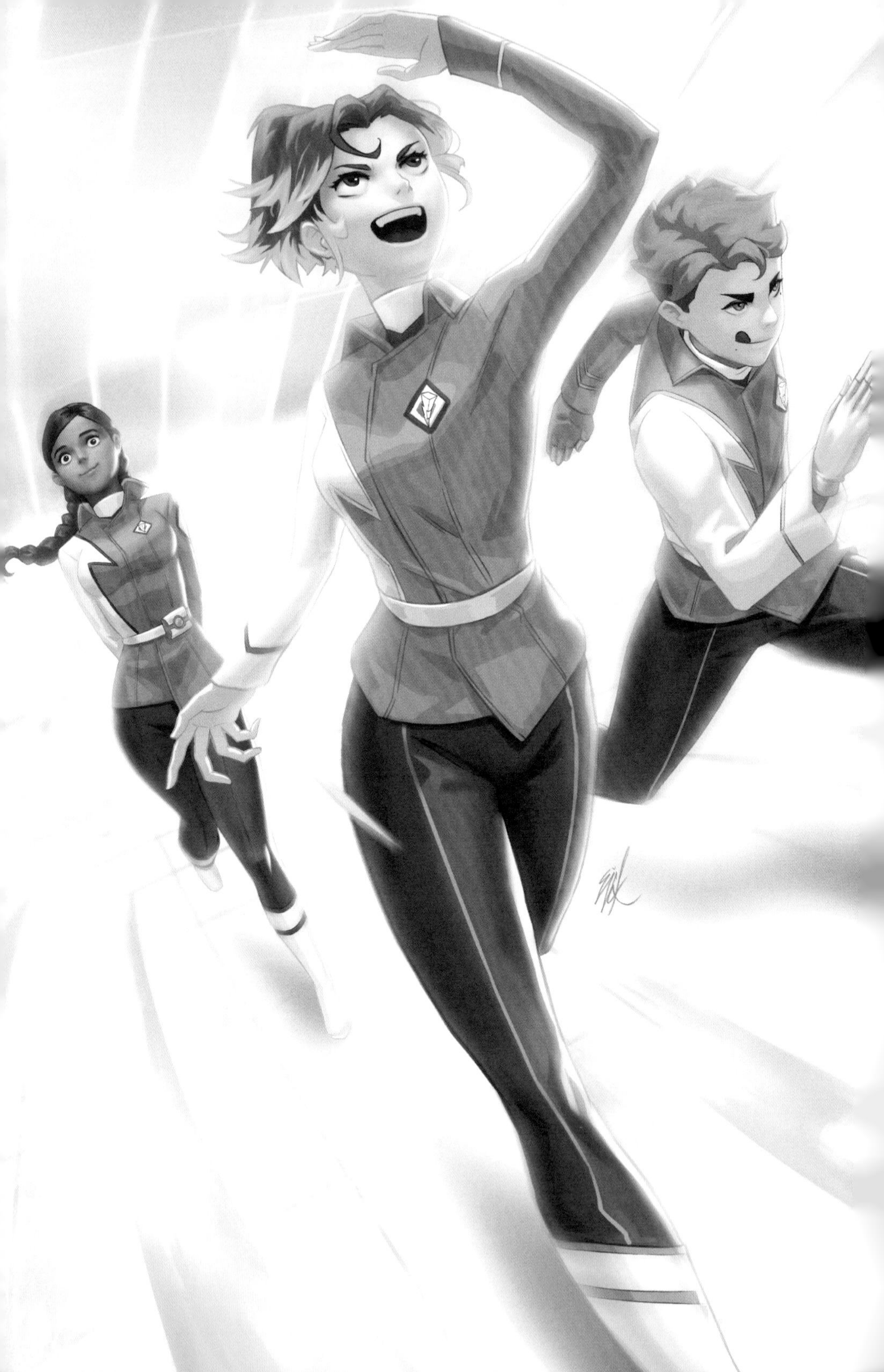

ISSUE ONE VARIANT COVER BY **EJIKURE**

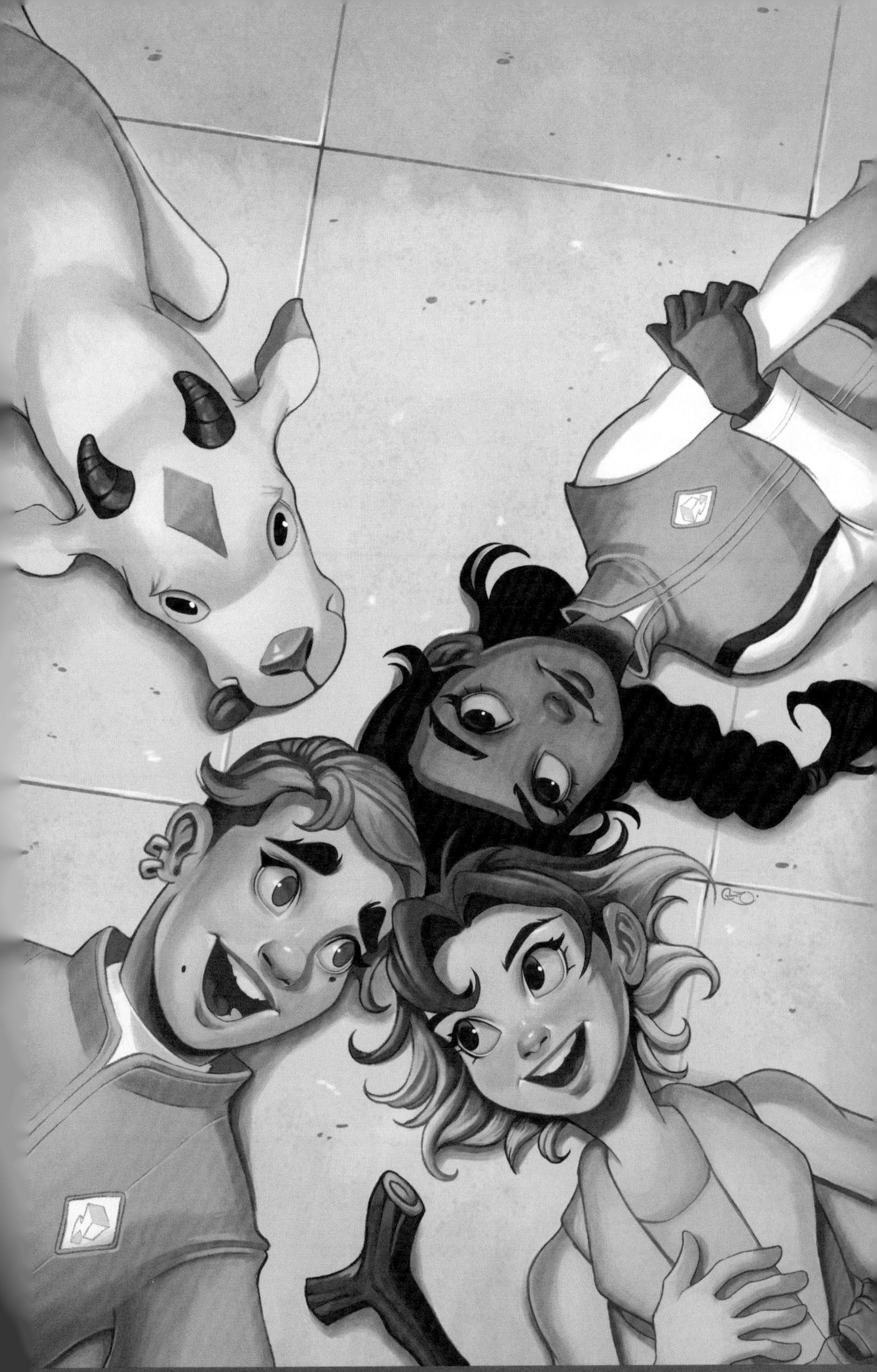

ISSUE ONE VARIANT COVER BY CHRISSIE ZULLO

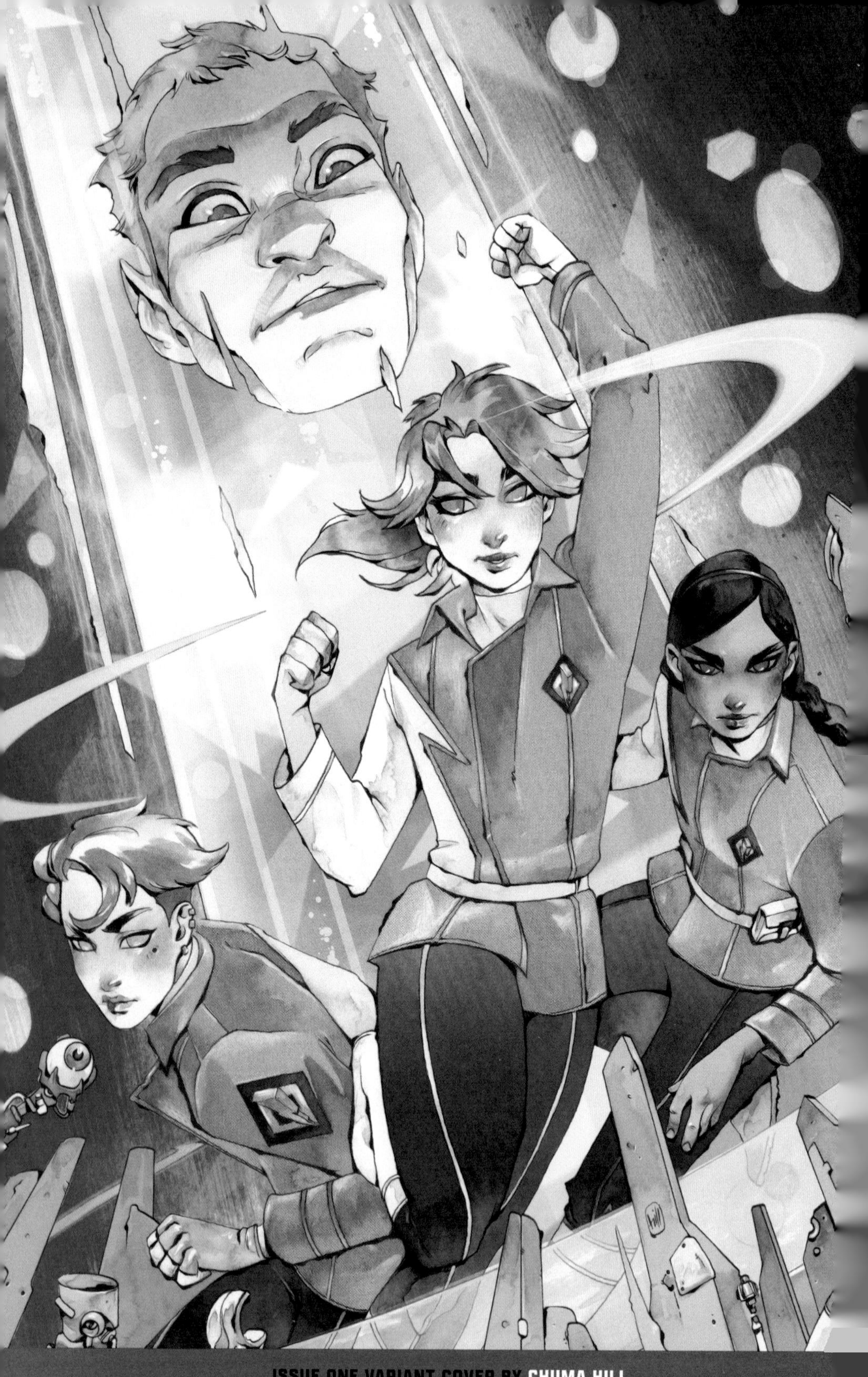

ISSUE ONE VARIANT COVER BY **CHUMA HILL**

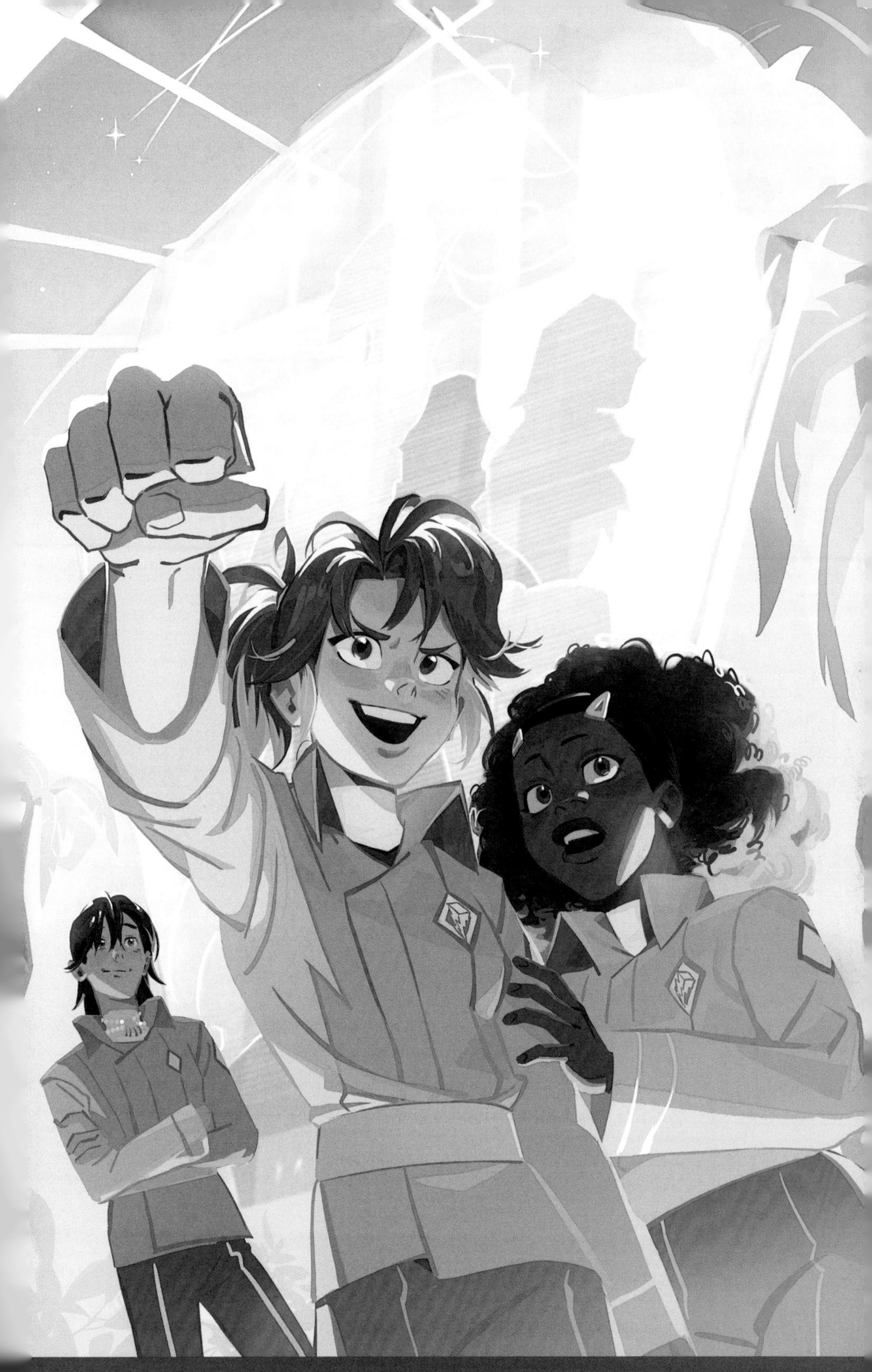

ISSUE ONE VARIANT COVER BY ALICIA SÁNCHEZ

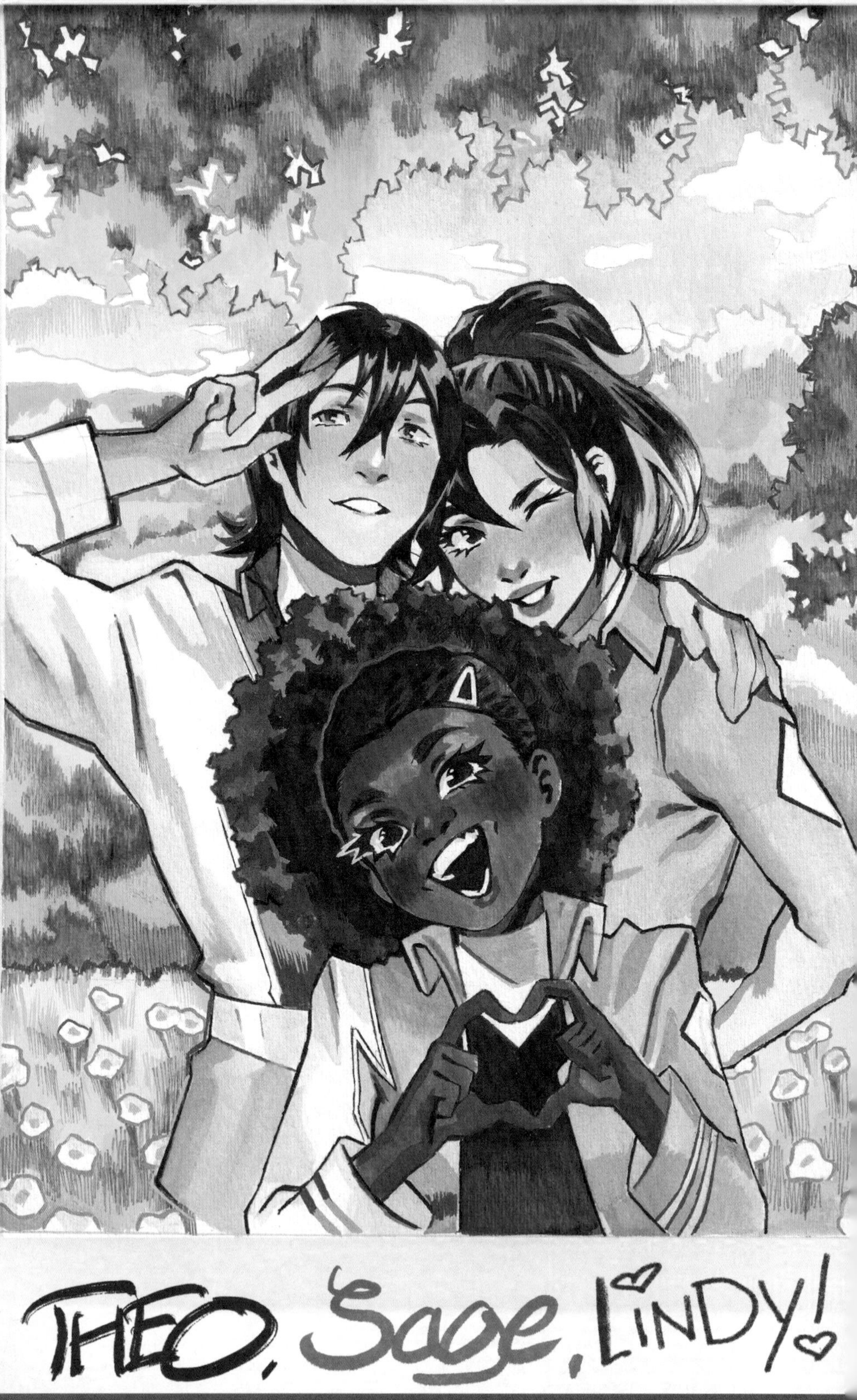
THEO, Sage, LINDY!

ISSUE TWO VARIANT COVER BY RIAN GONZALES

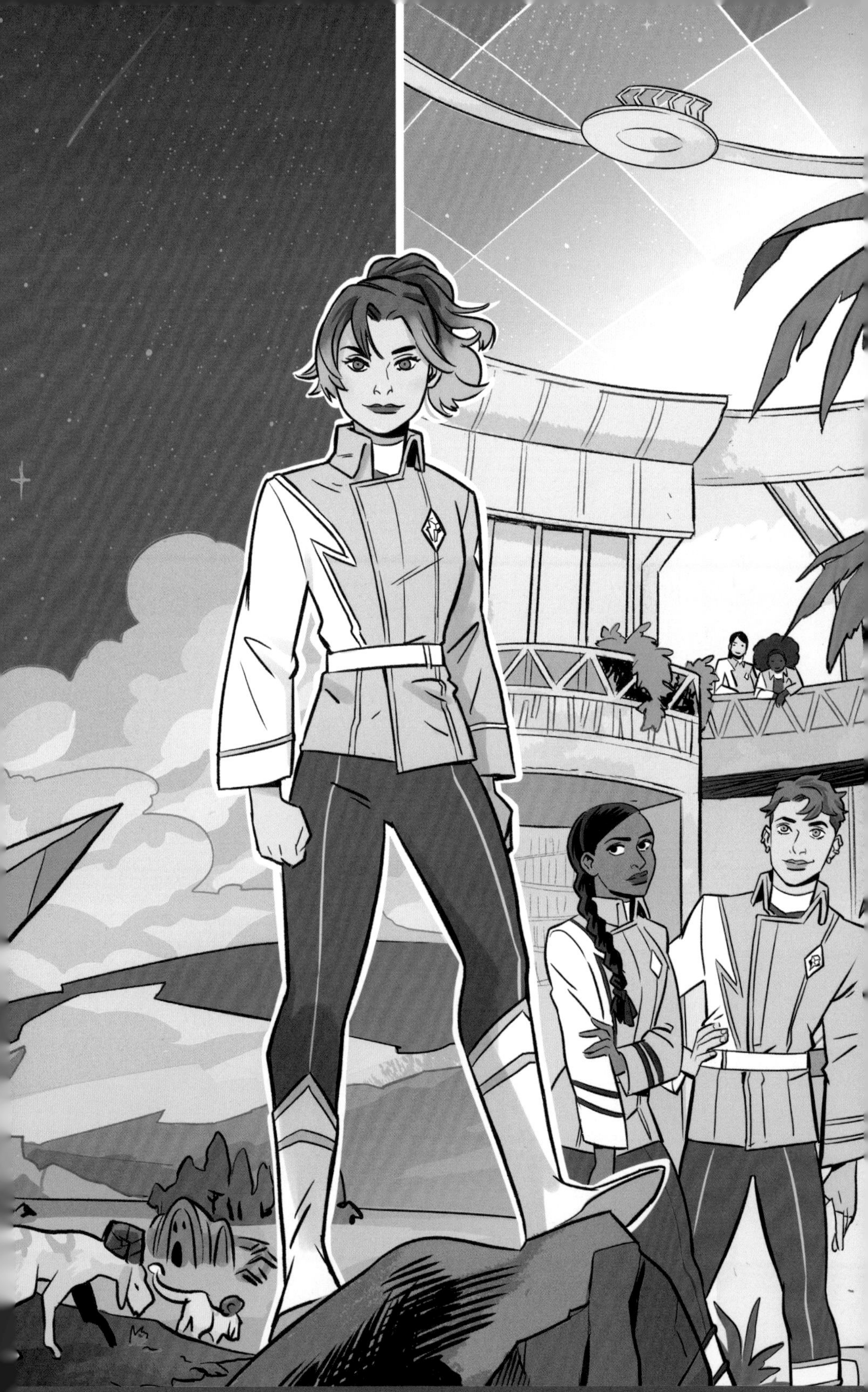

ISSUE THREE VARIANT COVER BY NATACHA BUSTOS

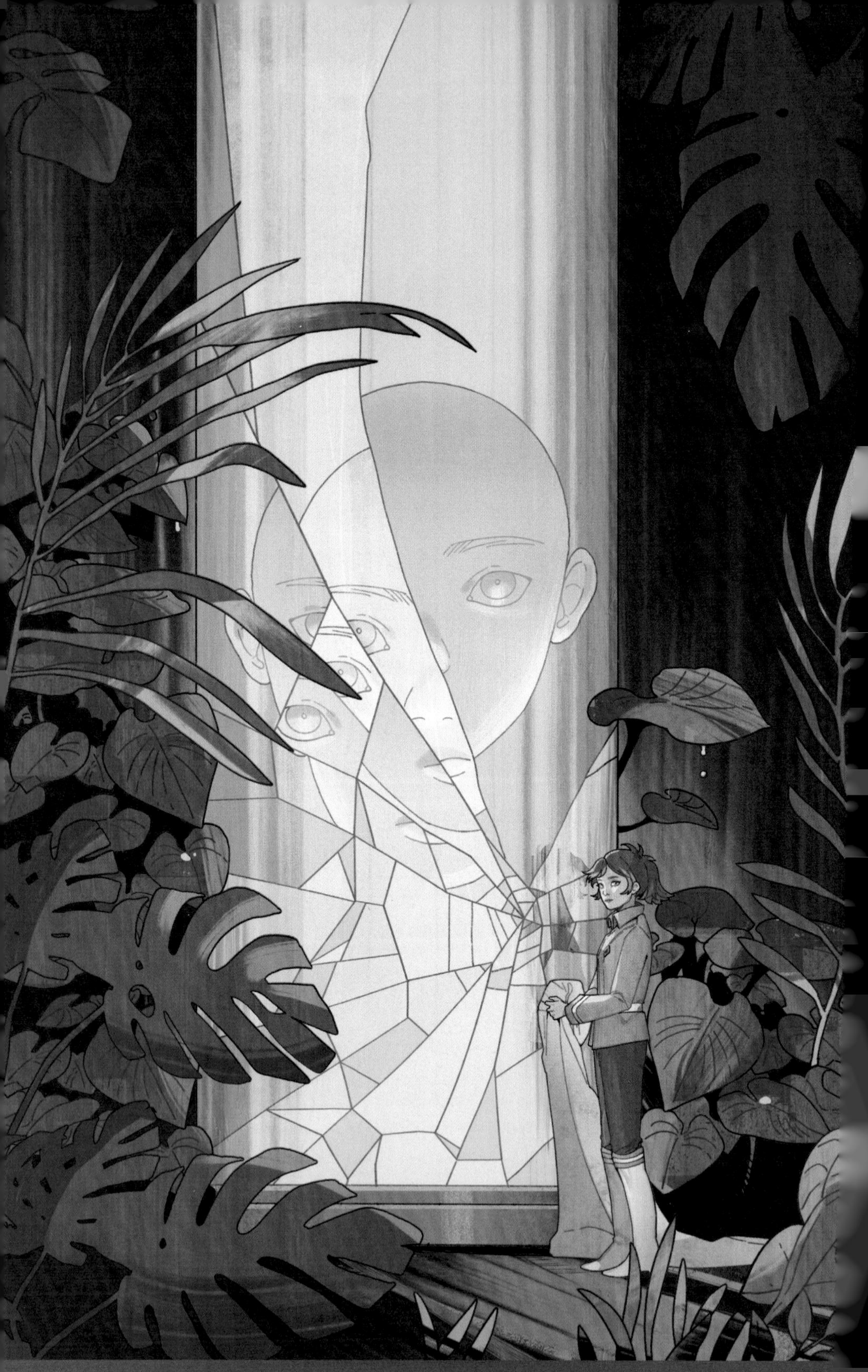

ISSUE FOUR VARIANT COVER BY **YEJIN PARK**

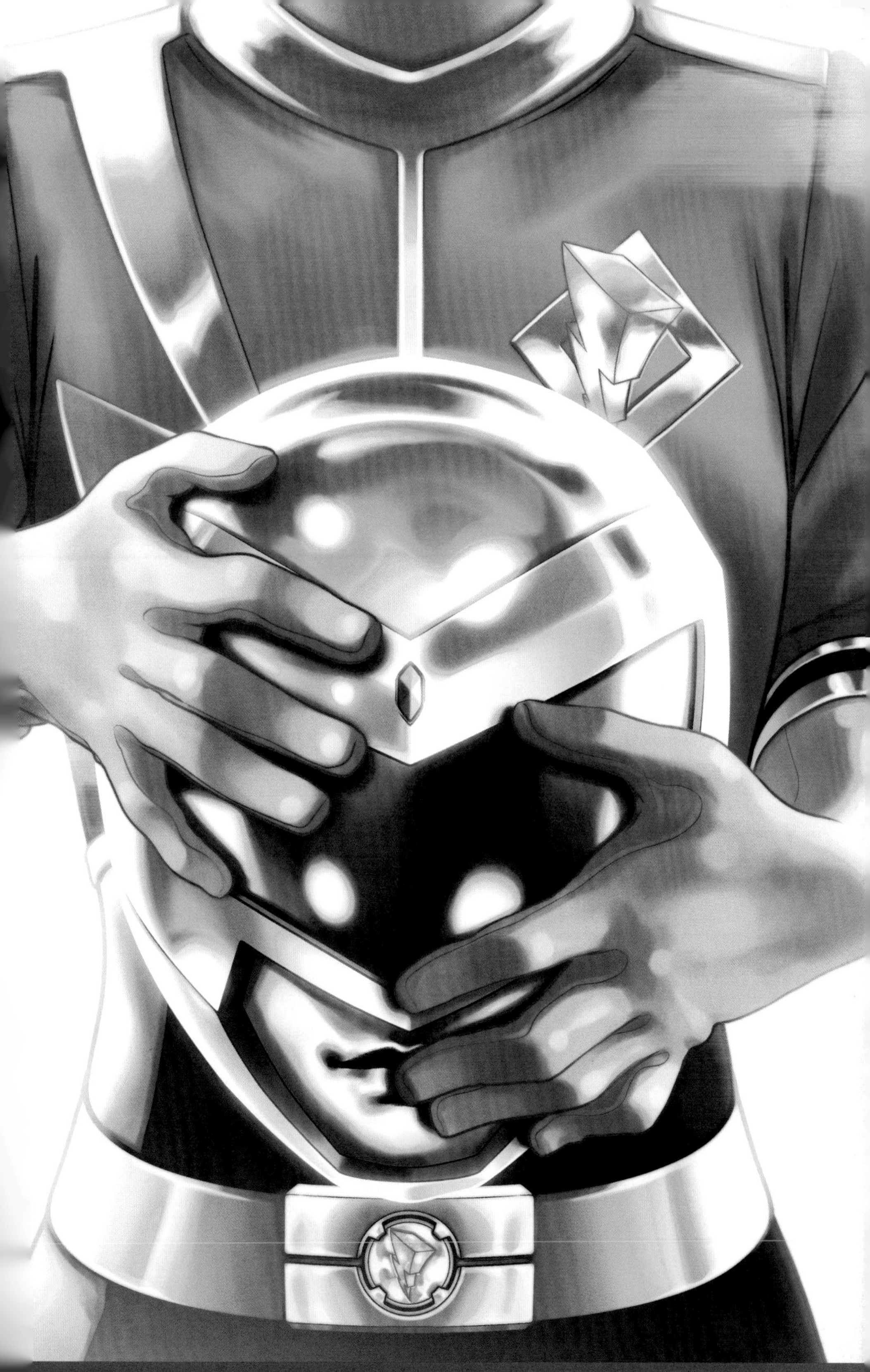

ISSUE FOUR VARIANT COVER BY GOÑI MONTES

ADVANCE YOUR WAY THROUGH *FENCE*
THE GLAAD MEDIA AWARD–NOMINATED SPORTS COMIC

ISBN 978-160886-137-8 | **$14.99** US

ISBN 978-1-68415-297-1 | **$14.99** US

ISBN 978-1-68415-334-3 | **$14.99** US

ISBN 978-168415-538-5 | **$14.99** US

ISBN 978-168415-843-0 | **$14.99** US

ISBN 978-160886-137-8 | **$14.99** US

FROM USA TODAY BESTSELLING AUTHOR
C.S. PACAT

AND

ACCLAIMED ARTIST
JOHANNA THE MAD